Terror
Hits
Home

A novel by
John Guntner

For my Mom and the Lulas, Big and Little. They are the most important people in the world to me.

(Newspaper clipping)

Maysville Gets New Police Chief

Maysville, Virginia - August 1, 2000

By Mary Johnson
May County Chronicle Staff Writer

Mayor Phillip Marston officially announced today Maysville has a new police chief. He is former New York City Detective First Grade Richard A. Harris, 49. Harris actually took the Maysville chief's job in earlier in the year when he began a lead undercover role in the much publicized investigation of a local dog fighting ring. 217 people from all over the United States were arrested in a raid on a large dog fight, July 5, 2000, held on a farm in the county outside Maysville.

Of the group, six were already wanted on federal and state warrants for crimes allegedly committed all over the country. One of the men, Amos Greenway, 38, was wanted for Murder for Hire in Georgia.

Some of those arrested have already pleaded guilty and been fined. Trials for the others are expected to begin in November.

Harris, a 26 year veteran of the New York City Police Department, was twice awarded the department's highest decoration, the Medal of Valor. The most recent medal was awarded for his role in a drug arrest on New Year's Eve of the Millennium. Although his partner had been killed, and he was seriously wounded, Harris managed to shoot and kill a wanted drug dealer in a furious gun battle on a city street.

The job of Maysville Police Chief has been vacant since long time Chief Wesley Barnett, 68, died suddenly of a heart attack last March.

"Maysville is growing," Mayor Marston said. "Policing the new mall is going to be a major undertaking for our small police department. The city council decided we needed to find the most experienced law enforcement officer we could get to head up this new effort. Chief Harris is the prefect choice for this important job." All 142 stores in the new regional mall are expected to be open by Thanksgiving 2001.

Chief Harris and his wife, Dr. Sandra Harris, have already moved to town. Dr. Harris, a former professor at Columbia University in New York City, is hard at work on a book about Susan B. Anthony and the other early leaders of the America women's movement.

1

A reception, where local citizens are encouraged to come meet the couple, is planned in connection with the next town council meeting to be held on August 11 at 7:00 p.m. at the Town Hall in Maysville. Everyone is invited to attend.

Chapter One

The problems of the world became all too personal on that warm September Friday. Just three days after the planes flew into the World Trade Center in New York the terror hit home. The day was more like Spring than Fall in Virginia's Shenandoah Valley. Every living thing close around us was a deep, rich green. But due to some trick of light refraction the distant green mountains appeared to be a deep blue. I pointed this out to my wife Sandra. "Probably why they're called the Blue Ridge," she said. The white cumulus clouds against the deep blue sky looked like the huge backlit ad for Kodachrome film they used to have in Grand Central Station. The colors were much too vivid to be real. Confused flowers were blooming again thinking summer was coming instead of snow. It was the kind of day that reminded me how lucky I was to be alive.

Sandra and I were driving on a winding two lane country road which appeared unchanged since her 1966 Mustang convertible rolled off the assembly line. Driving this car it was easy to pretend we were still the teenagers we'd been when it was new. I often teased Sandra we should park and fool around. We wouldn't get into trouble. Any noisy cop who shined his flashlight into the car window would be working for me.

My name is Rick Harris and I'm the Chief of Police in the little town of Maysville, Virginia. The town is located in the middle of the Shenandoah Valley. There is a comfortable cushion of rural life between us and the scattered cities in this part of the state. The population in and around the town is 15,000 give or take. It is a quiet, comfortable place, usually isolated from most of the problems of the world. If a kid busts three mailboxes it's a crime wave, our small town version of "drivebys." We know, and like, our neighbors. My wife pretends the town is Mayberry and I'm Andy Taylor. She is very naïve. I have been working at becoming more naive myself.

We've been through a lot in the past couple of years and pretending has become extremely important to us. We both nearly lost our lives and, more important to me, we nearly lost each other. One of the things we pretend is we're sure we will both be alive tomorrow morning.

But I'm not really a pretending sort of a guy. I know what's out there. Before coming here I'd been what I often call without thinking, "a real cop." I'd spent nearly 25 years on the NYPD. "The

3

Job," as its members modestly call it, before losing a gun fight in the street on the eve of the new millennium. Technically, I suppose I won the gun fight. The other guy is dead and I'm not.

But I'd come within a few centimeters of becoming a Jeopardy question. "History for ten, Alex". "The answer is 'Rick Harris'." "Who was the last cop killed in the twentieth century?" "Correct. You have control of the board."

I'll tell you about all that and more about Sandra and me later. But first, let me tell you what happened that incredible September afternoon.

Sandra and I had been to lunch at a barbeque place called Bubba's located a few miles outside of town. We have both taken to southern cooking with the zeal of television evangelists and eat there much more often than is healthy. Everything they serve is dripping in a delicious, artery clogging sauce.

For the past three days we'd been like everyone else in America: zombies, unable, or at least unwilling to take our eyes from the news on television. Prior to seeing it with our own eyes neither of us could have even imagined the horror we, and the rest of the country, had witnessed. September 11, 2001 was a day, like November 22, 1963, no American will ever forget.

I'd gone through the motions of making sure the crossing guards were at the schools, but that was the extent of my law enforcement efforts in Maysville. Fortunately the local miscreants were also preoccupied with what had happened. They were apparently also glued to their television sets. There had been no real crime in Maysville since Tuesday morning when the airplanes deliberately flew into the buildings many miles from here. There is never much crime in town. But even the drunks and spousal abusers seemed to be preoccupied, not leaving their television sets even to go out for booze.

Before moving here Sandra and I had lived less than a mile from "Ground Zero" in New York City. One of my last NYPD collars had been a dope dealer in the subway under the World Trade Center. Sandra and I ate at the Windows on the World restaurant our last day living in the city to take a final look at what we were leaving. We had happily abandoned the city that never sleeps for a town that never seems to come completely awake. Now a major piece of the city is gone. Surprisingly, I had not known any of the cops who were killed doing "The Job" as I would have been doing that day were I still on the force.

My father had been a New York City firefighter but he was retired even before the first attack on the World Trade Center in the early nineties. He's gone now, having died peacefully in his bed an old man.

Having been in New York City in the 1990s I shouldn't have been surprised at the attack. We saw plenty of terrorist activity

4

then. Many people seem to have forgotten the first, February 1993, attack on the World Trade Center. Four Middle Eastern terrorists set off a bomb in a parking garage under the North Tower. The damage to the building was minor considering what could have happened. Six people eating lunch in a cafeteria directly above the bomb were killed. When the mastermind of the plot, Ramzi Yousef, was later being brought back from Pakistan for trial he told a Fed guarding him the group had believed the bomb would cause Tower One to topple, hit Tower Two and bring them both down. Yousef boasted the group had hoped to kill a quarter of a million people in the instant after the explosion.

The possibility of this happening had been downplayed by officials. The public had been assured nothing could bring down the twin towers. I wasn't directly involved in the investigation but several of my friends were. Cops talk to each other. Engineers who had studied the bomb site had written reports saying had the bomb been a little bigger and placed in a slightly different position it could have brought the towers down just like one of those building demolitions they show on television. A half dozen of the participants in the plot were arrested, tried, and sent to prison.

But even before those guys were all caught there was another plot in June of that year to blow up the United Nations building, tunnels under the Hudson River and a federal government office building in Manhattan. Eight more militant Muslim fundamentalists were arrested, and later convicted, in this plot.

While Yousef was in the wind following the first World Trade Center attack he went to the Philippines. There he was involved in a plot to kill the Pope during a planned visit. He also was involved in a plot to blow up eleven American airliners within a forty eight hour period. This horrendous disaster was avoided completely by chance. Yousef was experimenting with explosives in a Manila apartment when he did something wrong. Unfortunately he didn't blow himself up but he did literally smoke himself out of the building. He left behind a laptop computer which contained plans for the highjackings. America had been very lucky, but even a blind squirrel finds an acorn once in a while. Given enough chances even the most incompetent terrorists eventually succeed.

But terrorism seemed far removed from this beautiful day in rural Virginia. It was an incredible day for September, the convertible top was down and we promised ourselves we were going to get our lives back to normal. While I was lying in the hospital after being shot in New York the previous year, with tubes coming out of every possible opening, Sandra asked me what I would change about my life if I could. I told her truthfully, "Nothing, if I didn't end up with you holding my hand. Everything, if it means being with you." I meant it then and I believe it now.

It had been eerily different at Bubba's that day. The large

gray shack of a building was as crowded as usual but the crowd was quiet, subdued. Bubba's wife Big Mary greeted us cheerily from her high stool behind the cash register as she always does. Big Mary is a tiny woman. The "Big" before her name is to distinguish her from her daughter "Little Mary," a pretty high school senior, who works in the restaurant on Saturdays. "Little Mary" is taller than "Big Mary". Although this is confusing to me it appears to be a local custom.

The television high on the wall in the corner was tuned to CNN instead of "All My Children" as it usually was. People nodded but didn't come over to talk. Everyone seemed to be deep into their own thoughts. Only the rich smell of cooking pork seemed to be the same. Sandra and I deliberately took seats with our backs to the television set.

The folks in the kitchen had apparently not been distracted by world events. The succulent platters of dripping slow cooked meat piled high with thin fries and fat onion rings were still nearly impossible to balance on the trays. Huge cups of syrupy sweet tea or freshly squeezed lemonade were served with the food. The cups were constantly refilled by Bubba himself moving through the room with a pitcher in each hand. Nothing in New York City was ever like this. No food anywhere else had ever tasted this good. And lunch for the two of us was less than ten dollars.

After eating too much as usual we started driving back toward Maysville. On the way home we discussed the urgent need to finally get the Nordictrak unpacked and start using it. We had discussed this so many times before. I had even gotten as far as moving the box to the front of the garage. I didn't light the after lunch cigarette I would have had if Sandra were not with me.

I slowed down as we drove past the home of the mother of a local dirtbag who owed many thousands of dollars in child support. He was number one on my personal most wanted list. Sooner or later someone in the department would see him. And bust him. This is how police work really goes, slow but thorough. This case is not in the least important to the world but vital to his ex-wife and three small children. In New York the cops concentrate on locking up the bad folks. In Maysville we concentrate on helping the good ones.

The speed limit was 35 and I was going about 30 when the black Lincoln Town Car slammed on its breaks behind me starting a deadly skid. It must have been going at least a hundred miles per hour. Had I not stomped on the gas, and the powerful old engine not responded instantly we would have been rear ended and probably killed.

Before I could find a place to pull over and stop, the Lincoln straightened up and came after us. At first I assumed it would fly by us and had my cell phone in my hand to call the Maysville police dispatcher. No one was going through my town this fast.

I don't know if it was the cell phone, and the driver's

6

realization I was probably calling the police, that further enraged him but I quickly realized he was going to ram my wife's prize possession unless I could out run him. Actually I was assuming "he" since I couldn't see who was behind the car's dark tinted windows. The Mustang was over 35 years old but had been a hot rod in its day. If the engine didn't quit or one of the old, historically accurate bias type tires didn't blow we would have a chance. It seemed "road rage" had come to Maysville. I tossed the cell phone into my surprised wife's lap.

The black Lincoln filled my mirror. It was so close I couldn't see the huge car's front tag. We were going nearly 100 miles per hour in an instant. There was nothing I could do but try to stay in front of him on the winding two lane country road.

Holding the wheel with my left hand I pulled my little Italian .380 pistol from my pants pocket and stuck it between my right leg and the seat. It had been too warm for a jacket so my "real gun", a heavy 9mm pistol and shoulder rig were locked in the trunk of my cop car sitting in our driveway at home. There was no way I could even get off a shot while trying to drive at this speed. I didn't know what use the little gun, designed more to hide than shoot, would be, but it was all I had. I realized my wife and I might both die because of our naïve belief in Andy Taylor's theory of being a gunless cop. But there was no time to dwell on it.

By now Sandra had the Maysville dispatcher on the cell phone and was repeating the instructions I was yelling to her over the wind. I was asking for marked units to intercept us before we got into the little town itself. The elementary school on Main Street would be letting out soon, and I was not going to allow anyone to go into my town at this speed.

After a long couple of minutes of being able to stay just far enough in front of the Lincoln not to be rammed I saw a state trooper's car coming out of a side road on the left. It pulled in behind the Lincoln, blue lights flashing and siren screaming. I tried to slow down hoping the Lincoln would pull around me in an attempt to get away from the trooper. But he bumped me instead of trying to pass. I sped up again.

The trooper pulled beside the Lincoln now but it still refused to stop. Had I been alone in a cop car, instead of in an antique with a civilian, the trooper and I would have both slowed down until we stopped the Lincoln. But it was not going to be that easy. I prayed we wouldn't meet any traffic coming the other way. Visions of a school bus loaded with children filled my head.

Sandra was still on the cell phone with the dispatcher. I told her to tell the dispatcher to tell the trooper I would floor it when we came to the flat straight by Finley's Farm and he should hit the Lincoln in the side, hopefully making him wreck before we got into town. We were at the straight before I had time to get an answer. I

7

didn't look at the speedometer but I could feel the Mustang's ancient but mighty engine push the car even faster forward when I floored the accelerator. Good old American muscle cars!

In the mirror I saw the gap widen between us and the Lincoln for just an instant. Then I saw, and heard, the trooper hit the speeding car. The cop car was smaller, but physics favors the bumper rather than the bumped. The Lincoln wobbled in the road behind me for a split second before careening off the right shoulder, flying clear over a ditch, and finally landing in a field of corn stalks. Amazingly the big car stayed on its wheels as it plowed through the field parallel to the road until it could go no further.

By the time I got stopped, turned around and back to the shoulder of the road near where the car had flown off, the trooper was making his way across the field to the smashed up Lincoln. After ordering Sandra to move the Mustang further down the road and stay with it, I made my way down the bank and toward the car clutching my toy gun in my hand.

I was still way out of my effective pistol range when the driver's door of the Lincoln popped open and a man came out shooting. His first shot hit the trooper in the chest. He went down hard.

Hopefully, for both our sakes, he was wearing his vest despite the heat of the day. The Lincoln driver probably knew about the vest too. He was taking slow, careful aim at what I assumed was the trooper's head. Everything was happening in slow motion. I remember thinking the driver looked like the photos I had seen of Ramzi Yousef. This was not a comforting observation.

Before he could fire at the trooper again, I screamed something to get his attention and let loose all seven rounds from my pistol in his direction. I knew I didn't have a prayer of hitting him. And I knew I didn't have any more bullets. It wasn't the smart thing to do, but it was the only thing I could do.

I had bet my life, and Sandra's, on the trooper being able to recover and shoot the guy. It seemed to be working at least for the moment. The Lincoln driver was looking at me now instead of at the trooper on the ground. His gun was coming around in my direction. He must have realized I was out of bullets, and he was taking slow, careful aim with his pistol to kill me. He was also starting to smile.

Just then the trooper fired from his knees hitting the man twice in the chest. He wasn't wearing a vest. He went down in a heap like one of those huge balloons when it is punctured. I had seen men go down like this before. I knew the driver of the Lincoln was dead before he hit the ground.

He was a slight young man, almost delicate, probably in his twenties, with a swarthy complexion. I might have thought he was Hispanic until a few days before. He lay on his back, his dead eyes staring at the sun.

I had been right assuming the driver of the Lincoln was a man. But to my surprise the trooper was a petite young blond woman with her short hair tucked under her hat. She was standing there holding her smoking pistol with a blank look on her face. I was sure this was the first man she'd been forced to kill. I had previously killed three, and it doesn't get any easier.

Ignoring my orders, as usual, Sandra came running down the bank and grabbed me in a bear hug leaving the trooper, gun ready, to look inside the wrecked Lincoln. I watched over my wife's shoulder still holding my empty pistol. There was no one else in the car.

The trunk lid was ajar from the crash. The trooper moved around to the back of the car and lifted the lid with her gun barrel.

"Chief," she said in a surprisingly steady voice, "you might want to take a look at this."

As I walked to the rear of the wrecked car I was surprised to see two of my shots had actually hit the car. The little dents looked more like hail damage than bullet holes. I looked into the open trunk and saw a green cloth bound book and a bunch of documents which appeared to be written in Arabic. There was also a cardboard box which had broken open in the crash. A large pile of hundred dollar bills was spread all over the carpeted trunk. The young man still lay dead on the ground beside the wrecked car.

Before last Tuesday I don't know what I would have thought of this. But since that awful day every cop in America was looking under the bed for terrorists. I seemed to have found one. He might turn out to be an apolitical dope dealer but anybody with a gun and papers in Arabic would be assumed to be a terrorist until it was proven otherwise.

I was the ranking police officer on the scene. I knew important things needed to be done immediately, people needed to be notified. Elaborate traps needed to be set to catch the other terrorists I was certain were still out there. He was taking the cash to someone. Time was of the essence! I needed to do many important things immediately.

But I didn't have a clue what I should do to start the wheels rolling. I was sure we were all in deep, deep trouble and, in this situation, pretending otherwise would not help at all. This was way beyond my, and Andy Taylor's, experience.

I was standing there with my cell phone in my hand wondering whom to call when I heard the screaming sirens of the approaching cop cars. The rest of the cavalry was arriving, too late as usual.

Chapter Two

The young trooper had holstered her weapon and was making her way toward the road. She was rubbing the hole in her shirt where the bullet had hit her. She probably had broken ribs but neither of us mentioned it. I knew from personal experience how much it hurt to be shot even if a vest stopped the bullet from actually penetrating.

She was looking back at Sandra and I still standing in the field. I knew she wanted to protect the crime scene but was too polite to tell me to get away from the car. I nodded to her and took Sandra by the arm. We made our way back to our car parked on the highway's shoulder. Sandra clutched my arm as we leaned against the trunk together. I was still holding my cell phone as I watched the mob begin to arrive.

I thought about the "Alice's Restaurant" littering case where more police officers arrived at the "scene of the crime" than the town had police officers. "It was the biggest thing that had happened in twenty five years and everyone wanted to get into the newspaper story about it." Then it occurred to me, I was "Officer Obie". But no one shot Arlo Guthrie for littering in the song. Then the war had been half way around the world instead of on American soil. Those were simpler days even if they had not seemed so at the time.

Cop cars, blue lights flashing, kept arriving. My cops, sheriff's deputies, and state troopers just kept coming. Soon police cars were parked as far as I could see on both sides of the narrow road. The officers milled around not having any more idea of what to do than I had. When my cops approached me for instructions I told them it was the trooper's crime scene and to stay out of the way.

I was still standing there with Sandra clutching my arm, trying to decide whom to call when a state police sergeant arrived. He was a middle-aged gray haired man whose demeanor exuded confidence. He immediately took charge. He sent troopers to drive stakes into the ground and string yellow crime scene tape around the wrecked Lincoln and the body of the dead man. He sent other troopers to direct passing traffic around the congestion of police officers and police cars. He sent my crime scene tech and those of the sheriff away. He was a total professional and just naturally seemed to take total charge. No one challenged his authority; they just instantly did as he told them to do.

Watching his cool professionalism I suddenly I realized whom I should call. I found Captain Robert White's cell number in my cell phone's directory and hit the "send" button. I transferred the phone to my right hand since Sandra was still holding on to my left arm. When White answered I could barely hear him for the loud motor noise in the background. When I told him who was calling he said, "Ricky, are you okay? I understand you were in a trooper involved shooting out your way. She says you saved her life."

I told him I was fine, and he said, "I'll probably lose this call pretty soon. I'm in a chopper on my way to the scene now. Stick around we'll talk when I get there. I'm glad you're okay. Thanks again for saving my trooper."

I immediately felt better. Captain White was on the way. I have to admit, having spent so many years on the NYPD, I am somewhat of a snob about other cops. New York City is the big leagues of law enforcement. "If you can make it there you can make it anywhere" the song says.

Don't get me wrong, my cops in Maysville are perfectly adequate for the law enforcement challenges they face on a daily basis. But this was going to be way beyond their abilities. Maybe I was too caught up in the terrorist hysteria and the guy was simply a dope dealer on his way to buy drugs. But whatever he was, this was going to be a real mystery; and, like most cops, I hate mysteries. And to be brutally honest, it was probably going to be way over my head as well. But I was confident Captain White would be able to handle it, whatever it turned out to be.

I first met White shortly after I came to Maysville, before I publicly took over as police chief. He had needed an experienced cop, who was not known in the area, for an undercover assignment to break up a ring of "sportsmen" who were staging dog fights. Dog fighting itself is only a misdemeanor in Virginia and those arrested for it are usually just fined. But White had bigger plans for these folks.

The investigation started when someone stole a tiny white poodle named "Buttercup" from the fenced yard of Miss Mamie Tate. Officially Miss Mamie was the previous police chief's secretary. She's now mine. Unofficially she runs the Maysville police department and is known by nearly everyone in town to be the long term "significant other" of the county sheriff, and a force to be reckoned with.

After Miss Mamie spent several days putting up posters, featuring photos of Buttercup with pink ribbons on her ears, on every pole in town, a local petty criminal and ex-con named Byron Tuttle called her at home. He told her he knew what happened to Buttercup.

Tuttle was, and is, pretty much of a lowlife. But Miss Mamie had been unexpectedly kind to his wife the last time he was locked up so he told her the story. A guy with the picturesque name of Jesse James Porter had stolen Buttercup to use in training the fighting dogs he raised. Tuttle claimed he had gone so far as to try to buy Buttercup back from Porter, but it was too late.

The following morning Miss Mamie walked slowly around town taking down the reward posters. She stayed in her house completely inconsolable for several days. As her grief dissipated she began to get angry. Someone, she decided, was going to pay big time for murdering her Buttercup.

She got the usual runarounds at first. Dog fighting, if you could catch them in the act, was a misdemeanor. She had gotten Buttercup from the animal shelter and could not prove she was worth a hundred dollars to make stealing her a felony. The only witness was a convicted felon.

People told her about the practical problems but Miss Mamie simply didn't care. She had embarked upon a blood feud. She was going to put some serious scum, in her opinion, in prison for some serious time. The fact that she was held in high regard by so many people in law enforcement in Virginia made her unstoppable.

First she talked to the local prosecutor who owed the sheriff for his political career. She talked with one of her former Sunday school pupils who is the nearest federal prosecutor. After she got all her research done, enlisted all the local allies she could think of, she drove to Richmond to visit with Captain White at State Police Headquarters.

He listened to her without comment for nearly half an hour. When she had finished outlining her plan he smiled at her and said, "Let's get them, Miss Mamie." "Operation Buttercup" was underway.

A few days later Porter, driving his pickup, was pulled over by Captain White dressed as a trooper and driving a marked Virginia State Police car. It took Porter less than three minutes to flip on his friends and associates and agree to cooperate. The sting was underway.

Word quickly spread through the dog fighting world that Porter would be hosting the Super Bowl of dog fighting on his Virginia farm a couple of weeks later. When the big day arrived I was there pretending to be the New York lawyer for a Columbian drug dealer who was interested in buying some champion quality fighting dogs at outrageous prices. It was an amazing scene. The field around Porter's barn was filled nearly to capacity with motor homes, expensive pickups and luxury cars.

We arrested 217 "sportsmen" at the big fight. They were charged with the state dog fighting misdemeanor as well as conspiracy and numerous federal racketeering charges. Conspiracy to commit a misdemeanor is itself a felony in Virginia. Six of those arrested were wanted on outstanding warrants from around the country. One was facing a murder for hire charge in Georgia. He

12

quickly began confessing to, and naming his accomplices in, everything he'd ever done in Virginia which couldn't result in a death sentence here.

Both the feds and the state cops quickly began playing games of "trade up" with the less involved arrestees. A bank robbery in which a clerk had been killed was solved. Literally a ton of stolen property was recovered. A farmer from Mississippi decided not to contest the forfeiture of his $200,000 motor home, paid a $100 fine for participating in the dog fight and left town on a Greyhound bus.

A bucket full of Rolex watches, a dozen farms and over 100 luxury cars were also seized. I am using one, a huge Chrysler 300, as my official police car.

Thinking about my cop car brought me back to the present and reminded me of something I needed to do. I looked around until I found one of my officers. I motioned to him to come to me.

"Cunningham I need you to drive my wife home in her Mustang and bring back my police car," I said.

"Yes, sir," the officer said reaching for the keys I held out.

"I'm not going anywhere," my wife said firmly, never taking her eyes from the dead man and the activity in the field or her hand from my arm.

"Cunningham," I said calmly, "I need for you to get another officer to drive you to my house and bring back my police car."

"Yes, sir," he said again, trying not to grin, taking the keys and trotting away toward the group of my cops standing on the side of the road. Sandra renewed her grip on my arm. I didn't like being defied by my wife in front of my subordinate; it is bad for discipline. But I should have known better than to give her an order in the first place.

My excuse, to myself, was I was in my police chief mode instead of my husband mode. In my mind I pictured the President of the United States in the White House giving orders. He could put ships to sea and planes into the air. He could order cities bombed and men to their deaths. His orders were instantly obeyed by everyone. Everyone except, of course, the First Lady. I need to get a dog so someone who lives at my house will do what I tell them to do.

I pulled loose from my wife, put my arms around her, kissed her on the forehead and said, "I'm sorry, darling. I have to leave you and go to work now. If you want someone to drive you home later get one of my cops to do it. I love you more than anything."

Sandra had tears in her eyes. "He could have killed you," she said.

"No, darling," I lied. "I wasn't in any danger. Bubba's cholesterol is more likely to kill me. It's over. Please go home. I'll call you when I can."

Talking to Cunningham had reminded me I was the Chief of Police in Maysville and responsible for the safety of my town.

13

Hopefully no one had robbed the bank while my cops and I milled around gawking on the side of the road.

I walked over to the group of Maysville police officers. Their conversations stopped immediately. "Don't you guys think maybe you should get back and protect the town?" I asked.

They all looked at me sheepishly until one of them said, "Chief, we're the day shift. It's past three and Miss Mamie has the evening shift out patrolling."

I continued to look at the officer until he said, "We probably should get some of these cars back though in case they're needed." I nodded my agreement and the officers dispersed toward their vehicles.

I should have known. As long as Miss Mamie was around, the Maysville P.D. would run just fine without much input from me.

The roar from the approaching helicopter was deafening. It came from the east, a few hundred feet over the road, staying well away from the crime scene so as not to blow evidence away. The pilot found a spot he liked a hundred yards or so from the taped off area and gently set the machine on the ground. White was the first one out, followed by a photographer and a crime scene tech carrying their heavy equipment. All three men trotted toward the crime tape as the pilot lifted off, flying away in the opposite direction.

I just stood there watching Captain White as he took over the investigation. I was, after all, outside my jurisdiction and only a witness to what had happened. Both the involved trooper and the sergeant quickly came over to their superior. I could see him asking questions, getting answers, and giving orders, but could not hear what was being said. The photographer moved around behind him, circling the taped off crime scene, taking pictures from every conceivable angle. Officer Obie's "27 color 8x10s" were being made. A trooper stood outside the tape watching the trunk of the car, safeguarding the spilled cash on the carpet.

After completing his circuit outside the tape the photographer moved inside for close-ups of the body still lying where it fell. When he'd gotten the photos he wanted he walked over to White and said something I couldn't hear.

I saw the captain nod to the patiently waiting evidence tech. The young man took rubber gloves from his pocket, putting them on as he walked to the body. He went through the dead man's pockets placing the contents into a plastic evidence bag. Then he began examining the stack of documents in the car's trunk, lifting each page carefully by the corner so as not to destroy any fingerprints which might be on the papers. When he was done he placed the documents in a larger evidence bag.

After checking to make sure he had everything, the tech returned to his boss with the bags. White looked around, then he and the evidence tech started toward the sergeant's car parked on the

14

shoulder of the road. He motioned for me to join them. I met the two men at the car.

I was utterly surprised when White put his arms around me in a bear hug. "Ricky," he said, "my trooper says you saved her life."

I gave him my best "aw shucks, it's all in a day's work" expression and said nothing. The young man handed the larger bag to White. "Boss, all these papers are in a foreign language. I guess it's Arabic."

White took the bag, motioning to a trooper waiting by his car. The trooper hurried to his boss. "Take these to the FBI office in Richmond."

"Yes sir," the trooper responded. He ran back to his car and was gone in an instant.

While this was happening the tech placed a large white plastic mat on the hood of the car. At White's nod of approval he emptied the evidence bag onto the plastic.

The captain took rubber gloves from his back pocket and two sets of tweezers from the tech before beginning to examine the contents of the dead man's pockets. The tech stood watching to preserve the chain of evidence should the matter ever get to court. I was impressed with their professional handling of the possible evidence. Although the driver was dead I knew this was just the beginning of something big, although at the moment I could not have possibly guessed the spectacular way it would end. Or what Sandra and I would experience while it ran its course.

There was a wallet, a green passport with Arabic writing on it, half an inch of folded U.S. currency with a one dollar bill on the outside, a few coins, and several small folded pieces of paper. White started with the passport. It was from Yemen and had been issued to a "Nawaf Alghamdi." The photo appeared to be of the dead man. White wrote the information on his pad.

Then the captain started unfolding the small papers. The first one was a receipt for gas from a station in Greenbelt, Maryland. Someone using a credit card in the name "Robert Downs" had bought eighteen gallons of premium at 8:22 that morning. The next paper had only a phone number on it. 917-555-9911 was the number. I knew this was a New York City number and I knew the first "9" in the last group of four numbers meant it was a pay phone.

White made a small hand signal to a young man in a dark blue windbreaker and sun glasses leaning against a car parked across the road. His hair was a little too long for his military bearing. The man walked across the road, joining us. No introductions were made. White showed him the information from the passport and the phone number. The man copied the information onto a pad from his pocket, nodded and walked off down the road. He apparently knew what to do without any instructions from White. He was the first of many men whose names and jobs I would not be told during the course of this investigation.

The next slip of paper had the words "Starlite", "Maysville" and "Robert Downs" written on it in block letters. "It's a mom and pop motel in town," I said.

"Do you want to send one of your cops?" White asked.

I shook my head. He then pointed to a state police investigator I knew by sight across the road. The man, dressed in civilian clothes, joined us. White showed him the slip of paper, holding it by the corner with the tweezers to preserve any possible fingerprints.

The investigator wrote the information from the slip onto a pad he pulled from his jacket pocket. "Talk to the owner quietly. We may want to try to set up there," White said. The investigator nodded his understanding. White took his pad and wrote his cell phone number on the page. "Call me as soon as you know something."

"Yes, sir," he said. He turned and briskly walked toward where I assumed his car was parked.

White pointed to the pile on the car hood, "See anything else of interest, Ricky?"

I shook my head. We had looked at everything on the hood. White returned the stuff to the evidence bag, returned the bag to the evidence tech and walked toward the wrecked Lincoln in the field. I followed along behind.

We looked at the money lying on the trunk's carpet for a minute. Then White, still wearing his rubber gloves, picked up the green book with the Arabic writing on it. He leafed through it looking for whatever might be stuck between the pages. "It's a copy of the Koran," I said.

White looked surprised. "Have you read it?"

"Just a little of it," I said. "We had a death we'd put down to suicide in New York. But the dead guy's brother said it couldn't be. His brother was a devout Muslim and devout Muslims do not commit suicide any more than devout Catholics do. Turned out the victim's business partner killed him for his share of a roofing business. He would've got away with it but for the brother and the Koran."

"So how did the devout Muslim air plane hijackers commit suicide?"

"Same way so-called Christians who claim to believe in the absolute "right to life" bomb abortion clinics and kill people I guess. They think God told them to do it. And Pat Robertson and Jerry Falwell have said that abortionists, feminists, gays and liberal groups were partly responsible for the terrorist attacks," I said.

White shook his head sadly. "So in addition to Virginia's home grown fanatics, now we're importing them." White's cell phone rang. After a brief conversation he said, "My guy says there has been a call to the motel for Robert Downs. The clerk told the caller he hasn't checked in yet. Maybe he'll call back. Come on, I'll ride with you."

We trotted down the road to where my Chrysler was parked. Officer Cunningham was leaning against it. He handed me the keys. I looked around for Sandra but didn't see either her or the Mustang. I made a mental note to call her as soon as I got a minute. Hopefully she'd gone home and was not off somewhere playing Nancy Drew.

I immediately opened the trunk to get my 9mm pistol and shoulder holster. It is a blue steel Browning which holds 14 rounds of ammunition. When I first started carrying it in New York the range supervisor had said, "If you can't do it with 14 shots you probably can't do it." Although the gun is heavy, it was a comforting weight under my arm. If I was involved in another gun fight today I could now do more than throw spit balls to distract the other guy. I covered the gun with a dark windbreaker from the trunk. It was still a little too warm for the jacket. But worrying about discomfort had nearly cost me my life earlier in the afternoon. My first firearms instructor on the NYPD had drummed into us, "It is better to have a gun and not need it, than to need a gun and not have it."

With the pistol under my arm I felt like a cop again. I called Miss Mamie to tell her I would be tied up for a while but would be in touch. I also asked her to call Sandra and tell her I would call when I got a chance.

As soon as we were strapped into my big Chrysler, White was on his cell phone. I could only hear cryptic bits of his side of the several conversations which took place continually until we pulled up at the Starlite Motel on Main Street in Maysville.

The Starlight Motel is a relic from the 1950s, before the Interstate highway, when all the through traffic had come right down Main Street and the middle of town. It was now a little run down but still open for business, mostly renting rooms by the week to construction workers from the huge outlet mall being built near the Interstate. It was still early afternoon and the parking lot was nearly empty.

I pulled past the office, parking in front of the first unit. The Starlite's design, with the parking lot visible from Main Street, kept it from being popular with the "afternoon delight" crowd. My Chrysler didn't look like a cop car so it should be okay parked in plain sight.

White and I entered the lobby. We were met by the investigator and the owner of the motel, Harvey Joseph. Harvey is the son of the original owners. I knew him from around town. He nodded to me when we came in. The investigator reported to his captain, "The guy called right before I called you. Phone company security has taken the incoming lines out of service; he'll get a recording saying all circuits are busy, until they can get the tracing equipment in place. Here's the number for the security guy. He says call him on a cell phone so y'all can keep the line open."

White took the paper with the number on it and nodded his

approval.

I pulled my cell phone from my pocket, offering it to White so he wouldn't have to tie up his phone. He shook his head, handing me the paper. "You talk to him."

I nodded my agreement and dialed the number. I was glad to be given a role in the case.

The call was answered simply, "Security."

I told the unidentified person on the other end who I was and why I was calling.

"Hi, Chief," he said in a cheerful voice. "We just about have everything hooked up and will put the line back into service in a couple of minutes. We should be able to get the number and location of any incoming call in a matter of a minute or so. The further the calling phone is away from the motel the longer it will take. If it is international we're probably screwed."

I relayed the message to White. He thought about it for a minute. He took the phone from me and said, "I have my department on full alert. Can you call Sergeant Williams in Richmond? Wait a minute I'll find the number for you. Oh, okay." He handed my cell phone back to me. "He knows Williams and already has him on the line."

I'd always been impressed with the phone company's security in New York. The guys who run it are mostly retired detectives and feds. They were always cooperative in providing needed information. Since things have become computerized I've been amazed at the amount of information they have on telephone use. As a young beat cop I'd once written a parking ticket for a phone company truck only to be severely chewed out by my sergeant. I voided the ticket and have never seen one on a phone company truck since.

We stood around in the lobby, waiting. I had my cell phone to my ear. Everyone jumped when the motel phone rang. White picked it up, "Starlite Motel," he answered cheerfully.

Shaking his head, he looked at me and said, "It's the phone company guy." He had a short, cryptic conversation before hanging up the phone.

White sent his investigator out to wait in the car with another investigator across the street, where they had a good view of the motel and passing traffic, in case the bad guys drove by looking for the Lincoln. I went out to my car and found the tiny headset for my cell phone, still in its bubble pack from Radio Shack. I attached it to both the phone and my ear before taking a seat on the lobby couch, pretending to read the paper and waited. I hate to wait.

But I knew cops were waiting all over the state. If everything went according to plan the cavalry would swoop down on the caller while he was still on the line.

White was busy answering the phone and running the motel

18

with his usual efficiency. Several of the motel's resident construction workers returned from work and came to the lobby for ice. A couple of them talked with Harvey about various things. No one seemed curious about White standing behind the counter, answering the phone. A couple of them nodded to me on the couch.

I had been sitting there looking at the same newspaper page for nearly an hour when the call came. White answered it cheerily, "Starlite Motel." He nodded his head in my direction. Across the street I could see the investigators sit up straighter in their unmarked car.

"Yes, sir," White said. "Mr. Downs checked in a little while ago. Would you like me to ring his room? Please hold."

From the cell phone in my ear I could hear the phone company security guy, "Keep him on the phone. We're locked on and tracing." White was pushing the button on the antique switchboard so the caller could hear the ringing sound it made.

He waited as long as he dared before saying, "He doesn't appear to be answering. I can see his car outside his room. We've been having phone problems. Wait a second and I'll go knock on his door." He held the receiver away from his head. I could hear activity on my cell phone.

"We've got him," the voice said excitedly. "Let me give the location to the State Police in Richmond and I'll be back with you." There was a pause. "Okay it's a pay phone outside a Quicky Mart on Main Street in a town called Walton's Corner."

I wrote this on my pad, holding it up for White to see. He nodded while still holding the phone. Apparently the caller was still holding. He said, "He isn't in his room. Hold another second while I check the restaurant."

Sticking my pad in my pocket, I walked over to where I could hear what was happening on the phone White held. All I could hear was breathing. Then I heard a siren over the phone, it was getting closer and louder. Then there were a couple of excited words in a language I didn't understand, and finally a thud as the caller dropped the receiver.

Chapter Three

The investigators were running across the street toward us as White and I sprinted to my car. He told them to stay on the motel in case anyone showed up looking for Robert Downs. We strapped in and were out of the parking lot in an instant. It was about twenty miles to Walton's Corner.

It was infuriating driving slowly down the main street of Maysville. I noticed people waving to me out of the corner of my eye but was too focused to return the waves. I picked up speed as we passed the ball fields on the edge of town. One of my cops was sitting in his car, hidden behind the restrooms, pointing his radar gun at the traffic. Things were back to normal in Maysville. I was going twice the posted 30 mph speed limit.

As soon as I cleared the town limits I turned on the blue lights in the car's grill and stepped down harder on the accelerator. The huge, powerful machine leaped forward. White was talking on his cell phone, writing notes on his pad. I wanted to call Sandra but needed to keep both hands on the wheel at this speed. Plus I didn't know what to say to her. "Hi, darling, guess what? I'm driving down the road at 100 miles per hour on my way to a possible shoot out with a bunch of terrorists! How's your day?" That would cheer her up.

We sped through the Virginia countryside on a continuation of the two lane country road I had been on earlier with Sandra. I suppose the fields were still as green and the mountains still looked blue, but I didn't really notice. Too many things had changed. There was no longer room in my mind for the innocent observations I'd made earlier in the day. I had to deal with the fact this was not Mayberry, and I was not Andy Taylor. The world had changed too much for it to ever be that way again.

We arrived at the Quicky Mart in record time. The parking lot was circled with yellow crime scene tape. A Walton's Grove police car was parked just outside the tape with a Middle-Eastern looking young man sitting in the backseat cage. This all looked encouraging. I parked next to the other cop car.

An overweight, middle aged man wearing a uniform from the town's police department came over to the car immediately. He apparently knew Captain White and half saluted him.

"Good work," White said, walking toward the pay phone in the corner of the parking lot. "Did you see the guy while he was on

20

the phone?"

"No, sir," the officer replied. "He was already back in the store behind the counter when I got here."

White looked at the phone, its receiver back in its cradle. "Who hung up the phone?" The officer looked sheepish but didn't answer.

Suddenly another, newer Walton's Grove police car came flying into the parking lot, scattering gravel in all directions. Before the car was completely stopped a large, red faced man wearing a powder blue jump suit with the police department's patches on it and carrying a huge gun on his hip climbed out.

He nodded to White on his way to the other police car. White returned the nod. "Good to see you, Chief," he said.

The chief's face was getting even redder as he yanked open the rear door of the police car and lifted the prisoner out of the cage. I was stunned, not knowing if he was about to start beating the handcuffed man, and what I should do if he did.

Then he pointed his huge right hand at the other Walton's Corner police officer. "Barney," he bellowed, "get your dumb ass over here and take the cuffs off this boy!"

The officer started toward the chief but wasn't moving fast enough to suit his boss. "Run, you idiot!"

The officer ran with his keys shaking in his hand. He unlocked and removed the handcuffs. The chief took the released prisoner in a bear hug. "I am so sorry, boy," he said. "I was home after taking my wife over to Charlottesville to the doctor when I heard about this. Are you okay?"

"I'm fine, Chief," he said. "Thank you for coming."

"When your momma called I burned up the road." He turned to his subordinate. "Get out of my sight. I'll deal with you later." The officer slinked away.

Then he turned to White and me, sticking out his hand in my direction. "I'm Curtis Buford, the police chief here." I told him my name and title.

"You're the one who saved that little trooper girl's life. She is a sweet child and I thank you for saving her." I wondered if she'd be offended by him describing her as a "sweet child" after she'd won a gun fight with an armed terrorist. But he said it with such affection I didn't think she would be. I gave him by best "aw shucks" grin.

"I apologize for my idiot cop. The job doesn't pay much so we don't get much." He squeezed the released prisoner tighter and said, "This boy's family has been living around here for over 75 years. His grandmomma used to baby sit me. His brother is a Baptist preacher. Muslim terrorist my ass!" I couldn't help liking this plain spoken man.

He kept his arm around the clerk's shoulders to show the world the young man was under his protection. A little dark skinned girl about six years old appeared from nowhere, wrapping her arms around the young man's legs.

"Now, Captain," he said shaking his head. "I understand somebody called the boy the trooper killed from this phone?" White nodded his agreement. He turned to the young man, "Did you see anyone use the phone, David?"

"No. I was in the store watching CNN and not paying attention. But a dark skinned guy did come in the store earlier this afternoon. He said something to me in a language I didn't understand. I didn't answer. He bought a Diet Coke and left."

"What did he look like?" White asked.

"Dark complexion, twenties, six feet or a little less, wearing jeans and a plaid short sleeved shirt," the young man replied.

"If we get an artist here do you think you can help him with a drawing?" White asked. The young man nodded. "What was he driving?" White continued.

"I don't know. I didn't see it," he said.

"I know. I saw the car," the little girl said proudly. Everyone looked at her. "It was one of those big station wagons, dark green with blue and orange license tags."

"Do you remember the license tag?" White asked.

"The letters on the tag were R, A and G. I don't remember the numbers."

"What kind of car was it?" White asked.

"I don't know kinds. I just know colors and letters," she said, looking sad to have let us down.

Chief Buford patted the little girl on the shoulder. "She's bright as she is pretty, and she's pretty as a picture." She beamed at the attention.

White wrote the information on his pad. He turned to the young man again. "Who hung up the phone?"

He pointed to the Walton's Corner officer sulking on the porch of the store. Chief Buford's face got red again. He motioned for his cop to come to him. Before the chief could light into him White asked, "Why did you come with your siren blasting. Didn't the state police dispatcher tell you we wanted to catch the guy on the phone?"

"That wasn't my fault," the cop said defensively. "I was coming quiet as I could when I met the rescue squad coming toward me. It was their siren that scared him off."

White didn't ask him why he'd cuffed the young store clerk. That was between the cop and his chief. It was bound to get loud and ugly.

We were still standing there when White's cell phone rang. He answered it and walked away from us to keep his conversation private. The crime scene tape was taken down except around the phone itself. Soon the chief and his cop left.

When White returned he told me folks were on their way, and he needed to wait for them. I could go home or stay. It was up to me. I stayed.

We went into the store and both picked up Krispy Kreme doughnuts and diet drinks. In my opinion, based on my experiences, the stereotype of cops and doughnuts is usually accurate. We had to argue with the clerk, David, to let us pay.

Before we left the store White apologized to the young man for the local cop's behavior. David just shrugged it off and said, "I probably better get used to it. It's going to get worse for anyone who looks like an Arab before it gets better." Neither of us could argue with that.

Back outside we leaned against my car and ate. "They rerouted the trooper I sent to Richmond with the papers from the car," White said. "Now he's going straight to the feds in Quantico. Why didn't I think of that?" I smiled and nodded for no particular reason.

Then White said, "Ricky I want to tell you how much I appreciate you risking your life to save my trooper this afternoon. It was a brave thing you did." I gave him the humble, "aw shucks" look again.

"Don't make light of this," White continued. "I saw the tiny dings your little bullets made in the car's fender. Even if you'd hit the guy it wouldn't have hurt him at that range. You knew that when you drew his fire away from the trooper. It was a very brave thing to do."

Again I said nothing. To tell the truth I don't think I'd given any thought to the danger I was putting myself in before I did it. I'm a trained cop, and the training just took over. Besides, the trooper had just put her life in danger to save me and, more importantly, my wife Sandra. And if she hadn't stopped the guy before he got to town the main street could have been littered with the small mangled bodies of school children.

We stood leaning against my car for a couple of minutes, neither of us speaking. Then I went around and opened my car trunk.

I pulled the carpet in the right rear corner lose from its clip. I reached into the hole behind it, between the supports and the fender, and pulled out my treasure. The hiding place would not withstand a thorough, professional search, but no one would see its contents by merely opening the trunk.

I hid my treasure in my hands and returned to White's side. I opened my hands to show him the rumpled pack of Marlboro Ultra Lights, a disposable lighter, and roll of Certs I held.

White leaned back against the car, laughing loudly. Then he took a cigarette from the offered pack. I lit his, then my own. We stood there together savoring the smoke as only people who do not smoke on a regular basis can.

"We share a secret vice," White said laughing.

23

"Yeah," I replied. "I don't smoke much. Usually just after lunch if Sandra isn't watching me."

"I smoke a little more than that," White said.

"If we're telling the truth here, I do too," I admitted. "Sandra hates cigarettes, and I honestly think if I told her I had a girlfriend she'd say 'you didn't smoke a cigarette after you had sex with her did you?'"

White laughed again. "I really appreciate your help with this, Ricky. I hope you'll stay involved. I like hanging out with you; and if I partner with investigators from the state police I'm their boss, which isn't good."

"I'll be happy to do whatever I can. Miss Mamie runs the Maysville PD so I have lots of free time."

White laughed again. "Miss Mamie could run the state police investigators too. Fortunately for me it hasn't occurred to her yet.

"Ricky, everything has changed since the eleventh. You'd be amazed at what is going on just in Virginia. A bunch of the highjackers had Virginia drivers' licenses or DMV identity cards issued in fake names. There is a group of radical followers of some Muslim extremist from Pakistan living in a compound outside Charlottesville. Their leader back home was in prison until some of his followers high jacked a plane in India and traded the passengers for his release."

"A local cop stopped a car driving on a flat tire about 10 miles from Dulles Airport. The driver had aviation manuals, three different Social Security cards and driver's licenses from five different states showing different variations of his name.

"There are a bunch of Middle Easterners involved in dope and gun dealing all over the state. They're so close-knit I couldn't get an undercover in even if I had one who speaks the correct language. On the rare occasions we arrest one they never flip and testify."

"What about the feds?" I asked.

"The change there has been interesting. There is a lot more information sharing. They used to withhold information so they'd get the credit. Now they share it in order to avoid the blame when the next catastrophic event happens."

I laughed. I, and most other cops, share his distain for federal law enforcement. Most of them, in my opinion, are heavily armed bureaucrats. But I had worked with some good guys on the organized crime task force in New York. I try to look at other cops, federal and otherwise, as individuals instead of stereotypes. But when you know you may be running down an alley chasing a perp with a gun it's best to err on the side of skepticism in choosing whom you want with you. I'd decided I'd go anywhere with White.

"Things are better but there is still a lot of 'mushrooming' going on," White continued. "Mushrooming" is when the other agency keeps you in the dark and covers you with manure.

"They arrested three guys in Chicago who used to work for a company that provides meals to airlines. They still had their work IDs and could have gotten access to airliners. The Canadians busted a guy with a fake pilot's license and stolen Lufthansa pilots' uniforms.

"There is so much information being shared it is impossible to sort and prioritize it all. To make matters worse most of my investigators have more experience with radar guns than they do with computers. It is so frustrating."

I said, "I have been reading in the paper there is a lot of involvement by intelligence agencies in the investigations into the terrorists."

"Oh yeah," White said. "That is a whole other can of worms, some good and some bad. The CIA says thousands of men have gone through terrorists' training schools in the Middle East, and we have no idea where most of them are at the moment. We are getting a lot of helpful information, but there is also a lot of bugging and break-ins going on.

"And that's just our guys. There are foreign intelligence officers here from all over the world. There is a Canadian spook whose name is, I swear to God, 'James Bondsworth'. Who would have thought Canada even had an intelligence agency?" I couldn't help laughing.

"Yeah," White said. "But some of these guys are anything but funny. I heard from a fed I know there was plot to blow up a Jewish school outside Boston. They had some good evidence on the actual bombers but nothing at all on the guy everyone thought was behind it. There was an Israeli intelligence guy involved in the case. One day the suspected mastermind and the Israeli agent both just disappeared. There is some scary stuff going on."

I remembered what Ben Franklin had said about anyone who tries to trade freedom for security will end up with neither. Hopefully old Ben was wrong.

These intelligence guys are a whole different breed from normal people. Shortly after I'd taken over as police chief in Maysville the owner of a local bar was severely beaten one night in his parking lot after he'd closed. Surprisingly he wasn't robbed although he'd had a wad of money in his pocket. I went, with my lone detective, to see the guy in the hospital the following morning. I've never seen anyone as thoroughly messed up. His nose was broken, and his right ear was badly torn. I asked him if he had any idea who had done it.

He said, "I know exactly who did it. My former father-in-law did it."

I asked if he could identify his former father-in-law as

having been in the parking lot. He told me the father-in-law wasn't there. He had some other guy do it for him. He said the father-in-law was a retired CIA spook.

Back at the office I checked on the father-in-law with our crack, all knowing intelligence division. Miss Mamie said the father-in-law, whom everyone called "The Colonel", was indeed retired from the CIA. He lived in the large Victorian house on the right coming into town from the Interstate. She confirmed his daughter was now divorced from the bar owner, and our cops had been to their house on domestic calls often through the years they were together. I asked her if she thought the Colonel was responsible for the beating. She just shrugged.

I decided to go see the Colonel for myself. I parked in front of the huge white clapboard house with its well kept lawn. There was a child's "Big Wheel" on the porch. I knocked on the door.

A voice from inside said, "Come in. The door is unlocked."

Through the foyer I could see a man of undeterminable age sitting in a wheelchair in the middle of the room. There was a catheter bag hanging on one side of the chair and a small oxygen tank mounted on the other. A clear tube fed oxygen to one of those little things under his nose. Next to him on the floor was a little dark haired girl with large green eyes, who looked about three, quietly playing with her Barbie dolls.

I introduced myself. He asked what he could do for me. I told him his former son-in-law had been badly beaten early that morning and asked if he knew anything about it.

He looked at me with his bright green eyes for a long time, then reached in his shirt pocket and handed me a Polaroid picture of a young dark haired woman. Her nose was broken and her right ear showed the stitches that had been used to reattach it. I could not see the color of the woman's eyes, but I was sure they were green. When I looked up from the photo he quickly took it out of my hand and returned it to his shirt pocket. I held out my hand and asked him if I could keep the photo. He simply said, "No." I stood there for a while looking at him. His return gaze was steady. I thanked him for his time and left.

A few months later Miss Mamie told me the Colonel had died in his sleep the night before. Apparently he'd been putting his affairs in order and getting ready to leave his family.

No one was ever arrested for the beating. There wasn't any evidence. I sincerely hope the bar owner is smart enough to know a man like the Colonel would have left his daughter a number to call if she should ever need to do so. He wasn't the type of man to leave her and his granddaughter unprotected.

"So I need to be careful with these intelligence guys," White said bringing me back to the present. "Some of them are really strange so don't be offended if I don't introduce you to them. They won't talk in front of you but I'll get you up to speed on what you need to know when we are alone."

I nodded my agreement. "Whatever I can do to help is fine with me."

White said, "This is probably going to be a waste of time here. I wish the trooper hadn't had to kill the guy so we could question him."

"It seemed like a good idea at the time," I said. He laughed again. I was as excited as a little kid on Christmas Eve about being involved in this investigation. I wanted to be part of whatever was going to happen. It would certainly be a big improvement over hanging around the police station in Maysville pretending I was in charge.

Maybe I could be a real cop again, if just for a little while. Sandra would not be happy about this. Thinking of my wife reminded me to call her. I was reaching into my pocket for my cell phone when the convoy arrived.

In front was a marked Virginia State Police car, its blue roof lights flashing in the twilight. Following were three other unmarked, but obvious, police cars. They all came to a stop in the parking lot.

A technician was the first one out from the front passenger seat of the marked car. He trotted over to White carrying his heavy looking work box. The captain pointed toward the pay phone and the tech trotted to it. He set his box down just outside the crime scene tape, put on surgical gloves, and went to work looking for fingerprints.

Men were climbing out of the other cars. White went to join them. I went over, sat down on the porch and dialed my home number. It was nearly 8 p.m. and I had not talked with my wife since the crime scene hours before.

"Hi, darling," I said cheerfully when she answered. "How are you?"

"Fine," she said curtly.

"Did you get home okay?" I asked.

"Yes."

This was not going to go well. But like any experienced husband I blindly plowed ahead. "I'm sorry I haven't called. I got tied up in the investigation. I'm in Walton's Corner with Captain White. This is the first chance I've had to call you." The truth is a good thing but I didn't see any point in being a fanatic about it.

"I was worried about you, Ricky," she said.

I looked at my cell phone. It didn't show any messages so I said, "You should have called me."

"You know I don't like to bother you when you are working."

"It is never a bother when you call, my love. It's usually the highlight of my day." There was only silence on the phone.

"Anyway I should be leaving here in a couple of minutes. Have you eaten?"

"No. I was waiting to hear from you."

"There is salmon in the freezer. Pull it out and I'll cook it on the grill when I get there," I said cheerily.

"It'll be too frozen to cook. I think I'll go to the Widow's. They're open later and have fresh fish on Friday nights."

"Okay. I'll meet you there before you finish eating. Tell him to save me some fish. I love you more than anything, darling," I said.

"I love you too, Ricky." She sounded a little warmer than when she answered the phone.

I walked over toward where White was talking with the other men. I stopped far enough away so I could not hear their conversation. One of the men facing me glowered. White saw this, then saw me. He stopped talking and started toward me.

"I need to get back to Maysville. Call me if I can do anything to help."

"Trouble?" he asked.

None you can help me with I thought but said, "Not really but I need to get back."

White promised to call and I started walking to my car. I stopped and turned around when he called my name. He was coming toward me. Maybe he had an important job for me. "Can I have another cigarette before you go?" he asked. I took the pack out of my shirt pocket and offered it to him. He took one.

I was glad he'd reminded me. I went to the trunk of my car and put the cigarettes, lighter and Certs back in the hole. I tucked the carpet back in its clip to conceal the evidence.

I started the car and was up to 85 mph in a few seconds. The country road was totally dark. I turned on the high intensity driving lights which lit the road for several hundred yards in front of the huge, speeding car. Sandra says if I'd just get an Asian driver I can pretend I'm the Green Hornet.

Driving fast is one of my newer vices. Growing up in Brooklyn I didn't learn to drive until I went on the police department. And there is no place in the city where even a cop can drive very fast. But it was different in rural Virginia.

Just as I was starting to enjoy the speed I saw flashing blue lights in my mirror. At first I thought White had sent a trooper after me with an important message. Then I realized he would have called my cell phone. I slowed down, reaching under the dash until I found the switch. I flipped it. The small blue high intensity lights in the corners of my rear window began to flash. Extra strobe light bulbs hidden under the tail light lenses began to pulse. I could see the lights reflected from the front of the police car behind me. It began to drop back and the emergency lights went off.

28

There is a police radio in the car, but I wouldn't have a clue as to how to talk with the state police on it. I turned it on, however, and listened to the channel for the Maysville PD. There was nothing going on. I picked up the mike and pushed the button. "Maysville One to Maysville Base."

"Yes, Chief," came the immediate reply. "What can we do for you?"

"I'm just checking in. Is anything going on?"

"That's a negative. Are you coming to the station?"

"Not right now," I replied. "I'm going to eat at the Widow's and then go home. I'll either be on my cell phone or at home."

"Roger that. Have a good evening, boss."

I put my foot back down hard on the accelerator and enjoyed the speed for the ten miles to the town limits sign. New York was never like this.

Chapter Four

Let me tell you a little about our previous lives in New York City and how we came to be in Maysville. I was born in the Fort Hamilton Parkway section of Brooklyn, the only child of a firefighter and a housewife. I was an average student in high school. After graduation I attended classes at a local community college. But I was really just putting in time until I turned 21 and could go work for the city.

Most of our family's male friends were also firefighters, and it was drummed into me from the time I was a small boy that I should become a firefighter, too. The security of working for the city was the dream of every family in our neighborhood. Other little boys dream of being firefighters, and their parents hope they will outgrow it. But my family not only embraced the idea, they encouraged it every way they could. It was their dream for me.

After a number of part time jobs while I was at the community college, most involving brooms and all involving minimum wage, I could appreciate the salary and benefits of a city job with both civil service and union benefits. But I do not like heights, or ladders, and the idea of deliberately rushing into a burning building completely terrified me. But there was another city job, with the same security and benefits, I did want. I wanted to be a cop.

The NYPD was accepting applications. The department had just gone through one of its periodic corruption clean ups so there were vacancies. I submitted my application and passed the physical. Then I went back to brooms and minimum wage jobs until I was old enough and a new recruit class was starting.

I loved the NYPD from the first day. The police academy, to me, was the most exciting summer camp a boy could ever attend. I had never touched a gun before, but I was taught to shoot them and then given one of my own to carry with me at all times. I had never driven a car before, but I was taught to chase bad guys at high speeds on the pursuit training course. The classes on law and procedure were not as interesting, but I was able to do the required work fairly easily.

On my dresser at home I still have my graduation photo with my parents. I'm standing between them in my stiff new police uniform looking like the cat that swallowed the canary. It wasn't until after I was shot that I noticed the worry on my mother's face in the photo.

30

My training officer was a veteran of twenty five years, plodding steadily toward his thirty and full pension. He was still a patrolman, never having even attempted the sergeant's exam. He shared what he believed to be the secret of success on "The Job" with me. "Never do anything that will cause anyone above your immediate supervisor to learn your name," he told me time after time.

I was happy at my first assignment, walking a beat near where I'd grown up in Brooklyn. I walked along the neighborhood's middle class, low crime streets twirling my nightstick like Pat O'Brien in one of those old movies on cable television.

But I never took an apple from a fruit stand. There is corruption in the NYPD. Some cops do take bribes. But I was fortunate never to be in a position where a bribe was offered to me. I hope I wouldn't have accepted it, had it been offered, but I later saw the pressures other cops were under to go along with their fellow cops so I can't be sure.

Besides I was living at home with my parents and, even paying them a modest rent every pay day, I had more money than I could spend. I was dating girls from the neighborhood and partying with my high school friends. I was on course to eventually marry one of these girls, have some kids, put in an uneventful thirty years on the NYPD, take my pension and move to Florida. But one day everything changed.

I'd been in the department for just over two years on the morning my world, and all my plans, changed. I was walking a foot beat on a warm Spring day in a mostly middle class, ethically mixed section of Brooklyn, happily twirling my nightstick when I noticed a car double parked in front of the Hadid's small market. The driver was behind the wheel so there was nothing really unusual about it. As I walked by the store I saw the Hadids with their hands in the air behind the counter. The robber had his back to the door.

My training immediately took over. I drew my pistol and as quietly as I could, stepped into the dark store. "Police officer," I shouted. "Drop the gun and . . ."

According to the way I'd been trained the robber was supposed to do as I told him and no one would get hurt. Apparently he hadn't been trained to be a robber and he didn't do it. Instead he turned toward me with his pistol raised. I did as I was trained to do. I pulled the trigger.

My first shot killed the slushy drink machine on the robber's left. My second shot killed the New York State Lotto machine on the robber's right. But my third shot killed the robber. He fell in a heap to the floor. I was standing there taking in the enormity of what I had just done when I noticed Mrs. Hadid pointing behind me, screaming something in a language I didn't understand.

I turned to see what she was yelling about. The driver of the double parked car was rushing toward me with a pistol in his hand. I dropped to one knee before he fired. His bullet went over my head into a beer cooler at the back of the store, shattering the big glass door. I fired back. My bullet struck him in the middle of his chest. He went down on the sidewalk. He later died in the emergency room of a nearby hospital. I had been extremely lucky.

I was stunned. Mrs. Hadid brought me a chair while Mr. Hadid dialed 911. I was still sitting there holding my pistol in my badly shaking hand when the other cops started arriving.

The shooting was ruled justifiable. Under normal circumstances I would have received a medal, had my picture in the paper accepting it, been offered psychological counseling for having to kill two people, then returned to my foot patrol beat in Brooklyn.

But the circumstances were not normal. The night before my shooting three of New York's Finest had brutally beaten a handcuffed African American male in Harlem. This had nothing to do with me, or what I'd done. But the brass decided they could make a hero out of me and, hopefully, distract the media from the other story.

This was my first experience with the inner-workings of the NYPD. It would not be my last.

There was carefully orchestrated media coverage about me, the Hadids, and the two robbers. The driver was the younger brother of the other stickup man, which explained why he came into the store instead of speeding off at the sound of gunfire as any competent getaway car driver would have been expected to do.

I not only received a Medal of Valor, I was also taken out of uniform and promoted to the rank of detective third grade. My assignment was moved to a precinct in Manhattan. Fortunately I never really bought into the hero stuff and went into my new assignment with pretty much the same attitude I'd previously had while in uniform. True, everyone now knew my name, but I intended to continue just doing my job as well as I could while slogging along toward retirement.

Being a detective in Manhattan was totally different from wearing a uniform in Brooklyn. Before the NYPD had been simply a wonderful job. Now it was an amazing adventure.

My first detective job was on the surveillance squad. This mainly involved watching a location until someone wanted by the NYPD showed up. Then I was supposed to call the detectives whose case it was to come and arrest the person. Wearing jeans instead of the stiff uniform with its choker collar and sitting in unmarked cars I felt like a secret agent. I loved every boring minute of it.

After a couple of years of this I was transferred to another detective squad. This transfer probably had nothing to do with my job performance, and I certainly didn't request the move. There was an opening; and since I had not done anything to embarrass the department in my previous assignment, I got the job. Although I was nervous about it at first, being assigned to a precinct detective squad was even more of an adventure than the surveillance squad had been. Not only did we not wear uniforms, we didn't even have to check in for roll call at the beginning of our shift. I was assigned a partner, and we investigated crimes committed in our precinct. Unlike on television, this usually involved taking reports from the victims of burglaries, robberies, assaults and rapes. Then we'd go back to the precinct and compare the crime to others previously reported. There were very few mysteries. Most of the time we had a suspect fairly quickly and just had to wait for him to be arrested for something else or the surveillance squad guys to tell us he had come home. We'd make the arrest, do the paperwork, and occasionally testify in court in the rare cases the public defender didn't plead the perpetrator out for a reduced sentence. I was making more money than I had in uniform and had moved from my parents' house to a tiny apartment in Manhattan. Life was good.

I met my future wife Sandra during an investigation. She was a graduate student at Columbia working on her doctorate in American History. Her room mate was also a graduate student, but in social work. The room mate was raped in the laundry room of their apartment building one afternoon. My partner and I caught the case.

I was impressed with how kind and concerned Sandra was with her room mate from our first meeting when we went to the apartment to do the follow up on the statement the room mate had given in the emergency room. It was love at first sight, at least on my side. I was also fascinated by the book filled apartment. I had never seen so many books outside a library. A woman who was studying for a doctorate and read so many books was so exotic and different from the women I had grown up with or dated later.

As usual we could only add our rape report to a half dozen others which appeared to have been the work of the same perp and wait until we had a suspect. Time was on our side. Statistically every time a criminal commits a crime he increases the chances the cops will catch him. This rapist had the bad luck of not being caught by the cops, however.

Less than a week after raping Sandra's room mate he was in another laundry room in a building a few blocks from the previous attack. He found a pretty, petite, young blonde with pigtails sitting on the folding table, reading a magazine while waiting for her clothes to dry. She was wearing a huge pink tee shirt with a picture of a teddy bear on it. She must have looked to be about twelve years old to the rapist.

He grabbed her and pushed her back on the table. He was attempting to rip her shorts off when she stuck a nine millimeter pistol against his crotch and pulled the trigger. She was not a twelve year old child. She was a twenty two year old Deputy United States Marshal named Kaitlyn O'Brien. She'd heard about the rapes committed in laundry rooms around the neighborhood and decided to

33

bring her gun with her while she did her wash. The responding officers told us later the rapist was cowering on the floor in the corner trying to stop the bleeding with a towel and begging her not to kill him when they arrived.

A young woman doctor in the emergency room completed the genital removal the marshal had started. The doctor told us she treated so many rape victims this was a pleasant change for her.

If this had been the end of the rape case I probably would never have married Sandra. Fortunately for me the case had some unexpected developments.

I had assumed a public defender would plead the rapist guilty for a twenty five year to life sentence, he would go off to prison, and that would be the end of it. But this rapist was the son of a rich, prominent Manhattan psychiatrist. There was no public defender involved. Instead Daddy hired one of the heaviest hitters in the New York criminal defense bar. He was pleading "not guilty by reason of insanity."

Usually having to do all the additional paperwork and prep the witness, Sandra's room mate, would have been a bad thing. But in this case it meant I would be spending more time with Sandra as well as with her room mate. This was a good thing.

Never did a NYPD detective spend so much time preparing a witness. The room mate was a total basket case. Part of the problem was, prior to the rape, she had seen the police, though her compassionate social worker eyes, as fascist bullies who sadistically enjoyed mistreating the less fortunate members of society. She didn't think the police should even have guns. After the rape she thought the police should be given nuclear weapons and allowed to use them any time they wanted. I think she knew intellectually neither of these positions made any sense, but her problem was emotional not intellectual.

Sandra went to her room mate's psychologist's appointments with her. I tagged along. We got better acquainted while we waited. When the room mate decided New York City was not for her, and went back home to Atlanta, I moved into the apartment with Sandra. I don't remember either of us ever proposing to the other. We just started on the wedding plans.

Eventually the rapist's lawyer made his deal and the rapist went off to Attica to serve at least 25 years. I'm sure he got a whole new perspective on rape there.

After a large wedding at her parent's country club in Connecticut we started our lives together. Sandra received her doctorate degree and became an associate professor in the history department at Columbia. I worked cases and was promoted to detective two. Things went along amazingly well. I could not have been happier.

Sandra was never happy about me being a cop. I knew she

worried constantly when I was working, but she rarely complained. Even if I had wanted to give up being a cop, which I didn't, I don't have any other job skills. I came home one night to find her reading a book called "I Love A Cop" by a psychologist from California. Sandra believed she could learn to understand anything from a book.

On the day after Labor Day in 1999 our lives changed forever. And it was not a good change. Although Sandra had worried about my safety through the years, she was the one whose life was now in danger. At a scheduled doctor's appointment before she went back to teaching, following a routine mammogram, small lumps were found in both her breasts. We spent the Fall in doctors' offices for months of tests, biopsies, and specialists' opinions. I was bewildered by it all. My concern for her was all consuming but there was nothing I could really do.

I tried always to go to her doctors' appointments, most of the time I made them. I remember one fight we had after an appointment. A new doctor was not very forthcoming in responding to Sandra's questions. I leaned on him harder than the law would ever allow me to lean on a suspect. I'm sure the doctor believed I would cause him great bodily harm if he did not answer the questions. He was right. Sandra was furious.

Taking a clue from her "I Love A Cop" book, I read everything available about being supportive to breast cancer victims. Most of it was too vague to be of any use; many of the books seemed to me to contradict each other. But I have never tried harder to do anything right in my life. Fortunately Sandra gave me credit for trying. Afterwards she said she had always been an easy grader in her college classes, too.

Finally there was absolutely no choice other than the surgery. Waiting was becoming too dangerous. We could not put it off any longer. She decided to have the surgery during her Christmas break from university teaching.

Doctors' schedules were coordinated and it was decided she would go into the hospital on December 27, 1999. If things went well she would be home, cured, by the first days of the new millennium. I planned to take vacation time so I could be with her every second.

We went to visit her mother Rose on Christmas Day. Rose has Alzheimer's. She doesn't always know who Sandra is, but fortunately she is always happy to see anyone who comes to visit, so it was not as bad as it could have been. She lived with her sister Carol in the big house where Sandra had grown up in Connecticut. Sandra's father and both my parents were already gone.

When we came home from Connecticut we spent the next day in our apartment alone. It was some of the best times we ever had together. Everything was going to be all right, but just in case it wasn't, we cuddled and made love for twenty four hours straight.

But every time I touched her breast she would cringe. At

first I thought I was hurting her but she said I wasn't. She cried and told me it was because after tomorrow she would not have them any more. She wanted to know if I would still love her. I told her that was a silly question. I would still love her as long as there was breath in my body no matter what. I tried my damnest to be warm and supportive when what I really wanted to do was find someone I could hold responsible for doing this to her and beat them to death.

Very early on the morning of December 27 Sandra and I took a cab to Gilbert Memorial Hospital in uptown Manhattan. Later the fact that her doctor performed his surgeries at that particular hospital would prove to be fortuitous.

I waited outside her room while they prepped her for the surgery. When they finally let me back in all I could do was sit by her bed, holding her hand while she slept. About 11 a.m. they took her to surgery and sent me to the waiting room.

At noon my partner Todd Markum showed up. He looked awful. He was pale, and there was a sheen of sweat on his forehead. He told me he had a cold and some kind of flu which he could not seem to shake. Todd had brought lunch for both of us from my favorite deli. My sandwich was left untouched, but I did drink the cream soda. I didn't feel like talking so Todd sat there and helped me stare at the wall.

I don't know any other successful partners on The Job who are as different as Todd and I. Although he has a wife and three kids he is the biggest woman chaser I have ever met. After work he hangs out with a bunch of hard drinking cops who make Wambaugh's "Choirboys" look tame by comparison. I used to tell him he was going to get caught, and fired, some day. But my warnings didn't affect his behavior so I eventually stopped nagging him.

The reason we got along so well even though we are so different, I think, is because we both absolutely loved to be out on the street chasing, and catching, bad guys. And we both knew we could count on the other no matter what the circumstance. Either of us would take a bullet for his partner without giving it a second thought.

Todd was theoretically working and about 3:00 p.m. his cell phone rang. You are supposed to turn them off in the hospital but I've never met a cop with any respect for other people's rules. We are the Princes of the City.

I walked out with him. He gave me one of our cigarettes he was carrying. I smoked it and chewed the Certs to cover up my crime. I had taken the uneaten food with me and gave it to a homeless man hanging around outside the hospital. This was something I had picked up from Sandra. Whenever we ate in a restaurant she would collect any food left on the table in a "doggy bag" and give it to the first homeless person she saw. Initially I was embarrassed by this but I soon realized if everyone were as kind as my Sandra the world would be a better place.

When I got back upstairs the nurse was looking for me. Before I could panic she told me Sandra was in the recovery room, the operation had gone well, and the doctor would be down to talk to me in a moment. The "moment" turned out to be an hour and eleven minutes. I know because I spent the entire time staring at the clock on the wall, constantly checking it against my watch to be sure the clock had not stopped.

The doctor was a short, tired looking man with salt and pepper hair, more salt than pepper. He had a good bedside manner and did his best to reassure me that Sandra had come through the surgery fine. He had removed both breasts as planned. Sandra should recover in time as he had previously explained to us. Although she would never be her old self, she would survive. Being who I am, I gave him my best cop stare as I asked my questions. I have read too much about patients dying in hospitals due to gross negligence. I wanted everyone to know that any negligence in my wife's case would certainly result in immediate, withering gunfire. Cops are trained to be assertive and this often leads to them being bullies. I am no exception.

I thanked him for his efforts and went back to staring at the waiting room wall. Around five the nurse came to tell me Sandra was back in her room. I moved in there. Sandra was asleep, but at least I could hold her hand while I stared at that wall.

She was still asleep at nine when a nurse came in to tell me I would have to leave. I was leaning back in the chair, the butt of my pistol in clear view under my left arm, holding Sandra's hand. I simply said, "No." and went back to staring at the wall.

A little while later the floor's supervising nurse came in. She had apparently been chosen to be the hospital's negotiator. I don't think she had volunteered for the job. She calmly explained to me that Sandra would sleep through the night so I should go home and sleep myself. She promised me I would be called if my wife woke up. I wrote my cell phone number on the back of my business card, explained her personal responsibility to be sure I was called if necessary, kissed Sandra on the forehead, and left.

I called Sandra's Aunt Carol from the sidewalk, explaining the surgery had gone well and Sandra was still asleep. I promised to call back when she woke up the following day. Then I took a cab back to our apartment, placed the cell phone in its charger, put a frozen dinner in the mircrowave, and lay down on the couch to wait seven minutes until dinner was ready. I woke up at six the next morning.

This was later than I'd planned to sleep. I quickly showered, dressed, armed myself and left for the hospital. On the street outside our apartment building the rush hour had already begun. Two empty cabs in the center lane ignored my waves and passed me by. I didn't look like I wanted to go to the airport. The next empty cab was in the curb lane. I banged my fist into the fender and held up my badge for the turbaned driver to see. He stopped.

Outside the hospital I bought coffee and sweet rolls from a sidewalk cart. It was a cold morning, with a strong wind blowing, cutting into me like a scalpel. I asked the cart's proprietor if he wasn't freezing. He said, "Is better to be freezing in New York than freezing in Moscow." I couldn't argue with that.

Inside the hospital, I walked past the sign saying "No Visitors Until 10 a.m." and retook the chair next to my wife's hospital bed. She opened her eyes, smiled weakly at me, then went back to sleep. I was shooed out of the room several times while various things were done for Sandra. Each time when I returned she was asleep again.

A little after nine my partner Todd showed up with coffee. He looked even worse than the day before. He was pale and sweating. Just as he caught my attention from the hall the doctor arrived. He needed to examine Sandra so I went to the waiting room with Todd.

As I sipped my coffee he told me the news. There was buzz around the squad that all leaves would be cancelled for New Year's Eve. A couple of Middle Eastern terrorists had been arrested near the Canadian border with a big bomb in their van. Somebody in authority thought the thousands of people who flock to Times Square to watch the ball drop might be the target. The department was going to put as many of its 39,000 members on the street as it could, in uniform! I groaned at the idea of wearing my uniform. It later saved my life.

No place outside the Middle East has had more experience with terrorism than New York City. In the more distant past we had every one from Puerto Rican separatists to sixties radicals setting off bombs in the city.

We had been experiencing Islamic Jihad since at least 1990. Terrorists gunned down a radical Jewish activist named Meir Kahane on a city street. In 1993 the World Trade Center was attacked for the first time. In the summer of that year a plot was foiled to blow up the United Nations, the tunnels under the Hudson, and a federal office building in Manhattan. Early in 1994 some Lebanese terrorists shot up a van full of Hasidic students on the Brooklyn Bridge.

Then in 1997 a Palestinian teacher killed seven tourists at the Empire State Building before committing suicide. I was at the crime scene, and it was the worst I have ever seen. Later in the year two Palestinians and a Pakistani were arrested on a tip. Bombs and suicide notes were found indicating they intended to blow up the city's subways. It would have been a bloodbath had they struck during rush hour. Hundreds, if not thousands, would have been killed.

Whether all this is because New York is "Hymie Town" as

38

the Reverend Jesse Jackson put it, or because Israeli targets are too well protected. New York City is high on the terrorist hit list. I remember reading Ramzi Yousef had told his interrogators, "If you can not attack your enemy, you should attack the friend of your enemy." Anti-Semites call it "Jew York City" and it was paying a price.

The precautions the city was taking for the Millennium celebration were certainly understandable to me. I just hoped they would work and not involve me personally.

Every sworn officer on the NYPD is required to have a uniform in wearable condition. I had worn mine last nearly three years before to a funeral for a guy I knew slightly who was killed in the line of duty. I'd actually lost a little weight, in spite of my awful eating habits, since Sandra got sick so I knew it would fit. I hated to leave Sandra alone in the hospital on New Year's Eve, especially since it was the start of a new century. Since I was off, maybe the department wouldn't be able to notify me, and I wouldn't have to go.

The doctor came out and joined us in the waiting room. I introduced him to Todd. He told us Sandra was doing wonderfully, and she would just need a little time to get stronger. He hoped to take the drains out of the incisions on the first of January, and then she should be able to go home.

Todd slapped me on the back, told me he was thrilled Sandra was doing so well. He said to tell her he'd love to see her but he didn't want to come around her and give her his flu. He promised to be back later.

On my way back to the room I met a delivery guy with a huge arrangement of flowers. They were from the Hadids. We had kept in touch through the years even though seeing them always reminded me of the two young robbers I'd been forced to kill in their store. Sandra had helped their daughter get a scholarship to Columbia, where she was a prize pupil in the history department. Siena Habib had probably heard about the upcoming operation from Sandra.

Sandra was awake when I returned to her room. She smiled weakly at the flowers. I had to tell her they weren't from me. I sat down next to the bed and took her right hand. There was a bottle of something dripping into her other hand. "How do you feel, my love?" I asked.

"Like crap," she said. "But I must be getting better. I'm hungry."

"Dominos?" I asked pulling out my cell phone, trying to show her a happy go lucky leer.

She did at least laugh softly, shaking her head. "Go ask the nurse what I can have."

They brought her some sort of clear broth. She was perking up. We spent the afternoon watching old movies on television. They bought her dinner just as the bell was ringing for Clarence's wings. My life was nothing like Jimmy Stewart's, but it was wonderful none the less. I was with Sandra and would be for years to come.

I helped her cut up her food. Both arms were weak from the cutting done on the muscles in her chest. But she could eat without assistance. As soon as she finished dinner she told me I should go home so she could sleep. I protested. I would have been perfectly happy sitting there watching her sleep. But she insisted, so I agreed. Before I left she asked me to bring the tote bag full of books by the front door in the apartment when I returned in the morning. One day of television was apparently enough for Professor Sandra. She was ready to get back to her usual, more intellectual pursuits.

I was at the hospital before seven the following morning. Sandra looked much stronger than she had the previous evening. Her hair was combed and she had on lipstick. She was glad to see me but probably gladder to see her books. She organized her pad, pen and highlighter on the hospital bed, put on her reading glasses and got to work. Sandra is a historian by training. She has been working for years on a scholarly book about the suffragettes. She is interested in the supporting players to Susan B. Anthony of silver dollar fame. She has read everything available on them, has filing cabinets full of material, but has never found the angle that is exactly right for her book. But she never gives up.

I sat by the window reading a book of my own, a 1966 novel called *Darker Than Amber* by John MacDonald. I don't think I ever read a book that wasn't assigned to me in a class before I met Sandra. Her father, Ned, had introduced me to McDonald and Travis McGee. I had read all the books in his McGee series except this one. He is a wonderful writer who filled my head with amazing quotes. "You can be at ease only with those people to whom you can say any damn fool thing that comes into your head, knowing they will respond in kind, and knowing that any misunderstandings will be thrashed out right now, rather than buried deep and given a chance to fester." This described my relationship with Sandra so well. He was such a perceptive man.

Of course later in the same book he wrote, "Carrying a gun, especially a very utilitarian one, has the bully boy flavor of the ersatz male, the fellow with such a hollow sense of inadequacy has to bolster his sexual ego with a more specific symbol of gonadal prowess." Hey, I don't agree with everything anybody writes!

The book also had me thinking about retiring in a few years, moving to Florida, and living on a houseboat with Sandra. I hadn't told her my plan yet because she would just roll her eyes at me.

I was in and out of the hospital room throughout the day. I knew I didn't need to watch Sandra every minute, and it was obvious she did not want me to watch her every minute. Things were getting back to normal.

When I got home on the night of December 29 there was a message on the answering machine from my lieutenant telling me about the canceled leaves and that I was to report at three for a roll call in uniform on the last day of the millennium. He also said all necessary overtime had been pre-approved and I might be in for a long night.

At the hospital on the morning of the next to last day of that December Sandra seemed relieved I was going back to work. My constant vigil was apparently wearing on her. I would have been happy to do it every day for the rest of my life. When I went home that night she told me to try and rest the next morning and just come by on my way to roll call so she could see how handsome I looked in my uniform.

We both knew she wanted to satisfy herself I was wearing my vest.

Chapter Five

I slept late on the morning of the last day of the twentieth century. Then I just hung around the apartment drinking coffee and reading a book. I had finished the one from the hospital and started another Florida novel, this one by Carl Hiaasen. It was bitter cold in New York which made the Florida story more inviting. Around noon Sandra called to ask me to bring her laptop computer on my way to work. I promised I would.

My uniform was hanging in the closet. I finally located the black cop shoes I had not worn for so long. They looked pretty good after I polished them. I hung the heavy wool "bag" as it is called in the department in the bathroom while I showered. It looked better after I spent a considerable amount of time pressing it. I had nothing else to do.

One of the television networks was showing New Year's Eve celebrations from around the world. By noon in New York, Hong Kong was already in the twenty first century. The new millennium was rapidly moving west. There were fervent hopes being expressed of a new beginning for the whole world, not just Sandra and me. I could not imagine the new year not being better for us than the one coming rapidly to a close had been.

I ate lunch standing over the sink. Sandra hates for me to do this, but she wasn't there. Then I began to dress in my heavy, scratchy police uniform.

The pants were still long enough and even roomy in the waist. My vest, "bullet resistant" they called it instead of "bullet proof", still fit. I wear it occasionally when we are doing something I think might get me shot at. When we take down doors we wear heavy vests that look like those of a baseball umpire. Those are "bullet proof". But it was not possible to wear one of these all the time without announcing I was a cop.

The tunic also fit fine. I pinned my detective's badge through the reinforced holes on the left side in my chest. I was not going out on the street with the .38 caliber service revolver I had carried when I used to wear this uniform. It took me a while with a razor blade and shoe polish to modify the belt holster to fit my nine millimeter pistol.

I retrieved Sandra's laptop computer from the hall closet and realized I had a serious problem. It was bitter cold outside and I do not own a department regulation great coat. The one I'd worn so many years ago had moths so I'd thrown it out. I found Sandra's father's old baggy tweed overcoat hanging there. She had said many times she should give it away but never got around to parting with it. He was a much bigger man than I am so it was plenty large enough to accommodate my vest, tunic and gun belt. He was also taller so it was a little long as well. The choker collar of my uniform looked odd if I didn't button the coat all the way to the top so I found a grey wool scarf in the coat's pocket to finish off my ensemble. I was sure I'd be able to find a more suitable, departmental issued coat at the stationhouse.

I picked up Sandra's laptop case and started for the hospital. The weight of my pistol felt strange on my hip instead of under my left arm where I usually carry it.

The street was crowded with holiday revelers even this early. There was no hope of getting a cab. I walked two blocks to the underground entrance and took the subway to the hospital. It was jammed as well.

Sandra was taken aback at the sight of me wearing her father's overcoat. I quickly explained why I'd worn it. She assured me it was okay, but I could see the tears in her eyes from having seen the coat and being reminded she would never see her father again. She had me take off the coat and model my uniform for her. Neither of us mentioned the vest.

She popped her laptop open and sat up in the hospital bed. "We both need to get to work," she said.

"Happy New Year, I love you more than anything in the world," I replied. "I'm looking forward to spending the next century with you." Sandra teared up again, returning my words to me. I kissed her and left for work.

Outside the traffic was even worse than it had been earlier. There was still no chance I'd be able to get a cab. While trying to decide which subway stop was closest, a NYPD radio car from my precinct came out of the emergency entrance of the hospital. I didn't recognize the cop driving so I unbuttoned my coat to show my uniform and waved to the driver. He stopped next to me. I asked for a ride to the station. He told me to hop in.

The detective squad room had a surreal quality to it. The lieutenant and several of my fellow detectives had obviously been much thinner men the last time they'd worn their uniforms. The pants of the guys with potbellies were also too short. Nearly all of them had my problem of no longer having the departmental overcoat and were wearing a diverse collection of warm coats over their uniforms. And, unlike me, many of them no longer had the regulation shoes. They were wearing everything from penny loafers to cowboy boots.

My partner Todd was sitting in the corner staring out the

window. He looked even paler and sicker than he had the day before. I knew he probably felt as bad as he looked. I wondered why he didn't call in sick. Maybe he didn't have any more sick days and didn't want to be docked. His philandering life style was expensive plus needing to support the family he had at home. But his personal life is always such a mess I don't pry into it. I make myself available to help if he wants me to do so but have learned not to insist. I took a seat next to him and waited for him to speak.

When he became aware of my presence, he forced himself to smile. "How's Sandra doing," he asked? I told him my good news in as exhilarated a manner as I could, hoping my joy would rub off on him. It didn't. He still looked sick and glum.

He and I moved together to gather around the lieutenant with the other guys. Todd had lost so much weight his uniform just hung on him. His tunic was so big I could not see the outline of his vest beneath it. His brown civilian overcoat looked like a tent on him. The squad, most of them outstanding detectives, was a motley looking crew in uniform.

The lieutenant read our assignments. Todd and I were told to direct traffic a block apart until eight. Then we should take a dinner break and afterwards go to the staging area a couple of blocks from Times Square by ten. The mayor and other big shots were coming to watch the ball drop. Todd and I were to be part of the security detail. The squad might look like a clown college class reunion, but we would do The Job.

The traffic was already near gridlock when you got out onto the street. It took us nearly an hour to go the few blocks in the unmarked car to our first assignment. I parked illegally in the middle of the block between the two intersections. It was bitter cold, and we couldn't wear our civilian overcoats while directing traffic. Todd looked so bad I suggested he stay in the warm car. I would walk between the two intersections. The traffic was in a nearly complete gridlock anyway, and waving our arms in the middle of the street wasn't going to help in the least. Todd was shivering even in the warm car, so I got the blanket from the trunk and covered him. I would walk back and forth until I couldn't feel my feet, then I would return to the car.

By eight the traffic had somewhat sorted itself out, due to absolutely nothing I had done, and was moving, if slowly, again. As I was pulling the car into the traffic I suggested to Todd that I take him back to the station. He was too sick to be out in the bitter cold. He could rest in the dormitory until I was done. Then I would take him home.

He refused. He said he needed to see a guy a little ways uptown. He suggested he drop me off at a diner on the way. I could order carryout for both of us and he'd pick me, and the food, up in a few minutes.

44

I refused. I told him he was too sick to drive. I assumed he wanted to tell one of his girlfriends "Happy New Year" so I said I would drive him and wait in the car. He appeared reluctant but relieved as he accepted my offer.

Todd directed me to a loading zone in front of a large, slightly rundown apartment building farther north in Manhattan. He got out of the car and then leaned back in. "Thanks for everything, buddy," he said "I really appreciate it." I assumed at the time he meant driving him to see his girlfriend.

A car load of lost tourists recognized the car as being an unmarked police vehicle and stopped to ask directions. If I hadn't had my window down talking to them I probably wouldn't have heard the shots. The tourists heard them too and quickly drove off. Before I left the car I had the presence of mind to pick up the mike for the police radio, report the shots and give the location.

Then I leaped from the car and started toward the building entrance. The normal human response to danger is to run from it. Cops are trained to run toward it. Before I reached the door I could hear the sound of pounding feet running toward me. I ripped open my overcoat as I ran. Buttons flew in all directions.

I was reaching under my left arm for my nine millimeter when the fleeing perp and I first saw each other. The gun wasn't there. In the time it took me to remember my gun was on my hip the man had stopped and was aiming one of those machine pistols that are so popular with drug dealers at me. They spit lots of small caliber bullets extremely fast. By the time I had my gun out and pointed at him he was firing. His first bullet ripped into my left shoulder. The pain was indescribable. By the time his next three rounds hit me in the chest I was firing back. I don't know how many times I pulled the trigger but I didn't stop until he did. I was still on my feet when he hit the sidewalk, but barely.

I started toward him to remove the machine pistol from his reach in case he was still alive. I must not have taken more than a step or two before I passed out on the sidewalk.

I woke up nearly twenty four hours later in a new century. I was in a hospital bed with tubes running everywhere. Sandra sitting in a wheelchair, IV hanging on a pole beside her, was holding my hand.

When she saw my eyes open she asked, "Tough day at work, dear?"

"I quit," I answered. I remained conscious long enough to see her smile.

When I awoke the following morning Sandra was not there. I was able to check out the damage to my body and was pleasantly surprised. The only place the bullet had penetrated was my left shoulder and that wound seemed to be high enough to avoid most of the muscles. The pain was intense, but I could move the fingers on that hand. Because I'd been wearing the Kevlar vest my chest had suffered broken ribs instead of fatal bullet wounds. The perp's choice of the smaller caliber machine pistol had also been helpful. If he had shot me even once with a heavy magnum I would have been dead.

The hospital staff fussed over me. I kept asking for Sandra and was promised she would be told I was awake. I was in no shape to intimidate anyone into going to get her immediately. A harried looking young resident examined me and said I had been remarkably lucky. I already knew that.

I was still waiting for my beloved wife when the guys from the squad started arriving. They all assured me I'd be back on The Job in a month. I didn't dissuade them.

When I asked about Todd the cops shook their heads sadly. When I asked how the fiasco which had nearly killed me had come about, they all just shrugged and remembered some place they urgently needed to be. I could live with having killed the man who had apparently just murdered my friend and partner. It was what cops call "a public service killing."

I thought about going back to work. If I was able I knew I wanted to do it. Playing cops and robbers with real robbers, and real guns, is the ultimate adrenaline rush. But I knew I lacked both the courage and capacity for cruelty to tell Sandra I was going back out there. If I had to I could live with the Florida houseboat idea for her sake.

But I didn't think I would have to totally give being a cop. I'd always been a good cop, a team player, and the NYPD would take care of me. They would find me something I could stand to do, that wasn't dangerous; while I put in the years I needed for full retirement benefits. I'd still be sort of a cop and would be able to keep the health insurance we needed. I would not be a real cop, but I had to choose between that and Sandra. I chose Sandra. I would still be safer on the streets than most New Yorkers. I'd still be carrying a gun.

They told me Sandra was exhausted and had developed an infection in her incisions so she could not come to visit me. I made a deal with the nurse. If I would eat all the unappetizing slop I'd been served for lunch they would take me, in a wheelchair, to see her.

I had only managed to eat a couple of spoons full when my lieutenant arrived. I explained my need to get rid of the lunch. He scraped the rest of it into a plastic evidence bag and hid it in his pocket. Cops have a natural ability to conspire with each other against non-cops. It's called "The Blue Wall" and it was just beginning to be put into place.

"The big brass will be here shortly, Ricky," he said. "So I don't have time to blow smoke up your ass. Here it is plain and simple. Your partner committed suicide last night and damn near got you killed in the process."

46

I was stunned. "Why," I asked? I had run so many possible scenarios through my mind for what had happened last night, but I hadn't even come close to this one. It was literally unthinkable.

"It's complicated," the lieutenant said. "You know old Todd would have humped a bush if he thought there was a snake in it?" I nodded my agreement with his assessment of my now dead partner.

"So he was HIV positive and apparently had been that way for nearly a year. We've quietly checked the records. He took a lot of personal days and lost time lately." I had been so wrapped up in Sandra's cancer and taken so many days myself I hadn't noticed.

"Apparently he had recently developed full blown AIDS so he hatched this plan," the lieutenant continued. "If he could manage to get himself killed in the line of duty his wife and kids would get a hero's pension. If he'd gone out for non-job connected health reasons they would have gotten very little except for some Social Security chump change. I don't think he meant for you to get shot in the process."

"No, I am sure he didn't," I said. "He tried to get me not to come with him. I was waiting in the car. I assumed he was stopping by to tell one of his girl friends 'Happy New Year.' I jumped out of the car when I heard the shooting and ran into the perp."

The lieutenant nodded his agreement, continuing. "I think he was getting sicker faster than he'd thought he would and couldn't afford to wait any longer. He looked so bad last night I shouldn't have let him go out.

"So anyway, he John Wayned the door of this crack dealer's stash pad all by himself and the dealer killed him. Unless the perp was brain dead he quickly realized he had just killed a cop and immediately fled. He was beating feet when he ran into you. He shot you. You killed him."

"So what's the department going to do, Lou," I asked?

"If you'll go along, they're going to buy Todd's plan." You'll both get Medals of Valor. Todd's wife will get the hero's pension. You'll be promoted to Detective One and the full thirty year retirement at that rank."

What would happen if I'd didn't go along was left unsaid. I'd be screwing Todd's widow out of any possible financial security as well as screwing Sandra and myself out of more tax free retirement than my current take home pay. The brass was being generous with the taxpayer's money. I'd like to think I went along for Todd's family. I know there was never any question in my lieutenant's mind that I would go along. I nodded my agreement and the deal was done. The Blue Wall was up. If organized crime families were as effective at maintaining their code of silence as the cops are the nation's prisons wouldn't be so overcrowded.

The lieutenant looked relieved.

"But," I said pressing my advantage while I still had it, "I'm too young to go fishing. I want to work and don't want to be another ex-cop doorman on the west side. I need some help finding another job."

The lieutenant nodded. I knew the nod was as good as a written, signed and notarized contract. "The brass would probably be happier if you left the city anyway. How about a law enforcement job someplace warm? Maybe a small town police chief?"

I nodded my acceptance, sealing the deal.

"I'll be in touch. What about the funeral, Ricky? He's going to get full honors, an inspector's funeral, the day after tomorrow."

"I think I'll pass, Lou."

My lieutenant nodded understandingly. "Okay, I'll tell the widow you aren't up to it. The brass is waiting to give you the medal. There are photographers and television cameras with them. You're doing the right thing, Ricky. You won't be sorry."

As I waited for the circus to begin I thought back over the past months. I should have been aware something was wrong with Todd. We'd been together a long time. Besides, I am a trained investigator, a man who should have taken nothing for granted. There were two signs on the squad room wall. One said: "If your mother tells you she loves you, CHECK IT OUT." The other was even more direct, "In God we trust. Everybody else we polygraph." But I had taken my partner purely on faith. It had nearly cost me my life.

While most cops are chronic complainers, they only whine about impersonal things. Bad coffee, bad hours and the stupidity of the court system top the list. I knew Todd would have died for me in some alley, if necessary, but he had not shared his health problems. Of course his silence had also saved me from becoming an accessory to my partner's plan to defraud the pension system.

Several deputy chiefs swept into my hospital room surrounded by a swarm of television cameras and reporters. The cameramen all turned on their portable lights at once. The room's temperature went up twenty degrees. I was nearly blinded. I lay still, trying to look sedated. If this charade blew up later I'd be able to claim I'd slept through it.

The police brass quickly deployed to both sides of the bed with practiced ease for the best photographic coverage. The only reason there was even a semblance of order was no one dared shove anyone who outranked him from the picture.

A deputy chief made the presentation, looking at the cameras, over my semi-conscious form, prone under a dingy sheet. He placed the Medal of Valor on my chest, on top of the bandages and sheet. After a final round of blinding flashes from the still photographers the group swept from the room. My lieutenant was the last to leave. He smiled at me and winked as he went out the door.

48

Alone again I examined the medal. It was a chunk of brass hanging on a bright green ribbon. It did not look as impressive as the one I had received for the Hadid shooting. The leather folder with it contained, I knew, the citation which enumerated the reasons for the medal. Since I was sure it didn't say "for assisting brass in covering up an embarrassing situation" I didn't bother to read it. I tossed both the medal and leather folder onto the bedside table. I knew I would never wear this medal. I also knew I would never be able to look at any of the other cops who had received one without wondering if they'd earned their medals merely by being a convenience to the department.

I remembered a movie I'd seen a long time before about an Indian, Ira Something, who had received a Congressional Medal of Honor he didn't feel he'd deserved. I remembered Ira had come to a bad end. As I pondered where my life would go from here I fell asleep.

When I awoke it was dark outside and another alleged meal was on my bed tray. I was hungry enough to eat the Jello but not the mystery meat. So I started to get out of the bed to flush it down the toilet. When my feet hit the floor I suddenly realized I was now twenty feet tall, very thin and had absolutely no sense of balance. I leaned against the bed until my balance partially returned and my height shrunk to a more manageable ten feet. I was finally able to stand but discovered I was tied to the bed with wires attached to metal plates on my chest as well as by the plastic line running into the back of my hand. I sank back onto the bed covered in sweat from the exertion.

I reached for the button to call the nurse. I might have to eat the toxic waste dinner but I wanted to make sure my deal to see my wife was in place before I did it. I realized I was making a lot of deals lately, but there didn't seem to be anything I could do about it.

It was nearly an hour later when I was finally rolled into my wife's room. I hadn't liked negotiating with the nurse from a subservient position. I am too much of a cop for borderline whining to civilians. I prefer dealing with people I can shove against the wall before I start talking to them. But I couldn't do it that way here. And the nurse looked as if she could have kicked my ass, even before I got shot, anyway. The deal had turned into an almost unconditional surrender, but I'd finally made it to Sandra's room.

From my wheelchair in the doorway I saw my wife looking tiny and vulnerable in her hospital bed. Her color blended into the dingy sheets that surrounded her. Her eyes were closed so I could observe her unnoticed. My eyes were drawn to the flatness of the sheet across her chest. It had been a double mastectomy. She had not had a bulletproof vest to protect her chest from the assault of the surgeon's knife. There had been no one I could shoot to prevent it being done to her or even to avenge it.

She opened her eyes and smiled as best she could. "I saw you on the news. They said you were retiring."

I smiled. She hadn't mentioned the Medal of Valor, not

because she knew I hadn't deserved it, but because she had her own priorities. And she hadn't asked about the man I'd killed or Todd's death. She focused on what was important to her; I was not going to be a cop in New York City anymore.

"They promoted me and are giving me credit for the full thirty years," I said. "We still have all of our insurance and more take home pay than before. We can get out of this city and live some place warm."

"But, I know there is a 'but' in there somewhere."

I looked sheepishly at my wife. "Well, I'm really too young to retire. The lieutenant promised he would help me find a job as a small town police chief somewhere. We'd have my NYPD retirement plus what I'd make at a new job. We'd be rich."

"But you'd still be a cop, Ricky. You promised me that . . ."

"No. No, I wouldn't really be a cop anymore. Not like I was here. I'm talking about moving to Mayberry. I'd be Andy Taylor and you'd be, I don't know . . ."

"Aunt Bea?"

I laughed, "Not exactly Aunt Bea, although I did always wonder about their relationship. You'd be more like whichever Gabor it was on 'Green Acres', a glamorous woman with a husband who adores her."

Sandra smiled, "Could we have a pig like whatshisname?"

"Just like whatshisname."

Maysville didn't turn out to be exactly like Mayberry and we didn't get a pig. But it was light years away from the NYPD. The small town didn't have the type of crime I'd seen entirely too much of in the big city.

Only one cop had been killed there in the last 100 years. And rumor was he'd been shot by his mistress' husband. In the twenty some years the current chief had been on the small police department there had only been two deaths in town which had not been from natural causes or accidents. One drunk had stabbed another drunk in a beer joint. There was one unsolved murder from the last ten years still on the books. Rumor is the old chief had known who'd committed that one, but could never prove it.

Maysville was growing and changing, which was why the council had been looking for a new, more professional police chief from the outside. The old chief had come up through the ranks of the small department. The growth was also the reason they had the money to pay a $50,000 salary. But the growth had also brought some crime. And would bring more when the huge shopping center was completely up and running.

One point eight miles of Interstate 81 ran through the northwestern corner of the town. At various times, the short stretch of road had been a notorious speed trap. In past, less prosperous times, the contributions of out-of-town speeders had accounted for a large percentage of the small town's budget.

The highway bisected a farm of approximately 1000 acres which belonged to an old man named Granger. Mr. Granger had fought the politicians twenty years before when they'd annexed his property into the town's limits. The compromise had been to give him an extremely low tax rate as long as he farmed the land. So while the town looked big on a map, nearly one third of its area had been of little use to the tax base. It had contained a population of one old man and a few hundred cattle.

But to the delight of the local growth boosters the old man had finally died and the property had been sold for development. And what development it had been.

On one side of the Interstate a syndicate of Canadians were building what they claimed was to be the latest "Largest Outlet Shopping Mall in the World". Across the highway a developer from Oklahoma had built a huge "truck plaza" capable of fueling over a hundred cars and trucks at a time. Next to this was a new motel.

The beginning of construction on the projects had brought the first boom. Literally hundreds of construction workers had flooded the area for the well paying jobs. Many of them brought campers and trailers with them, and a rowdy city sprung up on the construction site. The construction workers made good money, and they spent a lot of it locally. The bankers, lawyers, merchants and insurance executives who made up the city council were largely happy with the prosperity. One member, a lawyer named B.J. Cunningham, ran radio ads for the small convenience store he owned on the edge of the excitement which sang, "Where you gonna get your next six pack? B.J.'s! B.J.'s!" And being a born entrepreneur he also made money defending the construction workers on their drunk driving charges for $1,000 a pop. Some Saturday nights Maysville seemed to be a Yukon gold town. But the "rowdy element" kept mostly to themselves so the locals didn't really mind. The money was rolling in.

When we first visited Maysville we'd driven into town from the direction away from the new development. We came down the wide tree-lined street past the 1930s houses with their large, well kept yards. At the intersection just before the town square a large black dog was asleep in the roadway. He didn't bother to move as I negotiated the rental car around him.

Sandra's first comment on our potential new home was, "If Elvis is alive in the Federal Witness Protection Program this is probably where they have him stashed."

The interview with the town council had gone well. I was wise enough not to ask, after having been given a tour of the new mall and truck stop, why these people seemed intent on turning idyllic Mayberry into suburban New Jersey.

Sandra had been left at "The Widow Marsh's Bed & Breakfast" while I had visited with the powers that be. She had quickly been taken in hand by "the Widow", a large middle-aged, obliviously gay, man named Leigh, "never Lee", Williams. Williams told me he had been fully briefed by the mayor's wife and would take good care of Sandra.

By the end of the afternoon I had agreed to become the new police chief contingent only on Sandra agreeing to move to Maysville. I returned to the B&B to find Sandra having tea with the Widow, the mayor's wife, the commonwealth attorney's wife, and the other women who passed for local society. Sandra was ensconced in a large wingchair in front of the fire in the tasteful parlor. The others were paying her court.

That night, under a handmade quilt on an antique brass bed, we discussed our respective days. I thought this was a perfect opportunity for us. I didn't mention the problems from the new development I knew were down the road a bit. It wasn't really going to be Mayberry. But it wasn't Spanish Harlem either.

Sandra told me she loved the area. Before serving tea the Widow had taken her on a tour. He had even shown her a little green Queen Anne house with white trim he owned a block from the B&B. We could rent it for less than half what we now paid in monthly fees for the small apartment we owned in Manhattan. If we liked the house we could buy it later. She told me the Widow was the last surviving member of what had been a fairly rich old local family. For years he had lived in various cities around the world as a classic remittance man, accepting an allowance as payment for remaining absent from home. Finally his last homophobic relation had died, and he'd come home to Maysville. He'd opened the B&B and restaurant. He considered himself to be the center of small town society.

We made love that night for the first time since we'd gotten out of the hospital giggling like teenagers as we tried to keep the antique brass bed from squeaking. When Sandra began to kiss me in a way which had always signaled she wanted to have sex I had been pleasantly surprised. But as my hand had instinctively gone toward where her breast used to be she had caught my wrist and moved my hand downward. After we had both satisfied our needs for each other we lay back to catch our breath. Sandra leaned over and kissed my nose. "I think I'm going to like Maysville," she said softly.

"I already do," I answered.

Over the Memorial Day weekend we moved into the little green house. I officially became Maysville's police chief on June 1 although it wasn't announced until much later. In July we busted the dog fighters.

Sandra had finished her chemotherapy before we left New York. The doctors were optimistic about her recovery. Her hair was growing back as curly as it had been when she was a baby. We were both happier, and more optimistic, than either had been for a long time.

Although my new job wasn't "The Job" I was reasonably

content with it. Over the summer I had reorganized the small department to face the problems the new mall would bring when it opened in October. This mainly consisted of making suggestions to Miss Mamie. She accepted, and implemented, some of them.

When I pulled up in front of the Widow's on Main Street that Friday night Sandra's Mustang was parked in front.

Chapter Six

It was nearly 9:30 p.m. when I walked into the restaurant. In addition to my wife's Mustang there were half a dozen other cars parked in front. While Maysville has two sometimes rough beer joints, a new "sports bar" with big screen televisions, and a half dozen fast food restaurants this is the only hangout in town for the Merlot drinking crowd.

The restaurant is in a huge old house built in the early nineteen hundreds. Members of the Widow's family had lived in it until the nineteen fifties when it had been converted into a funeral home. The building then sat empty for a number of years after the funeral business went broke. When he came back to town Leigh Williams had bought it and spent more money than he could ever hope to get back turning the abandoned building into a beautiful, elegant restaurant. Although couples in Volvos and BMWs come from miles around to eat here I don't think a large majority of Maysville citizens have ever been in the place. Local homophobia did not die out with his last relative.

Sandra once told me Williams calls himself "The Widow" because he had lost his long time partner, the "Marsh" in the establishment's name, in a boating accident in Europe shortly before he returned to town. The Widow is my wife's very best friend, and I am sometimes jealous of how close they are.

Inside I found a few couples sitting at small tables scattered around the beautifully decorated room under soft lights. Waiters dressed in black hovered near the walls. A patron need only raise his eyes to summon one of them. They were all attractive young men. I exchanged nods with the diners and waiters I know. Sandra was at the larger table in back, which is reserved for the owner, with the Widow himself.

I bent over and kissed my wife. Leigh Williams leaped to his feet, as if he too intended to kiss me. Then he apparently remembered I had promised to shoot him if he ever kissed me again. He shook my hand enthusiastically. "Ricky," he said in his usual effervescent way, "Sandra and I have been so worried about you. Are you okay?"

I nodded, turning to my wife, I said, "I'm so sorry, darling. I got tied up. I know I should have called sooner. I promise I will do better in the future." By the time I had said all this, a waiter was there with a bottle of Commonwealth Ale. He showed me the label, and only after I had nodded my approval, did he open and pour it expertly down the side of the frosted glass. Another waiter was standing behind him holding a salad with my preferred dressing. He placed it in front of me. New York City must have restaurants with service like this, but I had never eaten in one of them.

Sandra nodded her acceptance of my lame excuse. She sipped her wine and looked at me.

I dug into the salad so I didn't have to grovel any more for the moment. Besides it had been a long time, and a lot had happened, since Bubba's lunch. As soon as I put my salad fork down the waiter placed a platter of sautéed white fish, with tiny boiled potatoes and broccoli, in front of me. Given the choice, I would have ordered it fried but it was delicious none the less.

While I ate, Sandra and the Widow discussed Maysville society; who had done or said what recently. When I set my empty beer glass on the table the waiter was there with another bottle and fresh frosted glass. "Ricky," the Widow said when I was finished with my dinner, "I was telling Sandra, before you arrived, the Peters' House is about to come on the market. It is the renovated red brick on Maple. The county school superintendent lives there. Do you know which one I mean?"

I nodded I did. "They are moving somewhere," he continued. "He got a new job. The house is beautiful, and I believe the price will be reasonable. Sandra is interested. Would you like to go look at it tomorrow?"

My mind was full of terrorists, living and dead, while Sandra and the Widow were concentrating on everyday life. They were the wiser. As far as I'm concerned she can have any house in town she wants. We had sold our tiny Manhattan apartment for a large sum and needed to buy another house or pay taxes on the profits. My salary as police chief is ample, and my retirement from the NYPD is even larger. Sandra received a sizable inheritance from her father, although I don't know how sizable. I'd never asked.

Whatever problems we might have, money is not one of them. Besides, I've never been good with money anyway. It has always amazed me how people will accept green pieces of paper and give me something shiny I want in return. "Whatever Sandra wants is okay with me," I said to the Widow. "As long as I get to live there with her the place doesn't matter."

Both Sandra and the Widow smiled. "I'll call them first thing in the morning," he said happily.

I covered my empty beer glass with my hand as soon as I put it down to avoid receiving another. I motioned to the waiter for the check, giving him my credit card, waiting to sign it. Most of the restaurant's regular clients are sent a monthly bill. I don't want, as police chief, to be seen walking out without paying. The Widow kissed Sandra on both cheeks. I stuck out my hand, "It was delightful as always, Leigh," I said.

He shook my offered hand, turned to my wife and said, "I will see you tomorrow, and we'll go house shopping! I love to spend other people's money for a change."

While following Sandra the few blocks to our little house I checked in with the dispatcher again. He might need me. Even Miss Mamie presumably has to sleep some time. But things were quiet as usual. The town's high school football team was playing an away game. According to the radio, the dispatcher said, they were losing badly so there wouldn't be any late night adolescent celebrating in town. I told the dispatcher to call me at home if I was needed.

Sandra seemed to still be upset with me so I apologized again when we were in bed. "I am sorry I didn't call you. I'll try to do better. You're the most important person in my life."

She looked at me for a while before she answered. "Ricky, I am not mad at you because you did not call. I am furious at you because you almost got yourself killed this afternoon. You knew you could not stop that man with your tiny little gun but you shot at him anyway. I had to stand there and watch that man aim his huge gun at you. If the trooper had not shot him when she did you would be dead now. I do not want you taking stupid chances, and I do not want you to get shot again. I want you here with me."

I could have explained all the rational reasons I had for doing what I did. I couldn't let that guy kill the trooper. If, for no other reason than he would have then killed us. But Sandra knew all this so I played the card which is always a winner in any argument with her. "If you want I will quit my job, and we can spend twenty four hours a day with each other seven days a week. I can fix things around the new house, and we can garden together. I will never leave your side again." Sandra knows I cannot fix anything around the house, and she hates gardening as much as I do.

"God, no," she said laughing. "Come here and make love to me. That is one thing you can do exceptionally well.

"Okay," I agreed. "But are you sure I won't get hurt?"

"You'll get hurt if you don't," she replied. "Besides, it is okay if I hurt you. I just don't want anyone else to do it."

Later when she lay snuggled in my arms she asked, "Do you want a new house?"

"If you do," I replied. "You should have anything you want we have the money to buy. You can have any house you want as long as I can live there with you. I love you."

"I love you too, Ricky, even if you do stupid things," she said before going to sleep.

The ringing phone woke me a little after seven the following morning. It was Captain White. He apologized for calling so early but wanted to invite me to a terrorism task force meeting outside Charlottesville which should be starting at nine. I quickly accepted his offer. Sandra ran "Mapquest" on her computer to get the directions while I was showering. I hate to admit I don't know my way around Virginia very well.

While I was sitting on the bed putting on my shoes she came into the room carrying my shoulder holster rig between two fingers as if it were something unpleasant she was forced to pick up. I stood up so she would have to hold the harness for me like you would a lady's coat. After I had it on I removed my nine millimeter pistol from the bedside table drawer. After checking to be sure it was loaded, with a round under the hammer, I slipped the gun into its holster. I got my light weight blue jacket from the hall closet. Sandra handed me my coffee in a to-go cup and gave me a passionate kiss, "If you come home safely you can have some more of that," she said.

I kissed her again and went outside. I turned and said, "You know if you let me quit working and we were together all the time we could. . ." She slammed the door.

The dispatcher told me, when I called on my police radio, there had only been one crime the previous night. Someone had broken into a construction worker's pickup out near the new shopping center. The owner of the vehicle was evasive about what had been taken. A couple of uniforms were there now filling out the report for his insurance company. And a reporter from the May County Chronicle had called me about yesterday. I don't like to talk to the press, but I felt I should praise the trooper for her bravery. There was no hurry; the paper doesn't come out again until the next Thursday.

I told the dispatcher I would be out of town for part of the day on cop business. He could reach me on my cell phone. I drove through town slowly, returning all waves. I'd ignored them yesterday when I was busy but doing it two days in a row would have the whole town gossiping. There were teams in bright colored uniforms playing on the ball fields at the edge of town. Little kids were everywhere. Minivans lined both sides of the road. I understood my obligation to protect these people better than I ever had in New York.

There was no real hurry, so I only abused my authority by driving ten miles over the speed limit on the highway. Since I didn't see a single cop anyone would have gotten away with speeding. I enjoyed my coffee while listening to "The Car Guys" on NPR. I'd overdosed on news about the attacks.

I found the place without much trouble. The meeting was being held in a deserted looking office building on a two lane road west of the City of Charlottesville. The feds had probably taken it in a forfeiture case. They love to do that; and, I must admit, I do like my seized Chrysler better than I would some stripped down Ford.

Just before I arrived I realized I had committed another offense as a loving husband, so I called home. When Sandra answered I said, "Whatever you want to do about the house is okay with me. If you like it, buy it." Most men think if they settle something the night before they don't have to mention it again the following morning. I know better.

"I love you, Ricky," Sandra said.

"Anybody would," I replied. She laughed and hung up the phone.

There were twenty cars parked in front of the rundown office building. None of them were obvious cop cars, although many had several antennas on their tops and trunk lids. The building's large front windows were completely covered with "For Lease" signs hiding what was going on inside. The door was locked. I pushed the button next to a speaker by the door.

"Yes,"

"Harris," I said. "I'm the police chief in Maysville." There was only silence so I continued. "Captain White asked me to meet him here." The silence continued for another full minute before the door was buzzed open. There was a man my age dressed in casual clothes sitting at a desk in the reception area in front of another door with a speaker next to it as well.

"White will be with you in a minute," was all he said. I sat down on one of the rickety chairs and read the sports section of a week old newspaper until White stuck his head through the door, motioning for me to join him.

The room I entered seemed to take up most of the first floor of the building. There were rows of narrow tables with telephones on them. A huge map of Virginia covered the front wall with pins sticking in it in various places. There were small, cubbyhole offices with large windows into the main room around three sides. Men were on the phones in several of them.

"We are just about to start. Get a cup of coffee and come join us," White said, motioning to a group of maybe twenty men sitting in a cluster in front of the map. I did as he said.

Like most of the law enforcement people I'd met since coming to Virginia the group was all male and mostly Caucasian. It was warm and many of the assembled men had their coats off. All appeared to be armed. I recognized a few of them. The state police investigators from yesterday were there as was the man to whom White had given the phone number at the shooting scene. The May County Sheriff was not there, and I didn't recognize anyone from his department.

White was standing in front of the map. He began the meeting. "First let me thank all of you for coming so early on a Saturday morning. The terrorists' attacks of last week have set up an unprecedented problem for law enforcement in this state and throughout the country. You men in this room will have a major role in what is happening in Virginia. There are some extremely dangerous people out there, and we need to get them off the streets as quickly as possible. I'm sure you've read about aliens being arrested and held all over the country. A lot of them have connections to Virginia. Seven of the nineteen hijackers had identification from the state.

58

"Due to the way the Division of Motor Vehicles operated, before last week, Virginia was an easy state in which to get either a driver's license or an I.D. card. All you needed was someone with an I.D. showing a Virginia address to sign an affidavit saying you live in the state too. This has been corrected. It also appears that several of the hijackers had student I.D. cards from state community colleges. We need to find any of these folks who are still alive, who have the I.D. cards, and make sure they are not working on future terrorist attacks.

"Before the attacks commercial sailors off cargo ships were routinely allowed to come ashore in Norfolk. Since the attacks those from countries on the watch list have not been allowed to do so. There are still a dozen of them unaccounted for, some from ships that have sailed.

"Due to the need for tight security you will be given information only on a 'need to know' basis. However, we have all seen the problems this has sometimes caused in the past." There was laughter from several of the men in the audience.

"So," White continued, "Special Agent Andersen and a group of his people will be in charge of coordinating all information collected in Virginia." He pointed to a tall, young looking man sitting off to the side. "Both he and I will be available twenty four seven for the foreseeable future. Before you leave I will make sure you have the list of phone numbers and email addresses which will be constantly monitored and responded to at all times. We would prefer emails for written reports since the information can be added to the data bases more quickly. If you are not used to using computers then partner with someone who is.

"We are attempting to computerize all the information we have now or will receive in the future. To start with we are concentrating on collecting and sorting names and last known locations of suspected terrorists. Within the next few days we hope to be able to run any name anyone comes across and give them all the information we have on that person and a list of their known associates in an extremely short period of time."

From working drug cases in New York, I know how important this can be. One of the biggest drug dealers in the city was taken down after his name kept coming up as a minor associate of a number of mid level dealers who had been arrested. He was the common link between them all and the big boss of the entire drug operation. Without computers he might never have been noticed.

"Amazingly the INS has a list of over 400,000 illegal aliens who have had their hearings and could be deported if anyone could find them. The data base of these folks has not, in the past, been connected to NCIC or any of the other law enforcement databases. This is being corrected as we speak. I expect many of the people you interview will have INS problems and can be held on those.

"As you all know," White continued, "the Pentagon is in

59

Virginia so we have already had a direct attack. And most of you know one of my troopers was in a gun fight with another suspected terrorist yesterday. Thanks to the help of Ricky Harris here she won," he said pointing at me. "Harris is currently chief of police in Maysville but before that he retired from the NYPD where he received the Medal for Valor."

I would just as soon he hadn't brought that up. In fact I would have been happier if I had not been mentioned at all.

"The young man who was killed yesterday was carrying a passport from Yemen in the name of "Nawaf Alghamdi ". Osama bin Laden himself is from Yemen. The real "Nawaf Alghamdi" is currently at the University of Florida in Gainesville. He has his passport which is identical except for the picture. His mother is Jewish, he is not a Muslim, and claims not to know how anyone could have gotten the duplicate passport. We found a phone number on the man's body. It is a pay phone in a pizza parlor across the street from a mosque in Brooklyn. The blind Egyptian cleric Sheik Omar Abdel-Rahman, who's in prison for plotting to blow up the United Nations, used to preach there. Thousands of people have access to the phone every day. The feds are watching the mosque and now the phone as well.

"Just down the road from here, between Lynchburg and Danville, we have a group of approximately 300 Black Muslims. I'm sure many of them are fine upstanding citizens. But a number of the men converted to Islam in various prisons, and some of them are very bad guys. They are part of the Muslims of the Americas group from upstate New York. This group has settlements scattered all over the country.

"In the last couple of days the feds in Roanoke have arrested three of their members on gun charges and say they are linked to an obscure, very violent group called Al Fuqra from Pakistan. Members of Al Fuqra have been linked to murders and fire bombings all over the country in the last couple of years.

"Hamas, the group that often claims credit for suicide bombings in Israel, has an office for one of its front groups in Herndon, just a couple of miles from Dulles Airport. We have no shortage of people to investigate.

"Just this morning we learned that a guy who was in custody in Minnesota before the attacks was supposed to have been the twentieth highjacker. He had taken flight training and had manuals for crop dusting in his possession. Crop dusting airplanes would be a highly efficient method of spreading biological, chemical or even radioactive materials over a city. The feds have grounded all crop dusters and are looking for anyone who may have recently shown an interest in flying these airplanes.

"So here is what we're going to do," White went on. "We have divided up our suspects geographically. Form into groups with others from your areas, take the information, decide who is going after which ones and go lock their asses up. Don't worry about charges. As I said, many of them have visa problems and the INS will be able to give you charges to hold those on. If this doesn't work out for a particular guy we will find another reason to hold him. Nearly 200 people were killed when the airplane hit the Pentagon and anyone who assisted the highjackers in any way can be arrested on the state charge of conspiracy to commit murder.

"Once we have suspects in custody we plan to set up an interrogation team we can fly around the state to grill these guys. The interrogators will have more of the whole picture and should be able to better know what information we can expect to get out of them. Our goal is to keep any potential terrorists from being able to commit another attack.

"Let's go get them before they kill anybody else. Agent Andersen and his guys have the information for you at the front of the room." The others made their ways to the waiting feds.

I didn't really seem to fit into the plan anywhere so I just hung around waiting to hear what White wanted me to do. When I stood up I noticed a group of eight tough looking, Middle Eastern looking, men sitting in the back of the room. I assumed they were some of the spooks I had been told about. A small dark man appeared to be their leader. He looked tough enough to strike matches on. He returned my glance with a stare. I was glad this man was on our side. He looked like he would make a bad enemy. I got another cup of coffee and waited for White.

It was only a few minutes before he joined me. "Sorry if I embarrassed you, Ricky," he said. I shrugged. It was done.

"Where do I fit into your plan?" I asked.

"I want you to be part of the interrogation squad. You and I can do the initial interviews to see who we should turn them over to feds for the follow-up. You are more experienced than most of my investigators. Can you spare the time away from your town?"

I smiled, "As long as nothing happens to Miss Mamie the town should be okay."

White laughed, "I thought about getting her to head up all this. She'd do a great job and bring cookies too." He gave me a folder full of papers; he said it was general "open source" stuff. In law enforcement this generally means information from publications. He asked me to read all of it and said he would be in touch. I told him I'd be at home. We shook hands and I started to leave.

On my way to the door a white haired man I didn't know, with a state police badge on his belt, stopped me. "That little girl you saved yesterday is my wife's niece. I really appreciate what you did."

"You've got it backwards," I said. "She saved my wife's and my life, not the other way around. She's the hero, not me. Thank her for me when you see her. How is she taking this?"

He shook his head, "Not real well. She has a teaching certificate and her husband is on her to quit the state police and go back to teaching." Her husband and my wife think alike.

"Did you see the article in the Richmond paper today about the shooting?" he asked. I shook my head so he handed me the paper. It was a short article identifying the dead man as "Robert Downs" and describing the incident as "Road Rage". Neither my wife nor I was mentioned. Apparently the Virginia State Police is as good at managing the media as the NYPD.

I drove back to Maysville at a more leisurely pace than usual, enjoying the beautiful day and thinking about what I had heard in the meeting. I was not really comfortable with the idea of picking up Middle Easterners in wholesale lots just because they were Middle Easterners. I had seen that happen yesterday with the clerk from the Quicky Mart. It was wrong and it was also extremely inefficient. While the clerk was being cuffed and put in the cage in the backseat of the cop's car, the guy we wanted had gotten away. I understand we were living in dangerous times and I would rather see some people's rights violated than see another terrorist attack. But White had said the system was already overloaded with information and soon it might well be paralyzed with locked up folks who presented absolutely no danger to us. I knew I could only mention this to White and keep it in mind for my own activities. Maybe this was a case where it was better for the net to catch too many than too few. I guessed time would tell. I was glad I was not the one responsible for making the decisions.

Besides, I have always had mixed emotions when I read news stories about "racial profiling." Every time I went up to any one I didn't know working cases in Spanish Harlem I was guilty of racial profiling. I would never have looked at a blonde Swedish looking woman and thought she might be a crack dealer, armed robber, or rapist. I knew what the neighborhood perps looked like and they were the ones I went after. This doesn't mean I think African-American drivers should be stopped in large numbers on New Jersey's highways. But it does mean I think anyone who fits the profile of the September 11 hijackers should receive more attention than other innocent looking passengers before he is allowed to board a plane.

After the first bombing of the World Trade Center I remember other cops on the squad were furious the feds hadn't been all over the group before it happened. They had held rallies where they preached the destruction of America. But I knew the feds were restricted to investigating actions not words. In the 1970s the FBI was embarrassed by some of their activities in investigating the civil rights movement. Hoover had illegally bugged Martin Luther King everywhere he went, even though King preached, and practiced, non-violence. But, I thought, the resulting restrictions on law enforcement went too far and we had just paid the price for not watching some of these groups. Common sense is not all that common when it comes to Congress, or

62

much of any place else for that matter.

Hopefully it would not be like it was during World War Two when the United States government locked up thousands of Japanese, many of them U.S. citizens who'd been born here, in camps. It might make more sense this time than it had then, but I hoped no one in authority had the stomach to do it again.

I was excited about being involved in this investigation. Catching terrorists before they could strike was surely more fulfilling than catching rapists after they had committed their crimes. And it was certainly more interesting than locking up the occasional drunk spousal abuser in Maysville.

I think I am pretty good at interrogating suspects. I have never been one of the cops who thinks they have to beat things out of people. And I could rationalize, under the present circumstances, turning those I felt had valuable information but wouldn't give it to me, over to someone who would do whatever was necessary to make them talk. I couldn't help thinking of the exchange with Jeff Goldbloom in "The Big Chill" about rationalizations being more important than sex. I know I have never gone a week in my adult life without a rationalization.

And I could further rationalize I would not be acting as a cop outside the town of Maysville anyway. I would be a secret agent! I wish I could say images of James Bond or Matt Helm came to mind. Actually I immediately thought of the cartoon character "Secret Squirrel."

It was another beautiful day so I drove home, with the car window down, wondering what the future would bring. I knew Sandra would worry, but I didn't know what could be safer than interviewing people already in custody. I listened to the police radio but, as usual, nothing was going on in town.

One of the three police cars which are usually out during the day on a Saturday was working his radar by the ball fields on the way into town. I waved to him. I knew he would alert everyone else I was back in town. On the way home I drove by the Widow's. My wife's Mustang, with the top down, was parked in front so I stopped and went inside.

It was too early for lunch on a Saturday, the place was empty. Sandra and the Widow were sitting at his table, which was covered with decorating magazines. As I walked to the table the Widow leaped up, went into the kitchen, and returned with a cup of coffee for me before I was finished kissing my wife.

"Did you like the house?" I asked.

"It's way too big for us, but I loved it. Everything is new within the last couple of years. There's a library where I can write my book. There is even an exercise room!"

I thought an exercise room would be a good place to store the NordicTrak neither of us ever used but I said, "That's great. Did you buy it?"

"No," she said. "I want you to see it first. Can you go this morning?"

Were it up to me I would simply show up at the house after Sandra bought it and had all our stuff moved in, but I said, with as much excitement as I could muster, "I would love to go see it."

Arrangements were made, and Sandra and I went to see the house. The Widow did not join us. He needed to get ready for lunch. When we arrived the husband was gone with the kids. The wife greeted us. I didn't have a clue as to their names. It was called the "Peters' House" which was the name of the people who had built it so many years ago.

I quickly saw why Sandra wanted the house. It reminded me of the one where she had grown up in Connecticut, but it seemed bigger. We entered through the front door. To the left was a library with floor to ceiling golden oak book selves covering most of the walls. Sandra was already planning to write her book in this room. To the right was a large formal dining room with a table which looked big enough for twelve. I couldn't think of ten people I would want to have for dinner, but I said nothing. In the back wall there was a pass through to the kitchen. Every room had shiny, golden oak floors.

We went straight down the hall and came into a huge "great room" with a fireplace. To our right, behind the dining room was a modern kitchen with stainless steel appliances, expensive looking cabinets, granite counter tops, and a round oak table surrounded by four chairs. I could see the deck and a large, well kept lawn through the windows. I've never operated a lawn mower in my life and have no intention of ever operating one. I assumed there was someone in town we could hire to cut the grass.

There were stairs going down to the basement from the kitchen. Down there was a large family room with a big screen television. Several pieces of exercise equipment where scattered around. Unlike our NordicTrak these looked as if they were actually used. The lady of the house then took us into a large side room, explaining I could have a workshop in this room. There were wooden benches and peg boards on the wall for tools. She explained her husband had never gotten around to organizing a workshop in the room. Neither Sandra nor I laughed, but I certainly wanted to. There was also a bedroom and bath on this level.

Back in the kitchen she showed us the two car garage. There was a vintage Corvette parked on one side and room for the mandatory family minivan on the other. The lady told us her husband liked to work on his car here and change the oil in both cars. Both Sandra and I knew I was more likely to fly than do these things, but neither said so.

Then we went upstairs to see the bedrooms. There were four on this level. I saw the two kids' rooms and the guest room first. They were all spacious. There was a bath between the two occupied by the kids and another for the guest room. I made approving noises.

The master bedroom suite, as I am sure it was called, was huge. There was room for a king size bed, built in cabinets, and four closets. But the most amazing thing was the master bath. Outside was a huge marble counter with two sinks. Inside was a toilet and bidet in a little room which could be closed off by a pocket door. In the main part of the bathroom there was another marble sink and the largest shower stall I have ever seen in a house. It had three shower heads, one of them on a chrome hose, and a tile bench that could be put to all kinds of interesting uses. I smiled, and I knew from the way she blushed, Sandra was also remembering the times we'd made love in the cramped bathtub in our old apartment.

But sadly that appeared to be in the past. I have not seen the scars from Sandra's double mastectomy and do not expect I ever will.

We both thanked the woman for the tour. Sandra promised her she would get back to them as soon as we had discussed the house. We drove home in our separate cars. I went into our current home thinking more about the information in the large envelope I carried and the terrorists who were out there than I did about the house we'd just seen.

But as soon as Sandra was in our now cramped feeling house she said, "Well, what do you think? Don't you love the house?" she said, giving me the necessary clue as to what my answer should be.

Chapter 7

Given the clue I didn't have to be a genius to say, "I love the house. Please buy it for me." I said it with no hesitation. I like to think I'm getting the hang of being married. Sandra beamed. Trying to be practical I asked, "Can we afford it?"

She laughed, "Darling, this house is over $100,000 less than we got for our apartment in New York. We can buy the house, put in a pool, and we'll still have to pay taxes on the money we made from the apartment."

"Do you want a pool?" I asked, surprised.

"No, I don't want a pool. That was just an example," she said. "Do you want the house?"

"Yes, I want the house. But isn't it awfully big for the two of us? Who is going to cut the grass and keep that oak floor so shiny?"

"Yes," Sandra replied, "It is bigger than we need. But that is better than if it were smaller than we need. It is a good investment, and we will always be able to sell it for more than we paid. "

I shrugged my agreement. "What about the grass and cleaning?" I didn't ask why she was thinking about selling a house we hadn't even bought yet.

"Miguel can cut the grass," she said.

"Who's Miguel?" I asked.

My wife gave me a look of pure exasperation. "Miguel is the nice man who cuts the grass here as well as at the restaurant and the other houses the Widow owns," she said. "Miguel's wife Maria can do the heavy housework. Didn't you ever wonder how the grass gets cut here?"

I just looked at her sheepishly. If I answered her honestly I would be forced to admit I had never once wondered how the grass managed to always be neat in our small yard. It just happened, and I just accepted it. In my defense I could have said my mind was occupied with saving the world from terrorists, and I could not spare the time to think about mundane things. But if I'd said this she would have asked what my mind was occupied with before last Tuesday. Since I didn't have an answer to that question I simply said, "Let's buy the house."

"I love you, Ricky," she said with a grin.

"Talk is cheap," I replied. "Come into the bedroom and show me."

66

"Just as soon as I call and tell Silvia we want the house. Go and wait for me on the bed." Now I at least knew the first name of the lady who'd shown us the house.

I went into the bedroom and put my pistol into the drawer in the bedside table. I'd taken off my jacket and shoulder rig when I first came home. The pistol was stuck down the back of my pants. Before yesterday Sandra would have given me a dirty look for doing this. But now she seemed to accept the fact I needed to keep the gun close at hand. I lay down on the bed and flipped on the television.

Although I hate to admit this, since we'd come to Virginia I have become a "car guy." Maybe I would use the garage of the new house to work on Sandra's Mustang, or at least if not actually work on it, to change the oil myself. I had even started watching NASCAR races on television and was secretly planning to attend one in Richmond next Spring! I'd begun to look forward to spending my weekend afternoons watching stock car racing on television. But due to the events of the previous week the weekend's races had been postponed. So I lay there watching a MASH rerun and listening to Sandra talk excitedly on the phone, waiting for her to join me.

It was after six when I woke up. Sandra was sitting on the couch in the living room with her decorating magazines spread out around her. "I called about the house," Sandra said excitedly. "Silvia talked to her husband and they have accepted our offer! The Widow has a standard real estate contract on his computer so we are all meeting at the restaurant tomorrow afternoon to formalize the deal."

"What happened to our date for some sweaty marital stuff?" I asked.

"You slept through it, darling. Maybe you'll get another chance someday."

Since I never beg for sex, unless I think there is a chance of being successful, I said, "What about dinner?"

"The salmon is defrosting. You can cook it on the gas grill. Come and help me pick out furniture for our new house," she said motioning to the magazines.

"I would love to, but I have to read all this stuff from this morning," I said picking up the packet White had given me.

I plopped down in my old leather recliner. I've had it since I got my first apartment, before I met my wife. "We can't put any of this ratty old furniture in our new living room," Sandra said. "We will need to buy all new stuff. The Widow has a decorator friend in Richmond who will give us very good prices on top quality furniture."

I wanted to ask her exactly who was not going to allow us to put our furniture in our new living room. Are there "furniture police" who come to the house and check? But I didn't say it, of course. Hopefully I could keep the recliner in the basement since I have gotten used to lying back in it to read. The house I'd grown up in was small and cluttered, not unlike the one we lived in now. But Sandra had

67

grown up in a large house with a formal living room which did not appear to have ever been used. I know I never sat on any of the furniture in it on my numerous visits. It looked like we were going to have a living room like that one as well. Again I wanted to ask why she wanted a room full of unused furniture but knew better than to ask.

All the material in the packet White had given me was "open source information." It had been collected from newspapers, magazines, and various organizations' web sites. All of the two inch thick collection of information I managed to read was interesting. Much of it was also extremely frightening,

There were stories about the three members of the Islamic compound near Lynchburg who had been arrested on gun charges. They were said to be connected to a group called "Muslims of the Americas" based in Hancock, New York. Who, in turn, were said to be linked to the radical Pakistani group "Al Fuqra" White had talked about which in turn had been connected to fire bombings and murders, including the shooting of a deputy sheriff in California, over the last ten years. There was an "Anti-Defamation League" report on the "Muslims of the Americas" group citing writings on the group's web site by "notorious anti-Semites and Holocaust deniers, including Michael Hoffman and former Klansman David Duke." American "White Power" types and Islamic Fundamentalists seemed like strange allies to me but I guess it's the old "my enemy's enemy is my friend" logic. Both groups do share a passionate hatred of Jews.

There was an article about a huge Muslim gathering at the Oklahoma City Convention Center which had featured many kinds of radical printed material including coloring books instructing children on "How to Kill the Infidel." Other stories said international terrorist organizations like "Hamas", "Hizballah", "Al Qaeda", "Islamic Jihad" and the "Muslim Brotherhood" have groups of supporters in mosques all over the country. The media didn't even seem to try to draw distinctions between the groups.

I was surprised to learn that Islam is the fastest growing religion in America. There are seven million people in the country who consider themselves to be Muslims. Although there are a lot of immigrants among the congregants nearly one third of them are converts. And the article said many of these converts are African-American males who converted to Islam while in our nation's prisons. Not all of them are dangerous extremists, of course, but Jihad appears to be actively taught in many mosques around the country and tolerated in the others. According to the articles it is difficult to separate the moderates from the more extreme, not unlike among "Christian Fundamentalists." Many are fine people, but others belong to the "Army of God" and blow up women's clinics. I also remembered previously reading about the guy who is charged as the "Green River Killer" in Washington state. He was said to have carried a Bible with him at all times. I assume he had it with him when he committed the

49 murders he's charged with.

Other articles pointed out the United States government had actively encouraged, and spent millions of dollars promoting, Jihad in Afghanistan during the Soviet occupation of the country. The U.S. backed "Mujahedin Freedom Fighters" became the Taliban and al Qaeda after they forced the Soviets out of their country. As so often happens, the U.S. won the war but lost the peace. I was also surprised to learn the U.S. had been doing business with the same Taliban leaders building an oil pipe line right up until September 11. Now, less than a week later spokesmen for the administration were calling them "extremists" and "terrorists" who provided refuge and support to terrorists.

The president, another story said, trying to demonstrate his understanding all Muslims are not extremists or terrorists, invited an influential American Muslim scholar named Hamza Yusuf to the White House to pray with him a few days after the attacks. It was later learned two days before the attacks Yusuf had made a speech saying the United States "stands condemned" and would face a "terrible fate" because of its mistreatment of minorities.

Mainstream Islamic cleric Iman Fawaz Damra was shown in a ten year old video tape, according to one article, saying Muslims should point "all the rifles at the first and last enemy of the Islam nation, and that is the sons of monkeys and pigs, the Jews." He later apologized. "Mainstream Muslims" throughout the country condemned the radicals in other articles, but I could see it was going to be extremely difficult to separate the law abiding Muslims from the terrorists even with a score card.

Fortunately, I did not have to understand all this. All I have to do is take anyone who commits some overt act in support of terrorism off the street. But I couldn't help remembering the Christian slogan from the Crusades, "Kill them all and let Allah sort it out." Things didn't look good for David the Quicky Mart clerk, who is not even a Muslim, but whom many people would think looked like the terrorists. And there are thousands of others like him who would suffer for the foreseeable future.

About half way through the pile I gave up and went to start dinner. I had plenty to think about as I stood on our tiny deck grilling salmon. I had the turner in one hand and a flashlight in the other as I cooked. It would be nearly eight by the time dinner was ready, and it was already dark. My mind was full of what I had read about Jihad and what was likely to come. I now had no doubt that among the millions of peaceful Muslims in America there might be literally thousands who were planning more attacks. It was not a reassuring thought. The best I could do to help stop them would have to be the best I could do.

As usual I didn't cook the fish long enough and Sandra had to nuke it before we could eat it. Just as we sat down to dinner the phone rang. It was Captain White.

He apologized for calling me on Saturday night, but one of his troopers had stopped a New York rental car for speeding on Interstate 95. There were two Middle Eastern men in it. The driver had a fake Virginia driver's license in the name of "Francis Xavier O'Brien" and the other man had no identification at all. The trooper had separated them and they were now being held on different floors of the Hanover Jail. White asked if I wanted to question them with him.

I tossed my napkin on the table and told him I would be right there. White laughed and said, "Just come at eleven. We need time to get some equipment in place and an Arabic speaker from the feds. Plus it's my daughter's birthday. There are a dozen ten year old girls at my house for a slumber party, and I need time to get those little terrorists under control before I leave my wife alone with them."

I told him I would see him then and tried to go back to my dinner. I was like a kid on Christmas Eve. I tried to conceal my excitement from Sandra. As a rule, anything about police work which excites me worries her.

I explained to her I would simply be helping White interrogate prisoners who had already been caught, disarmed and locked up. I could think of no safer job in law enforcement.

We finished our dinner. I carefully steered the conversation to the new house. Sandra said she thought the house would be empty shortly after Christmas and we could move in by New Years. New Years had become a significant holiday in our lives.

We washed the dishes together and talked about only pleasant things. Afterwards I tried to read the rest of the articles but had one eye on the slow moving clock. At nine thirty I told her I needed to leave to drive to Hanover to meet White and the suspects. She asked if I was coming back that night. It had not occurred to me until she asked the question that we had not spent a single night apart since we both got out of the hospital in New York over eighteen months before. I didn't want to break our streak so I assured her I would be home before morning.

I armed myself, got my jacket and kissed my wife good by. I hated to leave her, but I was excited about interrogating the potential terrorists. I was going to be a real cop again. I checked with the dispatcher on my way out of town. Things were quiet as usual. The mayor's ninety year old mother had backed into another pole in the Star Market parking lot. Since she only drove a couple of blocks to the store and church, and had never hit anything while going forward, no one was too concerned about her driving. One of her nephews owns the shopping center and takes the position the poles she hits are his property anyway, so she's never ticketed. I told the dispatcher I could be reached on my cell phone. I knew I should try to spend some time at the town police department since it paid my salary. Next week for sure, I promised myself.

It was pitch black with widely scattered stars as I traveled on the two lane road through rural Virginia. I was in no hurry. I had plenty of time to get to Hanover by eleven. When I got to Walton's Corner I saw the newer of the town's police cars sitting in the parking lot of the Quicky Mart so I stopped. Inside the police chief, wearing his powder blue jump suit and heavy pistol, was playing checkers with the clerk, David. We exchanged, "Chiefs" in greetings.

"I heard from the feds about the pay phone," the other chief said. "There were no calls for half an hour before the first call to the motel in your town. And there were no calls between the two calls made there." I shook my head to show my disappointment.

"But," he continued, "it is a toll call from here to Maysville and the guy used one of those long distance cards." He pointed to a display on the counter. I nodded my understanding. "The one he used came from a convenience store within spitting distance of the offices of one those Islamic groups in Herndon. They're still checking to see where else he called on the card. These fellows don't seem to realize that computers keep track of all this stuff nowadays."

The computer could tell us everything except where the guy is, I thought. "Keep me posted, Chief," I said. I made small talk with David for a minute, bought a Diet Dr. Pepper and went on my way.

The rest of the trip was uneventful. I sang along with Jimmy Buffett until I arrived in Hanover. Coming into town from the west I first went through a section of neon signs, fast food, and a huge truck stop. But once I crossed over Interstate 95 the town became a lot like Maysville. I followed the signs for "Hanover Courthouse" and found the much newer jail behind the historic building. It was a couple of minutes before eleven when I arrived.

Inside the building I showed my badge to the deputy at the counter and told him I was supposed to meet Captain White. "Yes, sir," the deputy said excitedly. "I'll get him right away." He picked up the desk phone and dialed. Apparently the deputy was as energized as I was about the potential terrorists in his jail.

Almost immediately I heard a buzzer and saw a light come on over the door behind the deputy. He went to the door and looked through the reinforced window before sticking his huge jail key into the door. A voice from inside said, "Come this way, Chief."

I went into the room. I heard the door lock behind me. There was equipment to take mugshots and fingerprints in this room. The new deputy pointed to the bank of small gun lockers on the wall. I placed my pistol in one of the lockers, locked it and put the key in my pocket. When I had done this he unlocked and opened the door into the jail itself. "First door on your right," he said. I thanked him and walked down the hallway. White was seated at a desk, talking on the phone in a small office. There was a tiny, attractive woman with an olive complexion sitting in a chair beside the desk. In front of her on the desk was a tape recorder, a pair of earphones and a yellow legal pad.

White held up his free hand toward me until he finished his phone conversation. Then he said, "Ricky, this is Selma." I nodded my greeting. "Selma is fluent in Arabic and is going to help us out here." He didn't tell me her whole name or say who she worked for, and I didn't ask. This was more spook stuff.

"Is she going to translate for us to question the two men?" I asked.

"No," White replied shaking his head. "They both speak English, but they probably won't talk to us anyway. They've been kept apart so far but after we attempt to interrogate them they're going to be accidentally placed in holding cells on this floor where they can talk with each other. I figured they would talk in Arabic so Selma is going to translate what they say to each other then. They haven't been allowed to call anyone yet so hopefully whoever they were supposed to meet is also getting nervous."

I nodded my agreement. The U.S. Supreme Court has ruled prisoners have no expectation of privacy concerning what they yell to each other in jail. They could be monitored for jail security reasons without a warrant so the only question was: Would they be dumb enough to say something helpful to us?

"After we're done with them here they'll be transferred to a federal lockup near the pen in Petersburg," White said. "We've cleared all the prisoners from the top floor and the surveillance equipment is being installed now. Hopefully we can put everyone we arrest in Virginia in there together and overhear what they say to each other. And we have a federal warrant to bug the phone in the day room so we'll let them call anyone they want. The system will not let them call pay phones so we may get some new numbers out of it too. Maybe we'll learn something."

There was a deputy outside the small office. He escorted White and me through the ground floor of the jail, unlocking and relocking doors as necessary. Eventually we came to a small interrogation room on the other side of the building. The room contained a table, which was bolted to the floor, and three chairs. The deputy showed us four empty holding cells, separated only by bars, along the corridor around the corner past the interrogation room. "Go get us the driver," White said to the deputy.

When he was gone White said to me, "This is probably going to be a waste of your time, but I called you before I thought through what we were going to do."

"Not a problem," I said. "I have plenty of time. What do you think these guys could tell us if they talked?"

"I don't know. There has to be some reason the guy the trooper killed was coming to that motel in Maysville and why the guy was calling him from Walton's Corner. Neither place is on a direct route anywhere so they weren't just passing through," White said. "Besides the powers on high have apparently decided we just need to lock up as many of these potential terrorists as we can find. Maybe they will tell us something. It should at least make their friends nervous every time we catch another one. Besides, they will not be blowing up stuff while they are in custody."

There was a knock at the door. The deputy brought in a compact, muscular, dark skinned, tough looking young man with a smirk on his face. White motioned to the single chair on the far side of the table and told him to sit. He sat. His hands were still cuffed behind him but no one mentioned it.

Without telling the prisoner who we were White started in, "What's your name?" The prisoner just looked at him, the smirk was steady. "Suit yourself," White said. "We have you on the false driver's license, a gun found under the seat, and several pounds of what appears to be cocaine hidden in the trunk. You are looking at least twenty five years. You might as well go back to your cell and start getting used to it." The U.S. Supreme Court has also ruled it is okay to lie to prisoners to trick them into cooperating.

"I demand a phone call," he said in a confident voice. "I want a lawyer."

White laughed, "You're in no position to demand anything. When you tell us who you are, and we check to see if you told us the truth, then maybe you can call a lawyer."

White opened the door and said to the deputy, "Take him back and bring the other one." The deputy took the prisoner by the arm and led him from the room. We could see the deputy turn away from the elevator back up to the jail. A few seconds later we heard the door to a holding cell slam shut.

A couple of minutes later another deputy brought us the other prisoner. He was smaller than the first one. He had long eyelashes and an almost pretty face. His hands were also cuffed behind his back.

"I'm going to give you one chance to tell me who you are and what you know, sweet face," White said menacingly. "If you don't, I am going to tell the deputy to put you in the sex offender tank and let you entertain the bad boys. Most people in this country are extremely pissed off about the attacks. I'm sure these guys would love to take their anger out on you in their own special ways."

Pure fear showed on the prisoner's face but he didn't speak. "Are you going to talk to me?" White asked. The prisoner shook his head. I wondered what he was more afraid of than being gang raped in jail. "Then off you go, sweet thing. I'll ask you again in the morning. Sleep tight, precious." White opened the door. The deputy came in. White told him to put this one in with the sex offenders. The deputy nodded. He had to lift the prisoner from his chair. This deputy too turned away from the jail elevator. We heard him say to the prisoner, "I need to stick you in here while I tell your new room mates to get ready for you," as he put him in one of the other holding cells.

As soon as the deputy was gone the two men started yelling to each other. The deputy came back into the interrogation room. "We put them in the cells on either end of the block so they have to yell through the two empty cells between them." White nodded his approval. We sat in the little room listening to them talk excitedly in a language, we hoped was Arabic, for twenty minutes. Then the conversation gradually petered out. While we were listening White had called on his cell phone to confirm they were ready for them in Petersburg. Then he called someone in the sheriff's department to confirm there were two deputies waiting to transport the men separately. He wasn't going to let them talk to each other when we could not record what was being said.

The deputy took White and me back through all the locked doors to the little office where Selma was waiting for us. She had covered a number of pages on her legal pad with small precise handwriting. We closed the door in case the prisoners were brought out of the jail this way.

"What did they say?" White asked.

"It was impossible to tell which one was talking when," Selma said. "But one of them kept asking the other about cocaine and a gun. The other kept saying he didn't know anything about either one. I don't think the first one believed him."

White and I both laughed. "You never know what will work," he said. Then to Selma, "Did they mention any names?"

"Only 'Ahmed', one of them said they needed to call Ahmed as soon as possible. The other one told him to shut up and never mention that name again."

"Who's Ahmed?" I asked.

White shrugged, "I don't know. It will be interesting to see who they call when they get to Petersburg. Maybe the phone number will give us Ahmed. What else did they talk about?" White asked Selma.

"Just about how much trouble they were in and how much more trouble they would be in after it happens."

"After what happens?" White asked.

"They didn't say, just 'after it happens'. Let me go back and transcribe the tape. Parts of the conversation were hard to understand the first time I heard them. I'll call you in the morning."

White nodded his agreement. Selma collected her paraphernalia and left.

It was nearly one in the morning. White said, "It's late. I am exhausted. Do you want to come home with me? I only live about ten miles from here."

I shook my head. "I need to get home. We're buying a new house, and we have to go sign papers tomorrow. I'll get a cup of coffee and be fine to drive." I really wanted to question him on what he thought the "it" was that was going to happen. But I was an outsider in this and reluctant to push anyone, especially White.

74

White suggested we get coffee, and maybe something to eat, at the "Truckstops of America" on the other side of Interstate 95. I quickly agreed. We retrieved our pistols from the gun lockers, asked the deputy behind the front desk to thank the sheriff for the use of his jail, and left. I followed his plain dark blue Plymouth to the truckstop.

Inside White went immediately to a booth in the smoking section of the restaurant. He pulled a rumpled pack of Marlboro Lights from his jacket pocket and offered me one. I took it. He lit it just as the waitress arrived with two coffee cups and a thermos of coffee. She pointed to the menus in the little rack on the table, saying she'd be back in a minute for our orders. Since I rarely pass up a chance to eat I looked at the menu while I asked, "What do you think the 'it' is that's going to happen?"

"I don't have a clue," White said, sounding as tired as I felt. "But we can be sure "it" isn't going to be good, and there must be a connection to Virginia."

I nodded my agreement. "There are plenty of places to hide in the Shenandoah Valley, out of the way farms and industrial buildings. But I would think 'foreigners' would stand out and attract attention, especially if they make a habit of speeding in out of state rental cars."

White laughed. The waitress came and we both ordered huge truck driver breakfasts with enough cholesterol to kill us.

"I would like to talk to all the police chiefs and sheriffs in the area," White said. "But if I do, I'll read about it the next day in the paper. I will call the ones I can trust on Monday. The troopers are 'profiling' motorists big time. We always tried to be sure our troopers didn't do that in the past against African-American drivers, but I don't see how we can avoid it against Middle Eastern looking drivers. We have got to get these guys off the street before they kill somebody else." I nodded my agreement, but we both knew that was easier said than done.

Our food came as I asked, "What do you make of the second guy not telling his buddy about your threat to put him in with the sex offenders?"

"I don't know," White said, "But we may be able to use that against him later. I thought he was going to wet his pants he was so scared. He is the weak link in this so far. I'll talk with the department's shrink about how to exploit this guy's fears."

Sportsmanship is not a big factor in law enforcement in general and particularly not when lives are at stake.

We finished our breakfasts talking about trivial, personal things. White told me this truck stop brought back memories of his days as a trooper. He said he'd written a million radar tickets on Interstate 95 and eaten enough grease in this restaurant to kill a lesser man. He also showed me pictures of his children. One boy was through college, one girl was a college senior and his ten year old daughter whose birthday it was had the face of an angel. He said she had been a pleasant surprise to both him and his wife.

It was after two when I got my large "to go" coffee. We were walking out when I noticed the tapes in the truck stop's store. White said his goodbyes and left me to shop. I found a tape of NASCAR racing songs and Willie Nelson's Greatest Hits. I bought both, peeling the wrappers off as I walked out to my car.

It had been a long day and I still had over an hour trip home. I had my window part way down, singing along with Kyle Petty's rendition of "Old King Richard" about his legendary father all the way home.

The Maysville town limit had never looked so welcoming. I checked in with the dispatcher. Everything was quiet as usual, but the mayor had dropped off an envelope for me about ten the previous night.

I decided to swing by the PD to see what the envelope was about. At first I insecurely thought he was firing me for not coming in for so long. But then I realized it had only been just over 36 hours since the shooting on Friday afternoon. It seemed like a month to me.

I dragged myself from my car in front of the municipal building and forced myself up the steps. Inside I straightened up before the dispatcher saw me. I spoke to him, picked up the letter from the mayor and my other messages, before going into my office. My office is a plain, uncluttered place. It hasn't been painted in years and you can still see where the retired chief's pictures hung on the walls. Miss Mamie is after me at least once a week to have my medals of valor framed and hang them on my office wall. I know I'll never do that. There is a computer behind the desk. I receive tons of emails about various police subjects every day and am often bored enough to read many of them. I was too tired to even turn the machine on.

The mayor's letter was expressing his concern for both Sandra and me over the shooting ordeal and asking me to please cooperate with the reporter from the Mays County Chronicle. He explained she was his wife's niece which was enough for me to understand my need to call her. Everyone around this part of Virginia appears to be related to everyone else, and people have no problem asking for help for their relations. There were also four messages from the reporter asking me to call her, the first about five on Friday afternoon. Surprisingly none of the others were from reporters. The state police had done a good job keeping me out of the story. But someone had obviously talked to the mayor, who had talked to his wife, who had . . .

I stuffed the latest message with her home phone on it into my shirt pocket. I would call her after one Sunday afternoon. No one in Maysville would expect even an urgent call to be returned during church time. I told the dispatcher I would be at home on my way to my car.

I let myself into the dark house as quietly as I could. I took my clothes off, laid them on the floor with my pistol on top next to the bed and slid in with Sandra. She stirred so I knew she was aware I was there. I cuddled up against her warm back and put my arm around her. "Did you have fun at your play group with the other cops?" she asked. I was asleep before I could think of a witty answer.

Chapter 8

I slept until just after noon on Sunday. The voices of Sam and Cokie discussing the past week's attacks in ominous tones combined with the smell of cooking bacon woke me up. I staggered into the kitchen in my robe. Sandra was standing at the stove looking lovely, making breakfast. I kissed her on the forehead before getting a much needed cup of coffee. "You look awful, my love," she said.

"A late night combined with old age," I said. The huge Sunday edition of the *Washington Post* was on the table. Stories about the terrorists' attacks filled the top of the front page. I didn't open the paper. I'd overdosed on the national news and was now trying to concentrate on only what I could, hopefully, do something about.

We were discussing my choices for omelet ingredients when the phone rang. It was White. "Hope I didn't wake you, Ricky," he said. I assured him he had not.

"Okay, here's what's happening. I just received the transcript of last night from Selma. There isn't much in it, just the one mention of Ahmed. But when our boys got to Petersburg one of them tried to call the pay phone the dead guy had the number for in his pocket. Since they can only call collect the system will not let them call pay phones. So he then called another number in New York. A woman answered and he asked for Ahmed. She blessed him out and told him never to call there again before slamming down the phone.

"The feds are on the house, which is in Queens, as well as the pay phone. So far there has been no sign of anyone going in or coming out of the house or any phone calls since they set up the tap."

"So what do we do now?" I asked.

"We look at the other leads I guess. The car they were driving was rented at JFK Airport using a secured Visa card in the name of "Francis Xavier O'Brien". The card was obtained three weeks ago by posting $5,000 in cash. The bank references and addresses given were fake but they apparently weren't checked. The car the dead guy was driving was also rented with the credit card we found in the glove box of the wrecked car. It was a secured one too. The information on the application for that card is also fake. These guys spent a lot of time and money setting this stuff up before September 11. The credit card company is cooperating and checking for other false information on applications for other secured cards they approved. Maybe we'll get lucky there."

"What other leads can I help you with?" I asked.

"There was a story in the paper today about how Virginia is involved in a project to map the entire state using satellite photos. I tracked down the guy in charge of the project, and he agreed to help us. The images of the area around Maysville were taken within the last month. I thought we could get together tomorrow and try to pick out some likely places the terrorists may be using. I can have the military fly over them and photograph any cars that may be around them." It occurred to me I had not seen an airplane in the sky since the attacks. The country's civilian aviation industry was mostly shut down, and there had apparently not been anything up until this point in the area of interest to the military. I pointed this out to White.

"I'll see if I can get some airplanes to fly over the whole area tomorrow so the recon flights won't stand out so much. Good thinking, Ricky." White told me he expected some more arrests for visa violations shortly and would be in touch when there were suspects to question.

I finished my now cold omelet, took a shower, dressed and decided I should call the reporter back about the shooting on Friday. I would have been happier to have been totally left out of the story. My two previous brushes with fame had not been pleasant experiences. They too had involved dead men. At least I didn't kill this one personally. I know better than to lie to a reporter, but I was determined to be as uninteresting as possible.

Her name was Mary Johnson. She answered her home phone on the second ring. I could hear other conversation in the background from her end. Hopefully I had gotten her up from dinner and she'd rush through the interview. I told her who I was, and the mayor had asked me to call.

"I just wanted to ask you about the shooting you were involved in on Friday, Chief," she said.

"I was just a witness. That trooper saved my life," I replied.

"What happened?" she asked.

I decided to see if I could leave Sandra out of it all together. "I was driving back to town from having lunch at Bubba's in my personal car when this guy tried to run me off the road. I called the town police dispatcher who apparently called the state police. I was trying to stay ahead of the guy when the trooper arrived. The guy wrecked, came out of the car shooting, and the trooper was forced to kill him. She saved my life. I was just a witness."

"Chief, the car was from New York, and you were on the police department there before you came here. Is there any connection?" Thankfully the reporter was completely on the wrong track.

"Eight million people live in New York City alone. I never saw the driver before," I said truthfully.

"Why do you think he rammed your car then?" she asked.

"I don't know. I guess it was one of those 'road rage' deals you see on television. I guess I was just in the wrong place at the wrong time," I replied.

"Thanks for calling me back. If I have any other questions I'll call your office." I told her that would be fine and hung up.

Sandra was standing there with a grin on her face. "I forgot to tell her you were there too. Sorry," I said.

"There goes my one chance, I hope, to be on 'Oprah'," she said. "How did it go last night questioning those guys?"

"They didn't talk to us. They're being held for a fake driver's license and probably some immigration charges. We don't have any idea who they are or where they came from yet.

"What are those people doing around here?" she asked.

"I honestly don't know, Sandra," I said. I didn't add that I hoped to find out exactly what they were doing and stop whatever they were planning. "When do we go sign the contract for the new house?" I added, changing the subject.

"We're meeting them at the Widow's at four. His lunch rush will be over by then."

I put my arms around her. "Want to go fool around until then? It will make your hair curlier."

Sandra looked at herself in the mirror on the living room wall. "If you're sure about my hair, let's do it," she said with a smile.

I had showered again before we left for the restaurant. Silvia and her husband, whose name, I think, was Tom, were already there when we arrived. We all sat at the Widow's personal table in the back of the empty restaurant. He had the real estate contract program open on his laptop computer. Sandra and Silvia filled in the blanks. While they were doing this Tom told me all about his new job somewhere in either North or South Carolina and how much they hated to leave Maysville, but it was such a great opportunity and . . .

The ladies finished filling out the contract. The Widow took the disk into his office to print. We all four signed it. Sandra wrote a check for the deposit. The Widow made photo copies for everyone and we were done. The Widow promised he would take the papers to a local attorney the next day so he could do whatever was necessary to transfer ownership of the house. Then the Widow brought out Champagne, and we all toasted the deal.

It was raining and starting to get colder when we left the restaurant. I dropped Sandra at home and went to the police department to check my emails. There was nothing of any interest, but it took an hour to wade through them all.

I was back at home a little after seven for our Sunday ritual. It never seemed to vary since we'd come to Maysville. We always ate delivery pizza and watched HBO on Sunday nights, first "The Sopranos," then "Sex and the City" and finally "Oz." Sandra sat on the couch, also reading a book since television alone never seems to be enough to completely occupy her mind, while I sprawled in my old recliner. The pizza was gone, and we were in the middle of "Sex and the City" when White called.

He said he had the satellite photos of the area and would be coming to Maysville in the morning. He said they were each thirty six inches square, and there were hundreds of them. He did not want to bring them to the police department because they would attract too much attention. I asked Sandra if she could find something to do away from home in the morning so we could work at our house. She agreed. White said he knew where I lived and would be there by ten.

Before hanging up White added that he wanted the chief from Walton's Corner to see the photos too. The chief had spent many years in and around his little town and knew what was up every back road. If the chief could come he, White, would pick him up on the way.

I suddenly realized how little I knew about the area around Maysville and suggested we also include Miss Mamie in the meeting. She, like the Walton's Corner chief, was an expert on the surrounding area having spent her whole life here.

White was silent for a minute apparently thinking about this suggestion. Then he said Miss Mamie was a good idea, but that meant we would also need to include the May County Sheriff since the two of them were so close. White said he really should include the sheriff anyway since it was the usual practice of the state police to include local law enforcement when working in their jurisdiction.

We agreed he would line up the Walton's Corners police chief, and I would get Miss Mamie and the sheriff to be at my house the following morning. I immediately called Miss Mamie, apologizing for it being after nine on a Sunday night. She said it was fine. She was just lying in bed watching HBO. Apparently she was also a "Sex and the City" fan, but I thought better than to mention it.

I told her White and I would like her to come to my house the following morning to look at some satellite photos for some possible places the guy the trooper shot might have been going. I added White was hoping to bring the Walton's Corner police chief, and I would try to locate the sheriff and invite him as well. Miss Mamie said she knew where the sheriff was and would see that he was there.

I was just starting to hang up when she suggested we all come to her house instead of mine. She said she had a huge dining room table where we could spread everything out. Plus, I thought, the neighbors will not think anything about the sheriff's car being there. He drove the most police car looking police car I have ever seen. It had a forest of antennas on the trunk and top as well as blue emergency lights everywhere they could be attached to the car. I had hated to run Sandra out of her own house and besides, with Miss Mamie, there were always delicious cookies. I called White back to tell him to come to Miss Mamie's instead of my house in the morning.

When I got off the phone I told Sandra we had moved the

meeting to Miss Mamie's house. I knew Sandra was also concerned about what was going on. She had seen the man come out shooting last Friday and was as addicted to the news as I was. I needed to find something safe that she could do without causing me to breach any more security than absolutely necessary. I noticed the *Washington Post* was open to a story about a mosque in New Jersey and a radical cleric who had spoken there. It gave me an idea. I asked Sandra if she'd be willing to check the major papers available on the Internet and collect stories on possible domestic radicals for me. She quickly agreed. Later when I started to go to bed she was looking at articles in the *New York Times* from the last week. Her laser printer was spitting out pages.

When I asked her if she was coming to bed she said, "In a little while." I fell asleep waiting for her.

I woke up earlier than I usually do Monday morning. I guess I was excited about the possibility of finding these guys' hiding place and, hopefully, stopping whatever they were planning. I showered and dressed without waking Sandra. I don't know when she came to bed but there was a thick stack of newspaper stories lying on top of my shoulder holster rig on the dining room table. I took them with me to my office at the police department.

I rarely come in that early. The dispatcher and the couple of cops who were hanging around waiting to start the day shift looked surprised. I spoke to each of them in my best "carry on men" manner before getting a large mug of coffee and going into my office. Checking my computer, I deleted twenty five new useless emails, before starting to read the articles Sandra had printed for me.

The government was rounding up potential terrorists all over the country. Most were being held on INS charges and many, the articles said, would soon be deported. It didn't make any sense to me to send these guys back to wherever they came from so they could plot and conspire from there but nobody had asked me. The media was also beginning to mention that some of the terror suspects, still in the Middle East, had once been involved with the U.S. trained and financed "Mujahedin" in Afghanistan. They had been brave, freedom loving patriots when they were fighting the Russians. Now they were cowardly terrorists.

The NYPD was looking for suitcase size nukes. It would be easier to find a needle in a haystack than a suitcase in the city. I was just as happy to miss that hunt.

A little before 10 a.m. I told the dispatcher I would be available on my cell phone and drove to Miss Mamie's. It was foggy and drizzling rain. Miss Mamie lives in a large, square red brick house with a big porch on the front, on a back street two blocks from the police station. The porch was crowded with white wicker furniture and still blooming plants hung from the ceiling. It was getting colder, and I doubted the blooms would survive the day. The sheriff's cop car was in the driveway covered in dew.

Miss Mamie opened the door before I could knock. She is a short, round lady who looks like Norman Rockwell's idea of the stereotypical grandmother. But I knew from past experience she was extremely intelligent and tough as could be. She was followed to the door by a tiny white poodle. The dog wagged his minuscule tail in greeting.

The May County Sheriff was sitting in the parlor holding a tiny, delicate looking cup in his ham of a hand. Miss Mamie greeted me enthusiastically and motioned me to the silver coffee pot and plates of cookies on the sideboard in the dining room. I filled a tiny cup with coffee, placed it on an equally delicate saucer, added a couple of cookies to the tiny saucer and went in to talk with the sheriff. Our relationship has always been cool. Rumor is he thought his son, who is one of his deputies, should have been given the job as Maysville Police Chief. Before I made it into the parlor I saw White's car pull up outside. I set my coffee and cookies down before going to help bring in the satellite photographs.

White and Chief Buford were getting out of the unmarked Plymouth. I was glad to see Buford was dressed in jeans and a dark jacket instead of his usual powder blue jumpsuit. White opened the trunk of the car. It was stacked full with large photo paper boxes. I walked over offering my help carrying the boxes into the house. "Before we go inside, Ricky," White said, "I wanted to tell you the feds raided the house in Queens just before dawn this morning. No sign of Ahmed but there were three women and half a dozen kids in the house. They took two of the women into custody and left the third one, who is a U.S. citizen with the kids. She hadn't called anyone last time I checked. They may have left the wrong woman with the kids. They also found Mapquest directions to Walton's Corner. They took a computer out of the house and are going through the stuff on it now."

We divided the large boxes among us. Chief Buford, who I thought must be at least 80, took more than his share. When we entered the house the sheriff was still sitting in the parlor drinking his coffee. He spoke to White and Buford but didn't get up. He was as cool to them as he had been to me.

Miss Mamie greeted both men enthusiastically. She told me she and Buford had graduated from high school together. They were two of the 29 members of the senior class, the largest the school ever had up until that time. She had tears in her eyes when White picked up the tiny poodle. I'm sure she was remembering Buttercup and the justice she and White had brought down on those responsible for that little dog's death.

White stacked the boxes on the white lace table cloth. Each box had a number on its lid, and he had organized them into various piles on the large dining room table. He dug through the piles until he found the box he wanted and removed one of the photographs. The 36 inch square print showed a tiny cluster of buildings near its center with fields and wooded areas all around. "The collection of buildings is the middle is Maysville," he said. I located the town square on the photo and could figure out the location of other landmarks from there.

He pulled out two more of the large photos and placed them next to the first one. "This is the road to Walton's Corner," he said about the second photo, "And this is Walton's Corner itself," indicating another, smaller, cluster of buildings on the third photo. "I hope the place we are looking for is off the road somewhere between the two towns. If I'm wrong about that, this is hopeless. But if I'm right we should be able to locate these guys."

As I looked at the photos I could see the logic in White's theory. If the place was not in the immediate area there were much easier, more direct ways for the dead man to have gotten to it. Interstate 81 is to the west, and Interstate 64 is to the south. Interstate 95 is to the east, but much further away. It didn't make any sense to me they would come through Maysville or use the pay phone in Walton's Corner if there was a better, more direct way to get where they were going.

We spent the rest of the morning poring over the boxes of detailed photos looking for likely hideouts. Between Miss Mamie, Chief Buford, and occasionally the sheriff, we compiled a list of 30 possible places between the two towns. I carefully wrote the latitude and longitude numbers from the photos, as well as the names and numbers of the roads, for each of them in case White was able to arrange military over-flights. The sites ranged from small farms that had been sold to outsiders, an abandoned church camp, and several secluded industrial buildings, some of which had been used as drug labs in the past. I was surprised by Buford's stories about the amount of marijuana he said was grown in the National Forest around the area. He said since the government had started seizing property where marijuana fields were found many of the growers had moved their crops onto government property. He said there were probably also structures in the forest we could not see from the air. This meant there were probably others, beside the terrorists, out there who wouldn't want us poking our noses in their business. One of the stories Sandra had printed for me yesterday talked about all the drugs which had been found since border security had been increased looking for terrorists. We might find some around Maysville as well.

The weather was too bad to fly even if White could arrange the flights on short notice. Chief Buford suggested I come with him. We would poke around a little to see what we could find. He said we were coming up on deer and turkey hunting season, and there would be guys out looking for places to hunt so we shouldn't stand out. Buford said he had a personal pickup truck we could use.

White, Buford and I thanked Miss Mamie for the coffee, cookies, and use of her dining room table. She said she would go down and make sure everything was okay at the police department while I

84

was gone with Chief Buford. The sheriff moved back into the living room. Buford and I said "goodbye" to White outside. He promised to keep in touch.

Buford climbed into my cop car. "This is nice," he said, stroking the leather seat.

"It used to belong to one of the dog fighters," I replied.

Buford laughed, "Mamie and Captain White sure taught those fellows not to steal old ladies' poodles, didn't they? They must be really embarrassed when somebody in the penitentiary asks them what they're in for."

We stopped by my house so I could change into jeans and cowboy boots for our expedition. While I was changing I could hear Sandra and Chief Buford discussing computers. To my surprise Buford told her he had worked on electronics years ago in the navy and was now a computer enthusiast. He said he had built several of them from scratch, and when Sandra was ready to upgrade hers she should come see him. She gave me another inch thick stack of newspaper stories. I told her I would read them when I got back.

Buford asked if I would mind stopping for lunch before we left town. He said he was diabetic and needed to have his meals on a set schedule to keep his "sugar regular." I asked where he wanted to go, and he immediately said Molly's by the post office. I drove there and parked. We went inside.

Most of the people in town call the place "Eats" after the neon sign in the front window. There's no other sign on the building. This was where I was eating breakfast when I saw the first reports of the airplane hitting the North Tower of the World Trade Center. The Maysville Debating Society had been in the middle of their daily meeting arguing spiritedly over whether or not Congressman Gary Condit knew more about Sandra Levy's disappearance than he was saying. I haven't heard this subject discussed anywhere since. I rushed home that morning. Sandra and I watched the second plane hit, as well as all that followed, together. It seemed like so long ago, so much had happened, but it was really less than a week.

The restaurant was only about half full, but I knew the wait for our food would be considerable. Miss Molly, as everyone calls her, only prepares one order at a time. When it's on the ledge for the waitress to pick up she starts on the next one. Our lunches, and everyone else's in the place, were going to be further delayed by Miss Molly coming out of the kitchen to personally greet Chief Buford. After about five minutes of questioning each other about family members and such, Miss Molly said she needed to get back to cooking. No one in the place left or made any objection to the added delay. I couldn't even imagine what the reaction to this would be in New York City. As soon as Miss Molly left the waitress, who is the proprietress' daughter, brought us each a glass of tea. Buford's had a spoon in it to show it was unsweetened. She also took our orders.

While waiting for our food Chief Buford told me 60 years earlier he had been "sweet on" both Molly and Mamie. He told me he would hitchhike to Maysville from Walton's Corner every Saturday afternoon to take one of them out. He would have his date of the evening home by 10 p.m. and then usually have to walk back home, often arriving just in time to go to church with his mother. It wasn't that no cars would stop for him on the way back, he explained, there were no cars on the road late at night.

Buford said he was still trying to decide between the two young women when he graduated from high school and went off to the navy. It was 1942 and he didn't want the war to get over before he had his chance to fight. When he came back 25 years later he had a wife and two children.

I would have guessed Buford had never been a hundred miles from Walton's Corner. But he had lived all over the world during his navy career. I couldn't picture this plain spoken man working on the most secret, sophisticated electronics gear of his day. He told me some of the high tech security stuff he'd worked on back in the 1960s that was still secret today. Some detective I am.

While we ate our lunch he regaled me with stories of his world travels and navy adventures. He had retired as a Master Chief after 25 years and returned to Walton's Corner only because he was needed to care for his aged mother. She refused to leave her lifelong home to come live with him. Although he had a good pension from the navy, and didn't need to work, he had become bored hanging around the house. So he joined the volunteer fire department where he rapidly rose to be its leader. When the police chief job became available in 1970 the town council offered it to him, and he'd had it ever since.

He surprised me when he said casually, "I understand your wife had breast cancer." I must have looked startled because he quickly added, "My wife had the double surgery over 20 years ago. She did great afterwards." I'm sure I looked relieved. "My wife is sick with the cancer again now, "he said. "But the specialist in Charlottesville says it has nothing to do with her old breast cancer. We are both just getting so damn old something is bound to kill us."

We finished our lunch and then drove toward Walton's Corner. Buford pointed out the side roads he thought we should explore in his truck. I tried to keep track of them in my head. This area would be easy to hide in if those looking for you didn't know it as well as Chief Buford did.

His old pickup was standing behind the tiny police department building in Walton's Corner. It was a faded red except for the driver's door which was blue. I had expected to see Barney when we went inside. Instead there was younger man sitting behind the counter in a uniform that was too big for him. When we were in the chief's cluttered office I asked about Barney.

"The town found him a job more suited to his talents," Buford said. "You know the guys you see where they are fixing the road holding the poles with 'Slow' and 'Stop' attached to them?" I nodded that I did. "Well, they have given Barney one of them poles. I hope he doesn't kill anybody by showing the wrong sign at the wrong time." I could not help but laugh. Buford joined me.

The Chief went to a small refrigerator in the corner of his office. He took several items of food as well as a vial of what I assumed was insulin and a hypodermic needle out and placed them in a small padded cooler. He carried the cooler with him.

Buford stopped to open the trunk of his cop car on the way to the pickup. "You got a shotgun in your car?" I nodded that I did. "You might want to bring it," he said. I got the 12 gauge pump from my trunk. I also brought the box of extra shells. I'd learned my lesson and would, hopefully, never put myself in a position to be outgunned again.

I placed my shotgun in the rack under Buford's in the truck's rear window before climbing into the battered vehicle. "It runs better than it looks," Buford said. I was tempted to say, it would have to, but thought better of it.

We started back toward Maysville. I had the list of places to check. Buford suggested we hit the highest probability sites first since it would be dark in a few hours. He said he had to take his wife to the doctor on Tuesday, but we'd look at the rest of them the following day. If we got an early start we should be able to check them all by dark Wednesday.

We were about half way back to Maysville when he turned left onto a narrow lane leading toward the mountains to the east. We had driven a couple of miles when we came to a smaller road going off to the left. "A bunch of hippies bought this old farm a couple of years ago," he said driving slowly around the pot holes in the road. "They are probably growing marijuana but it is outside my jurisdiction. And the sheriff isn't what you'd call 'proactive' when it comes to law enforcement." We followed the narrow track until we came to a ramshackle old house. There was an ancient VW bus parked in the yard and another one on blocks partially covered with a tarp. The only structure I could see that was big enough to hold other vehicles was a dilapidated barn. It was open on the end facing us and empty.

Just as Buford started to turn his truck around in the first spot be found which was wide enough a middle aged woman with hair down to her waist wearing a long, flowered dress came out of the house. He stopped and waited politely while she walked over to the pickup.

"Howdy," he said. "We're lost. We turned into your road by mistake and didn't have room to turn around until we got clear up here to your house. Sorry to disturb you."

She was looking at the shotguns in the gun rack. "We don't approve of killing animals and don't allow anyone to hunt on our property," she said.

"That's certainly your right," he replied. "And we would never hunt on anybody's land without asking first. You have a nice day now." He pulled the pickup back the way we'd come on the narrow lane. "No terrorists here," he said.

Back at the road he turned away from the direction which we'd previously come. A mile or so further I saw a black Lincoln parked in the yard of large brick house with a satellite dish on the roof set back from the road on the left. Before I could get excited Buford said, "That's Mary Bane's car." I looked it over as we drove past. It had Virginia tags.

When I didn't react to the name he said, "Haven't you heard about the Bane family?" I shook my head.

"They are right famous locally. I am surprised you haven't heard of them. Her late husband Ronald was a big shot in the 'Dixie Mafia' back in the 1970s. Have you heard about the 'Dixie Mafia'?" Again I shook my head.

"Back in the 60s and 70s a bunch of southern criminals decided to run the Italians out of the organized crime business all over the south. They took over drugs, gambling and prostitution from here to New Orleans. A lot of them had been moonshiners back when that was a low risk, profitable business. They were a mean, violent bunch. They would simply move into an area, kill the mobsters running the various rackets and take them over. They also managed to shoot or blow up a bunch of innocent bystanders along with the folks they were after.

"Of course all the killings attracted a lot of attention from law enforcement and eventually there were arrests all over the place. I guess a lot of local cops were being paid off but once the feds came in it was all over for the bad guys. A lot of conspiracy cases and RICO seizures of property were brought throughout the south. This place had been in Mary Bane's family for years so they couldn't take it. Ronald died in prison a few years ago. I guess the Italians just took their rackets back after the rednecks were gone and operated them more quietly."

"Unless she has a good job it looks like they didn't get all of Ronald's money," I said.

Buford laughed. "The money she has didn't come from Ronald. It came from her two sons. Now that's a story."

I waited patiently to hear it. "Mary had two boys, Ronald Junior and Tad. They were about a year apart. When they were teenagers they were nasty little thieves, always in trouble with the law. But Mary always paid for everything they got caught stealing or destroying and most people were too afraid of her husband to press charges so they just skated along. By the time they reached their early twenties they just seemed to straighten up and fly right.

"Their daddy was already in the penitentiary so folks figured they had learned their lesson from what happened to him. I heard they
88

both had jobs away from here, but I'd see them around town from time to time when they'd come home to visit their momma. When I'd see the boys they were always respectful and polite. I was thinking maybe a leopard could change its spots.

Buford laughed again. "Then about ten years ago we all found out what they had really been up to all those years. The boys were in a high speed chase and shoot out with the police in South Carolina. They had pulled off a very professionally done bank robbery in some little town there. But their luck ran out. Just as they were coming out of the bank with their guns and stocking masks a state police officer turned into the parking lot and saw them.

"The newspaper story said they had apparently watched the bank for some time and knew it was far enough off the highway that the state police didn't regularly patrol in the area. The town just had some old town policeman like me and he didn't scare them. But it was their bad luck the bank had messed up the trooper's mother's social security direct deposit. He was stopping by on his dinner break to straighten out the problem.

"There was a chase followed by a gun battle. Junior was killed and Tad was sentenced to 40 years in prison. After it happened the feds came around. One of them told me the boys were suspected of having robbed over 200 banks during the previous 15 years. The feds, and the insurance company investigators, brought metal detectors and dug holes all over the Bane's property but they never found any money. There are still a couple of local guys with metal detectors who come out here looking for the treasure when they think Mary is gone on one of her frequent trips. No one has ever found any of it."

I told Buford about having spent three cold miserable days digging holes in Central Park once looking for a steel box of money from a robbery. It was backbreaking work, but we did finally find the money.

Buford just shook his head. "The manager from the hardware store in Maysville told me the boys used to come in and buy sections of that plastic sewer pipe, and the plastic caps that you use to seal off the ends, when they were in town. Nobody is ever going to find that money with a metal detector."

We were getting closer to the mountains. Buford turned off onto another side road. We followed it about a mile until it dead ended in the yard of a fallen down old house. There were beer cans and discarded condoms around the perimeter of the flat parking area. No terrorists were living here.

We went back to the road and drove further away from town. "There is a little old church camp up here a few more miles," he said. "They only use it in the summer so it's probably deserted now." As we approached the camp we were stopped by a chain across the road. Even though it didn't look like any cars had been past the chain in a while we got out and walked around it into the camp anyway. It was more an opportunity to stretch our legs than the hope we would find anything. It was deserted.

Darkness was fast approaching as we got back into the pickup. "This road only goes a little way further before it goes into the National Forest. There is no telling what we might find in there but it would take four wheel drive to get in so we aren't going to find any rented Lincolns."

I reminded the Chief the little girl had said the guy who used the phone at the Quicky Mart was driving an SUV. He said we couldn't go in there in the dark anyway so it would either have to be checked from the air or we'd have to come back.

We drove slowly back the way we'd come through the gathering darkness. There were lights on at the Bane's house when we drove by. "I wonder if anyone will ever find the money," Buford said, "Or if it'll still be there when, and if, Tad gets out of prison in about 2030." I wondered if the world would still be here in 2030 but didn't say anything. We each ate an apple out of Buford's little cooler on the way back to town.

Behind the police station we made plans to meet on the same spot at 8:00 a.m. on Wednesday. I told Chief Buford I had thoroughly enjoyed the day and was looking forward to doing it again. Maybe we'd find them next time.

I put my shotgun back into the bracket in the trunk of my car and dialed my home phone number. Sandra answered on the first ring. She'd been waiting for me to call. She wanted me to take her to the Home Depot to look for stuff for the new house. I wasn't crazy about shopping, but she said we could have dinner at the Italian restaurant on the way. That peaked my interest. I told her I would pick her up in half an hour. While we were at the Home Depot anyway maybe I could buy the necessary stuff to change the oil in the Mustang.

Chapter 9

Sandra and I had a great evening together. It was almost like a date. We had dinner in a chain restaurant that claimed to be Italian. The food was nothing like what's served in New York's "Little Italy" but it was good none the less. Then we went to Home Depot. First I picked out a complete set of power woodworking tools for my new basement workshop. I might not understand exactly what a "router" does but I certainly wanted one. Then I picked out enough mechanics' tools to completely rebuild Sandra's Mustang in my new garage. Intellectually I knew these tools would not get even as much use as the NordicTrack sitting abandoned in our garage, but I wanted them. I was going to become a "car guy" and a guy who built his own furniture. Fortunately, I decided I should wait to actually buy these things until after we moved into our new house since I had nowhere to store them until then.

Then I walked around, holding hands with Sandra, agreeing with her that she needed to buy a ton of stuff for the new house. We discussed the merits of various colors of paint and patterns of wallpaper. All we actually ended up buying was the pump thing for Miguel to fix the toilet in our present house to make it stop running. I was so into this stuff that I almost suggested I would fix the toilet myself. Home Depot is an amazing place. It's easy to completely lose control of your senses.

I checked with the dispatcher from the car as we drove back to town. Everything was quiet as usual in Maysville.

We were home before the news came on. Amazingly, no one had called either our home phone or my cell all evening long. Maybe things were getting back to normal. But I have to admit I was disappointed not hearing from White.

Printouts of more articles about domestic terrorists were piled on the dining room table. Seeing them reminded Sandra she needed a new cartridge for her printer as well as another box of paper. She said she had meant for us to get the supplies while we were out, so I could carry the heavy paper box for her, but she had forgotten.

Tuesday was shaping up to be an uneventful day in my personal war against terrorists. Chief Buford was taking his wife to the doctor in Charlottesville and, until I heard from White, there was nothing for me to do. So we agreed to meet at the strip mall in town for lunch. We would eat, and then get her stuff from the office supply store. She said she also needed to go to the grocery store so I could put the box of paper in the trunk of her car at the store and carry it into the house when I came home.

I was at my office at the police department early. After checking my email I spent the morning reading the terrorism articles Sandra had found. Some of them contained well researched connections to suspected terrorists in the Middle East, and some of them were pure "black helicopter" conspiracies which have become so popular since the advent of the Internet.

There were articles linking the Oklahoma City bombing to international terrorism, many of which seemed farfetched to me. I know more about that bombing than I ever wanted to know. My former partner in New York, Todd, was obsessed with the case and spent countless hours telling me about it.

One of the articles Sandra had printed said that "John Doe II" was a Middle Eastern terrorist. I knew this was wrong because I knew that "John Doe II" was an army private named Todd Bunting. Bunting had gone to Elliott's Body Shop in Junction City, Kansas to rent a truck to help his sergeant move the day after McViegh rented one. The sketch of "John Doe I" was actually the sergeant, Michael Hertig, not Timothy McViegh. The composite sketch of "John Doe I" does resemble McViegh but the man in it has a prominent cleft in his chin. McViegh did not. There were published photos of the sergeant and the sketch at the time. The people at the truck rental place had merely been confused as to which of the trucks they had rented was which. Neither Bunting nor Hertig was involved in any way with the bombing.

What upset my partner so much was the presumed reason for the mistake. The feds thought pretty much from the start the bombing was the work of some militia group and had asked the clerks if anyone who had rented a truck had been wearing army fatigues. So the clerks remembered and described the two guys wearing the fatigues. McViegh was shown in a McDonald's security tape a few minutes before he rented a truck wearing jeans. I particularly remembered all the statements about there being some sort of "Islamic symbol" on "John Doe II's" cap. It turned out to have been a Carolina Panther, the Charlotte football team.

Of course, if the government had not been in such a hurry to execute McViegh they might have been able to ask him more about the bombing. Prisoners with no hope of ever getting out make deals every day for better conditions in prison. Terry Nichols is still alive, serving a life sentence in a federal maximum security prison. But the State of Oklahoma wants to try him again and execute him too so there is no way he's going to cooperate. If politicians were more concerned about being smart about crime, instead of looking tough on crime, it would be easier for investigators to get to the bottom of things.

I expect any day now to see articles linking Osama bin Laden to both the Kennedy assassination and the Lindbergh kidnapping. But then, a week ago I would not have believed anyone could highjack four commercial airliners at the same time and fly three of them into buildings. I thought of a line from Lilly Tomlin, "No matter how cynical I get, it's never enough."

Miss Mamie came in to see me. We discussed our meeting the previous day at her house. I told her about my exploring the countryside with the Walton's Corner Chief. She told how she, and every other girl in her high school class, had been madly in love with him. In his day, according to Miss Mamie, Curtis Buford had been the hottest thing ever seen in May County. She still had a glazed expression in her eyes when she talked about him.

We discussed various police department matters. I knew she was just being considerate asking my opinions since she would do whatever she thought best anyway. The new mall was scheduled to open before Thanksgiving in time for the Christmas shopping season. They were building a substation for both the town cops and the sheriff's deputies inside the mall. There was a meeting we needed to attend about it next week. Both the sheriff and I would defer to her, but we'd be expected to show up for the meeting anyway.

The mall opening, and the added policing responsibilities that would come with it, would allow us to hire three more full time officers. We decided to first offer the new full time jobs to our present part timers if any of them wanted them. If they didn't, we would have to do something else. She also told me she was just about through with the grant applications to get federal money for a couple of different things. I would need to sign them when they were done. We agreed there would probably be new grants we could apply for in the new war on domestic terrorism.

I was amazed at how much money there is available to small town police departments around the country when I first became chief. Each grant seemed to require a ton of paperwork, but Miss Mamie was a wizard at getting both money and seized property, like my car, from the feds.

Sandra called a little after noon and said she was on her way so I should meet her at the pizza place next to the Star Market. When she arrived I was sitting in a booth chatting with the proprietor of the tiny restaurant. He was a large man with a full mustache and a heavy accent. I had never wondered before where he was from, but that kind of thing had become more important to me in the past week. He said he was from Albania which has more in common with Greece than the Middle East. I remembered some ethnic Albanians were involved in the current war in Bosnia, many of them Muslims, but didn't mention it.

Sandra was late because she had been on the phone with the Widow. A decorator friend of his had just finished a big project this side of Charlottesville, and he wanted her to see the house. They were planning to go that evening and both hoped I would join them. I told my wife I would try to come if I could and planned to find an excuse not to before it was time to go. Neither my wife nor the Widow go in for the frilly stuff I hate so I figured I could live with whatever they chose for the new house. Sandra told me of her plans for the decorating while I looked out the window at the town's residents in the parking lot. After spending the morning thinking about the new mall I wondered how many of the stores in this strip shopping center would still be in business this time next year. The world was constantly changing. Some of the change was good. Some was bad. But there was nothing I could do about it.

Both of us had the baked spaghetti. It is wonderful. But even while I was concerned about big business killing off the mom and pop stores in Maysville I had to admit the home delivered pizza from Domino's is better than what was served here. That's why we always eat the baked spaghetti.

After lunch we went into the office supply store next door. Sandra picked the correct cartridges for her printer and pointed out the heavy box of paper I was there to carry. After she paid, I carried the paper out to her car and placed it in the trunk.

"My hero," she said. We were standing in the parking lot talking when I saw something suspicious over her shoulder. There was a white van parked a couple of rows over. An elderly Middle Eastern looking man and two younger ones, who looked in their early twenties, were loading large bags of something into the vehicle. I instantly thought of Oklahoma City and fertilizer bombs. I took Sandra by the arm and we went back into the office supply store. I could see the van and its license tag from my new location. The tag was from Virginia but I called the dispatcher anyway. I gave him the tag number and he put me on hold. I watched the trio and the van while I waited.

I noticed one of the town's patrol cars pull up across the street. I could see Officer Cunningham talking on his radio. He had apparently been sent to be my backup. But if this was anything, I didn't want to confront these guys. I wanted to let them leave so I could follow them. Maybe they would lead me to the terrorist's local hideout.

When a voice came back to me on my cell phone it was Miss Mamie instead of the dispatcher. "That van belongs to Bob Murray," she said. "He was a couple of years behind me in school. The family used to have the small department store on Main Street. They have been around here forever."

I asked about the two young men with him. "Probably a couple of his grandsons," she said. "He has some greenhouses over on the other side of the Interstate in the county. He has a bunch of grandsons. They try to be available to do the heavy lifting for him. One of them is a state trooper." I thanked Miss Mamie, kissed my wife and was walking toward Cunningham in his cruiser when I heard the crash.

94

Although I'd been startled by the sound of the crash I was not surprised when I saw the cause. The mayor's elderly mother had been backing out of another parking space. But this time instead of hitting one of her nephew's poles she had hit a minivan driving past behind her. She could not have been going very fast, and the impact to the van had been behind the driver's door, so hopefully no one had been seriously injured. Maybe this would be the final straw, and the mayor would be forced to persuade her to stop driving. I was walking toward the accident when Officer Cunningham pulled his cruiser in front of the minivan.

Cunningham walked between his car and the minivan, approaching the driver's door apparently to see if the occupants were okay. Just as he got even with the door it came busting open, striking my officer in the chest, knocking him to the ground. Before I could react to Cunningham being hit a dark complexioned young man, wearing a bright yellow shirt leaped from the vehicle and ran across the parking lot toward downtown. Then I heard someone yell, "Freeze, police officer" at the fleeing man. I saw this also dark complexioned young man, wearing jeans and a dark sweatshirt, take off running after the first man. At first I didn't know what to think. Then I remembered Miss Mamie had said one of Mr. Murray's grandsons was a trooper. This must be the one.

Cunningham was getting up and appeared to be okay. I turned to go to see about the mayor's mother but Sandra, Mr. Murray and the other grandson were already at her car.

I ran to Cunningham's cruiser, picked up his radio mike and said as calmly as I could, "Maysville One to Base."

"Go, Chief," the dispatcher said.

"Attention all units, we have a suspect fleeing from a hit and run accident in the parking lot of the Star Market. He's a dark skinned young male wearing a bright yellow shirt. He was last seen on foot running in the direction of the elementary school. Be advised there is another dark skinned young man wearing a dark sweat shirt chasing him on foot. The second man is a police officer. I repeat, the second man is a police officer. Do not shoot at the second man under any circumstances. I repeat do not, repeat not, shoot at the man in the dark sweatshirt. He is a cop and is probably armed. The one in the yellow shirt is the suspect."

On a normal weekday there should be six patrol cars and my lone investigator out in town. Cunningham's car was here, but I could hear the sirens from the other cars converging on the area around the elementary school.

I called the dispatcher back, "Maysville One to Base."

"Yes, sir," came the immediate response.

"Call the elementary school. Tell the principal to keep all the children inside and lock all the outside doors. Tell him I'll be there in a minute."

"Yes, sir," he said again. "All units, give me your locations."
I went back over to the mayor's mother's car. The old lady was sitting in the driver's seat crying softly. I didn't see any blood or contusions. My wife and Mr. Murray were talking quietly to her. "I'll call for an ambulance," I said turning away, looking for my cop car.

Before I got to my car I caught Officer Cunningham's attention. "Call her an ambulance and stay here with them until it comes." I saw him turn and start toward his cop car as I sprinted to mine. When I turned on my police radio I could hear Cunningham requesting the ambulance.

I turned on my blue lights and started toward the elementary school four blocks away. I quickly pulled up in front of the school. I wanted the fleeing guy but my first concern was this didn't develop into some barricaded suspect mess at the elementary school. Hopefully the trooper could run fast enough to keep the guy in sight. If he didn't have an opportunity to hide we should apprehend him quickly.

I didn't want to leave my radio to go into the school. While I was trying to decide what to do one of the school's doors opened a crack, and I saw the principal slip through and walk rapidly toward my car. But before he could get from the building to my car I heard the dispatcher say, "Mrs. Synder on Queen Street just called. Two men, one of them with a gun, just ran through her garden. She says they are heading north in the alley behind her house."

Then I heard "Unit Four to Base. I'm a block away. I'll head them off."

"Roger," the dispatcher said.

I grabbed my mike, "Maysville One to all units. The one with the gun is probably the cop. I repeat, the one with the gun is probably the cop. Do not shoot the one in the dark sweatshirt."

By the time I said this I was pulling into the south end of the alley. A long block ahead of me I could see one of the town's police cruisers. The uniformed officer had the man in the yellow shirt spread eagle on the hood. The man in the dark sweatshirt was sitting on the ground.

My heart rate was dropping back to normal as I got out of the car. First I said to my cop, "Good work. Take him to the police station. I want to question him before we take him to the jail." The officer nodded, pulling his prisoner off the hood and pushing him toward the back door of the cruiser. The rest of Maysville's police cars were arriving.

I walked over to the man in the dark sweatshirt sitting on the ground. "Trooper Murray," I said, extending my hand. "I'm Rick Harris, the police chief. Thanks for your help. I am too old, overweight and I smoke too much to chase anybody on foot anymore. It's fortunate for me that you were there."

The young man laughed, "Actually my name is Burnside. Grandpa Murray is my mother's father. But I should thank you. When

I saw the cruiser it suddenly occurred to me that I am not wearing my uniform and don't know any of your town cops. All I could think of was, your guy was going to see two dark skinned guys running toward him and I was the one with a gun.

"I stopped, put my hands up, and was getting ready to throw my pistol as far as I could when your guy called me 'Trooper'. After he got the guy I was chasing on the hood he said you had been repeating over and over on the radio, 'The one in the dark sweatshirt is a cop, don't shoot the one in the dark sweatshirt.'"

One of my arriving officers handed Trooper Burnside a bottle of water. He twisted the top off, downing the contents in one long drink. Then he coughed most of it back up. I left him to get his breath and went to my car. I picked up the police radio mike. "Maysville One to Officer Cunningham." I didn't have any idea what his unit number was.

"This is Cunningham, Chief," came the reply.

"Please tell Mr. Murray his grandson is okay, and I'll drive him back over there in a few minutes."

"Roger that Chief. I'll tell him."

I went back to Trooper Burnside. "I had one of my guys tell your grandfather you're okay," I said. "Come on I'll give you a ride back." The first officer on the scene was backing out of the alley with his prisoner. I followed him back to the street.

"Why was that guy running, Chief?" Burnside asked. "Looked to me like that lady backed into him. I saw him knock your guy down and take off so I chased him but what did he do?"

I thought for a minute before I answered. This kid was a cop after all and he was now involved so I said, "This is just between us?" He nodded his agreement. "We think he's connected to that guy the female trooper had to kill last week over toward the Interstate. We don't know what they're up to, but hopefully this guy will tell us."

We were pulling into the shopping center parking lot when I said, "I'm going to put you in for a commendation for bravery. You deserve it."

Burnside was quiet a minute before he spoke sheepishly, "If you have any influence, Chief, I'd rather you help me get transferred somewhere around here. I need to spend time with my grandfather, and I'm as far away as I can get and still be in Virginia."

I asked him where he was stationed.

"Out near Grundy," he said. The name of the town meant nothing to me. It must have shown so he continued. "It's deep in the coalfields so I spend all day every day weighing coal trucks and ticketing the ones that are overweight. It is dirty, backbreaking work and not what I joined the state police to do."

We pulled up by the minivan. It was now surrounded with crime scene tape. His grandfather was waiting. "Come by my office in a couple of hours. Captain White from the Investigative Division should be here by then. I'll ask him to help you."

"Thanks, Chief," he said. "I really appreciate it." When he got out of the car he was gathered up in a bear hug by his grandfather. They walked away together with the old man's arm still around his grandson's shoulder.

Cunningham came over to me. "Chief, we taped off the minivan and are waiting for the state police crime scene techs. Miss Mamie said since they processed the other scene we should have them do this one too." I nodded my approval.

He pointed to another officer and asked him to watch the car for a minute, then he said, "I want you come with me to talk to the store manager." I nodded again and followed him. As we entered the store we passed a grocery cart stacked high with brown paper bags of food which had been pushed out of the way and taped off with yellow crime scene tape. Another of my cops was watching it. The manager, whom I didn't know because I never go to the grocery store, came out to meet us. He looked to be in his middle thirties, harried and tired.

"Chief, this is Bob Williams," Cunningham said. I shook the man's hand. "He says the guy who ran was shopping with another guy. He says he noticed them because they bought $112.29 worth of groceries and paid with two one hundred dollar bills. The cashier brought them to him to be sure they were real before she gave them change. He said the cashier told him the guy had a thick roll of the bills in his pocket."

My head spun from my own stupidity. Why did I go tearing off after the guy who ran? I should have checked to see if there was someone waiting with a grocery cart while he drove around to pick them up? This was a total rookie mistake. How could I be so stupid? I asked the store manager, "Can you and the cashier work with a sketch artist on a likeness of the other guy?"

Cunningham answered for him, "They told me they could so there's a sketch artist coming with the crime scene guy. They're flying up from Richmond now. The pilot is going to land the helicopter on the ball fields. I sent a car to wait for them."

I told Cunningham he had done all the right things. When we were back outside I ask if the mayor's mother had gone to the hospital. "She went in the ambulance, Chief. Your wife went with her." In all the excitement I had not even thought about my wife.

"Which hospital did they go to?" I asked.

"Shenandoah," he said. I told him I was going to the hospital and walked quickly to my car. I was shaking I was so upset with myself. Not only had I messed up as a cop, I had also messed up as a husband which, truthfully, was much more important to me. While I drove through town at around the 30 mph speed limit I called the police department on my cell phone. There are several people in town, including the newspaper, with police scanners so we try to use cell phones for anything we want to keep private. I asked for Miss Mamie.

98

When she came on the phone I asked her what was going on. She told me the prisoner was in the interrogation room handcuffed to the ring in the table. I told her to leave him in there with his thoughts until I could interrogate him. She said White, a sketch artist, and a crime scene tech were on their way from Richmond by helicopter. White said he wanted to be in on the interrogation. I said I wanted him there. She said Mrs. Marston, the mayor's mother, was experiencing an irregular heart beat and the doctors were going to put in a pacemaker. The mayor and her other son were on their way to the hospital. She said Sandra would stay at the hospital with the old lady at least until her sons got there. By then I was out of town on the two lane highway toward the Interstate. I told Miss Mamie I would call her from the hospital. I broke the phone connection, turned on my blue lights and put my foot down hard on the accelerator. I made the 20 mile trip in less than 12 minutes.

At the hospital I pulled up in the fire lane behind an illegally parked state police car and rushed inside. I was pulling my badge case out of my pocket, heading for the information desk when I heard a familiar voice. It was the Widow.

"What are you doing here, Leigh?" I asked with some surprise.

"Sandra called me," he said. "She's up on the fourth floor with Mrs. Marston. The mayor and his brother just arrived and went up there. I am waiting to take Sandra home when she's done."

"Don't you need to get back to the restaurant?" I asked.

"It's Tuesday, business is always slow on Tuesday. Andre can handle whatever we do have. The only reason we're even open the middle of the week is I like to try new dishes. Besides the waiters and I have to eat somewhere. I assure you I have nothing more important to do than wait and take Sandra home."

"Sandra and I are both lucky to have a friend like you, Leigh," I said starting quickly for the elevator before he could hug me. I didn't fully appreciate how true my statement would turn out to be when I made it. When I got off the elevator on four I saw my wife, the mayor, and his brother talking to a doctor wearing surgical scrubs in the waiting area.

I went over and put my arm around my wife. I arrived in time to hear the mayor say, "Do whatever you think is best, Doctor." The doctor nodded and hurried quickly away.

"How's your mother, Mr. Mayor?" I asked still holding on to Sandra.

"The doctor says she should be okay once they get the pacemaker in," he replied. "I know I should have stopped her from driving when she started hitting things, but it means so much to her. It's all the independence she had left."

"You know the accident really wasn't her fault," I said. "There was a big van parked beside her on the side the minivan was coming from. He should have stopped when he saw her backing out instead of trying to speed to get past her. It could have happened to anybody." Okay, I know I didn't actually see the accident and didn't have the slightest idea what kind of vehicle was parked next to her. But what I said might make the mayor feel less guilty about his mother's condition. And, if we got lucky, her running into the guy might help us stop a bunch of terrorists from doing whatever "It" turned out to be.

"I don't understand why the guy ran if the accident wasn't even his fault," the mayor said. "What did he say when you caught him?"

I knew the mayor is technically my boss and I didn't want to tell him an outright lie. But I also knew whatever I told him would be all over town, including his wife's niece at the newspaper, by tomorrow so I said, "I haven't had a chance to question him yet. But he probably has some outstanding warrants from someplace and thought we'd arrest him on those as soon as we checked."

"And who was the officer who caught him? I heard he is some kind of undercover narc in a dirty sweatshirt and jeans."

I couldn't help laughing at this. "He's Bob Murray's grandson. He was helping his grandfather pick up stuff for his greenhouse when he saw the guy knock Officer Cunningham down and start running. The grandson is also a state trooper."

The mayor nodded as if this last bit of information cleared up everything. I turned to Sandra. "How are you doing, my love?" I asked.

"I'm fine. Thanks for coming to check on me." She had not been fooled for a minute about the purpose of my trip to the hospital. "The Widow is waiting downstairs to take me home when I'm done here." I nodded.

"Well, I need to get back to work. I'll probably be late getting home tonight," I said.

"The Widow and I are supposed to go look at that house tonight. We may put it off, but don't worry about me. I'll see you later," she said.

I kissed her on the mouth and said, "I love you, Sandra."

"You'd be a fool not to," she replied.

On my way back through the lobby I waved to the Widow. He was chatting on his cell phone so I didn't have to stop and talk. He waved to me as I went out the door.

Just as I was getting back to my illegally parked cop car my cell phone rang. It was Miss Mamie.

"Chief," she said, "I just wanted to let you know Captain White and several of his people are in town. They're at the Star Market interviewing the manager and cashier."

"Tell them I'm leaving the hospital for there now and should arrive in a few minutes. Is anything else happening?"

I heard her laugh, "Chief, this is the most excitement we have had in Maysville ever. You drive carefully."

The traffic was heavier going back. People were getting off from work and going home. I didn't run my lights so the trip took about 25 minutes. When I pulled into the Star Market parking lot I saw the crime scene tech was lifting finger prints from one of the paper bags in the taped off cart. Inside I found White and the sketch artist together with the manager and cashier in the raised office in the front of the store. White came down to meet me. "This could be the break we've been looking for, Ricky," he said motioning to someone behind me. The swarthy, hard looking spook from the meeting on Saturday came to join us.

White introduced the man to me simply as "Ari." I nodded my greeting.

"Miss Mamie faxed the mugshot of the guy you have in custody with his finger prints to the feds. Ari thinks he's a Jordanian named Zlad Al Alhazmi. They're checking his prints now to be sure. Tell him about the guy, Ari."

"Zlad Al Alhazmi has been knocking around the terrorist world for some time. We believe he was trained at one of the camps in the Sudan. He was involved in an operation against my government a couple of years ago. Last I heard he was believed to be in Berlin with some other group. My government is checking the prints now. If the guy is Zlad Al Alhazmi they will send us photos of his known associates and maybe we can make the other guy from them."

"So what do we do now?" I asked.

"I guess we wait awhile to see if we get confirmation on who the guy is," White said. "It should shake him up if we know his name when we question him."

I shrugged my agreement. "He's not going anywhere. How are we going to handle questioning him?" I asked.

White looked at me sheepishly, "Well he is your prisoner, Ricky . . ."

"But," I said, "If it were completely your decision how would you handle the questioning?"

"I'd let Ari do it alone. If he's the guy we think he is he'll make Ari as Israeli Intelligence immediately," White said. "And I can not imagine anything we could think of to do that will scare him more than that."

"Suits me," I said. "I just want to know what he knows." I turned to Ari. "But I can't let you torture him in my interrogation room you know."

Ari smiled, "I won't need to torture him. It's all psychological. Once he knows who I am he will either talk or not talk no matter what he thinks I will do to him. Interrogation is all a mind game." I must have looked skeptical because he continued, "Have you not ever had a suspect tell you everything you wanted to know without laying a hand on him?" I nodded. "Well, an American criminal suspect will talk even though he is pretty sure you will not beat it out of him. But he is not totally sure, so he talks. This man will be absolutely convinced I will do whatever is necessary to get the information so he will either give it to me or promise himself he will die without telling me what I want to know. It is all in his head. Of course, we can eventually make anyone talk with drugs given enough time. But that isn't going to be practical in your interrogation room."

I was still thinking over what Ari had said when White's cell phone rang. He listened a while, then went over and asked the store manager if he had access to the Internet from the store. The manager said he did. White told whoever was on the other end of the conversation to email the photos to him at a personal Yahoo account.

"We should have the photos in a couple of minutes," White said. The manager took us to a larger office in the back of the store. It took him several minutes to establish a dial up connection. White quickly accessed his email account but it took several more minutes for each page of color mugshots to print. We just stood there starring at the printer, willing it to go faster. Finally we had two pages with six photos on each page. The photos were numbered. "If they can ID one of them I have to call back with the number to get the name. Security, I guess." The manager looked at the sheets and almost immediately picked number four as the guy who had been in his store earlier in the day. He called the cashier over the intercom to come to the office. As soon as she looked at the first sheet she also picked number four. There was no hesitation. White hit the call back button on his phone. When someone answered he said, "Number four." After a slight pause, White began to write a name on the pad from his pocket: "Khalid Suqami."

Ari shock his head, "Doesn't ring a bell. Will they send us all they know about both of them?"

White nodded, "We can get it when we get to Ricky's office." We all thanked the manager for his cooperation. I started to tell him not to talk about what had happened at his store but I knew that was hopeless. I would just have to stick to my "outstanding warrants" story when anyone asked me anything.

Chapter 10

Ari and White rode back to the police station with me in my car. It was long past time for the shift change. But none of my day shift cops wanted to go home. They were canvassing the strip shopping center and its neighbors trying to find someone who'd seen where the second guy went. I had left Cunningham in charge. Four evening shift cops were out patrolling the town looking for unfamiliar faces.

When we arrived at the police station Miss Mamie was waiting to brief me on where everyone was and what they were doing. She said all the cops who were not scheduled to work had called to offer to come in. We seemed to be back to "Officer Obie" and "every one wanting to get into the newspaper story." Hopefully there wouldn't be a newspaper story. For the first time since I'd come to Maysville Miss Mamie actually asked me what to do and listened to what I said. Fighting international terrorism seemed to be beyond her experience too.

I led Ari and White past our one jail cell, it was full of stuff the town used in its frequent parades, past the closed door of the interrogation room and into a small store room at the back of the building. I did not turn the lights on in the room. I opened a hinged wooden panel to reveal an air conditioning grill. Everything that happened in the interrogation room could be seen, and heard, through the grill. It's low tech but it works. Our prisoner was sitting at the table in the middle of the room with his left wrist cuffed to an iron ring bolted into the table which was, in turn, bolted to the floor. He was leaning back in the chair with his eyes closed. He didn't appear to have a care in the world. Hopefully Ari would soon change his attitude.

I carefully closed the panel and the three of us went into my office. I pointed White toward my computer. It has an "always on" high speed connection and he quickly accessed his email account. It was another unseasonably warm evening and hot in my office. I took off my coat and hung it on the coat tree by the door.

White was busy on the computer. Pages of photos quickly began pouring from my laser printer. Then out came pages of information on the men in the photos. Everything went quickly until White tried to open an email with "Ari Eyes Only" in the subject line. The computer showed an error message and stopped. Once again I thought, security is going to prevent us from getting important information.

But Ari leaned over White's shoulder and rapidly began closing some things and opening others. After a few seconds he said to me, "I need to restart your computer." I nodded my agreement. The screen went black for a second and then came back on showing the Windows opening page. He stepped away from the computer and asked White to pull up the email again. This time it displayed its contents on the screen. It was in a foreign language I assumed to be Hebrew. White hit the print button and pages began to come out of my printer. "The Hebrew fonts weren't installed, "he said. "Happens to me all the time."

White and I looked at the photos again. My printer is better than the one at the Star Market so the photos were crisper. We read the information on each of the pictured terrorists. "We should make about a dozen copies of these photos so my people will know who to look for." I nodded my agreement and White went back to the computer. More pages came spitting out of the printer.

The printer was still going when Ari finished reading and said, "This is all interesting stuff. What are a couple of hardcore killers like Zlad and Khalid doing here?"

Neither White nor I had an answer so he continued, "Both of them have been all over the place. We barely missed Zlad in Ramallah on the West Bank last year after an attack. We killed six of his associates including one who was either his brother or his cousin, we aren't sure which. Before that he was in the Philippines when the plot to kill the Pope and hijack all those planes was going on. He spent some time in Afghanistan and bragged, to one of our informants, about sitting at the feet of Osama himself. In the past Zlad always managed to slip away. But we have him now.

"I think it is time to go chat with our prisoner," Ari said with a smile.

The police department lobby was crowded when we came out of my office. Some of the men I recognized and some I didn't. Trooper Burnside, dressed in clean casual clothes, was one of the ones I recognized. A tough looking, dark haired man I had never seen before caught Ari's eye, and they exchanged almost imperceptible nods. Apparently Ari had sent for backup as well.

White stopped in front of Miss Mamie behind the counter and said, "Don't you think we should ask Chief Buford to join us? If this guy gives us a location Buford will be the one who knows the most about the place." I nodded my agreement and asked Miss Mamie to call him. She dialed the number without having to look it up.

After a brief conversation she covered the phone with her hand and said to me, "Curtis says he doesn't see well enough to drive at night anymore. Can we send someone to pick him up?"

I nodded again. "Tell him they'll be on their way in a minute." I hated to take any on my cops out of town. Then I thought of Burnside. I motioned for him to join White and me. When he came

104

over I introduced the two, "Trooper Burnside this is Captain White of the Virginia State Police. Captain White this is Trooper Burnside. He's the one who ran the guy down this afternoon. I plan to put him in for a commendation."

"I'll see he gets it," White said. Burnside beamed.

"Do you know Chief Buford over in Walton's Corner?" I asked.

"Yes, sir," he replied. "I went to high school with his granddaughter and used to hang around his house while he tinkered with his amateur radio gear."

"Do you have a car?" I asked.

"Yes, sir," he said again. "My personal car is outside."

"Well then," I said, "Please take your personal car to Chief Buford's house, pick him up and bring him back here."

"Yes, sir," he said again. "Do you want my cell phone number in case you need to reach me, Chief?"

Every kid cop I encountered today seemed to be smarter than I am. First Cunningham found the grocery cart and now Burnside reminding me I should have his cell phone number. "Just give it to Miss Mamie," I said. He quickly did so and ran out of the station on his assignment. "I am getting too old for this crap," I said.

White laughed, then said, "If you can use the help, I'll have the boy assigned to me tomorrow and leave him here with you," I nodded my agreement. "What's his assignment now?" White asked.

"Weighing coal trucks in some place called Grundy," I replied.

White laughed again. "I'm sure he'll hate to give that up."

Ari was standing outside the door to the interrogation room waiting for White and me to get into position in the storeroom. He looked impatient. We were just starting toward the storeroom when Cunningham burst into the lobby and called my name. I tried to brush him off but he insisted it was urgent he speak with me.

"Chief, we just found a witness who says the second guy from the market got into a green Chevy with two other Arab looking guys who were waiting in the parking lot. She remembers because she saw the guy walk away from the cart full of groceries, get into the car, and drive off without the groceries. She thought he just forgot his stuff."

"Can she describe the other guys in the car?" I asked.

"No," he replied. "Just two Arab looking guys, she said. She also didn't see the tag on the car. But she says there was some damage to one of the front fenders. Maybe it was on the driver's side, she isn't sure. The headlight is broken."

"I'll get my guys on it," White said pulling out his cell. I turned to Miss Mamie, "Get the word on the car out to our people. Tell them if they see it do not approach it. Just watch it and call for the cavalry. Tell them the guys in the car may have robbed a bank and are armed and dangerous." She nodded her agreement and picked up the microphone.

Ari was standing there, taking the new development in. I looked at him inquiringly. "More grist for the mill," he said. "Let's do it." White and I made our way into the storeroom and raised the cover from the vent. We would have to stand to see what was going to happen but I was sure neither of us was going to miss a word.

Zlad was starring at the wall when Ari entered the room. He gently closed the door and took a seat across the table from the prisoner. After he had settled as comfortably as he could into the straight backed chair he said in a calm voice, "Well, Zlad, we finally meet." If the prisoner was surprised that his interrogator knew his name he did not show it. Ari continued, "I once met your brother or was it your cousin? Anyway it was in a safe house in Ramallah." Ari laughed. "I will never forget him. I was standing too close when I put the bullet into his head and his brains completely ruined my suit. But my friend, I learned a valuable lesson that night. Now I always stand further back when I kill one of your kind." Zlad's face still showed no emotion, but he was paying close attention to what Ari was saying to him.

"Do you know who I work for?" Ari asked. Zlad nodded. "Then you know I have no more regard for your life than you have for mine. I am sitting here politely questioning you so the soft Americans will believe this is how we do it and turn you over to me. When I walk out of this room, and you do not have a mark on you they will be convinced.

"That is silly, of course, we both know you are much too tough for me to beat anything out of you. But you are not a stupid man, so you know that given time, and the proper drugs, you will tell me everything you know. Bravery is no defense against drugs. Your body will betray you, and you will betray your friends."

Zlad was starring at Ari but his expression still did not give me any clue to what he was thinking. "My people already have your friend Khalid and he is not as brave as you. They may already know what they need to know about what you are doing here. And they were close to having your other two friends in the green car when I left them to come talk with you. Those two can also tell us what we need to know about the attack you are planning. One of the four of you will certainly talk." Zlad continued to stare.

"This brings me to why the Americans sent me to talk with you. They are soft and weak. They do not understand this is just one little battle in a war that has been going on for many years. They only care about saving the lives of a few of their citizens. So they have asked me to offer you this deal: If you give us the information we need to stop your local operation they will put you into their witness protection program. They will give you an American Green Card and a place to live in the American city of your choice. They will even bring your wife and son from Germany to join you."

I saw a momentary reaction in the prisoner's face. But I didn't know if it was to the offer of the new life in America or to the news Ari knew where his wife and son were living.

Ari continued, "I want you to understand I am only bringing you this offer from the Americans because my government ordered me to do us. If your friends are successful in your planned attack it will only open this country's eyes further to the need for them to totally support my country in our war against you. My country has lost too many of its citizens to your terrorism and I will not cry for the few Americans you manage to kill. Had the Americans understood this is their war years ago we would not be here today." There was still no response from the prisoner.

"But, as I said, one of the four of you is going to take this offer and the Americans do not care which one it is. You can live here with your family or you can return to the Middle East with me."

Zlad licked his lips and took a deep breath. Something Ari had said to him had caused this reaction but I didn't have a clue to what it was.

"I need to go talk with my people now. You will be here when I get back. One of the others may have already talked, and it will be too late for you to accept the Americans' generous offer. If that is the case we will spend the next several months together, you and I, while you tell me everything you know about every terrorist you have ever come into contact with in your life. This information is more valuable to me than the lives of a few Americans."

Zlad had still not said a word. Ari rose from his chair. "Oh," he said when he'd reached the door, as if this was an afterthought, "when one of the others talks, my friend, I will see to it that there is a newspaper story in my country saying it was you who gave us the information. What do you think your friends will do to the wife and son of such a traitor?"

When the door had closed, and he was alone, the prisoner slammed his right fist hard into the table. He leaned back in the chair and sucked on his lower lip. Ari had made some progress, and it now seemed likely Zlad would talk in time. But there was no way for me to know how much time this would take and, more importantly, how much time we had before "It" happened.

I silently closed the hatch over the vent. White and I went back into the police department lobby. Chief Buford was standing there talking with Trooper Burnside. I nodded to them. I asked the dispatcher where Ari was, and he pointed to the front door. I went out onto the stoop and found Ari, smoking a cigarette, standing on the sidewalk talking with a man I had never seen before.

When he had finished his conversation the other man walked away, and Ari joined us on the porch. White had just come out the door. Ari offered us both cigarettes from a metal cigarette case. They were unfiltered so I said, "Those are much too strong for weak, silly

Americans like us."

Ari laughed. "I was just reinforcing what Zlad already believes," he said. "And I wanted him to have a clear choice between your offer and mine. He knows I would gladly cut his heart out with a dull knife. If he believes you will give him and his family a new life in Cleveland he will be much more likely to choose that alternative. I think his family is the key that will open him up. We just need to figure out how to turn that key."

I nodded my acceptance of this logic. I took a cigarette from the pack White offered. The three of us stood there silently smoking for a few minutes.

We went back into the police station. There were still people milling about, awaiting orders. I stopped to ask Buford to join us in my office. As we were going in the dispatcher said, "Chief, your wife called and asked you call her back." I nodded that I had heard the message and hoped I would remember to call her when I got a minute.

White introduced Ari to Chief Buford by just his first name, without saying who he worked for, and was telling the chief what had happened in the interrogation room when there was a knock on my office door. I went to the door and found Officer Cunningham standing there. "We found the green Chevy with the busted headlight." I pulled him into the office and closed the door.

"One of the patrol guys found it in the driveway of the vacant house that's for sale on Maple Street." I shook my head to indicate I didn't know which house he was talking about. "It's two blocks down from Miss Mamie's almost behind your house. Officer Wilson rode by a couple of times and didn't see anyone." Cunningham looked sheepish. "So he parked on the street behind the house and went to check it out. The car has a broken headlight. Wilson still didn't see anyone so he went back to his cruiser and called me. He's sitting as far away as he can get where he can still see the driveway and waiting for instructions."

"Call him back and tell him to stay there," I said. "He is not to approach the men if they come back to the car. If they leave he is to just call us and tell us which way they're going. Tell him we will drive by and check it out in a few minutes."

White was saying, "Let's go," but I knew I needed to do something to secure the prisoner and the police station before I left. There were three terrorists at large somewhere in my town. I quickly made the best plan I could on short notice. First I went to the gun safe in the corner of my office. When I opened it I saw there was only one shotgun in it. The others were in the trunks of the various cars. The one remaining was identical to the one in the trunk of my car. I pulled it, and a box of shells, out and relocked the safe. I grabbed my jacket from the coat rack on my way out.

The lobby was too full of people, some of whom I didn't know, to make any kind of general announcement. I grabbed Trooper

Burnside with my free hand and took him back to the storeroom. I spoke to him in a low voice so the prisoner in the next room would not hear me. "Can I use your car?" I asked.

He handed me the keys without hesitation. "It's the blue Firebird out front, Chief." I nodded my understanding and handed him the shotgun.

"The guy who got away this afternoon and a couple of others appear to still be in town," I said. "If they are they may be planning to come get their friend in the interrogation room. If anyone tries to go into the interrogation room use the shotgun. Understand?"

He nodded that he did. White and Ari were waiting for me in the lobby. I showed them the keys. I told Cunningham to call Wilson and tell him we'd be coming by in minute in a blue Firebird.

When we started to get into the car I could see Ari was not happy crawling into the backseat of the small two door car. If there was shooting he would be trapped. But he didn't mention it, and we set out.

I turned, away from the direction we needed to go, toward the Interstate to see if we were being followed. I didn't see anyone so I turned into the last residential street before I got out of town and made my way through the older neighborhood until I was one block in back of Maple Street. As we passed I pointed the backside of Miss Mamie's house out to White so he'd know where we were.

I continued down this street for three blocks. The houses were too close together to see through to the yards of the houses behind them. I turned around the block and we drove slowly down Maple Street past the house. It was easy to recognize from the real estate sign next to the curb. I kept my eyes on the road but White said, "There's a car in there, but it is too dark to see if it is the one we want." I nodded to Officer Wilson in his cruiser as we passed. He was a block and half down the street parked under a huge oak tree. Unless someone drove past they wouldn't see him.

"My cop went in from the street behind and says it is a green Chevy with a broken front headlight. I think we have to assume it is the right car." Both White and Ari agreed.

I stopped in the parking lot of the Star Market on Main Street. "So what do we do?" I asked. "I don't think they're setting up any kind of ambush. Maybe they just dropped it there and left town in another car. But maybe they'll come back. If they do, I'd like to catch them."

There really was no workable plan I could come up with using the resources of my tiny police department. This was a populated neighborhood where I certainly didn't want bullets flying if the bad guys didn't immediately surrender. White was silent too. Apparently he was having the same problems coming up with a plan I was. Finally Ari spoke.

"Let my associates handle this," he said. "Several of them are in town. They have been trained to get into an area without being seen or heard. They will wait quietly and if the terrorists show up they will capture them as quietly as possible. I don't think this is a situation where we want people yelling, 'Police, Freeze' and shots being fired."

"I think that's our best option," I said. "At least we don't have to worry about the story leaking out later. Nobody would ever believe an ambush by Israeli Intelligence agents against a group of suspected Muslim Fundamentalist terrorists in Maysville, Virginia." But no one, including me, laughed.

We parked in front of the police station. White helped Ari from the tiny back seat. He stopped in the middle of the sidewalk to light a cigarette. The headlights of a van parked down the street flashed briefly. "Let me get my associates to work on our problem. I will be back shortly." He walked off toward the parked van.

"I'm glad he's on our side," I said to White as we walked up the steps. There were fewer people in the lobby than when we'd left. Miss Mamie and the dispatcher were still behind the counter. I asked where Chief Buford was. The dispatcher said he was in the storeroom with the trooper. White and I started into my office. The dispatcher held up a pink message slip and said, "Chief, Leigh Williams called. He said it is extremely important you call him back immediately." I stuffed the message into my shirt pocket. The Widow's idea of important and mine, at the moment, were not likely to be the same.

White went to my computer to check his email. I hung my jacket up again. If anything it was warmer than it had been earlier. White hit the print button and paper came out of my printer. He got up to give me my chair behind my desk. "What do we do now?" I asked him.

"I guess we wait for Ari to come back and then decide. I imagine he'll want to take another crack at our prisoner," White replied.

White occupied himself reading the emails he had just received. I'd leaned back in my chair, closing my eyes when I heard the knock on the door. "What is it?" I asked in a loud voice. The door opened a crack and the dispatcher stuck his head through. "Chief, I'm sorry to bother you, but Leigh Williams is here and he insists on seeing you right now."

Before I could reply Williams had pushed the door open and was in my office. "Ricky," he said, "Something awful has happened to Sandra."

I told the dispatcher to close the door. "What?" I asked.

"I don't know exactly, but I called her a little while ago to reschedule our trip to look at that house. When she answered she said, 'Leigh, how are you. I am sorry Richard is not here. I think he is at his office. I know he will be sorry he missed your call. Try him at his office." I was stunned. I had never heard her call him "Leigh" and she had never called me "Richard" since I have known her. Something serious was wrong.

"So I called and they said you weren't here," he continued. I thought of the ignored phone message in my shirt pocket. "So I drove by your house on the way over here. Her car is in the driveway. But, Ricky, the living room drapes are closed tight."

I must have looked pale. White asked, "What about the drapes?"

"The pulley thing on them is broken. The last time Sandra closed them we had an awful time getting them open again. They have only been closed the one time since we've lived in the house."

"I keep meaning to get over there and fix the rod but . . .," the Widow said.

"It's a good thing you didn't," I said. I grabbed my jacket to cover up my gun and said, "Come on. Let's go." White and the Widow followed me outside. We jumped into my Chrysler, and I pulled out. I saw Ari standing by the van across the street. I stopped and said, "Ari, get in. We need you." He didn't ask any questions. He just ran across the street and jumped into the back seat of my car with the Widow. I made myself drive away in the wrong direction again to see if anyone followed. I hoped there was someone there now because I could grab them and make them tell me what was going on with my wife. Sandra's life might depend on it.

White was telling Ari about the strange phone conversation and the closed curtains when I turned off the main road to circle through the neighborhood to my house. The cell phone in my pocket beeped loudly. I popped it open but it wasn't a call. It was telling me I had a message from earlier. I pulled over to check the message. It seemed to take forever to get to where I could hear my wife's voice say, "Richard, when are you coming home? I'm waiting dinner for you." Someone was definitely there with her. I repeated the conversation to the others as I drove slowly toward my house. When we went by I could see the curtains were closed just as the Widow had said.

Something was seriously wrong, and I needed to get in there and save my beloved wife. My first impulse was to stop and kick down the front door with Ari and White for backup. But I knew that wouldn't work. Even if I didn't mind risking my life and my friends' lives Sandra would surely be hurt in the resulting shoot out. I needed a plan. But I didn't have a clue as to what to do.

We drove back toward the police station without stopping. No one in the car said a word. This was my wife, and they would let me decide what to do. I knew both Ari and White would be perfectly willing to risk their lives to help me save Sandra. But I knew they would want me to figure out exactly how I wanted to do it. If this went wrong it would be my responsibility. Sometimes even ordinary men rise to the extraordinary challenges they are forced to face. Sandra's life depended on me doing just that.

We arrived back at the police department and went inside. I said to the Widow, "Leigh, sit down over there and wait for me. I need you to help me some more. I'll be right back." He took the seat without comment.

I started down the hall toward the interrogation room. Ari said, "What are you going to do, Ricky?"

"I am going to make him tell us what he knows about this," I said. I turned away and immediately felt Ari take hold of both my upper arms. I might outweigh him by a hundred pounds, but I had no doubt he was tougher than I could ever hope to be.

"Before you do that," he said calmly, "Come into your office so we can make a plan. I don't believe the prisoner will know anything of value about this." He was pulling me back away from the door so I agreed.

I plopped down into my desk chair. "Ricky, you two discuss possible plans while I send my associates to see what is going on at your house. They are the best in the world at this type thing. They will not be seen and we will have a better idea what is happening inside." I nodded my agreement, and Ari left the room.

"Ari is right about the prisoner," White said. "He was in our custody when this plot was hatched. I assume they want to trade you Sandra for him."

I hadn't thought about why this was happening, just about rescuing my wife. Maybe we could swap them. But the logistics would be a nightmare. The terrorists would not trust me any more than I would trust them.

"I don't see any way we could try a swap without putting Sandra in even more danger," he said. I also knew he'd be putting his career with the state police in the toilet if we tried something like that without his first getting approval from his superiors. Neither of us mentioned it.

"The only thing our prisoner could give us is the two other guys' names. We have to assume Khalid is one of them," White said. "This information will not help us and will probably take a long time to get. I don't think we have that kind of time."

I nodded in agreement. "Forget the prisoner, "I said. "I don't see any way to get Sandra out of there without me walking up to the door. Maybe I can distract them and get them into position for Ari's boys to kill them. If there were only two of them I might be able to handle them. But if the three are spread out I'd never be able to get the third one. But if they are concentrating on me maybe Ari's boys can get the third one before he can shoot Sandra."

White and I both knew if we followed this plan I would likely die before the third terrorist. Neither of us mentioned it. This was my wife and my town. We would follow my plan regardless of how unlikely it was to work. I couldn't think of any better way to do it to save my life. The irony of that thought didn't escape me. I would save my beloved wife's life or I would die trying. If I failed I'd have nothing to live for anyway.

Ari came back into my office. He was wearing a small headset with the wire disappearing into his shirt pocket. He was also carrying a shopping bag from Macy's. "I dropped my associates off a block from your house," he said. "Two will check from the front and the other two from the rear. They will tell me what they see as soon as possible. What have you decided we are going to do?"

I did not tell him how much I appreciated the word "we" in his question. "I don't see anything for me to do but walk up to the front door and go inside. I want you and one of your guys right behind me. I will draw their fire away from my wife, and hopefully between us we can kill all three of them before one of them can shoot Sandra."

"Is there a back door?", Arie asked. I nodded.

"Then my men will crash through the back door just as you start into the house from the front. I will be right behind you. The crash might distract at least one of them. And if things are not going well for our side they can finish the bad guys off." I nodded my agreement. Ari also knew there was a real chance he would not survive this shoot out either, but he was going anyway. It was certain there would soon be some dead people in my living room. The only question at this point was how many and who they would be.

Ari held up a finger and then tapped his earpiece. He listened intently for a moment, asked a question in a language I assumed to be Hebrew, then listened again. "Things are better than we thought. One of the bad guys is on a little porch in the back of the house. He is staying in the shadows so it must be his job to guard the back. There is a screen door from the porch into the house that is closed, but the door behind it is open. I asked if they could take this man out ahead of time and go in the back while we created a diversion at the front. My friend said he could not be sure they could kill the man on the porch silently and suggested they take him out as soon as you went through the door. Then they will immediately come in the back door.

Ari continued, "I think it would be better if you go in the door and I crouch just outside behind you until my friends start coming through the back. Then I come in and we will have them in a cross fire."

I nodded my agreement. It was a plan that could work. Ari reached into the Macy's bag and pulled out a Kevlar vest. "Do you have one of these?' he asked.

I nodded, "Hanging in my hall closet at home." Ari smiled. I took off my jacket, my shoulder rig with the nine millimeter in its holster, my shirt and tee shirt. I could feel the sweat under my arms. I put the vest on, then the tee shirt and outer shirt.

I was reaching for my gun and holster when White said, "You need to go in there with your gun in your hand Ricky. There isn't going to be time for any fast draw cowboy crap."

Again I nodded my agreement. I pulled my shirt from my pants. "I can put the gun in the back of my pants."

White shook his head. "You need to have the gun in your hand pointed in the right direction. I know you've won gun fights in the past, but this is the most important one you have ever been in. We need to find something you can carry to hide the gun." He thought a minute then said, "How about a bag of groceries? We can cut the bag so you can hold the gun in your right hand and shoot through the bag."

"How am I going to get the door unlocked and open while holding the bag and my gun?" I asked. "I guess I can let go of the gun while I open the door."

"No," Ari said. "You should not let loose of the gun for any reason. I will sneak up and be waiting by the front door. When you come up I will unlock the door and shove it open for you. Then I will come in behind you on the signal of my friends coming in from the rear. You should also duck on that signal and move to the right away from the door."

I shook my head. "There's a wall to the right. I'll have to go to my left."

"Go to your left then," Ari said. "Just go down and out of my line of fire."

Again I nodded my agreement. "The groceries will also tell Sandra I know something is wrong so she'll know to duck. I haven't been to the grocery store since she's known me."

White went out and conferred with Miss Mamie. A couple of minutes later he returned with a paper bag from the Star Market, a gallon jug of spring water, and a huge economy size package of toilet paper. Ari produced a razor sharp knife from his pocket. We slit the bag around the back right corner as well as a little way across the bottom and up the back. I tried holding the bag with my gun in bottom, the water and toilet paper on top of it. I had to turn the gun sideways which meant it would probably be impossible for it to eject the spent shell from my first shot. This would jam the gun making it useless. We considered me using a revolver but I didn't want to try and do this with an unfamiliar gun. We decided when his guys started in the back door I would drop the bag while holding on to my pistol. This might take an extra split second, but we could not figure any other way around the problem. We cut on the bag some more until we were satisfied I could get the gun free when I needed to.

White stopped me as I was starting toward the door. He pulled out his nine millimeter pistol and handed it to me. "Put it in the back of your pants in case you need it. I have had it for years and it's never jammed." It would be difficult for any one who has never been a cop to understand what it meant for White to give me his pistol. I was touched but I remembered what my old shooting range instructor in New York had said. If I couldn't do it with fourteen shots, I couldn't do it.

"You better keep it," I said. "You might need it."

"I have another one in my car," he said.

"Where's your car," I said with as much of a smile as I could manage.

"In Richmond," he replied. "There are guys out there who work for me. I'll get one of their guns. You take this one."

I stuck his pistol in the back of my pants and covered it with my shirt tail. I rolled up my shirt sleeves so they wouldn't restrict the movement of my arms. I picked up the grocery bag, and we went out of the office.

The Widow was still sitting in the chair where I'd put him, it seemed like hours before. He could see we were going to attempt to rescue Sandra. "Can I do anything to help, Ricky," he asked in the quietest voice I have ever heard him use. I started to say no but changed my mind.

"Actually you can, Leigh. Drive your car over and park as far away as you can from my house where you will still be able to see me park in front and go up the walk. Punch our phone number into your cell phone. Just as I start to open the door hit the send button. If Sandra answers, tell her to hit the floor when she hears a noise coming from the back porch. Can you remember all that?"

He nodded. "Thank you Ricky for letting me help," he said as he hurried out of the front door, toward his car. Ari said to give him a couple of minutes to get into position and brief his friends. He said he would be beside my front door when I got there. I took the key to my front door off my key ring and handed it to him. As he was turning to go I said to him in a low voice, "If this goes badly, my friend, I want you to kill Zlad for me."

"If this goes badly, my friend," he said quietly. "I will do a lot worse to Zlad than kill him." He slapped me on the shoulder and was gone. I saw White take an automatic from one of his investigators. He released the clip and jacked the slide back to be sure there was a round under the hammer. He replaced the clip and stuck the gun into his holster. He walked to my car with me. "I'll lie down in the back so I'll be close by." I nodded my agreement. When I opened the car door the inside lights came on. We both laughed nervously as we pried the plastic covers off and removed the bulbs. Then I started driving toward my house.

We had a good, well thought out, workable plan. So, of course, it didn't work.

Chapter 11

I drove slowly away from the police station, wondering if I would ever see it again. It surprised me how much the rundown little building, and the people who worked in it every day, meant to me. White was lying flat on the back seat of my big Chrysler below the window level. The extra pistol he insisted I take was digging painfully into my lower back. As I drove down the street we live on I saw the Widow sitting in his old Jaguar parked a block before I reached our house. I pulled the car into the driveway behind Sandra's Mustang, backed up, and parked at the curb in front of the small house. I heard White say from the backseat, "I'll see you in a few minutes, buddy."

I got out of the car, pulling my pants up to cover pushing the gun in the middle of my back into a more secure position. I reached across the driver's seat and picked up the grocery bag. I slid my finger into the trigger guard and balanced the heavy jug of water on top of the pistol. Sweat was pouring off me making the Kevlar vest stick to my ribs. It was a warm evening, but I knew the sweat came more from fear than from the weather. I was not afraid that I might die in the next couple of minutes. I was afraid I would not be able to save Sandra before I died. I thought about how small and vulnerable she had been in the hospital bed in New York. I couldn't save her from the surgeon's knives, but hopefully I was a little better equipped to defend her against terrorists' guns.

As I started up the walk I saw Ari, dressed in dark clothes, come from the corner of the garage. He stayed low as he made his way to the side of the front door, flattening himself against the wall. As soon as I stepped onto the porch he opened the storm door far enough for me to get my knee and shoulder inside it and push it further open. He stuck the key I had given him into the lock, turned it and pushed the front door open just far enough to clear the latch. As I was beginning to push the door the rest of the way I heard the phone ring. I quickly shoved the door all the way open. It hit the stop instead of banging against the wall.

I saw two men in my living room with my wife. They both had guns in their hands. I saw Sandra picking up the phone. Both of the men were looking at her. When they heard the door they quickly turned toward me.

In that split second I could see neither of the men was pointing his pistol at my wife. Both guns were pointed down, toward the floor.

116

At some point in their lives they had both apparently been taught elementary gun handling safety.

They were quickly raising the pistols now. But they were coming around to point them in my direction. The closer man was only a couple of feet in front of me.

I instinctively knew this was the best opportunity I could possibly hope for. Using my left hand, I shoved the grocery bag at the man nearest to me as hard as I could. The pistol in my right hand tore free from the paper bag. I heard a grunt of surprise from the man I'd hit with the jug of water as I took a step to my left swinging my gun toward the second man.

This one was further away from me but closer to Sandra. My gun was pointed dead at him while he was still bringing his into firing position. I instinctively aimed for the biggest part of the target, the center of his torso, as I had been trained to do. To this day I don't know why, in the split second before I fired, I realized he was wearing a vest too. I jerked my gun higher and shot him in the middle of his face. His finger pulled the trigger on his gun by reflex as my bullet hit him. I knew he was dead and didn't wait to watch him fall.

Turning back toward the man at whom I'd thrown the jug of water and toilet paper taking aim at his head, I fired again but missed him entirely. During the split second after I fired my first shot I heard several more shots which sounded as if they'd come from the back of the house. I could not worry about these. I had a more immediate problem.

Ari told me later the first man had instinctively jumped back when the groceries hit him, pulling his arms back. He had apparently thought he had been hit by something more lethal than water and toilet paper. By the time he realized whatever had hit him was not going to hurt him, and started to bring his pistol back toward me, Ari was in position in the doorway. Before the second man could react to me shooting at him and missing I heard the soft "phft" from Ari's silenced .22 Berretta as he shot the man in the face. Even before the second terrorist could fall down dead one of Ari's guys was in through the back door from the porch. I heard another "phft" as he shot the man in the back of his head as well.

It was over in a split second. Sandra was still standing where she had been with the phone in her hand. I could hear Leigh Williams saying, "Get down, Sandra. Get down, Sandra," through the phone. I handed Ari my pistol, took the phone from my wife, hugging her to me with my free hand. Her head was against my shoulder, both her arms were around me and she was hugging me back with all her strength. "Stay on the phone, Leigh," I said. "I'll get back to you in a minute." I dropped the phone into the chair and put my other arm around my wife. White came through the front door with his borrowed gun drawn. He surveyed the situation, put his gun away and closed the front door. He was grinning from ear to ear.

117

"Are you okay, darling?" I asked Sandra.

"I am not shot if that's what you're asking," she replied. "I am so glad to see you, Ricky." I hugged her tighter. Then she said, "Ricky, you are without a doubt the bravest fool in the world."

Foolhardiness and luck become bravery and skill when the fool manages to come out on top. "I am nobody's fool but yours," I said to my wife. The others were milling around the small living room, trying not to step in the blood that was seeping from the dead men on the floor. One of Ari's associates was dragging the third body into the house from the back porch and closing the door.

I knew there were many things we needed to do, some of them quickly. But my first concern was still my wife. I picked up the phone from the chair. "Are you still there, Leigh?" I asked.

"Yes, Ricky," he answered. "Is Sandra okay?"

"She's fine. Can you pull your car down in front of our house? I need you to take her home with you for a little while."

"I'll be right there," he said.

Sandra was calmly looking around the living room. In addition to the three dead bodies on the floor, there were three men she'd never seen before dressed in black and Captain White standing by the closed front door. "We need to do something about this mess," she said.

I took her by the shoulders and guided her around the dead man in front of her to the front door. White opened it for us. "We'll take care of it, darling," I said. "Leigh is going to take you to his house while I do some things. I'll be there as soon as I can." For once in her life she didn't argue with me.

As soon as we were through the door Leigh Williams was out of his car and running up the walk. He grabbed Sandra in a bear hug. "Are you all right? I was so worried. I heard the gun shots over the phone and . . . "

"Leigh," I said, "you can not mention what you heard on the phone or anything else about what happened here tonight to anyone. It is part of an ongoing investigation and I promise I will tell you all about it when I can. Everything has to remain as secret as possible. Do you understand?"

"Yes, Ricky, I understand," he said with a sigh. "The best gossip in the history of this town, I know about it but can't tell anyone."

Sandra laughed, "We pretty well trashed your house, Widow. Some tenants you picked. It's a good thing we are moving anyway."

"We'll fix the damage to the house," I said quickly.

Leigh Williams made a motion of dismissal with his hand. "I don't care about the house. All I care about is you two are okay." I kissed Sandra. Leigh Williams put his arm around her shoulder and walked her to his car. Not for the first time, I was glad the Widow is gay. He loves my wife nearly as much as I do.

118

I started back into the house. One of Ari's associates came up the walk with me carrying an instant camera. He gave it to Ari when we were both inside. "I am making a scrapbook for Zlad so he can remember his trip to your little town." The other man turned the body of the man I had killed over and Ari took a picture of what was left of his face.

I went over to White. "What do we do now," I asked.

"We keep this all under wraps as best we can," he said. "I've got several of my cops out looking for the bullets that got away. I don't care about recovering them, but we need to find out what they hit.

"Ari's guy was apologetic about the shots from the porch," White said. "He said he had shot the terrorist in the back, aiming for his heart, but the man was wearing a vest. So he had to shoot him again in the head. The bad guy got off three rounds from his machine pistol between shots." I nodded my understanding. I had almost made the same mistake. But if I had made it, it would have been much more serious. I would be dead now.

"I have people on their way who will take away the bodies and the blood soaked carpet," White said. "You can get someone local to replace it." He pulled the curtain back to show the bullet hole in the picture window. There were cracks radiating out from the small hole. "We should take something and break this out a little so it doesn't look like a bullet hole." I went to the kitchen and found my entire tool collection in one of the drawers. I brought both the hammer and pliers back to White. He stuck the pliers in the hole and twisted them until a piece of glass fell out. The hole was bigger but it no longer looked like it came from a bullet.

I looked around the room at the furniture. There was a smear of congealing blood on the corner of the couch where one of the men had fallen and blood spatter on the chair behind the other body. "Can you have your people take all this furniture? Sandra isn't going to want to see any of it again."

"No problem," White said. I went into the bedroom and got a box computer paper had come in and started going through the drawers in various pieces of furniture. There was nothing important except a few family pictures. I put everything I thought Sandra could conceivably want in the box and took the box back into the bedroom.

White had pulled the carpet up in the corner of the room. "There's a concrete slab under this so we should be okay, "he said.

Ari was busy going through the pockets of the three dead men. There was a lot of cash and a few scraps of paper. Two of them had cell phones. Ari held them up and grinned. These phones were potential treasures. The companies that provide cell phone service could provide us with a computer record of every number the phones had ever called or that ever called them. None of the three men were carrying any identification, but the one I had killed also had a prepaid long distance card in his pocket. We could get more phone numbers from this. White had been right at the Saturday meeting. We were becoming buried in much more information than we could ever hope to utilize. But the break we needed had to be in there somewhere so we had to keep looking.

One of White's guys came in with the bullet that had gone through my front window. He held it up proudly. "It hit the tree between the house and the street, Boss," he said. That was a relief. I could just imagine finding the nice old lady who lived across the street dead from a bullet wound in the morning. But my luck was holding, at least for now.

We were just standing around waiting for the guys to come get the bodies when another of White's investigators came in with news of the other three bullets from the machine pistol. "Two of them hit a car window on the street behind here. They flattened out on impact. The third one probably went into the trees beside the house. They're small caliber, low velocity and probably didn't hurt anything. I didn't want to wake up the people in house looking for it."

"Fine," White said. "What did you do about the car window?"

"I broke the glass out around the holes so they don't look like bullets did it," he said. I wondered if these guys were as good at preserving evidence as they were at destroying it.

I called the dispatcher on my cell phone. When he answered I asked him if there were any of my cops around. He said Cunningham was still there. When I got him on the phone I asked him to get Carl and his tow truck to go pick up the damaged Chevy from the driveway behind my house. I told him to try and do it as quietly as possible, no flashing lights.

He didn't ask why I no longer wanted to watch the car in case the men came back. He did ask if I wanted Carl to lock it up in his storage building with the vehicle from the earlier wreck. I had forgotten all about the van from the Star Market. I asked Cunningham if they'd searched it.

"I did it myself, Chief," he replied. "It's a rental, and the only stuff in it that appeared to belong to the guys who rented it was two small soft suitcases. Each of them had clothes for a few days and shaving stuff." If I had looked in the van at the time of the accident I would have known there was a second guy and we could maybe have grabbed him up at the Star Market. Of course, I still would not have known about the other two and we could have had our gun battle in the parking lot with a lot of dead citizens too.

"Where are the suitcases now?" I asked.

"Locked in the trunk of my cruiser, Boss," Cunningham said. "I didn't know whether you'd want me to voucher the stuff into the property room or not."

I told him to bring the bags to my office after they'd picked up the car. The Maysville Police Department did not have a formal chain of command. Miss Mamie generally runs things, then comes whoever

120

is the Police Chief, and all the officers are, in theory, equal. But some of them take more initiative than others. With the opening of the new mall we'd be hiring more cops, and I had thought we should have a sergeant to help manage the department. I decided I would give the job to Cunningham.

We hung around for a while more before White checked with the people he was expecting to come remove the bodies and clean up the house. They were still a good ways away so he suggested we go back to the police station. He said he'd leave someone to watch my house. I quickly agreed. I asked White if one of his guys could drive him and Ari back so I could stop at the Widow's and see my wife. Ari promised they'd wait for me before he took another crack at our prisoner. I wanted to hear what Zlad had to say, if Ari could use our new leverage to make him talk, but I wanted to see my wife more.

Until last Friday Sandra had never seen a dead body except in a coffin at a funeral home. Now she had seen four men killed in front of her. Ironically, we had come to Maysville to get away from the violence in the big city.

The Widow lives in an apartment over his restaurant. The Bed and Breakfast where Sandra and I stayed on our first visit to Maysville is directly behind the restaurant in another old house that is bigger even than the one the restaurant is in. When I drove up in front, the restaurant was dark, but there were lights on in the front of the second floor. I had never been in the Widow's apartment, and had no idea where the entrance was, so I called on my cell phone. It was after one on Tuesday morning.

He came down and let me in through the restaurant. As I went up the stairs behind him I noticed he had a .45 caliber automatic stuck in the back of his pants. I asked him about it. "Well, Ricky," he said, "I was in the army and know how to shoot it. There are terrorists running around all over the place. They've already threatened Sandra once tonight you know." I told him I thought it was a good idea and appreciated his concern for my wife. Apparently there was one more man in town than I had thought with a gun ready to protect my wife.

The Widow's living room was exactly as I would have pictured it. The ceiling was high, the lighting was soft, and there was a conversation area of overstuffed furniture in the middle of the room. Most of the floor was covered by a huge oriental rug. The walls were a purplish color with matted black and white photographs evenly spaced around the room. Sandra was curled up on a big, soft sofa with her shoes off, her bare feet tucked under her. She patted the space beside her, inviting me to sit down. I sat and hugged her to me as tightly as I could. "How're you doing?" I asked.

"What did Mary Todd Lincoln say when they asked her how she enjoyed the theater that night?" Her speech was little slurred, I assumed from the nearly empty brandy bottle on the coffee table. I laughed and hugged her again.

121

"But seriously, Ricky, you have got to stop bringing your work home. It is going to be the death of us both."

"I'll quit my job as soon as I get back to the station if you want," I said.

"Is this all over?" she asked.

"No," I replied.

"Then you know damn well you will not quit your job when you get back to the station. Don't tell me you will do something you have no intention of doing."

All I could do was look sheepish. The Widow offered brandy, but I declined, saying I didn't know when I would be able to go to bed. He went into the kitchen and soon the smell of rich coffee filled the room. I hugged Sandra to me while I waited for the coffee to brew. I needed to ask her questions, but I needed to hug her more.

The Widow came back from the kitchen carrying three steaming mugs of coffee on a silver tray. There were also silver sugar and cream dispensers and spoons. He placed the gleaming tray on the coffee table next to his blue steel .45, which was resting on a copy of "Gourmet Magazine." The mug he handed me said, "We're Queer, We're Here, GET USED TO IT," on the side.

"Ricky," he said as I was getting sugar for my coffee, "tell us what happened. Who were those awful men and why did they kidnap Sandra?"

Although I was concerned about security, both the Widow and Sandra were too deeply involved for me to "mushroom" them. First I got them to agree again that they could not tell a soul what I was about to tell them. Then I told them as little of the truth as I thought I could get away with.

"I don't know yet what happened at our house before I got there," I said. "So let me tell you what I do know that led up to it." They were both sitting forward in their seats.

"You both know we have been trying to figure out why the guy who tried to run Sandra and me off the road last Friday was coming to Maysville?" They both nodded.

"Since he was Middle Eastern, and everybody is on edge over the World Trade Center attacks last week, Captain White of the state police thought there might be a connection. He set up a task force to investigate. I went to a meeting of it Saturday morning and then went with him to interview a couple of other Middle Eastern guys one of his troopers had arrested following a traffic stop." They both nodded again.

"Okay, yesterday in the Star Market parking lot I saw a couple of Middle Eastern looking guys loading bags of fertilizer into a van."

"Fertilizer," the Widow said. "You mean like the bomb they used to blow up the courthouse in Oklahoma City?"

I nodded. "The guys I saw turned out to be Bob Murray's grandsons, and the fertilizer was apparently for his greenhouse. But it

122

turned out to be a lucky break they were there in the parking lot."

"I know Bob Murray," the Widow said. "I buy all the plants for my restaurant from him.

"So," I continued, "I had just gotten off the phone with Miss Mamie, checking out Murray and his grandsons, when the mayor's mother backed into the minivan. How is she by the way?" I asked.

"She's going to be fine, Ricky," Sandra said in an impatient tone. "They put in a pacemaker, and she should come home today or tomorrow. Get back to the terrorists."

"We don't really know they're terrorists," I said. "We don't know why they came to town. Anyway, Officer Cunningham had pulled up across the street to give me backup when I called about Mr. Murray's grandsons. When Mrs. Marston backed into the minivan, he came over to see if the driver was okay. But his cruiser blocked the minivan in. This apparently panicked the driver. When Cunningham came up to the minivan's door, the driver knocked him down and took off running. I was standing a ways back, and he had no reason to suspect I was a cop too.

"I stopped to see if Cunningham was okay. Then I was going to get my car and go after the fleeing driver. But one of Mr. Murray's grandsons is a state trooper, and he took off running after the suspect. He and one of my cops finally caught him in an alley."

The Widow said, "I heard they both had guns and ran through Mrs. Snyder's garden over on Queen Street shooting at each other."

"Only the trooper had a gun, and no shots were fired, but they did run through her garden," I corrected him. "So they caught the bad guy and took him to the police station. When I got back to the Star Market Sandra had gone to the hospital with Mrs. Marston. Officer Cunningham had learned there had been a second guy with the one who had run. A couple of hours later we learned the second guy had hooked up with two more young Middle Eastern looking guys in another car, and they had all gotten away.

"Before I found out about the second guy, and the two other guys, I saw you both at the hospital. From there I came back to the police station. We were attempting to question the one who'd run after the wreck when the Widow came in and told me of his concerns for you, Sandra."

"I just knew there was something seriously wrong when I called Sandra," he said. "She called me 'Leigh' and you 'Richard' and acted as if I was calling for you! She told me to call you at the police station so I did, but they said you weren't there. So I drove by your house and when I saw the curtains closed I knew something was wrong so I came to get you immediately."

"You did the right thing," I said. "I couldn't have gotten Sandra out of there without your help. The phone ringing as I opened the door distracted them just enough that I was able to do what I did. I could not have done it without your help. You saved Sandra's life,

Leigh."

"No," he said. "You saved Sandra's life but who was the guy dressed in black who opened the door for you and went in behind you? I had my birdwatching binoculars in the car, and I was surprised to see him when you went up the walk."

I had hoped to be able to leave Ari and his friends out of my story. That was impossible now, but I wanted to play down their presence as much as possible. "They are intelligence agents who are helping with the investigation," I said.

"American intelligence agents?" Sandra asked. "Both the one who came in behind you and the one who came in through the back had foreign accents."

"Israeli intelligence agents," I admitted sheepishly. If the gossip had been good before, now it was many times better. Israeli secret agents shooting it out with Middle Eastern terrorists in Maysville! "But," I said, "you both need to forget I told you that. Lives could be lost, and our investigation could be ruined if anyone finds out the Israelis are involved. I need both of you to promise me you will never mention the Israelis." They both nodded their promises.

"Sandra tell us what happened with you and those guys?" I asked.

"Well, let me start at the beginning. When the ambulance came for Mrs. Marston, Miss Mamie hadn't been able to locate the Mayor so I decided I would ride to the hospital with her. She was so upset, the poor dear. She kept saying she knew she should not be driving at her age and now she had hurt someone. I tried to reassure her she'd just done some minor damage to another car, and no one was hurt.

"On the way to the hospital she was complaining of chest pains so they called ahead for the cardiologist. I just sat with her and held her hand until her sons got there.

"I knew you'd be tied up so I called the Widow and asked him to come get me. Miss Mamie offered to send one of your cops, but I didn't want to do that. Then you came to the hospital, and I could have come back with you but the Widow was already there, and we needed to make plans to go see the decorator's house so I came back with him. He needed to check on the restaurant, and I wanted to take a shower so he dropped me off and said he'd call before he came by.

"I checked my email and was just starting to get ready to take my shower when there was a knock at the front door. I opened it, and the first of the three men forced his way inside. He had a gun. He told me to sit down and be quiet. He made a call on his cell phone and a couple of minutes later the other two men arrived. The first man was the only one who ever spoke. He said you were holding a friend of his, and he was going to trade me to you for his friend.

"He assured me I would not be harmed and asked if I knew where you were. I told him I did not, but for some reason I told him I

124

expected you to come home for dinner in the next few minutes. Would you have traded his friend for me, Ricky?" she asked.

"In a heartbeat, darling," I said truthfully. "I just couldn't figure any safe way to do it. It was still an option in my mind when I came into the house. But thanks to the Widow's phone call they didn't have their guns pointed at either of us so I took what appeared likely to be the best opportunity I was going to get."

"Anyway," Sandra continued, "one of the men closed the front drapes when they first came into the house. It seemed like we were there together forever. Two of them stayed, watching me, but when it got dark the third went out on the back porch, I suppose to watch the back of the house. One the ones with me kept watch on the front by looking around the side of the drapes.

"When the Widow called I tried to let him know something was wrong. After that the men were getting impatient so they had me call you. I called your cell phone and left the message calling you 'Richard' which I hoped would tip you off."

"It did when I finally heard it," I said. "It was hot in the police station and I had my jacket off and left the cell phone in the pocket. By the time I got that message the Widow had already arrived to save the day."

"When you pulled up in front the one watching out the window said something in a foreign language to the other one," Sandra said. "We heard the key in the door, and the man at the window moved back into the center of the room. They were both pointing their guns at the front door until the phone rang. I instinctively grabbed the phone and both men turned toward me.

"When I saw you with the groceries, Ricky," Sandra said, "I knew you were coming to save me. You never bring home groceries! Imagine a kidnapping plot foiled by the clever use of toilet paper. You are a genius." I laughed.

"I've been thinking," she continued, "If you want to keep this quiet we need to do something about our house." She didn't mention the three dead bodies that were taking up most of the living room floor when she'd left.

"There are some people taking care of that now," I said. "They'll take the carpet and the living room furniture with them when they go. Tomorrow you get painters in and new carpet installed. You wanted all new furniture for the new house anyway." I hoped she would buy the furniture intended for the new rec room instead of the never to be sat on furniture for the new living room furniture. I did not want to have to stand up until we moved.

"There's a hole in the picture window so we need to get someone to come replace that as well," I said. "If anyone asks tell them an old lamp caused a small electrical fire. You got it out okay but it singed the carpet and couch. You don't know how the window got broken in the confusion." She nodded her agreement.

"Widow, I promise we'll put your house back better than it was before," I said.

"I don't care about the house. I'm just so glad Sandra is okay."

"Can she stay here with you for the rest of the night?" I asked. "I really do need to get back to work"

"Of course," he replied. "She can sleep in that guest room there," he said pointing to the far end of his living room. He pulled a single key from his pocket and gave it to me. "I wouldn't want you to get into the wrong bed by mistake when you come back. The key is to the front door of the restaurant."

I thanked him and hugged my wife to me again, "I love you, Sandra," I said.

"I love you too, Ricky," she replied. "You are so brave and so stupid."

"It's what I'm famous for," I said.

On my way out of the room, I stopped and squeezed the Widow's shoulder. "I couldn't have done it without you, my friend," I said.

"Oh, Ricky," he said, "if only you weren't so straight."

"Probably my loss," I said and left them both laughing.

Chapter 12

I drove back by our house on my way to the police station. The front door was closed, and the porch light was off. The curtains were still closed. Two full sized, windowless step vans were parked at the curb in front. One was shut up tight, but I could see rolled up carpet sticking out the back of the other one. There were no unusual lights on in any of the neighbors' houses so they must have been performing their tasks quietly. I didn't stop.

It was after two in the morning, and the street in front of my office was nearly deserted. Seeing his Firebird reminded me to check on Trooper Burnside. I had left him in the storeroom, holding a shotgun, guarding the prisoner hours before. There was no sign of the van belonging to Ari and his associates.

I'd been thinking about the Widow, his .45 caliber pistol and the fact he would be willing to risk his life to save my wife. But I really hadn't given any thought to Ari and his associates. I didn't even know Ari's last name. But he had come through the door right behind me, into a gunfight, and saved both Sandra's and my life. And I didn't know the first names, or even how many of them there were, of Ari's associates. But one of them had killed a man on my back porch on his way to rush headlong into the gunfight.

I've spent my entire adult life around cops and like to think I understand them to some degree. But these men were not cops. They were soldiers and I didn't understand soldiers at all. America, and I personally, had been fighting a full scale war against terrorists for less than a week. These men had been fighting that same war their entire adult lives. There didn't appear to be an end in sight for any of us.

Once inside the police station I went down the hall to check on Trooper Burnside. He was still at his post in the storeroom where I'd left him hours before. When he saw me he held a finger up to his lips, stepping away from the door to close the vent cover in the interrogation room. He opened the door and came out into the hall, still carrying the shotgun. I could see Chief Buford asleep in a chair in the storeroom, his huge cannon of a handgun next to his right hand on a box. These two were also good men to be in a war with.

We moved down the hall away from the interrogation room door. "You don't need to guard the prisoner any longer," I said. "We're going to take another crack at questioning him, then transport him to Petersburg. Wake up Chief Buford, ask him if he wants to go back to sleep on the couch in my office or if he wants you to take him home."

Burnside nodded, "What about the other three?"

"They won't be coming to break him out," I said. I liked the fact Burnside accepted this as a fact and didn't ask any questions.

In my office I found White typing on my computer and Ari sitting on the couch with his feet propped up on the low table in front of it. There were two soft suitcases sitting on my desk.

White spoke first, "My people are just about done at your house. They'll take the carpet and furniture to the landfill in Richmond and the bodies to the State Medical Examiner's Office. One of your guys brought the bags from the van. There's nothing but new clothes from a discount store and shaving stuff in them." I tossed the bags into the corner.

Then Ari said, "How is your lovely wife?"

"Pretty good considering," I said. "She's at a friend's house, hopefully sleeping by now. I can't thank you and your associates enough. My wife and I would both be dead if you hadn't done what you did. I don't even know the name of the one who came through the back door."

"His name changes so often I have trouble keeping up with it myself. I am glad we could help," he said modestly.

There was a knock on the door, and a sleepy looking Chief Buford stuck his head into my office. "If you don't mind I am going to have your boy take me home. I don't like to leave my wife alone too long," he said.

I walked out with him and thanked him for his help. I promised I would be in touch before the day was over. He didn't ask any questions about what had happened either. Burnside was waiting in the car.

Back in my office Ari said, "Let's go chat with Zlad again."

On my way to the storeroom I stopped to ask the dispatcher where Cunningham was. The dispatcher said he had gone home but would be back for his shift at 7:00 am. He said Cunningham had told him to tell me they had the Chevy locked up at Carl's lot. He also said to tell me he'd left a note on the car with the broken window asking the owner to call him in the morning. Cunningham would go to the house and take a report for the owner's insurance company.

White was waiting for me in the storeroom. I closed the door to the hallway and opened the hatch behind the vent into the interrogation room. A minute later Ari walked into the little room with the prisoner and took his seat on the far side of the table. Zlad had been handcuffed to the table for nearly 12 hours but he hadn't asked for even a drink of water.

"Well, Zlad," Ari said cheerfully, "I see you are still here. I have good news and bad news for you. Which do want first?" The prisoner didn't speak. Ari removed the Polaroids from his pocket and

128

laid them on the table.

"If you do not have a preference we will begin with the bad news then. The bad news is your friends will not be coming to get you." Zlad's expression upon seeing the photos was the first time I had seen the prisoner visibly react strongly to anything since he'd been here. This was not lost on Ari.

"The further bad news is that one of your associates killed a policeman during the gun battle which cost him his life. Now the State of Virginia wants to charge you with capital murder since you were part of the conspiracy and put you in their electric chair." The threat of the electric chair didn't seem to scare Zlad so Ari bushed it aside and continued.

"The good news is the Americans are still willing to offer you their witness protection program. I have not talked to my people in several hours, but we should have your wife and son by now. The Americans are willing to bring them to this country. After you are all finished helping them, you will be reunited, given new papers and a place to live. The alternative is you will go back to the Middle East with me and spend the last few months of your life telling me everything you know. If you go home with me we will release your wife and son before we put out the story you are cooperating with us.

"Either way," Ari said. "I am bored with this, so you must make a decision now. Either the Americans will come get you or I need to arrange your transportation. Would you prefer smoking or non-smoking?" Zlad was visibly sweating. His family seemed to be the hot button. I know I should have been highly upset Ari would use them like this against him, but I couldn't help remembering three of his friends had been pointing guns at my wife a short time before. The world appeared to be becoming a tougher place and any humanitarian ideals I may have had were taking a severe beating.

Ari waited for what seemed like a long time before yawning and starting to get up from the table. He walked around the table. Zlad stopped him before he got to the door.

"Wait," he said. "I am not afraid of what you will do to me. But if I agree to tell you what I know it may not be enough to satisfy the Americans."

"Okay," Ari said, "Then we will make a temporary arrangement while we see what you know. I will have your family released, and we will not put out the story that you are willingly cooperating with us. If we do this, you will tell me everything you know?"

"How do I know I can trust you?" Zlad asked.

"How do you know I will not pull out my pistol and shoot you in the face like I did your friend Khalid?" Ari replied. I think Khalid was the one I shot but Ari never seemed to let the truth interfere with what he was trying to accomplish. "You don't have any other option but to trust me," Ari continued. "And, as bad as I hate to say this, I am the best friend you have in the world at the moment."

Apparently Zlad had come to the same unfortunate conclusion. "I don't know what exactly is going on here and I don't know where the base of operations is," he said. "Khalid and I came down from the northern part of the state on Monday. We stayed at the motel by the truck stop for a night. Yesterday the two others met us and we were supposed to follow them to their base. We stopped in this little town to buy supplies. The two others went somewhere, I do not know where, while Khalid and I went to the grocery store. The others said their errand would be quicker than ours, and they would meet us back in the parking lot. You know what happened in the parking lot?" Ari nodded he did.

"I have been here ever since," Zlad said. He sat back in his chair pretending to believe this meager amount of useless information would satisfy Ari.

"You insult my intelligence, Zlad," Ari said. "You expect me to believe you know nothing? Why were you sent here?"

"I only know what I was supposed to do. I was supposed to meet the others and go with them to their base. I was told I would be briefed about my role in whatever they are planning when I got there."

"Were you told specifically to rent a minivan?" Ari asked.

"Yes," Zlad replied. "I want to cooperate. I was not told this specifically but there have been rumors that we are planning to hit a dozen or more targets around this part of the country at the same time. The rumor was they would be large stores: Walmarts, Kmarts, Targets. The attacks are scheduled for some time next Saturday afternoon when the stores would be crowded with shoppers. I do not know what type of bombs are to be used. I think it was going to be my job to pick up some of the devices and take them back to Northern Virginia to distribute them to the people who would place them in the stores. Truthfully, that is all I know."

"How long have you been in the country?" Ari asked.

"Nearly three months," Zlad replied. "But I have not done anything since I have been here but wait."

"What American cities have you been in?" Ari asked.

"New York and then outside of Washington, D.C. in a place called Herndon."

"Someone will want to ask you about the places you have been and the people you have met with since you came to this country," Ari said. "Will you cooperate and answer their questions truthfully?"

"Yes," Zlad said in a low voice.

"They will be here shortly to take you to a prison where a number of your friends are being held. You should not tell them Khalid and the other two are dead. They will want to know why you were spared. When this is over you will be released and given papers by the Americans. In the meantime you are to pay careful attention to what is being said by the others. In a few days we will take you out of

130

there and move you somewhere else. When we take you out we will expect you to tell us what you have been able to learn. We would very much like to know what these men are talking about among themselves. It is very important we learn this. The more you can tell us, the more grateful the Americans will be. Do you understand?"

"Yes," Zlad said in a low voice.

Ari got up and went to the door. "We will be talking again," he said. Zlad nodded his acceptance of that fact. Ari left the interrogation room, I closed the peep hole, White and I returned to my office.

"What do you think," I asked as soon as the door was closed.

"He did not really tell us anything of value," Ari said, "And, of course, he will betray us as soon as he gets with his friends in Petersburg. But maybe they will try to move their operation away from here and maybe we will catch them on the road. Maybe they will send more men to replace the ones they lost and we will catch them. Or maybe they will postpone their attacks and give us more time. I got what I could."

"Do you really think he'll betray us the first chance he gets?" I asked.

"Think it? I am counting on it," Ari said. "He is higher up in the organization than the others we have and may call someone further up the line than they have. If we don't try to get every little detail we can as quickly as we can though, it will make him suspicious." He turned to White. "Can you get someone to question him for a few hours on the way to Petersburg?"

White nodded, "I'll call Andersen from the FBI and let them have some time with him in Richmond. It will be good for interdepartmental cooperation."

White was still on his cell phone making arrangements with the feds when two of his men arrived to take the prisoner. They were carrying transport cuffs connected to leg chains. White told them to take Zlad to the FBI office in Richmond, wait while the feds questioned him, then take him to Petersburg.

The two cops went into the interrogation room and returned with Zlad hooked up in the chains. He had to shuffle his feet because of the short chain between his ankles. His hands were in front of him connected to another chain around his waist.

Ari asked White if he could speak privately to Zlad once more. White motioned for his cops to step away from the prisoner. Ari told me later he told Zlad not to mention his deal for the new identity and green card to the feds. They might not approve and figure out a way to sabotage the deal. Since, in reality, there was no deal, it would also keep Zlad from learning that fact. Truth is said to be the first casualty of war. Once again, deceitful though he might be, I was glad Ari was on my side.

It was past four in the morning when I watched Zlad being put into the back of a police car and leave my town, hopefully forever. Ari, White and I stood on the police department's front stoop until the car was out of sight. As it disappeared White yawned and said, "Since we're supermen and never require sleep, what do you want to do now?"

Ari laughed, slapped me on the back, and said, "I need to go check on my associates. I have some of them checking the parking lots of motels in the area for rental cars with out of state tags. Had we done this last night we might have found Zlad and Khalid sooner."

As he started to walk away I said, "Ari, I can never thank you and your guys enough for what you did last night. You saved our lives."

"I am glad we were there when you needed us," he replied as he walked away. It occurred to me I didn't have the slightest idea how to reach Ari. He always just appeared when needed, like some kind of guardian angel.

As we entered the building I could smell strong, fresh coffee brewing. It was tempting, but I hoped to be able to go to bed soon so I passed it up. There was a man I didn't recognize asleep in a chair in the corner of the lobby. White said he was one of his investigators waiting to drive him back to Richmond.

In my office White checked his email and printed several. "Well, it's been quite a day," he said. "I don't know if we are better, or worse, off than we were this time yesterday." I didn't know either. "I'm going back to Richmond, hopefully to bed. Several of my cops will still be around checking this and that. What are you doing today?"

"Chief Buford and I are going to check out some more places on the list and I need to help Sandra get something done about our house. Did your guys get everything out?"

"Yeah, that was one of the emails," White said. "Everything is cleaned up, ready for new carpet and furniture. It will be interesting to see who Zlad calls when he gets to Petersburg. Maybe we'll learn something from that. If he's telling us the truth about the operation being on Saturday I would think they'll begin moving stuff Thursday or Friday. If the weather clears up maybe I can get some military recon flights over the likely places. I'll get as many of my cops as I can in the area and we'll stop anybody who looks Middle eastern I guess. I don't know what else to do."

"Speaking of your guys, don't forget about Trooper Burnside", I said. "He's good to have around."

"Where is he now?" White asked.

"I sent him to take Chief Buford home so he should be on his way back here," I said. I found the phone number list Miss Mamie was keeping updated on my desk and dialed Burnside's cell phone. He said he should be back at the Maysville PD in a couple of minutes so White decided to wait. We went back out onto the stoop to smoke a cigarette. It had stopped raining but was still foggy and gray.

We had just finished our cigarettes when Burnside arrived. He trotted from his car to the stoop and stood up straight in front of White.

"When are you next scheduled to work?" White asked.

"Midnight tonight in Buchanan County, sir," he replied.

"What kind of cop car do you have?"

"A marked one, sir," Burnside replied.

White frowned, "Okay, I hate to waste the day but can you get someone to drive you down there to get your cop car?"

"Yes, sir, my cousin will take me."

"Good, try to sleep some in the car. Get your car and come to headquarters in Richmond. Turn the car you have now in to someone in the patrol division and then come to my office. Someone there will give you another, more suitable, vehicle. Then you are to report to Chief Harris here Thursday morning. Orders from him are orders from me."

"Yes, sir," Burnside said, "I'll see you Thursday morning Chief." He sprinted to his Firebird and drove off to wake up his cousin.

"I'll put him in for the commendation as soon as I get a minute and will try to keep him in the investigative division when this is over. He is a good kid," White said, then laughed. "I'm showing my age. I saw you wince when Chief Buford called the trooper from the shooting a 'sweet little girl'. Hopefully they will both realize we're old and not be offended." White yawned, "I need to go wake my guy up and get him to drive me back to Richmond. I'll talk with you later today."

After White and his cop drove away I stood on the stoop for a while reflecting on the events of the previous day. I didn't know if we were any closer to finding the terrorists or not. At least, if Zlad had told us the truth, we knew what "It" was but we were no closer to stopping "It" from happening. Maybe Chief Buford and I would find them today. If we didn't find them there would be a blood bath Saturday afternoon. If it was the terrorists' goal to damage the American economy I couldn't think of a better way than making shoppers afraid to go to their local discount store.

I wanted to sit in my chair, lean back and close my eyes for just a moment, but I knew that would mean I wouldn't wake up for several hours. I felt guilty about leaving Sandra alone after what she had been through earlier in the evening. I knew it was harder for her to watch three men killed in her living room than it had been for me to kill one of them. It surprised me how little emotion I felt about the man I killed. The previous shootings had bothered me much more. I don't know if this one was easier because I truly believe anyone who threatens my wife's life deserves to die or if it just gets easier every time I kill someone. I hope for my sake it is the former.

Sandra's safety was still a concern. Fortunately in Virginia local police chiefs issue concealed weapons permits. I got the paperwork for the Widow to carry his .45 on my way out. I signed it in the appropriate places. It was hard to picture Leigh Williams as armed and dangerous.

As I drove toward my wife, and my temporary bed, I thought how, until the last week, I had mellowed since coming to Maysville. I no longer had the "Prince of the City" swagger I'd had in New York. What I'd read in the John McDonald book while Sandra was in the hospital about men who carried guns was truer than I'd been willing to admit when I read it. My focus had shifted from catching bad guys after they committed crimes to preventing the crime. Even with Ari, White and the others that was still going to be a monumental job against these terrorists. I hoped we were up to it. Maybe Chief Buford and I would find something later today.

When I pulled up in front of the Widow's I could see one dim light on in his living room on the second floor. I quietly unlocked the front door, made my way through the restaurant and up the stairs. Sandra was asleep right where I had left her, tucked into the corner of the couch, covered by blanket. The Widow was also asleep in the chair where I'd left him. The .45 was on the table by his right hand. The brandy bottle was down a couple of more inches than when I'd left.

I leaned over and kissed my wife gently on the forehead. She opened her eyes slowly. "My prince," she said in a slurred voice.

"My love," I replied. "Why are you still up?"

"I was waiting for you," she said unfolding herself from the couch. "Let's go to bed." As I started to follow her toward the bedroom I saw the Widow was also awake.

I took the application for the gun permit over and placed it on the table next to his pistol. "If you will fill this out and take it to Miss Mamie at the police department they will issue you a permit which allows you to carry a concealed weapon," I said. "I would appreciate it if you'd carry your pistol when you're with Sandra until this is all over. I don't think she's in any more danger, but I can't be with her all the time. Knowing you're there to protect her would be a big load off my mind." The Widow nodded his agreement.

It was after four in the morning, and I can never remember being so tired, but I said, "I need to be up by eight. I have a million things I have to do in the morning."

Sandra asked, "Is our living room cleaned up?" I nodded that it was. "Then I want to go home. We don't have anything here, clothes or toothbrushes or whatever, so let's go sleep at our house. I don't want us parading through the streets of Maysville looking like we have been on an all night drunk."

This suited me fine. I wanted to be home in my bed with my wife for whatever stability it might provide. My world was out of control. I was facing the biggest responsibilities of my life. And I didn't have a clue as to how to handle things. I quickly agreed.

Sandra gathered her things, kissed the Widow on the cheek, and we started for home. I thanked him again for all he'd done.

"I'll be over before you leave in the morning, Ricky," he said. "We need to get the people to work on the house." The Widow was

134

taking his body guarding responsibilities seriously. I nodded my agreement.

We went down the stairs and out into the cool September predawn. The town slept peacefully as we drove the few blocks to our little house.

When we pulled up in front the house looked deserted. The living room drapes were closed tight, and there were no lights on. I took the flashlight from the door pocket of my car. I realized I did not have my key. The last time I had seen it was when Ari turned it for me. Sandra had hers, and our entry was much less eventful this time.

I flipped the light switch just inside the door but nothing happened. It had turned on a lamp in front of window but the lamp was gone, along with everything else that had been in the room. I walked across the bare concrete into the dining room and flipped the switch there. The hanging light over the table came on. With my back to the living room everything looked like home.

Sandra went down the short hall to our bedroom. She took the T shirt she sleeps in from the back of the door and went into the bathroom to change. I tossed my jacket, shoulder holster, and the rest of my clothes onto a chair on my side of the bed. I was sitting there in my shorts waiting for Sandra to come out of the bathroom so I could get in and brush my teeth.

A minute later Sandra came out. She held the front of her T shirt so I could read the message. It was an old one from a police union picnic in New York which read, "Feel safe at night. Sleep with a cop."

She came over, climbed into my lap facing me and kissed me hard. "Ricky," she said. "You saved my life. I love you."

"I had to save your life," I replied. "My life depends on you being here with me. I love you, too."

I woke up when I smelled coffee a little after eight on Wednesday morning. Sandra was already up. It was raining again and overcast. Even if White could get the military to send a reconnaissance plane it wouldn't be able to see anything in this weather. I was as tired as I can ever remember being and would have liked to go back to bed. But I could not count on the bad guys to sleep in. If what Zlad had told us about the bombs in the discount stores was true there wasn't much time.

When I was dressed in jeans for my exploring trip with Chief Buford and armed I went into the living room. I found the Widow drinking coffee with Sandra. He was wearing a red flannel shirt and jeans which he'd accessorized with a tool belt full of hand tools. His .45 was stuck into the tool belt as well. He appeared prepared for whatever job he needed to do.

Sandra looked extremely tired. She had been through a lot. I kissed her as she handed me my coffee. I was worried about Sandra, but since I didn't have any idea what I should say, I said nothing. Hopefully I am a better cop than I am a husband.

"You look like you know what you're doing, Leigh," I said to the Widow.

"I look like one of the Village People," he replied. "But I do know what I'm doing. The window man will be here momentarily to replace the window. Miguel has gone to the store for the paint and stuff to fix the wall." He pointed to the gouge the shot I'd missed with had made. "Miguel will get started painting as soon as he gets here. I scheduled the new carpet people for tomorrow morning so Miguel needs to finish up today." I nodded my admiration. I kissed Sandra goodbye and thanked the Widow again for his help the previous day.

I was in my office before nine. Nothing had changed in the few hours since I'd left. I checked my emails. There was nothing of importance there either. I called Chief Buford and agreed to meet him at his office at ten.

I remembered to tell Miss Mamie that Leigh Williams would be in to have his picture taken for his gun permit. She looked at me funny but did not object.

Since I had a little time to spare before I needed to meet Chief Buford I drove through the streets of my little town. Everything looked serene. It was hard for me to believe there had been a battle fought here yesterday with international terrorists. And even now Israeli secret agents were nearby looking for more. Andy and Barney never faced this kind of problems.

A window company truck was parked in front of my house when I drove by. Two men were carrying a replacement for the picture window toward the house. The drapes had been taken down. I could see the Widow and a man I assumed to be Miguel working on one of the living room walls. I didn't stop.

My police radio was on but, as usual, nothing was happening in town. This was a nice change from yesterday. I was almost to Walton's Corner when White called on my cell phone.

After some small talk White said, "After his chat with the feds our boy Zlad arrived at Petersburg about seven this morning. When he first entered the cell block the driver of the car we interviewed the other night came rushing over to him asking questions. Zlad grabbed him by the throat and slammed him into the wall. Since then he has been asleep in a cell. He hasn't called anyone."

"Does this mean he is going to stick to his imaginary deal with Ari?" I asked.

"I hope not," White said. "We need him to call his friends. On another front, the feds have information that there is an attack planned against one of the tank farms on Interstate 95 somewhere between New York and Richmond." I knew the "tank farms" he was referring to are those collections of gasoline storage tanks you see from the highway. I remembered there was one in New Jersey just out of the city and another in Northern Virginia. They'd apparently been built so close to the highway for convenience but they would be impossible to

136

protect without shutting the major north-south corridor down completely. And even that wouldn't really protect them since any place they could be seen from, they could be shot at from.

"What are they doing about it?" I asked.

"You know the feds, it is all a big secret. We're trying to figure out what the state police can do about the one in Virginia now. I'm glad that's not my job."

I told White I was on my way to meet Chief Buford. He said he would call again later if he found out anything helpful. If it quit raining he thought he could get the recon flights organized over the area.

The rest of the drive to Walton's Corner I imagined terrorists up every side road plotting to kill people with bombs. Maybe Buford and I would find them before the day was over. If we didn't find them I didn't know what was going to happen. But I knew it would not be good.

I met Chief Buford at his office. We loaded our shotguns into his truck again and started searching the likely places the terrorists might have set up their bomb factory between our two towns. He told me about the people who lived in the various places and the history of the area. I'm sure his stories would have been fascinating under other circumstances, but I couldn't really focus on what he was telling me. My mind was on the consequences of us not finding the place in time. And I was worried about my wife.

She had been through a horrendous experience yesterday. First she was kidnapped, and then she had watched men killed in front of her. I knew I needed to say, and do something, but I had no more clue about that than I did about the location of the terrorists. But there were a bunch of other people also looking for the terrorists. Sandra was solely my responsibility. I hoped I would be able to live up to it.

We got back to the Walton's Corner just after dark. I thanked Chief Buford for his help and told him I would call him on Thursday. We had looked at all the likely places and neither of us had any good ideas about where we should look next. I called Sandra from my car.

She sounded in good spirits. The window had been fixed. Miguel had finished painting and she wanted to know if I had time to drive to Charlottesville with her to pick out new furniture. I wanted to say "no". I was bone tired, but I knew it was important to her so I said "yes". I told her I would be home in twenty minutes.

I enjoyed a leisurely drive back to Maysville. Things were quiet on the police radio. I checked with the dispatcher. He didn't have any messages for me. I told him I would be on my cell phone if anyone wanted me.

When I got home the living room was bright and clean from a new coat of paint. The paint smell hung in the air. There were new drapes hanging from a new rod over the picture window. The drapes were closed so the neighbors would not see the room was still empty.

The concrete slab floor had been scrubbed as well in preparation for the new carpet Sandra told me would be installed the following morning. Once the new living room furniture was in place no one would ever know the room had recently been the site of a gun battle where international terrorists had died violent deaths.

I took a quick shower and put on clean clothes. Sandra was once again holding my shoulder holster rig while I put on my shirt. She had changed her mind about me carrying a gun it seemed. Andy Taylor's theory of being an unarmed cop had been totally discredited in Sandra's eyes.

On the drive to Charlottesville Sandra told me about her day with the Widow and Miguel. She thought we should buy furniture for the family room of the new house and use it in the living room of the present house so as not to . . . I just nodded my agreement without really listening at all. I checked every car we met for out of state tags and Middle Eastern looking men, but it was too dark to see either.

We had a quick dinner at a chain steak house and then went to a large furniture store on the outskirts of Charlottesville. I quickly found a room grouping with a recliner in soft brown leather. As soon as I sat down I was sold. Like a good husband I asked if this furniture was okay with her. I knew she wanted to look at everything in this store and two or three more before we came back and bought this one. But she must have been exhausted too and agreed.

I leaned back in the recliner while she got out her diagram of the new house's family room and her tape measure. I don't know how long I had been asleep when she woke me to say the furniture would fit fine. She had decided she wanted two of the recliners and the matching couch. She didn't really like the tables with this grouping and took me to another section to see tables she liked better. I quickly agreed these were much better even though I didn't remember what the original tables looked like.

She didn't like the lamps with either grouping so we searched the store until she found the perfect ones. I agreed they were the most wonderful lamps I had ever seen. I went back and sat in the recliner while she found the salesman and made the purchases.

Sandra leaned back in her car seat and slept all the way home, her left hand on my leg. We cuddled in our bed but were both asleep before it could go any further.

138

Chapter 13

(Newspaper Clippings)
From the September 21, 2001 May County Chronicle
Road Rage Comes To May County, New York Man Killed
By Mary Johnson
May County Chronicle Staff Writer

Last Friday May County experienced its first reported "road rage" incident. It resulted in the death of a New York man.

Maysville Police Chief Rick Harris was returning to town in his personal car after having lunch at Bubba's Barbeque when he was repeatedly rammed from behind by a Lincoln Town Car driven by Robert Downs, age unknown, of New York City. Chief Harris called the Maysville police dispatcher on his cell phone for assistance. Virginia State Trooper Erica Knight was close by and quickly responded.

According to the Virginia State Police, Downs refused to stop when ordered to do so by Trooper Knight, and she ran him off the road and into a field on the Finley Farm near the town limits. State Police spokesperson Ron Dean said, "The elementary school was about to let out for the day and the trooper wisely decided it was unsafe to let Downs drive into Maysville at a high rate of speed.'"

According to Dean, Down's car came to a stop in the field and he came out of the car shooting. Trooper Knight returned his fire, and two shots struck Downs in the chest, killing him. "Trooper Knight did what she was trained to do. It is regrettable that she was forced to kill someone, but there was nothing else she could have done under the circumstances."

When reached for comment Chief Harris said, "The trooper acted with extreme bravery and saved my life."

Trooper Knight is a 1995 graduate of the May County Consolidated High School. She received a Bachelor's Degree in Elementary Education from the University of Virginia in

Charlottesville before joining the Virginia State Police in 2000. She has been assigned to patrol in May County since she finished her initial state police training.

Nothing is yet known about Downs or why he repeatedly rammed Chief Harris' car. Although Harris recently moved to Maysville from New York City, where he received two Medals of Valor while on the NYPD, Harris said he had never had any previous contact with Downs.

****

Fugitive Arrested in Maysville After Foot Chase
By Mary Johnson
May County Chronicle Staff Writer

Mrs. Sidney L. Marston, mother of Maysville Mayor Phillip Marston had just finished her grocery shopping at the Star Market in Maysville Tuesday when her car was struck by a minivan as she backed out of her parking space. Maysville Police Officer Robert Cunningham happened to be in the parking lot and heard the crash. He pulled his cruiser over to investigate what he believed to be a routine fender bender. But when he got up to the door of the minivan, the driver slammed the door into him, knocking him to the ground. The driver then took off running away from the accident scene.

Before Officer Cunningham could get back to his feet and give chase, off duty Virginia State Trooper David Burnside took off after the fleeing man on foot. Trooper Burnside is the grandson of local greenhouse owner Bob Murray. Trooper Burnside and his cousin Robby Murray were in the parking lot with their grandfather helping him load greenhouse supplies into his van.

The foot chase lasted for approximately eight blocks through yards and gardens until another Maysville Police officer managed to block the fleeing suspect with his police car in the alley behind the Frank Connor's house at 354 Astor Street. Trooper Burnside then placed the man under arrest.

According to Miss Mamie Tate of the Maysville Police Department the suspect gave up peacefully when he saw he had nowhere left to run. Miss Mamie said the man was wanted on out-of-state warrants, and that was why she believes he ran when confronted by police at the accident scene. The man's identity is being withheld until the incident is thoroughly investigated.

****

Maysville Car Vandalized
By Mary Johnson
May County Chronicle Staff Writer

Mr. Martin Svensen, of 687 Maple Street, awoke Wednesday morning to find the driver's side window of his 1987 Buick had been broken during the night. Svensen said he had not heard anything unusual but said his bedroom is at the back of the house.

Svensen also said when he went out he found a note on the car from the Maysville Police Department. An officer patrolling the neighborhood had discovered the broken window earlier and left the note.

Miss Mamie Tate of the Maysville Police department said this is the first case of vandalism she can remember in many years and added, "We don't know when it happened. It may have been done accidentally by a child with a baseball."

Chapter 14

I was pleased when I read the local paper Thursday morning. The Chronicle completely missed the real story all three times. Of course, no one in town would have believed the real story had it been accurately reported.

At exactly eight Miss Mamie called to tell me Trooper Burnside was at the police station reporting for duty. She wanted to know what she should do with him. I said give him a cup of coffee and a doughnut; I would be there in a few minutes. I quickly showered, dressed and got ready to face another day. If the bombings of the discount stores were still planned for Saturday the terrorists might start moving the bombs today. Since we still didn't know where to look we had to look everywhere.

Sandra seemed better that morning; less tired and happier somehow. She was vacuuming the concrete slab in the living room in preparation for the arrival of the carpet installers. Getting the house back together seemed to be therapeutic. I hoped it would keep her mind off what happened and would give her something to occupy her time. Although I love my wife more than anything in the world I simply didn't have time to spend with her. I was haunted by the vision of bombs exploding in crowded discount stores.

As I told her goodbye, and pretended to listen to her tell me about the new carpet, I tried to figure out something productive I could do that day with Trooper Burnside. Chief Buford and I had been up every back road between Maysville and Walton's Corner. We hadn't found anything of value. The terrorists were somewhere, but we still didn't have a clue where.

I kissed my wife again, hugging her tightly before I went out to my cop car. My cell phone was in my hand to call Chief Buford when it rang. It was Captain White.

"Ricky, "he said, "I need your help. We have some kind of meeting of suspected terrorists going on in Herndon, and I don't have enough men to follow all of them when they leave. You should be able to get here in an hour if you hurry. Can you come?" I told him I was on my way and said I would also bring Trooper Burnside. I asked if he wanted us to bring two cars.

"Come together," he said. "In the Northern Virginia traffic it takes two people in a car to watch the traffic and follow a car at the same time. Come Interstate 81 to 66 and get off at the Route 50 West

142

exit. About six miles on Route 50 you will see a McDonalds on your right. Go just beyond it. There are some warehouses back there where we're staying out of sight of the road. Hurry, we don't know how long the meeting will last."

I called the Maysville Police Department, telling the dispatcher to have Burnside meet me outside. I was pulling up in front by the time I completed the call. Burnside ran out of the building, jumped into the car, fastening his seat belt as he closed the door. I caught him up on what Captain White had told me as we made our way out of town. As soon as I hit the highway I turned on my blue lights and put my foot down on the accelerator.

Fortunately traffic was light between Maysville and the Interstate. I was able to tap the siren and quickly overtake the few cars we came up behind on the two lane road. As we passed the spot where the trooper had killed the first terrorist, it was hard for me to believe this had all begun less than a week earlier. It seemed like a year.

Once on the Interstate I was quickly up to 100 miles per hour. The big Chrysler engine just hummed along. The dog fighter who had originally bought this car had made a good choice. The car was capable of more speed, but I was not comfortable with my abilities to drive it any faster.

I got into the left lane and my blue lights cleared the traffic in front of us. By the time we turned on to Interstate 66 Burnside had found the state police frequency for the area on my police radio in case we blew through anyone's radar at this speed.

As we passed Gainesville the traffic became heavier, and I was forced to slow down some but we were still making good progress. Although the speed limit had dropped to 55 most of the traffic was going 70. No one slowed down when they saw my blue lights coming up behind them. A couple of miles before our exit my cell phone rang. I was busy with the traffic so I handed it to Burnside. He told me it was White checking on our progress. Burnside told him where we were and that we would be at his location in a few minutes. White gave him the tactical radio frequency they were using. Burnside tuned my police radio to it. All we could hear were cryptic snatches of transmissions.

I killed my cop lights as we got off the Interstate onto Route 50. We were still moving along at 55 with the traffic in the 35 mph zone but it seemed as if we were barely moving after the high speed on the highway.

Burnside pointed out the McDonalds. I turned just after it. I found the warehouses and quickly found the collection of vehicles parked at the end of a short road. There was a medium size, nondescript motor home with half a dozen cars parked around it. The motor home had a satellite dish mounted on its roof. Several men were standing around one of the cars which had a roll of blueprints spread out on the hood. Although it was another warm day, they were all wearing jackets. Before we were completely stopped one of the men started toward the car. I could see the wire coming from his collar to an earpiece. Burnside held his badge up to the car window. The man nodded slightly and went back to the blueprints.

Burnside and I got out of the car, walking over to the men. I asked where White was. One of the men pointed to the motor home. Burnside waited with the other cops while I went over to the motor home. I knocked gently on the door. White himself opened it. "Ricky," he said, "good to see you. Come in and I'll catch you up on what's happening."

Inside the motor home looked like the bridge of the Starship Enterprise. On one side there was a large computer monitor showing a street map with three green blips pulsating close together superimposed over it. Each blip was a number. Next to the computer monitor was a video screen showing the front of a warehouse type building like the ones I had driven through to get here. I couldn't read the sign on the building, but it appeared to be in Arabic. Another computer monitor showed a list of names. There was also a rack of radios off to the side. Two men, who seemed to be responsible for the equipment, were sitting in chairs. Two others beside White were standing around. As usual no introductions were made.

"Let me tell you where we are," White said. "A couple of days ago pairs of men in rented vehicles started showing up at a mosque the feds have under surveillance in Pennsylvania. Everyone seems to be avoiding the Brooklyn mosque since they raided that Ahmed's house. They parked the vehicles on the street which gave the feds a chance to place these GPS locators on them." He pointed to the flashing numbers on the screen.

"I don't know exactly how the devices work," White continued, "but, as you can see, we'll know exactly where the vehicles are at all times until the batteries run out in about another 24 hours.

"These three vehicles with seven men in them left the mosque in Pennsylvania last night at different times and drove here by different routes. They arrived early this morning. There were a bunch of vehicles in the parking lot when we got here so we don't know how many people are in the building or what other vehicles belong to them. Four of the other cars there are also rentals. We'll put locators on them if they're still there after dark. It's too risky to do it now."

I nodded my understanding. "What can Burnside and I do for you?" I asked.

"Assuming Zlad was telling the truth," White continued, "no one, as far as we know, has gotten to the bomb factory in your area yet to pick up the bombs. If one of these vehicles is going there we want to follow it and find the bombs. With all this Buck Rogers' electronic gear you don't even have to have them in sight to follow them. We'll track them from here and keep you informed by radio."

White pointed to the video monitor, "For once luck is on our

144

side. There is a retired FBI agent with an accounting office across the parking lot from the target building. We can see what's going on from his window and have a couple of agents in there as well. But, as you can see, the area is full of innocent people. So in addition to wanting to see where these guys are going, we can't safely go in and get them anyway. But we'll have plenty of notice when anybody starts to move.

"And, as I told you, we're short on manpower. The feds are running operations like this all over the country and every one of my cops in Virginia is working on terrorists' cases. So I need you as an experienced cop whether this goes back to your area or not."

I nodded again. "Let me go make some calls back to Maysville. Burnside and I are here for as long as you need us." White nodded his agreement, and I went back to my car to make the calls. When Burnside saw me come out of the motor home he immediately joined me. I caught him up on what White had told me and asked if he could stay as well.

"Sure," he said happily. "This beats weighing coal trucks in Buchanan County." When I was his age playing cops and robbers with real guns appealed to me more than it does now, too.

Although I was nearly 100 miles away from Maysville I was still its police chief and responsible for the town. And I was worried about my wife. I got on the cell phone to do what I could long distance to live up to these responsibilities.

First I called Miss Mamie. As usual she had everything at the Maysville Police Department under control. I told her Burnside and I were with Captain White following up some leads on where the terrorists were hiding. I told her I didn't know when we would be back, but she could reach me on my cell phone.

Then I called Sandra. She said the men were there installing the carpet and hopefully she would be able to get the furniture we'd bought the previous evening delivered before the day was over. She said she didn't have time to talk. I was glad she was occupied with the house. I told her I didn't know when I'd be home, but she could always reach me on my cell phone.

I was still worried about Sandra so I called Leigh Williams to enlist his help. When he answered at the restaurant I explained I was out of town and didn't know when I would be back. Before I could ask him to look after Sandra he volunteered saying he would get her to come to the restaurant for dinner and spend the evening with him picking out furniture on an interior design web site he'd found. I thanked him profusely. I honestly do not know what I would have done without Williams these past few days.

I shifted my thinking from good guys to bad guys. I stuck my head into the motor home. Nothing had changed on either the video monitor or the computer screen. The vehicles were still parked in front of the building.

White said, "Here's what I think we should do, Ricky. You

follow the first minivan that leaves. Set your radio to our tactical frequency. Someone from here will guide you so you don't have to be too close. With the GPS transmitters we will know where the vehicle is at all times regardless of where they go. What we are most interested in is if they stop and meet anyone plus where they end up. We'll tell you when they turn." I nodded my agreement.

"I would suggest," White continued, "you and Burnside go fill your car up with gas and get some drive through lunch so you'll be ready to move when they are."

I nodded again. "See you later," I said. Burnside joined me as I came out of the motor home. I told him the plan. We drove back to Route 50 and turned left, back toward Route 66. There was a gas station and mini mart a little ways down on the left. Burnside filled the car with gas while I bought bottles of water and junk food inside. Then we drove through the drive through at McDonalds, Supersizing our lunches. The police radio was tuned to White's tactical channel. We could hear them fine. Burnside checked to make sure they could hear us as well.

I found a parking place in the strip mall next door where I could still see the intersection the minivan would come out of and easily turn in either direction to follow it. Hopefully we would get going before the afternoon traffic started. I had been told suburban Washington's traffic is worse than New York City's.

Then we sat back to wait. I have spent many hours waiting on surveillances but usually I had to be constantly watching something. This time, with everything so high tech, all I had to do was wait. White would tell us when the subjects moved.

I had a lot on my mind and Burnside was a good partner for surveillance. He answered my questions when I asked about his background but didn't feel the need to talk all the time. I thought about the terrorists, but I thought more about Sandra. Although she seemed fine I knew seeing those men killed in front of her had to be on her mind. Maybe I would really quit when this was over. But we had just bought a house in Maysville, and there was no reason for us to stay there if I wasn't the police chief. We could move to Florida but I didn't want to take her away from the support and friendship the Widow provided. But . . .

"Ricky," I heard White's voice on the radio say, "the black minivan is moving. You'll be able to see it when it comes to the light." A moment later I saw the van. It turned left away from Route 66. Since I was driving Burnside had the radio mike.

"We see them and are going after them," he said trying to keep the excitement out of his voice. I was feeling the adrenaline too. Fight or flight is the human reaction to excitement. But we could do neither. We could just follow along in the heavy traffic. More cops die from hypertension than of anything else.

There were three lanes of traffic going each way. I moved

into the middle lane so I could be ready to go either way if he turned. I could still see the minivan ahead in the left lane. But, due to the traffic, he would either get much farther ahead or I would nearly catch up to him. Finally a huge delivery truck pulled up behind the minivan in the left lane and I got in behind the truck. I could see him if he started to turn left and Burnside would see him if he got over into one of the right lanes. We drove like this for several miles. Once we got caught behind the truck at a light which the minivan got through. We caught up again at the next light. Now we were approximately ten cars behind.

As we approached the sign for Route 28 the minivan got into the left turn lane. There were six cars between us when we stopped to wait for the traffic light. Burnside told White we were turning. He said he could see the minivan was stopped.

Only a couple of cars behind the minivan got through on the next turn lane light. We were still sitting on Route 50 behind four other cars. This was good for us. If the minivan driver was looking to see if he was being followed he wouldn't see us behind him. As long as the technology worked we were in good shape.

When we turned White said the minivan was still headed south on Route 28. After a mile or so we saw the outer reaches of Dulles International Airport on our right. There were still office buildings and hotels on the left side. We continued along in the heavy traffic. I saw the minivan stopped in a left turn lane going into a motel parking lot on my left before we heard he had turned on the radio. Since I didn't want to turn right behind him, I drove past and had to go nearly a mile before I could turn around and come back. The radio said the minivan was stopped, apparently in a parking lot adjacent to Route 28. I had turned around and started back when Burnside pointed out what was on the airport side of the highway. There must have been 50 of those huge fuel tanks you see in tank farms beside highways. These were probably full of highly explosive jet fuel. I could have hit the tanks with my pistol at this range. This was not a comforting thought.

The minivan was sitting in front of the motel in a space reserved for registering guests when we pulled into the parking lot. I parked around the building out of sight of the office. Burnside got on the radio and told White about the tanks. He also told him we could not see the minivan so we needed to know when it started to move. White assured him he was on top of it.

After several extremely long minutes White said they were moving again. They had turned back south. From where we were sitting we'd be able to see them if they got back on to Route 28. But they didn't come out of the parking lot. White told us they were stopped again. They had apparently parked in front of the rooms facing the road, and the airport tank farm beyond.

Burnside jumped out of the car and moved to a corner of the building for a look. He peeked around briefly and came back. "They've parked facing the building," he said as he got back into the car. He picked up the microphone and repeated the information to White.

"Stay on them," White said. "The others are moving so it is going to get a little hectic around here."

I moved the car back around front and parked facing Route 28 and the tank farm. I could see the minivan in my mirror. The two men were standing at the open rear hatch. I watched them while I told Burnside, "We'll sit here as long as we can, then walk to the office I guess. We need to see which room they go into." Burnside nodded his agreement. I pushed the button which controlled the outside mirror on the passenger side of the car until Burnside said he could see the men as well.

As we continued to watch, the situation suddenly changed drastically. The men were unloading something long and thin from the rear of the van. It was wrapped in one of those quilted pads movers use. I didn't know exactly what it was, but I was sure it was some kind of weapon, maybe a rocket launcher.

"What now, Boss?" Burnside asked.

I could hear talk back and forth over the radio about the other cars from the guys following them. I didn't really want to tell White what we were seeing over the radio anyway. The two men, carrying whatever it was between them, were making their way toward the stairs to the second floor. I had to make a decision. All my usual doubts and uncertainties quickly returned. I weighed the options and quickly made up my mind.

"We have to take them before they get inside a room," I said. "We'll go up the stairs behind them. When I say, 'Excuse me,' draw your gun and cover the one in back." Burnside nodded his understanding. "Let's do it." I could feel the sweat under my arms. No matter how many times a cop does something like this he never gets used to it.

As we walked as leisurely as we could manage across the parking lot, the two men were starting up the stairs. When we got to the bottom of the staircase they were on the second floor. They turned left on the exposed walkway in front of the rooms. By the time we got to the top of the stairway, they had stopped in front of a room door. The one in front was sliding the keycard into the electric door lock with one hand while still holding his end of whatever it was they were carrying. They were both staring at us.

I looked at my watch and then said the Burnside, "Good, we're in time to watch the Winston Cup qualifying from Dover." The first man was just starting through the open door as we came even with them.

"Excuse me," I said, drawing my gun and pointing it at the first man's head. He looked surprised. I heard a gasp from the second man confirming Burnside was pointing a gun at him as well. I didn't take my eyes off the first man to confirm this. "Careful," I said.

148

"Move slowly inside and set that down gently on the bed nearest the door. Don't make any sudden moves. Do it now."

The man started to say something in a language I didn't understand. "Shut up," I said firmly, "and do what I told you."

"He doesn't understand English," he said. "I was trying to tell him . . ."

"Shut up," I said again. "If I shoot you he'll get the idea." The men moved carefully into the room and set their load down on the bed. I kicked the door closed. "Put your hands up," I said. They obeyed. I pointed to the blank wall behind the door with my gun. "Grab the wall." The man who had been carrying the front of whatever it was did as I told him. The other man followed his lead. I nodded to Burnside.

Burnside holstered his pistol before approaching the first man. He first pulled the man's feet back further with his own foot so the man would be off balance if he tried to turn around. As he patted the man down, he tossed the contents of his pockets onto the bed nearest the door. There were money, papers, and a wallet in the pile. When he was finished searching the first man Burnside slapped a handcuff around his right wrist while telling him to straighten up and place his head against the wall. The man did as he was told. Burnside pulled the cuffed arm behind him and told him to bring his other arm back as well. He did as he was told and was quickly cuffed with the backs of his hands together. Burnside told him to step forward until his toes were against the wall. When he was satisfied this man was as secure as he could be Burnside turned to the second man and repeated the operation.

In addition to the usual stuff, this one had a small automatic pistol in his back pocket. Burnside showed it to me before placing it in his jacket pocket. When he was done with the search I handed him my cuffs. He was cuffing the prisoner when my cell phone started ringing. I flipped it open with my left hand without taking my eyes off the prisoners.

"Yeah," I said into the phone.

"Ricky," I heard White's voice say. "Are you guys okay? I have been trying to get you on the radio."

"We're fine," I said. "We saw the guys in the van carrying some sort of rocket launcher or bazooka into the motel and decided we should bust them before they got out of our sight. I guess they were going to shoot at the jet fuel tanks across the road."

"Damn," White said. "Good work. If we'd had to get them out of there with a SWAT team it would have been a mess."

"What do you want us to do with them?" I asked.

"Let me think," he said. There was a long pause. "Can you sit on them for awhile until I can have someone come take them off your hands? Things are happening. The meeting has broken up and people are going in all directions. We are spread real thin right now."

"Sure, we can hold them as long as necessary," I said. "Just call me before anyone comes. I don't want to be surprised by a knock on the door."

"Thanks, Ricky," he said. "I'll be back in touch when I figure out what to do." He hung up and I turned to Burnside.

"White says he'll send some people to get these guys as soon as he can," I told him. "The meeting has broken up, and he needs to deal with ones who are still moving around before coming to get these two. He'll call back."

Burnside said, "Fine. Like you said qualifying for the Winston Cup race at Dover is on television anyway." I couldn't help but laugh.

We moved our prisoners away from the wall, placing them on their stomachs on the floor. One of them was between the two beds in the room and the other at the foot of the bed with his head toward the bathroom. There wasn't any point in us trying to question them but I didn't want them talking to each other.

I took the keys Burnside had found in one of the prisoner's pockets and went out to make sure their minivan was locked. I didn't know what other weapons might be inside it, and I didn't want some local thief to end up with a box of rockets. I locked the minivan using the little gizmo on the keys so I didn't have to touch it. I went to my car and dug around in the trunk until I found several evidence bags for the gun Burnside had found and the other stuff from the prisoners' pockets.

When I got back inside Burnside was flipping through the channels on the room's television. Our prisoners were lying quietly where we had put them. Qualifying was already underway when Burnside found the right channel. We spent the next two hours watching the remainder of 48 cars compete for the 43 spots in the race.

The commentators were talking more about increased security at the track than they were about the race cars. Coolers and large bags had been banned, and fans were sure to be unhappy about having to buy everything inside the track at high prices seemed to be the main theme. The world had changed since September 11, and security was now a concern everywhere. Our prisoners lay on the floor without making a sound throughout it all. There was nothing any of us could do but wait.

Whenever I have time on my hands I think about my wife and miss her terribly. So I called her. I have been a cop for so long it did not seem strange to me to have two men with their hands cuffed behind them lying on the floor while I made small talk with Sandra. She told me the carpet was installed and new furniture was scheduled to arrive any minute. She said the house should be back together by the time I got home. I didn't want to tell her I had no idea when I would be home again.

Sandra spent the entire conversation asking my opinion about how I thought the new furniture should be placed in the living room. I did not care in the least about this. But I have too much experience as a husband to say that so I asked questions and gave opinions. I just wanted to hear her voice. I was sorry when the furniture arrived and she said she had to go.

When I hung up NASCAR qualifying was still going on. There were only a couple of cars left to run, and it looked like Dale Jarrett would hold onto the pole with a speed of nearly 150 mph, by the time White called back. He told me the feds were on the way to pick up our prisoners and they would call when they arrived in the parking lot. White asked me to call him when we were done with the prisoners so he could decide what he wanted us to do next.

I was placing the contents from the prisoner's pockets into evidence bags when my cell phone rang again. A man who identified himself as an FBI agent said he and his partner were in the parking lot. I gave them the room number and went to the window so I could see them come up the steps. They looked like FBI agents to me so I opened the door.

They both had their credentials in their hands when they entered the motel room. I saw them look at the men on the floor and then at whatever it was wrapped in padded cloth on the bed. "What have you got for us?" the one in front asked.

"We followed them from a meeting up on Route 50. When they stopped here and went in to register we were going to continue watching them. But they got whatever kind of weapon that is out of the van and started up the steps with it," I said pointing to the bed I pulled the curtain back so he could see the tank farm across the road. His eyes got very big. "We decided we'd better take them before they got set up in this room," I continued.

"I think you made the right choice," the agent said quietly. He looked around the room and said, "Let me call some bomb people to come get the weapon and whatever is in the van. Then we'll take your prisoners and you guys can go back to whatever you need to do." I nodded my agreement.

Both my handcuffs and Blackburn's use different keys than the fed's so we gave the second agent our keys and stood around watching as he recuffed the prisoners using FBI handcuffs. When we had our cuffs back we received a nod of dismissal from the lead fed. He had not asked us our names or whom we work for. Apparently this was not a matter which would ever go to court.

As we walked back to the car I had a strange feeling of anticlimactic disappointment. Burnside and I had just prevented a catastrophe. It was hard to even imagine what would have happened if terrorists fired a rocket into thousands of gallons of jet fuel. There would have been a river of fire for as far as the ground was reasonably level. The resulting loses of life and property damage would have been beyond belief. We had stopped this from happening but we were no closer to finding the bomb factory back home. We had succeeded in stopping a terrorist plot but not the one we had set out to stop. Those folks were still in business and we were running out of time to stop them.

Back in the car the tactical radio channel was full of cryptic conversations so I called White on the cell phone. When he answered I told him the feds had taken our prisoners and ask him what he wanted us to do now. He said all hell was breaking loose at the moment and asked us to hang around until he could call back. I drove us back to the cul-de-sac and the command center motor home.

I didn't see White's car when we pulled up. There were two guys sitting in a parked car beside the motor home. The one in the passenger seat got out as we came to a stop. Burnside held up his badge and rolled down the window. I could see the guy walking toward us visibly relax when he saw the state police shield. He said he didn't know where White was at the moment, but he wasn't at the command post. We thanked him, and I started driving back toward Interstate 66.

We found a Sonic Drive-in and were drinking cherry limeades and watching the car hops balancing trays while on roller blades when White called back.

"Thanks for being patient, Ricky," he said. "After what you found we decided to grab up the other minivans as soon as we could. We got one of them on a road that runs parallel to Interstate 95 opposite that huge tank farm just outside the Beltway. The other two stopped to go to the bathroom at a gas station near National Airport and we took them inside the bathroom." White laughed. I could picture the terrorists standing at the urinals when the cavalry arrived with guns drawn.

"Both groups also had rocket launchers and rockets." White paused to let this sink in. "We did a good day's work today, Ricky," White said. "Had these three groups succeeded in their attacks it was impossible for me to even imagine the devastation that would have occurred."

"But do we know anything more about the location of the bomb factory back near Maysville?" I asked.

"Maybe," White answered. "A local cop arrested a Middle Eastern guy in a New York rental car just north of Richmond a little while ago. He had a woman with him who claims to be his wife and an American citizen. We'd been watching them since they came into the state and intended to let them go so we could follow them. But they apparently had an argument at a restaurant and the guy was dragging her back to the car. A local cop happened to see it and busted the guy for assault."

"So they may not know they were being watched?" I asked.

"No, hopefully they don't know the cops suspect there's any more to this than a domestic quarrel. If that's the case we'll keep the guy, put a tracker on the car and turn the woman loose. We'll have all

152

the time we need to set up our tails on this. Just hang out. When we get set up I'll get back to you." I quickly agreed.

I told Burnside what White had told me. He suggested we make our way toward Interstate 95 since that was the route we'd probably use when we left Northern Virginia. I agreed and since we weren't in any hurry I followed Route 50, then Route 236, the ten miles through the suburban sprawl instead of using the Beltway.

Fairfax County was what the growth advocates in Maysville were going to get if they were not careful. While it does have jobs, good schools and a large tax base it also has bumper-to-bumper traffic and crime. Selfishly I thought even if Maysville did become like this it would be long after I was dead and gone.

Making my way slowly from red light to red light I was amazed at the ethnic diversity around me. All the signs in one strip shopping center appeared to be in Korean. It would be impossible for the local police to recognize potentially dangerous strangers. If the people who had set up their bomb factory in rural Virginia had been smarter they would have done it here instead. Of course, we had just busted a bunch of people who were using a building hidden among the sprawl as their base. Hopefully since September 11 no place was safe for terrorists. America had certainly lost some of its freedoms and rights to privacy in the past week. Hopefully we would get them back. But that didn't seem likely until things stopped blowing up.

We had still not heard from White when we got to the ramp for Interstate 95. Neither of us was hungry so we couldn't kill time eating as I usually did. Burnside said he knew of a video arcade close by. I drove there, and we spent an hour playing video games.

Burnside, to his embarrassment, beat me consistently at various games. Although my reflexes are at least as good as his, he understood the games better and obviously had more experience playing them. And after killing a man in a gun fight in my living room a few days before it was hard for me to take battling space invaders seriously. Of course, I probably would not have taken battling terrorists seriously a couple of weeks before either.

I was completely bored with video games by the time White called back.

Chapter 15

I am not by nature a patient person. It seemed as if we'd been waiting forever when the call finally came. I answered quickly, rushing out the closest door to take the call. I literally trotted across the huge parking lot, with Burnside a couple of steps behind, while I talked to White. I climbed into the car, where I didn't think anyone could overhear my conversation.

After apologizing for the delay White said, "I don't know exactly where we are with this, Ricky. The woman, Caroline Barns is her name, appears to be cooperating. But she says she doesn't know why her husband brought her with him to Virginia. We've run her social security number, and she's a citizen. She says her father is retired from the NYPD. His name is Frank Barns. Do you know him?"

"No," I replied. "But there are over 39,000 cops on the department plus all the retirees. Do you have someone going to see him?"

"I've asked the feds. But they're as overwhelmed and shorthanded as we are so I don't know when they'll get around to it. There's another problem. The woman doesn't have a driver's license so she can't take the car."

"What's she going to do?" I asked.

"She's on the phone now making arrangements. Hopefully someone will come pick her up, and we can follow them. I'll keep you posted, but it's going to be awhile before anything happens."

"Should Burnside and I start toward Richmond or hang around in Northern Virginia?" I asked.

"You may as well hang around until we know how this is going to break," he said.

"We'll wait to hear from you," I said. I told Burnside what White had said. Since we didn't know when we'd get back to Maysville we both got on our cell phones.

I don't know who Burnside called, but I first called Miss Mamie at the Maysville Police Department. She told me nothing out of the ordinary was happening in town. Chief Buford had called to say he had exhausted all the places he could think of to look for the bomb factory. Since he wasn't accomplishing anything anyway, he said he was spending the rest of the day running errands with his wife. He'd be back in touch tomorrow. I told Miss Mamie I'd be reachable on my cell phone if she needed me but didn't know when I would be back to

154

Maysville. Miss Mamie assured me she would take care of everything while I was gone.

Then I called my house. Sandra answered on the first ring. The new furniture was in place, and she was back at work collecting information on terrorists from the Internet. She didn't sound tired at all, but I still went through my "don't overdo it, you need to rest" speech. She asked me where I was and how my day had been going.

I resisted the impulse to brag and tell her Burnside and I had foiled a plot to blow up thousands of gallons of jet fuel, saving untold lives and millions of dollars in property damage. I told her the day had been uneventful and we were hanging out in Northern Virginia waiting to see what White wanted us to do. It was now nearly five in the afternoon so I told her I wouldn't be home for dinner but would call her later. It was now late Thursday afternoon, and, as far as I knew, the plot to set off a bunch of bombs in discount stores around the northeast on Saturday afternoon was still underway and on schedule. This was not a comforting thought.

"I love you, Ricky," she said before we disconnected.

"And I love you," I replied. Burnside was apparently through with his calls and leaning against the hood of the car when I dropped the cell phone onto the seat. He got in the car on the passenger's side.

"We've got a bunch of time to kill," I said. "Do you have any suggestions?"

"How about Potomac Mills?" he said. "Have you ever been there?"

I told him I hadn't. "It is supposed to be the biggest outlet mall in the world," he said. "And it is the biggest single attraction in Virginia. More people go there every year than to King's Dominion."

I asked for directions and soon we were sitting in the afternoon rush hour traffic on southbound Interstate 95. It took us nearly an hour to go the 12 miles to Potomac Mills. The traffic was as bad as any I had ever seen in New York City.

When we finally arrived I was amazed at the size of the shopping center complex. It was immense. Burnside told me it was even bigger than it looked. The huge building also went off in other directions in the back which I could not see from where we were. We parked a hundred yards from the main entrance and walked across the parking lot. It was another warm evening and I was sweating under my jacket. But I had learned my lesson about going out without my gun. I just suffered the discomfort without complaining.

Inside the mall was incredible. The first thing I saw was a huge food court with fast food restaurants all the way around. There was also a map showing the literally hundreds of stores and how to get to them. With nothing to do but kill time we walked for what seemed like miles. Everywhere there were people carrying backpacks as well as packages. Some were pushing piles of stuff on carts furnished by the mall. Any of them could have carried in a bomb, placed it somewhere and simply walked away. I didn't have a clue how anyone could protect against this happening.

It was after eight and we were sitting in the food court eating huge sundaes in waffle cones when White finally called again. I made my way outside as I talked to him.

"Sorry for the delay, Ricky," White said. "I think something is finally happening with the Barns woman. Of course, we still don't know whether she's cooperating or blowing smoke. She made a number of phone calls; we'll have the information on whom she called shortly. A woman deputy is driving her to the bus station in Fredericksburg and putting her on the bus. The deputy will try to find out where she's going and we have another woman cop waiting to get on the bus with her. If she goes back to New York we'll let the feds deal with her there. If she stays in Virginia or goes to DC we'll stay on her. So basically, unfortunately, you guys need to hang out a little longer before we'll know anything."

"What has she said?" I asked.

"Just that she didn't know why her husband was coming to Virginia," White said. "And she claims she doesn't know what he's been up to in New York either. She says they have an on again, off again marriage. She claims she hadn't seen him in a month before he showed up at her apartment and insisted she come on a trip with him. She insists she doesn't have a clue why he wanted her to come."

"Probably because they have been losing all those pairs of guys they have been sending," I said.

"Probably," White replied. "Of course the guys who are making the bombs most likely have some type of transportation. If we keep intercepting people on their way to them they will eventually transport the bombs themselves. I have deputies from all the sheriffs' departments in Central Virginia looking out for Middle Eastern looking men so hopefully we'll get them if they try to come out of the area as well. But you never know, so I think we have to keep looking for the bomb factory." I agreed and was telling White this when he interrupted me.

"Ricky, this is truly strange," he said. "I just got the numbers she called from the pay phone in the police station. One of them is the main number for the United States Department of Justice in Washington! Why would she call there?"

"Maybe she is already cooperating with the feds, and we're wasting our time here," I said.

"We're checking on that now. Can you stick around a while longer? The intelligence guys think maybe your background with the NYPD might be useful since her daddy is retired from The Job."

"I don't have the faintest idea what I can do back in Maysville anyway so I might as well hang out here."

White promised he would call back as soon as he knew anything. I don't really like to shop, and I had already eaten way too

156

much that day, so I just walked around with Burnside. Since I knew I would soon have to figure out how my department was going to police the new Maysville mall I used the time to try and learn something about shopping center security. I had identified many more problems than solutions when my cell phone rang again.

It was White. "Okay, the Barns woman is on the bus. She bought a ticket to Springfield so we'll want to follow her when she gets off there." I asked Burnside if he knew where the bus station was in Springfield. He nodded he did. He said it was ten minutes away. I told White. He said he was a little further away but should be there in half an hour. He said he'd see us there.

Since we had more time to kill, and it might be a long night sitting in a car somewhere, we went back to the "Books-A-Million" store; and I bought the unabridged tape version of John Grisham's "Painted House".

On the way back to the car I tossed Burnside the keys. He knew where we were going, and I didn't. We got back on Interstate 95 and headed north, back toward Washington. I was dialing Sandra on the cell phone as we were passing the huge tank farm at Newington. I shuddered to think what the scene would be here if the state police hadn't busted the terrorists on the nearby service road before they could fire a rocket. Sandra answered on the first ring. She asked what we'd been doing, and I told her we'd been at Potomac Mills.

"What did you buy me?" she asked.

Like any experienced husband, I quickly lied, "It's a surprise. You'll see what it is when I get home."

"When will you be home?" she asked.

"I don't know. We're going to meet White now in Springfield," I said. "I don't know how long I'll be tied up here. But I should be home before you wake up in the morning."

"I'll miss you, Ricky," she said. I told her I would miss her too. That was true. I was bone tired. We had spent a long day playing "cops and terrorists" and there was no telling when the game would be over. I was just too old for this anymore. If I wasn't going to quit maybe I should stick to making sure Maysville's crossing guards were where they were supposed to be when they were supposed to be. That was what the town actually paid me to do. I thought I should tell White this when I saw him. I wanted to go home. But, if they talked to the woman again, maybe my background with the NYPD would be helpful. I would stick it out the rest of this evening but decided I would beg off tomorrow. It wasn't my job to protect the world, just Maysville. And I hadn't been doing my job lately.

Burnside got off the Interstate at the exit for Springfield. We looped around past another huge shopping center, went under a bridge and came to the subway station complex. "The bus station is here with the subway," he said. We drove around a large parking garage, taking the "Kiss and Ride" lanes.

The bus station was a tiny building situated off to the right before we came to the subway station. There were several cars parked near it, apparently waiting for the next bus to arrive. More cars were stopped beyond it apparently waiting to pick up arriving subway passengers. I was looking for White's Plymouth when he came walking out of the parking garage on the other side of the road. He climbed into the back seat of my car.

After a quick greeting he said, "The bus won't be here for at least an hour and a half." Then to Burnside, "We need to go pick up pizza for everyone." He directed the young trooper back past the shopping center and across the Interstate to a collection of small businesses on the other side. We stopped in front of a small pizza parlor next to a McDonalds. White handed Burnside several bills and sent him inside to pick up the previously ordered food. "Great pizza," he said. "I used to eat here all the time when I was a road trooper."

While we were alone in the car White caught me up on the day's events. "After what happened with the guys you were following we decided to take the other two cars before they could set up," White said. "They both had the same kind of rocket launchers as your perps. We were lucky and took them all without any problems.

"The feds are on the place where we were this morning. They've been grabbing up everyone who leaves. The other offices in the complex are clearing out for the weekend. The feds are planning on going in to get whoever is still there sometime before morning."

Burnside came back with the pizza boxes. White directed him to make another stop for drinks at a convenience store around the corner. While he was in the store White continued. "I also talked to the guys in Petersburg. The phone calls have dried up completely. No one is answering any of the phones the prisoners have numbers for anymore. Apparently whoever is in charge has written those guys off and cut all contact with them. Hopefully at least some of the prisoners are pissed at being abandoned. They plan on interrogating them all again starting first thing tomorrow."

I nodded my understanding and asked, "Do you have anything new on the bomb factory back in Maysville? Tomorrow is Friday, one day before Zlad said the bombs were supposed to be set off."

White shook his head, "There's nothing new on that front," he said. "But hopefully we have gotten all the guys they sent to pick up the bombs so they haven't moved them yet. Maybe this woman we are waiting for tonight will lead us to them."

"How likely is that?" I asked.

"More likely than I thought when I talked to you before," White said. "She has been arrested several times in New York at pro Palestinian rallies. The feds have a thick file on her. Nothing in her past indicates she has done anything violent, but you never know. These things have a way of escalating."

"Hopefully she'll lead us to the bomb factory tonight," I said.

158

"But if she doesn't, I have got to get back to Maysville anyway. I haven't been doing my job for the town, and I'm worried about my wife."

White nodded his understanding, "How is she dealing with the shootout in your living room?" he asked.

"She hasn't mentioned it," I said. "And that can't be good."

White was nodding his agreement when Burnside came out of the store with a bag full of bottled drinks. He drove us back to the subway station. White directed him through the parking garage until we found the rest of the group waiting for the woman to arrive.

Half a dozen men and two women were standing around in the mostly deserted parking garage. Burnside and White carried the pizza boxes and bag of drinks to the open side door of a minivan. It was unlikely anyone would be tipped off by our strange tailgate party. I was still full from my last meal so I stood around watching the others eat.

One of the men was monitoring the tactical frequency on the police radio with an earpiece. He told us the bus was about half an hour away and should arrive just a little after its ten o'clock scheduled time. The picnic finished and people began to get into place to follow whoever picked up the woman when she got off the bus.

White and I found a spot on the fourth floor of the parking garage where we could easily see the bus station. We were well concealed in the shadows. There were already several cars waiting. White said one of them, an old Pontiac, was one of his guys who would pick up the female trooper who was on the bus with the subject. As time for the bus to arrive got closer more cars arrived and parked to wait.

At about ten minutes after ten the bus arrived. The passengers were getting off on the side away from us so we couldn't see them until they came around in front of the bus. I moved forward to see the first young woman who came around. White told me she was his trooper. As soon as she was in the Pontiac she reported on the radio. The woman we wanted was wearing a dark jacket and did not have any luggage. A minute later a woman fitting the description came around the bus. She stopped by the parked cars looking for whoever was picking her up. Apparently she did not see them and began pacing up and down, looking in the direction a car would have to come from.

She was still there alone when nearly all the waiting cars had left. White told his people in the Pontiac to move out before she became suspicious of the car. They pulled out and a couple of minutes later an old, battered white Miata, with its top up, arrived. The woman quickly got into the car and it pulled away.

White was giving orders to his people over the radio. One of his units would be pulling out of the far side of the garage as the sports car came around. One of the guys standing farther down in front of the subway station read off the tag as the little car streaked by. He also told us the driver appeared to be a young woman.

The three of us ran back to my car. Burnside drove while we listened to the teams tailing the car on the police radio. We came around the shopping center again and back on to Interstate 95. The traffic was fairly light this late at night.

We were not part of the group actually following the little car. These cops knew their way around in Northern Virginia as well as the proper techniques for following a car. We would simply monitor the radio and meet them wherever the subject finally ended up.

The back and forth talk was constant on tactical frequency. "She's going north on 95."

"She's getting over to the left so she's not, not, repeat, not, going to follow 95 around toward Alexandria."

"She's getting on the beltway going west. Repeat, west on 495. She is flying."

White broke in to ask, "Has she made the tail?"

One of the units responded, "I don't think so. I think she just drives like a maniac. There is no way to get anyone in front of her."

"She's still going west."

Another voice broke in, "Boss, the car is registered to a Dana Addington on Virginia Avenue in McLean."

White answered, "Find out everything you can about her."

"Roger that."

We were also heading west on 495 several miles behind the little car and the units following it. A couple of minutes later we heard, "She's getting off onto Route 66 going east. Repeat 66 east bound." This was not good news for me. They were going away from Maysville and the bomb factory.

Burnside was just turning on to Route 66 when a voice on the radio said, "Boss, I have some additional info on the driver. I'll call on your cell phone." All our ears perked up, wondering what he didn't want to say on the tactical radio frequency.

White's phone rang. I could only hear his end of the conversation. After a couple of "uhuhs" he said, "Damn. Get on the feds right now. Find out who her boss is and where we can reach him." White disconnected from the call and said to me, "The woman who picked her up is an attorney with the United States Department of Justice."

"What does that mean?" I asked.

"Beats me," he replied. "Hopefully the feds will track down her boss and we can ask him."

A voice on the radio said, "She's getting off on Westmoreland, toward McLean. Catch up guys, we are going to be in neighborhoods from here on. Catch up."

"I've got a map," said another voice. "It looks like she is heading for the Virginia Avenue address."

"She's turning right onto Williamsburg." We were just

160

getting off Route 66.

"She's turning left just before the top of the hill."

"That's the most direct way to the Virginia Avenue address," said another voice. "Give them room." We were turning onto Williamsburg."

A minute later we heard, "They are stopping in front of the Virginia Avenue house. We're going on by."

'We've got them," said another voice. "We're turning down a side street before the house. Both women are going into the house."

"Somebody check if you can see into the house from the rear," White said.

"We're on it, Boss," came a voice.

We followed the route the Miata had taken. Two of the other cars were parked in front of a water tower when we got there. A cop jumped out of one of the cars and came over as soon as we pulled up. He pointed down the street to his left, "The house is about a hundred yards down that street, Boss, just over that little rise," he said to White. "Mary and Bobby can see it from where they are parked. Ronny is trying to see if he can get behind it and see anything." White nodded his agreement with the setup.

"Let's get out of here in case anyone else shows up," White said.

"Go to the bottom of the hill and turn right," the cop said. "There is a convenience store in a little shopping center on the right." All three cars moved out together.

At the store everyone dispersed. Burnside and the occupants of the other cars went inside. The clerk looked Middle Eastern to me. Lately everyone who wasn't blonde looked Middle Eastern to me. White went across the parking lot, sat on a brick wall, and started dialing on his cell phone. I got out, leaning against the car, I called Sandra. "What are you doing?" I asked when she answered.

"Watching the news and waiting for you to come home," she said. "Where are you?"

"We're still in Northern Virginia sitting on a house," I said. "I don't know how much longer we'll be but I should be home before morning."

"Are you okay to drive? You've had a long day."

'Burnside is driving."

"I forgot you have a Tonto now so you can be the Lone Ranger," she said.

I laughed, "I'll give you a silver bullet when I get home."

"Is that a euphemism for something dirty?" she asked.

"Count on it," I said. We swapped "I love yous" and disconnected.

Burnside was standing there offering me a Diet Dr. Pepper. I took it. White had finished his phone call and came over to my car. I popped the trunk and went to my cigarette stash. White took one, but

Burnside declined. I lit our cigarettes.

"Okay," White said. "The Addington woman is a civil attorney with the Justice Department. She's working on some Indian land case from out west somewhere. I don't know what she has to do with these Middle Eastern folks. The bureau is picking up her boss as we speak and bringing him here."

"What are we going to do?" I asked.

"Knock on her door, with her boss, and ask her what she is involved in here," White said.

"Sounds like a plan," I said.

One of the other cops came over to White. He had a radio earpiece in his ear. "Boss, Ronny says she has motion sensor lights in the back of the house so he can't get close enough to look inside."

White nodded, "Tell them just to sit on the house and make sure they don't leave. We're going to knock on the door in a little while. I think most of you can go home for the night as soon as we're inside." The cop nodded and went to tell the others.

We had only been hanging out in the parking lot for about 15 minutes when two Arlington County cop cars pulled up from different directions. White pulled his badge from his pocket and held it up for the driver of the closest patrol car to see. He said something into his microphone. The second car went on its way. After a brief conversation White and the Arlington cop went into the store together.

I could see them talking to the clerk. In couple of minutes White and the Arlington cop were back. They shook hands. The local cop got back into his cruiser and drove away. White came over laughing, "The clerk thought we looked suspicious hanging around in the parking lot so he called the cops."

"I was wondering if he was a terrorist," I said.

"It's the world we live in, Ricky," White said. "Let me call the feds and see where this woman's boss is." He walked away punching numbers into his cell phone. I stuck my hand into my jacket pocket, found my cigarettes, and smoked another one.

White was still on the phone when a heavy duty Ford with three men in it pulled up in front of the convenience store. The two in the front were obviously cops. The one in the back was apparently the woman's supervisor at DOJ. He did not appear to be happy about meeting with us in a parking lot so late on a week night.

He was a red faced, grossly overweight man still dressed for work. When he got out of the car White and I went over to talk with him. Before either of us could even introduce ourselves he said, "What has Ms. Addington gotten herself involved in this time?"

In a calm voice White said, "We don't know that she has gotten herself involved in anything. We had a surveillance going on a woman from New York. When she got off a bus in Springfield Ms. Addington picked the woman up and drove them both to her house. When I learned Ms. Addington works for DOJ I contacted the FBI. I don't know who was involved in the decision making process at the FBI but it was decided to bring you into this."

"What are you after the other woman for doing?" he asked.

I could see White deciding what to tell this guy. The truth is mostly irrelevant in this investigation. I knew White would tell him what would do us the most good.

"The woman she picked up is married to a Middle Eastern man who was arrested earlier today. She was with him when he was arrested. There was no reason to hold her, but we decided to see where she'd go and who she might lead us to."

"And she led you to Ms. Addington?" he asked. White nodded his head. "Does this have anything to do with 9-11?"

"Only peripherally," White said. "Any Middle Eastern men who come to the attention of law enforcement these days are getting a close look. What can you tell about Ms. Addington? She's a DOJ lawyer right?"

"She is one of a dozen lawyers working on an Indian land case in Arizona," the supervisor said. "It's a case that's been going on for twenty years and will probably go on for another twenty. She is a competent lawyer for what she does."

"Do you know of any connection she has with any Islamic groups?" White asked.

"No, and the DOJ does background checks on all its employees as well as regularly scheduled polygraphs." I could not help thinking about the recent case of FBI counterintelligence agent Robert Hanssen spying for the Russians, but I didn't mention it.

"Why exactly am I here?" he asked.

"Since Ms Addington works for DOJ we decided to take a direct approach with her. In a little while, you and I and Harris are going to knock on her door. I think she will be more forthcoming and cooperative with you there."

The supervisor nodded, "I need to talk to my boss before I do that," he said.

"Can you get him on the phone right now?" White asked.

"It's awfully late for me to call him at home," the supervisor said.

"Fine," White said. "We will just do it without you and put in the report you refused to cooperate. If we arrest her the DOJ can read about it in the *Washington Post*."

"I don't think you understand my position," the supervisor said huffily.

"And I don't think you understand ours," White said firmly. "We are chasing terrorists, and we are going to knock on your employee's door in the next few minutes. This is not going to drag out for twenty years. Every minute counts here. If you want to go with us, fine. If you don't, you can leave now."

I could see this midlevel bureaucrat's mind working. Which

163

outcome would be better for him personally was the question foremost in his mind. "I'll try to call my supervisor," he said.

"You've got 15 minutes," White said. "Then we're going." The man turned away, pulling out his cell phone. White looked at me and shrugged. It was hard for me not to laugh even though this was extremely serious.

"Want me to beat on him until he agrees to help?" I asked sarcastically when the other man was out of hearing range.

"That's Plan B," White replied. "Let's have another cigarette and then we're going." I gave him a cigarette, took one for myself, and lit both of them. We stood there watching the DOJ man talk on the phone.

When the cigarettes were finished White said, "Let's do it." I told Burnside to hang out with the guys who were not going into the house until I came out. Then White and I started toward my car. The DOJ man quickly finished his phone call and came to join us before I got the car started. He got into the back seat without being asked.

He didn't mention his phone call and neither did White or I as we drove the short distance to Ms. Addington's house. I parked in front. It was a warm night and both White and I tossed our jackets into the back seat of my car. Maybe our guns would add to the intimidation factor. We walked up to the door. Lights were still on in the small house. White knocked firmly on the door. It was opened with the safety chain on. "Who is it?" a woman inside said.

"Police," White said firmly. We both held up our badges for her to see through the crack in the door. The DOJ man stood behind us not speaking.

"Just a minute," the woman's voice said as she closed the door. I had assumed she would open it immediately but there was some delay. I could hear a toilet flushing somewhere in he house. When she opened the door again she had her DOJ credentials open in her right hand. "What can I do for you officer?" she asked. There was a sweet smell in the air.

"We would like to come inside and talk with you and your guest," White said.

"I don't know," she said. "What is this about?"

"We don't care about the marijuana," White said, stepping aside so she could see her boss standing on the porch with us. "We want to talk to you and Ms. Barns about her husband."

Chapter 16

Dana Addington was completely ignoring White and me while staring at her DOJ supervisor. I realized I didn't know his name. But his presence was certainly having an impact on his subordinate. I'd been concerned she would play lawyer games with us out of habit. But she appeared to be more interested in keeping her job than in showing off her legal knowledge at this point.

She reluctantly stepped aside and allowed all three of us to enter the living room of her small house. The décor was a hodgepodge of old furniture. The sweet smell of marijuana was thick in the air, adding to the college apartment atmosphere of the place. I didn't see the Barns woman anywhere. Then I heard a toilet flush. She was probably getting rid of the evidence. We all just stood there without anyone saying anything until Caroline Barns came out of a bathroom in the rear of the house, past the kitchen.

"I don't understand why you are here," Ms. Addington said to White.

"We are here to find out what your involvement is in a terrorist plot to manufacture and detonate bombs. You, an employee of the United States Department of Justice, picked up a suspected member of the terrorist gang at the bus station in Springfield and brought her to your home. When we knocked on your door to ask you about this the two of you were smoking marijuana and plotting who knows what."

It was Barns who spoke first. "I was questioned by the police earlier today and cleared," she said.

"No, ma'am," White replied calmly. "You were questioned by the police earlier today, then allowed to leave so you could be followed, hopefully leading us to other members of the terrorist gang. You led us to Ms. Addington."

"Wait a minute," Addington said. "All I did was pick up a college friend at the bus station and bring her to my house. I am an attorney with the United States Department of Justice after all." I could tell her nameless supervisor wanted to interject himself into the conversation. White gave him a withering look, and he thought better of it.

"And Robert Hanssen was an FBI agent who was spying for the Russians," White said. "You can either start cooperating here, or we can all go to the police station." Turning to remove his handcuffs from his back pocket White looked at me. This was my cue to play "good cop" to his "bad cop".

I focused my attention on Caroline Barns while I said to White, "Let's not be hasty here, Captain. Things are not always as they appear. Let's at least give them a chance to explain before we take them to jail."

Both women looked scared. Addington, as a lawyer, knew she didn't have to talk to us, that we had no grounds to arrest either of them. But we were not treating her like a lawyer. We were treating her like a perp and chances were pretty good she was scared enough to react like one.

But Barns spoke first. She was an overweight young woman, with a blotchy complexion, dressed in a shapeless black dress she mistakenly thought concealed her weight problem. "I don't understand," she said. "I cooperated with the police earlier today. I told them everything I know about my worthless husband."

"I'm sorry," I said, "but you need to tell it to us too."

She looked at me with a mixture of fear and annoyance. "Maybe I should get a lawyer," she said. "My dad spent his working life on the NYPD and I grew up around cops but . . ."

The word "but" hung heavily in the air. "I spend most of my life on the NYPD too," I said quickly. I hated to mislead her but we didn't have a lot of time before the bombs were scheduled to go off so I continued," I'm sure your dad would want you to cooperate with us."

"Who are you?" she asked skeptically. "If you are on the NYPD why are you here?"

"My name is Rick Harris," I said. "I was on the NYPD but I retired a couple of years ago. Now I'm a police chief in Virginia."

"Rick Harris," she said with a furrowed brow. "Are you the Rick Harris who got shot on New Year's Eve?"

Surprised, I nodded that I was. "My dad was one of the first cops on the scene after the shooting," she continued. "He got a commendation for holding his overcoat against your bullet wounds until the ambulance got there."

This was not happy news from the "isn't it a small world" department for me. From the corner of my eye I saw White was giving me an exasperated look. He knew as well as I did that I was not going to jam up the daughter of the guy who saved my life. My mind immediately went to work on a plan which would get us the information we needed while leaving Caroline Barns out of any possible legal repercussions. If I could question her alone I would simply forget to include anything dangerous to her in the report. I didn't want witnesses, so I quickly suggested, "Why don't you call your father and ask him what you should do?"

She still looked skeptical and I could tell she dreaded the thought of telling him she was in trouble with the law again. "I'll talk to him if you'd like," I quickly added.

This seemed to give her the needed push to make the call. She nodded her agreement and picked up a cordless phone from a nearby table. She also picked up a large purse and started digging in it. "Let me find my phone card," she said. Dana Addington said, "Just call on my bill." Caroline Barns nodded appreciatively, put the purse down, and dialed a number. It was well after midnight by this point.

I was sure she would rather take a beating than make this phone call. But she did it. After a number of rings the phone was answered.

"Daddy," she said in a tiny voice, "I'm sorry to call you so late, but the police have me again, and I didn't know what else to do." I could hear the sound of her father talking from the other end but couldn't make out the words. Caroline Barns seemed to get smaller, and younger, as she listened.

"I know what you think about Omar, Daddy, and I am beginning to agree with you; but he is not my immediate problem. The police just released me earlier so they could follow me and see who I lead them to. My college friend Dana Addington picked me up at the bus station, and the police followed us back to her house. They say they are going to arrest both of us for terrorism."

She paused, and I could hear her father talking again. When he ran out of breath she said, "I have cooperated with them, Daddy, but I don't know anything they want to know." The murmur from the phone was louder.

"Yes, Daddy, I understand all that. But the reason I'm calling is one of the police officers here is Rick Harris." After a pause she continued, "Yes, Daddy, that Rick Harris. Will you talk to him?" She listened again then handed me the phone.

"Officer Barns," I said. "This is Rick Harris. I understand you saved my life when I got shot. I want to tell you how much I appreciate what you did that night."

"All I did was slow down your bleeding a little until the ambulance got there," Barnes said. "It wasn't heroic. It was just what I was trained to do. But that was a long time ago. My daughter is what's important now. What do you want from her?"

He was a fellow cop, and one I owed big time regardless of what he said, so I decided to tell him the truth. "We think there is a bomb factory operating somewhere in Virginia. We think your daughter's husband came down here to pick up some of the bombs they have made to transport them back to the northeast. We need to know everything she knows about her husband and his associates. And we need to know it as quickly as possible."

Barns said, "I wouldn't put anything past the dirtbag she's married to, but I'm sure my daughter isn't involved with any bombs. She is too unassertive for her own good."

"I don't think she is involved in the plot," I quickly reassured him, "but she probably knows things we need to know. Time is running out, and people are going to start getting blown up if we don't find those bombs soon."

There was a long pause, "Can you get them to put off questioning her until I can get down there?" he asked.

"No," I said truthfully. "I really have very little influence here. I'm out of my jurisdiction and once they take her into custody I'll be completely out of the matter. I honestly believe I am your best advantage here so I think we need to do something now while I can still help your daughter. You saved my life, and I'm not going to let anyone jam up your daughter if I can help it. But once they take her into custody I can't help her anymore. Remember I owe you my life."

"My daughter is more important to me than my life," Barns said. There was a lengthy pause, followed by a sigh, "Let me talk to her and I'll tell her to cooperate."

I hated to do this to White, but I had to quickly prioritize my obligations so I said, "I think they will agree to that. Hold on and let me ask." I held the phone away from my mouth but where Barnes could still hear what I said, "He says he'll tell her to cooperate. But only with me, in private with no record made of what she says." White scowled at me. "It's either that or she will remain silent and wait for a lawyer. What do you want to do?" I could hear Barns chuckle softly through the phone. I had reinforced his faith in the notion members, past and present, of the NYPD stick together against all outsiders, cops or not. Nowhere is the Blue Wall stronger than the NYPD. White reluctantly nodded his agreement. He did not appear to be happy with me.

"Okay," I said into the phone. "They have agreed to your terms. I'll give the phone to your daughter so you can tell her to cooperate with me."

Caroline Barns took the phone back from me. She said, "Yes, Daddy" a couple of more times before disconnecting. Then she just stood there looking trustingly at me.

One of the realities of being a cop is that the job often requires you to lie to people. The U.S. Supreme Court has repeatedly held lying to suspects is an acceptable law enforcement technique. I have lied to many suspects in my career. I have made promises I never had any intention of keeping to get them to tell me what I needed to know. And I have lied frequently since we started chasing terrorists a week ago. I knew I would not lie to the daughter of the cop who had saved my life. But I also knew I held this young woman's life in my hands as surely as if I was pointing my pistol at her head. And I knew I would protect her at all costs to myself personally. Whether or not I would let the bombers escape with their bombs to avoid jamming this young woman up with the law was a dilemma I sincerely hoped I would not be forced to face.

I needed a place to talk privately with Caroline Barns. First I considered the deck I could see through the glass doors beyond the kitchen. But I didn't know where White's people were lurking outside so I thought better of it. The only safe option I could think was my car. I took Caroline Barnes by the arm, saying to White, "We'll be back in a bit," as I guided her toward the front door. She appeared to trust me completely and looked relieved to get away from the others. The DOJ guy had yet to say a word, but he was the most intimidating presence in the living room.

We walked to my car which was parked in front. Burnside suddenly appeared from a car parked on the dark side street in front of the house. He was waiting with some of White's other people in another car. I waved to him in a dismissive manner, and he got back into the other car.

I went around my car, opening the front passenger side door for Caroline Barns. She got in. I walked around and entered through the driver's door.

I suddenly realized how tired I was as I sank into the soft leather seat. It had been a long day and I was no longer a young cop who could run indefinitely on adrenalin and bad coffee. I moved the seat back to give me more room but heroically resisted the impulse to recline it for comfort. Hopefully this young woman was going to provide me with important information and I didn't want to fall asleep while she was doing it. I started the car, turning on the air conditioning. It was getting cooler outside but I thought if I was cold I could stay awake.

Caroline Barns sat up straight, giving me her undivided attention. I dug into my pants pocket for the crushed pack of cigarettes and offered her one. She shook her head, then dug her own pack from her large purse. I lit our cigarettes with my disposable lighter and cracked both front windows.

Eventually I had to say something, so I said, "You heard what I said to your father?" She nodded. "Okay, I owe your father my life so I promised him, and I'll promise you, that I will do everything I can to keep you out of this mess. But I need to know everything you know about what your husband and his friends are up to. People's lives depend on it."

"I don't really know much about what he has been doing," she said. "I haven't seen much of him for the last month or so. I don't really know any of his friends. He is very secretive."

"Just tell me what you can," I said patiently. "How did you get together with him in the first place?"

"I was doing some volunteer tutoring for English as a second language students," she said in a childlike voice. "Omar was one of my first students. He's very bright and didn't really need much help, but he was in the program. I was there really to meet somebody. Now, I think he was there for the same reason." There was a long pause. I didn't know what to say so I didn't say anything.

"I know I'm overweight and not very attractive. But I persuaded myself that Arab men look at women differently than

American men do, and Omar could appreciate my inner beauty. He's so handsome, and I was so proud to show him off to my friends from the neighborhood. He was so attentive before we got married. Afterwards he stayed gone for days and when he was there he was mean to me. I think he just wanted an America citizen he could marry so he could stay here, and I was it. Now you tell me he's involved with the terrorists. I wish I had never met the man."

I wondered how true that was. Once when I was a young uniform cop I pulled a husband off the wife he was choking to death. We were still struggling when she got her breath back. I was beating on her husband so she started hitting me with a broom!

"What does Omar do for a living?" I asked.

"He works in a pizza place on Long Island with a bunch of other Saudis. He delivers pizza for them. But I think they are involved in something illegal using the pizza parlor as a front."

But when some women do finally wise up they go to the other extreme and accuse their husbands of being involved in the Kennedy assassination. I wanted the dirt on this guy but didn't want to get suckered into wasting valuable time on charges that weren't true. "Why do you think that?" I asked.

"For various reasons," she said. "For one thing he always has a lot of money even though he never gives me any of it for the rent. Once I found some expensive looking jewelry in one of his pockets. And another time I found a beat up pizza box in the trunk of his car. I thought it was trash and was going to throw it away. But it was heavy so I opened it. Inside were two pistols. I think the pizza parlor is a front for a bunch of different criminal enterprises."

"Are all the people involved in the pizza parlor Arabs?" I asked.

She nodded, "All Omar's friends are Arabs."

"Do you think they are committing crimes to finance militant Islamic activities?" I asked.

She laughed at this. "Omar isn't much of a Muslim. I've never known him to go to a mosque. These guys look to Tony Soprano more than to Osama bin Laden as a role model."

I must have looked skeptical because she asked, "Do you remember the "Pizza Connection" cases in New York?"

I nodded that I did. The Pizza Connection was a massive drug conspiracy back when I was a young cop. Organized crime families, both domestic and from Sicily, were using a bunch of pizza parlors all over the country to sell heroin and launder money. It was a huge case. The famous "French Connection" case involved less than 100 pounds of heroin. The "Pizza Connection" case involved over a metric ton of heroin.

Both New York Mayor Rudy Giuliani and former FBI Director Louis Freeh had made their names as mob busting prosecutors on the case. It was also the beginning of the end for the Italian crime

170

families in New York. Large numbers of them went to jail and, probably more importantly, many of their soldiers flipped and testified against their associates. This was the end of *omerta*, the supposed "code of silence" in the American Mafia.

"Omar is fascinated by the Pizza Connection," she continued. "He has a bunch of books on the cases. They're the only books I have ever seen him read. I think he and his friends are using the books as a "how to" to do the same kind of things."

"Do you know why he came to Virginia?" I asked.

"Not really," she said. "He doesn't discuss his business with me. But I think he has come in the past to buy guns to resell in New York. There is a big flea market near Fredericksburg, and I think he buys pistols from some guys he meets there." This appeared to be another dead end as far as the bomb factory was concerned. The NYPD might be interested in crimes in the city, and the feds might be interested in the guns in other less hectic times; but the information didn't help me any at the moment.

I saw White and the DOJ guy coming out of the house and decided to wrap up my conversation with Caroline Barns just as my cell phone rang. It was after one in the morning. I grabbed my jacket from the back seat and dug out the phone.

It was Chief Buford. "Ricky," he said calmly, "I found the bomb factory."

"Hold on a second," I said as calmly as I could. Then to Caroline Barns, "I have to go. I will do all I can with the Virginia cops for you." I gave her one of my business cards. "Tell your father to call me if he wants to. But I need to go now." I got out of the car and motioned frantically to White. He hurried toward me.

"Sorry, Chief," I said into the phone. "I'm with Captain White now. What did you say?"

I could hear Buford was trying to maintain his calm as I held the phone away from my ear so White could hear too. "I said I found the bomb factory. Early this evening I dropped my wife off over toward Charlottesville to stay with a lady from the church who's sick. It wasn't dark yet so I came back by a round about way, just killing time. Well, I came to an intersection where an old friend named Cody Wilson used to keep a store. He's been dead for years. But I got to thinking about Cody and just decided to go by the old place."

I was getting impatient with the old man and could sense White was as well. But it was probably best to let him tell us in his own way, not that I seemed to have any choice in the matter. I did try to gently hurry him along a bit. "And that's where you found the bomb factory?" I asked.

"Well, first I found a van with three Middle Eastern looking men parked in front of the old store," he said. "They were standing outside the van with a map trying to call somebody on a cell phone. Cell phones don't work that far out in the sticks so I stopped and asked if I could help them.

"I was in my pickup, not wearing my uniform. I guess they thought I was just a harmless old fart. So they showed me their map." Buford chuckled at this. "I couldn't believe it. There was a big red X marking where they were going! And they were showing it to me!"

I couldn't help but join in his laughter. If news reports were to be believed brilliant terrorist masterminds had met in cities throughout the world and hatched intricate plots to attack America. They had provided millions of dollars, building a vast infrastructure to facilitate follow up attacks after 9-11. Many of the world's intelligence agencies were spending vast amounts of time and money tracking al Qaeda but the attack planning apparently slipped by them.

Then one of the highly trained terrorists showed a map of the secret bomb factory to a cop! Were I a more philosophical person it would cause me to wonder whose side God was actually on in this holy war. But I had no time for metaphysics. I just wanted to catch these guys before they killed anyone else.

"So where is the bomb factory," I asked trying to hurry this along.

"It's over between Walton's Corner and Charlottesville outside the area where we were searching," he said calmly. "Don't worry I have it pinpointed. Ari and some of his boys are on it. Nobody is going to leave."

"Ari's on it?" White asked over my shoulder.

"Yeah, when I couldn't get you on the phone I called Ari," Buford said, "I guess I'm still not a fan of the feds even in this new era of cooperation." Once again law enforcement had been unable to react quickly enough. It had come down to the Israeli spooks to save the day. But when I thought about the way Ari and his boys had handled the shootout in my living room I figured it was just as well.

"But you found the bomb factory?" I asked, again.

"Let me finish," Buford said, impatient with me. "I thought about drawing down on them and arresting them but there were three of them and I'm not as young as I once was. Plus I couldn't cuff them or transport them anyway. So I just looked at their map.

"What they'd done was turn off the main road too soon. Had they gone another mile they would have been on the right road, and I would never have seen them. I told them I lived over the way they needed to go so if they'd follow me I get them where they were going."

Buford was chuckling again, "I'm sure these boys were laughing about this dumbass old fool helping them destroy America. Anyway, I took them a roundabout way to the farm marked on the map. I found the driveway but couldn't see the house and other buildings back from the road in the trees. The driver honked his horn and waved when he turned into the driveway. They could never find their way back out the way I took them in.

"Then I was in a quandary. I didn't want to leave the place

but I knew I needed help. I got back out on the main road where my cell phone would work and called the local sheriff. I've known him all his life and he came out to meet me. While I was waiting on him I started trying to get you and White. When I couldn't get y'all I called a number I had for Ari. A couple of his boys were here shortly after the sheriff arrived. We've got everything under control.

"Where are you and White?" he asked.

"In Northern Virginia, McLean," I replied. White was motioning for his guys to come to us. The unmarked car pulled up and Burnside jumped out and joined us.

White, pulling his note pad from his pocket, said, "Get a number where I can call Buford back and let's get rolling." Buford apparently heard him and reeled off a very long phone number. "Ari's guys gave me this satellite phone I'm calling you on," he said. I noticed Burnside also wrote it down for us.

White was in the front passenger seat of a state police car and Burnside was behind the wheel of mine. I hurried around the passenger side while telling Buford I was getting off the phone so White could call him. As the two cop cars pulled out in sprays of gravel I noticed the DOJ man standing at the edge of the street looking bewildered. I don't know where Caroline Barns went.

The two car caravan went back through the neighborhood and onto Interstate 66 with blue lights flashing. Once on the highway the driver of White's car picked up speed. Burnside stayed right behind him. The landscape flashed by in the darkness. There were office buildings and shopping centers on both sides of the road, urban sprawl. Many of them were lit up even in the middle of the night. The blue lights from both our speeding cars parted the sparse traffic and bounced back from the cars we streaked past.

Even at this speed it would take nearly two hours to get where we were going. I was sure White was busy on the phone coordinating whatever needed to be coordinated. Next week's schedule for the crossing guards in Maysville had certainly been taken care of by Miss Mamie so I had nothing urgent to coordinate myself. I couldn't even call Sandra at this hour. It had been nearly twenty hours since I got out of bed Thursday morning so I closed my eyes and tried to sleep.

Chapter 17

I awoke with a start from what I first thought was a nightmare. Men with guns were in my living room threatening to kill my wife Sandra. Then I remembered.

Outside the landscape on both sides of the road had changed into one of total blackness. There was no other traffic, and the road appeared to be narrower than when I'd fallen asleep. We had left the Interstate behind and were now on a two lane byway through the center of Virginia, still traveling at a high rate of speed. I could still see the blue lights on the state police car in front of us. At least one other car was now behind us as well. Occasionally the blue lights from the high speed convoy would bounce back from some reflective surface hidden in the roadside darkness.

When I stretched and yawned Burnside saw I was awake and said, "We'll be there is another few minutes, Chief." I looked at my watch and it was ten minutes before four, the part of the night I always hated when I'd worked midnights in New York. It would be a couple of more hours before the sun came up bringing the new day. It's the time of the night when old people die in their beds.

"Do you know where exactly we're going?" I asked.

"No, I haven't heard a word since we left McLean," Burnside replied. I thought about asking if he were still okay to drive but there was nothing I could do if he said he wasn't since we were flying through the countryside at the moment. I thought about calling Sandra, but there was nothing I could tell her and I didn't want to wake her anyway. Fidgeting, with nothing useful to do I called the Maysville police dispatcher. He answered on the first ring.

I identified myself, and he assured me everything was quiet in town. The dispatcher had a long list of calls for me to return. Several were from Chief Buford from earlier in the evening. More were routine and could be returned on Monday. Sandra had called around one, asking I call her back on her cell phone regardless of what time it was. I quickly cut the dispatcher off and called my wife.

She answered in a sleepy voice on the second ring. I started the conversation with my usual apology, "Darling, I'm sorry I didn't call but I got hung up and . . ."

"I know," she said. "It's okay. I was just lonesome and wanted to talk to you. Where are you?"

"We're on the way back to meet with Chief Buford. There

have been some developments in the case."

"That's good," she said. I knew she wanted details but wouldn't ask. "When will I see you?"

"Later today I hope. Are you at the Widow's?"

"Yes, it was either spend the night at his place or he insisted on sleeping on our couch with his pistol. It was easier to come here. And breakfast will be a lot better."

I laughed. "I promise our lives will get back to normal soon. Hopefully this mess is winding itself up, and I can get back to staying in town like Andy Taylor."

"I can hear you are in the car. Are you okay to drive?"

I laughed again, "I don't drive. I'm driven. Burnside is driving, and I actually just woke up from a nap."

"Well you are getting along in years," she said.

"I realize that more every day," I said. "I love you and will be home as soon as I can."

"We can take a nap," she said in a sexy voice before hanging up. I felt old, tired and sincerely wished I was at home in bed with my wife where, it could be reasonably argued, I belonged.

I was far past tired, seriously considering going home. It was unlikely the operation's success would depend on my participation. The terrorists were not in my town after all. They were not my responsibility, and in fact I was shirking my responsibility by not being in Maysville doing the job I was being paid to do. But this was the most exciting thing that had happened during my long career in law enforcement, and I knew full well that I wouldn't miss it for anything.

As we sped through the night I broke another of my self-imposed rules. I dug into my jacket pocket, found a cigarette and lit it. I had never smoked in the car before tonight with Caroline Barns. I cracked the window to let the smoke out. The wind shrieked into the car making conversation impossible.

Before I finished the cigarette the convoy began to slow down. The cop lights on the car in front went off. Burnside quickly turned ours off as well. The caravan slowed down more as it turned right onto an even narrower two lane road which was totally dark. I didn't have a clue where we were. I asked Burnside, since he had grown up in the area, but he said he didn't know either.

We slowly made our way down the narrow road for a mile or so until we came to a medium sized, industrial building on the left. Faint lights were visible through several small windows. As White's car turned into the driveway toward the building a vehicle sized door in front began to slowly open, lighting up the driveway. Burnside followed White's car inside the building. The car behind us came in as well.

As soon as the third car cleared the doorway, the heavy door came back down. I got out of the car, stretched and looked around. The building had apparently been an auto repair shop not long ago.

Work benches lined the walls, and a lift was standing in a back corner.

There were several cars already parked in the building. A dozen men were doing various things when we arrived. The largest group was crowded around a large map spread out on a table. I recognized some of them from the meeting I had attended the previous Saturday. It seemed like much longer ago to me, but it had been less than a week. I didn't know any of their names.

Ari was also there. I knew I would never forget him, even though I was probably supposed to do so. He had saved Sandra's life, and I owed him much more than I did Officer Barns who had merely saved mine.

Ari was over on what I assumed was the south side of the building pointing the small dish of a satellite phone out an open window. Chief Buford and a young man I didn't know were standing next to him. As soon as White was out of his car he went directly to them. I stopped a few steps away and stood waiting until White motioned for me to join them.

Buford could barely contain his excitement. But his manners were stronger than his exuberance. Before he gave me the details of what he'd found, he took the time to introduce me to the young man who was standing there with him.

"Ricky, this is Robby McSwain. He's the sheriff here."

I shook the man's offered hand. "Good to meet you," I said. McSwain just smiled, apparently knowing I was dying to hear what Buford had to say about the bomb factory.

"Tell me everything, Chief," I said to Buford.

He grinned, "Like I told you, the guys on the road showed me their map and I led them to the place. Robby woke up the County Clerk and found out some corporation in New York bought an old farm about a mile from here nearly a year ago. There's a building, kind of like this one, on the property where there used to be a shop that made wrought iron railings and such.

"Ari's boys, and some other spooks who no one has introduced me to, have the building under surveillance." Buford pointed to a corner where two men I hadn't noticed before were standing by two television monitors with snow on their screens. "As soon as we get this hooked up we'll be able to see everything that's going on outside their building on TV," Buford said.

"It looks like you have everything under control," I said. "What happens now?"

"I don't know for sure," Buford said. "It's his show," motioning toward White, "and he just got here."

White nodded. He looked as tired as I felt. "This is going to be longer and more drawn out than I'd hoped.

"I don't see any other option but for us to go in with a SWAT team. The best time to do it is just before dawn. But time is working against us here. It is starting to get light already, but it will be hours before we can get all the needed resources and personnel into place. So if we have to go in it will probably be Saturday morning before we can do it." We all nodded our understanding.

"Maybe, just maybe, we'll get lucky, and the guys in the van will leave with the bombs," White continued. "There's nearly a mile of deserted road on the way back to the highway. We'll set up to take them somewhere along there. If they want to blow themselves up for Allah I think we can arrange it so no one else is hurt. There are people working on this plan as we speak."

I didn't ask what I could do to help since the answer would probably be "nothing." I knew I should go home to my town, and my wife; but this was way more exciting than making sure I had cops directing traffic at the school crossings. And Miss Mamie had already handled that anyway. I wandered back to my car, leaning against it to watch the activity in the garage. I was out of the way, and maybe someone would think of something useful I could do. White had given Trooper Burnside an assignment so he was at least busy and involved in the operation.

Men moved from group to group, joined in the ongoing discussion, then moved on to other groups in apparently random fashion. Years ago I had taken part in monitoring a wire tap in Manhattan. There was a building under construction across the street from the apartment we were using. I had spent many days watching workman apparently wandering about in random fashion on the construction site. It was rare to see anyone actually doing anything that seemed to be constructive. But the building rose in a steady fashion.

More men and cars arrived periodically. The building was getting crowded, and I was beginning to get claustrophobic. I also badly wanted a cigarette, but no one else was smoking in the enclosed space so I didn't either. And it didn't appear to be a good idea to go outside to smoke.

As it got lighter, sharper pictures appeared on the two TV monitors. They showed, from different angles, an industrial building surrounded by trees. When I wandered over to look at the pictures a young man with thick glasses and a headset was fiddling with the knobs on one of the monitors. "We'll have the infrared fixed before it gets dark tonight," he assured me. He was excited about what he was doing and began to explain the technology to me. I had nothing else to do so I listened patiently, nodding from time to time, even though I didn't understand any of what he was explaining.

The images on the monitors were oddly riveting. Nothing was happening that I could see; but I couldn't help but speculate on what was going on inside the building. Years ago a date had taken me to an Andy Warhol movie which showed a static picture of the Empire State Building for hours. I had left after only a few minutes and never called the young woman again. I tried to dredge up her name to occupy my mind.

I'd been hanging out for nearly an hour watching the screens when Ari came over to me. "Ricky, my friend," he said, "I need to go back to the motel by the truck stop in Maysville to meet some people. I do not have a car so could you please give me a ride?"

I was happy to oblige, "Let me tell White," I said.

"He suggested it," Ari replied. White and Buford nodded to me as we walked past them to my Chrysler. I started the car and backed toward the overhead door which opened behind me. Before I was turned around heading toward the road it came back down closing off the interior of the building.

"Take a left," Ari said. "I will show you where they are." I must have looked skeptical so he continued. "The building is far enough back from the road they will not know we have even driven by." I nodded and turned the car in the direction he had requested. I had never been down this road before so Ari gave me directions.

As we drove through the early morning in the outwardly serene Virginia countryside I wanted to thank Ari once again for saving Sandra's life a few days ago. But I didn't have the words to begin to tell him the debt I owed him so we rode along in silence. He called out the turns, and I followed his directions.

As we passed an abandoned store on the left and a partially burned house directly across the road from it Ari said, "Here is where White wants to set up to stop anyone who tries to leave."

The derelict buildings would provide some small cover for the men. I was glad I was too old to even be considered for this kind of John Wayne operation. I was sure White would have highly trained SWAT guys brought in for this. Waiting here would be something for the team to do until it was time for them to go in and take the bomb factory. "What if they go out the other way?" I asked.

"There is a narrow bridge over a little creek just past the place. You'll see it in a minute. White is having it blocked off with concrete barriers as soon as the highway department can get here to do it. Since we can see the vehicles outside their building on the TV monitors we'll have plenty of warning if they start moving."

I nodded my agreement. "What if more of them try coming in that way after the bridge is blocked off?" I asked. "I'd hate to see a car load of them wandering around lost in the countryside."

"We didn't discuss that," Ari said. "I'll call White." He tried his cell phone, but there was no service. I handed him mine, but it didn't have service either.

"We'll be back to civilization in a few minutes," I said. "You can call then."

Ari nodded his agreement. "The place is just up ahead on the left," he said after we'd traveled a little further. We were only going about 20 mph on the narrow, potholed road so I got a good look down the driveway, back into the trees. I couldn't see anyone from either side in the area. Ari apparently read my mind.

"Three of my associates with sniper rifles have them in a cross fire," he said. "They are very proficient at shooting long range." I thought about the one who'd taken out the shooter on the back porch of my house the other night. I didn't know his name or even which one of Ari's guys he was.

"Hopefully they will not have to do anything that will alert the people inside the building until the SWAT team is ready to go in," Ari said. "It will be better to have them contained in the building than running through the woods."

We drove slowly down the narrow road, finally coming to the small one lane bridge. It could be easily blocked closing off the bad guys from escaping in this direction. After crossing the bridge we came to a fork in the road. Ari was telling me to take the right turn when we saw the large blue trades van sitting pretty much in the middle of the road facing us. It had New York tags. Two dark skinned men were standing in front of it. One was holding a sheet of paper and the other a cell phone. There was a dark, medium size duffle bag resting on the hood. Both men looked at us as I started to turn. There was not room to drive past them on the narrow road.

"Go left, go left," Ari was shouting. I too quickly tried to turn my large car into the small road to my left. The turning radius of the car was simply too big for the narrow roadway. I threw the car into reverse, trying to straighten up to complete the turn. In the rear view mirror I could see the man who had been holding the paper pull a machine pistol from the duffle bag and take aim at the car. I could hear Ari cursing in a foreign language as he tried to get his seatbelt undone with his left hand while pulling his pistol from under his jacket with his right.

I was about to slam the gear shift into drive again when the back window of the car exploded. I felt something hit me in the back of my head and the right side of my face. I could feel blood pouring from the wounds, but since I was still able to function I assumed it was glass that hit me and not a bullet. I heard Ari moan in the seat next to me.

The burst from the machine pistol only lasted a couple of seconds. The shooter was standing in front of his van calmly reloading so he could finish killing us. I was loose from my seat belt and turning in the seat. I could see Ari was bleeding profusely from the back of his head. I was awkwardly trying to turn around in the seat to shoot back out of the rear window of the car when my foot slipped off the car's brake and we started rolling backwards. As soon as I realized the car was moving directly toward the man with the machine pistol I slammed my foot down as hard as I could on the accelerator.

The roar of the car's engine as it leaped backwards was soon drowned out by the screams of the man holding the machine pistol. He was pinned between the two vehicles. A less dedicated killer would have dropped his weapon from the agony. Not this guy. As I leaped out of my car door he was still trying to load a fresh clip into the weapon. As soon as I had my balance on the ground I shot him twice. The second round went a little higher than I'd aimed and his head exploded like a watermelon hit with a sledgehammer.

The other man was moving to the passenger side of the van. He seemed momentarily distracted by his gore covered friend dying so close to him. But he rapidly recovered at least some of his composure and snapped off a shot at me as he turned to run toward the rear of the van. The bullet didn't appear to hit anything. I let one round go in his direction. It didn't hit anything either, but it hopefully discouraged him from stopping and taking a better aim at me.

I was forced to backtrack around the front of my car to chase the fleeing man. As I went by the passenger door I wanted to stop and see if I could do anything for Ari, but I knew I had to deal with the armed man first. He was running down the road behind the van. I tried to run after him, getting as far as the side door of the van, before admitting to myself I simply I couldn't do it. I had no breath to run, and my pounding heart was pumping blood out of the wound on the side of my face. I was afraid I would lose consciousness and the man would come back and kill me, so I leaned against the side of the van. I took aim carefully with both hands and fired at the fleeing man.

It was a long shot for a pistol. My first round missed completely. But my second 9mm bullet hit him squarely in the middle of his back. He went down in a heap in the roadway. I could not tell from this distance whether he was dead or not. All my training said I should walk over to him and at least separate him from his pistol. But I simply didn't have the strength. I knew I needed to get help for myself and Ari as quickly as I could if either of us was going to live.

I didn't trust my balance so I was sliding along the van with my back to the vehicle to stay on my feet. I was not able to go very fast, but I could keep an eye on the shot man lying in the road in the truck's huge side mirror.

It seemed to take an eternity to work my way around the van's mirror and start sliding toward my car. When I realized I would have to go all way up the passenger side, across the front and back down the driver's side to get inside I almost gave up all hope. But as I got to where I could see into the passenger window I noticed Ari's breath was making bubbles in the blood pool his face was resting in. If he was breathing he was alive!

Needing to get Ari out of there was the motivation I needed to make me move faster, so I did. As I started around the front of my car at a little quicker snail's pace I looked back at the shooter who was lying in the road. He hadn't moved. But as my eyes traveled across side of the van I noticed the sliding door was now cracked open and appeared to be sliding slowly back. I fell to my knees in front of my car and rested my right hand holding my 9mm pistol on the hood.

The van's door was moving steadily, if slowly, back. As a

police officer I knew I should tell whoever was coming out of the van that he was under arrest and to drop his weapon. But I was in no shape to handle a prisoner. And I could not in good conscience leave him loose in the countryside. I sincerely hoped he had a weapon since I didn't know if I could shoot down an unarmed man. I wished once again I was at home with Sandra where I belonged.

It seemed to take forever for the man in the van to show himself. I was getting weaker by the moment. Blood seemed to be pouring from the wound in the back of my head. My vision was getting a little blurred, but things were not swirling yet.

If whoever was in the van wanted to die for the Jihad he was going to have to get moving. It takes nearly seven pounds of pressure to pull the trigger on my 9mm, and I did not know for sure I had that much strength left. And every minute that passed it was less likely that I did. But if I passed out now both Ari and I were dead for sure.

Finally the sliding door stopped at the rear of its track. From my angle I could not see inside the van. If the man in there was well trained he would leap from the doorway, sprint across the road and take cover in the ditch on the far side. I knew I had very little chance of hitting him if he did. And I only had two, or maybe three, bullets left in my pistol. I had another clip in a pouch on my shoulder holster but I knew I didn't have a snowball's chance in hell of getting the empty clip out and the new clip into the gun before he shot me.

Fortunately for me as he stepped out of the van the man, who was holding another machine pistol, was looking at his dead friend in the road behind the van. This was a fatal mistake on his part. While he was looking in the wrong direction I was able to take a steady aim at him. When he turned toward me I pulled the trigger on my pistol until the slide stayed back on the empty chamber. If there was another one in the van I was in serious trouble.

I was on my knees leaning heavily on the hood of my car. I made myself, through pure willpower, get the loaded clip from the pouch on my holster, release the empty clip and insert the new one. It took all the strength I could muster to release the gun's slide and jack a new round under the hammer. No one else had come out of the back of the van, and I was positive I could not go check.

I used the last bit of strength I had to pull myself to my feet, pushing against the hood of my car. Maybe my cop radio would work. It was the only chance we had. But as soon as I was upright I knew I could not take another step. As I collapsed in a heap I regretted that I wouldn't be able to get help for Ari. But my deepest regret was I would never see my beloved wife Sandra again. I concentrated on her for what I was sure would be my last minutes on this earth.

Chapter 18

I woke up pleasantly surprised to be alive. Once again I found myself in a hospital bed with blood running through a tube into my left arm. I had a headache I was sure would kill a lesser man. For a minute I wondered if I were back in New York and it was New Year's Day 2000. Maybe everything since I got shot in Manhattan the night my partner died had been a dream. But I could see a green mountain outside the window so I knew I wasn't in the City. My recent ugly adventure started to come back to me in all too vivid detail.

When I heard someone stirring on the side of the bed away from the window I was both excited and afraid it would be my wife Sandra. But when I turned my head I saw Trooper Burnside sitting in the chair. "How's Ari?" I asked in a strange croaking voice.

Burnside poured ice chips from a thermos into a plastic cup, handing it to me before answering. "He's alive and the doctor thinks he'll make a full recovery. He got a flesh wound in the shoulder, but luckily the bullet that hit him in the back of the head didn't penetrate the skull. The doctor says there's a lot of brain swelling but he should be okay when it goes down."

I tried to nod but it made my head throb even more. "How did we get here?" I asked in a little better voice.

"The highway crew coming to block off the bridge found you," the trooper said. "They said they heard shots so they must have been close. They called someone who called the state police who called White. We were there in a couple of minutes. By the time the ambulance arrived we'd cleaned up the mess."

"The mess" I realized was the bodies of the men I'd killed. Since I'd come to my tranquil small town to be Andy Taylor I'd killed four men myself and been involved in the killing of three more. Maybe September 11 was actually more significant than coming to Maysville, but none the less it was a lot of dead bodies. None of them had given me a choice. But it was still something I would never be able to forget. And something I did not ever want to be forced to do again.

"I've got to get out of this hospital before Sandra finds out I'm here," I said in a steadier voice.

Burnside looked sheepish, "She already knows. A trooper is bringing her here now."

I murmured a curse word and grabbed the telephone from the bedside table. I quickly dialed Sandra's cell phone. After a couple of rings I got the "We're sorry" message and hung up. "Okay," I said, "get my clothes. At least if I'm dressed and sitting up when she gets here. . ."

He shook his head, "Your clothes were soaked in blood. They cut them off of you . . ."

"Then get in your car and go to the Walmart down the road and . . ."

"I don't have a car," he said sheepishly again. "I came in the ambulance with you and Ari."

I was about to tell him to get on the phone to someone who could do something when the door of my hospital room burst open and my wife came rushing in followed closely by the Widow and a trooper in uniform. When she saw me sitting up in the bed she stopped and said calmly, "Another fine mess you have gotten us into, Ollie." She smiled in spite of the promise I was sure she'd made to herself not to do so. The Widow managed to hold on to his withering look however. He had made it his mission in life to keep Sandra from being hurt by anyone, including me.

I quickly said to my wife, "I didn't get shot this time. I swear. I just got cut by some broken glass. I'm fine. Just get me some clothes and we can get out of here."

She looked at the half empty container of blood hanging from the pole beside the bed. "I do not think you are going anywhere for a while," she said.

"How about we go when that thing is empty?" I begged like a little kid. "I just got cut from some broken glass and fainted from the blood loss. I'm fine, really. I just want to go home."

Sandra sat down on the side of my bed, took my hand and patted it reassuringly. "We will go home as soon as the doctor says you can," she said.

I don't really mind it when Sandra patronizes me. Remembering how I felt as I lay on that country road thinking I was going to die without ever seeing my wife again I realized once again being with her is the most important thing in my world. Someone else could stop the bombers. I was done playing cowboys and terrorists. And I was also done being a cop. The morning's brush with death was an epiphany for me.

"Sandra," I said, "I'm going to quit being police chief on Monday. You were right. I have no business doing this any more. I am too old, and it is too dangerous. I just want to grow old with you. We can move to Florida, get matching outfits, and eat dinner at four in the afternoon." Sandra laughed in spite of herself, making a face at me.

"Okay, maybe we can put off the matching outfits for a couple of more years," I said. "But we really should move to Florida."

Sandra said, "I could get a T-shirt that says, 'I'm with Stupid'." I smiled for the first time that day.

"But what about your new house?" the Widow asked. Sandra

gave him a look and he moved back away from my bed to stand by the door. Burnside got out of the chair and went to join him. The uniformed trooper was gone.

Sandra took the chair Burnside had vacated. My wife and I were holding hands, looking into each other's eyes when a harried looking young doctor rushed into the room carrying what I assumed was my chart.

He didn't take the time to introduce himself before he said, "I've looked at your head x-rays and there doesn't appear to be any fractures. You may have suffered a mild concussion, but I'm not worried about that. Your blood pressure was extremely low when they brought you in so it is likely you passed out from the blood loss. I sutured three cuts in the back of your head, and they should heal nicely in time."

He cut the turban like bandage from my head and examined the wounds. Apparently they met with his approval since he didn't feel the need to comment on them. He recovered them with smaller, individual bandages.

"When can I get out of here?" I asked as the doctor put the blood pressure thing on the arm that didn't have the blood going into it. He went through the procedure of pumping up the pressure and releasing it while listening with his stethoscope before he answered. "Your blood pressure is back close to normal," he said. "You can go as soon as this transfusion is done and they can process the paperwork." He left the room as abruptly as he'd arrived.

I reached for the phone again. "I'll call the Maysville dispatcher and have them send a car to take us home," I said.

"You don't need to," Sandra said. "Leigh and I came in his car. Can you take us back to Maysville, Leigh?"

He nodded without speaking. I didn't know if he was mad at me for upsetting Sandra by getting hurt or for saying we should move to Florida. But I was clearly not one of his favorite people at the moment.

"Would you please go to the Walmart and get me some clothes to wear home, Leigh?" I asked.

He nodded, "Give me the sizes," he said. Burnside pulled a pad from his jacket pocket and started to hand it to me. Sandra took it and began writing. When she was done she tore off the page and handed it to the Widow. She dug into her purse, handing him all the cash she had in her wallet.

"If that's not enough . . . ," Sandra began. The Widow nodded again and left the room.

I turned to Burnside and said, "Can you go see if you can get my stuff?"

The trooper retrieved a plastic bag from the floor next to the chair. He opened it and I could see my badge, wallet, cell phone, shoulder holster rig and two guns. I realized the other one was Ari's. I

184

dug into the bottom of the bag and pulled out my watch and wedding ring. They were both covered with caked on blood. The watch was a cheap one I'd bought on the street in New York. It wasn't running so I tossed it into the plastic lined wastebasket next to the bed.

If my epiphany was not complete before, it was when I dug out my blood encrusted wedding ring from the bag. I quickly poured water from the thermos into the palm of my left hand and scrubbed the ring clean. I dried the mess on my hospital gown and put the ring back on my finger. I couldn't look at Sandra so I don't know what her reaction was to this, but the silence in the room was overwhelming.

Finally Burnside said, "I'll go try and get the paperwork started," and left the room. When we were alone Sandra and I sat there silently watching the remaining blood drip into my arm. I didn't know what to say and apparently she didn't either.

By the time the blood bag was empty Burnside was back with a woman from the hospital's business office. Sandra gave her our insurance information. I signed everywhere she told me to sign. A nurse came in to take the needle out of my arm just as the Widow returned carrying a bag from Walmart. I could not help but smile at the thought of this elegant man, always impeccably and expensively dressed, shopping in the huge discount store. It was a reminder of what some people will do for their friends even when mad at them.

Sitting on the side of the bed I quickly dressed in the black knit shirt, gray cotton pants and slip on sneakers the Widow had bought for me. I retrieved my wallet and badge from the plastic bag, putting them in my pockets. I looked at the shoulder holster and gun but since I didn't have a jacket to cover the rig with it made it easier for me to leave them in the bag. If I stuck to the promise I'd made to my wife I realized I would never carry the gun again.

Finally I came to the moment I had been dreading. I had to stand up and walk out. I knew if I couldn't do it Sandra would insist I stay in the hospital. Once again fate intervened to save me. Just as I was about to attempt to stand up a teenaged girl, in a pink striped uniform, entered the room pushing a wheel chair. She informed us it was hospital policy for discharged patients to be wheeled out of the building. I tried to look disappointed. But by the time I had stood up from the bed and gotten into the chair I knew I would never have made it even to the room's door on my own.

Sitting in the chair with the plastic bag of guns in my lap I knew I had something else I needed to do before I left the hospital. I asked Sandra and the Widow to please wait for me a minute. Then I asked Burnside to take me to Ari's room. Burnside took control of my wheelchair from the young girl and pushed me down the hall and around the corner. As we approached the door I saw an unfamiliar tough looking man sitting in a waiting area at the end of the hall say something into his sleeve. "Show the guy your badge," I said to Burnside. He cupped it in his hand and held it toward the man in the waiting area. He nodded and said something else into his cuff. Burnside pushed the door open and wheeled me into the room.

Another man was sitting in a chair on the far side of the bed. He was one of the ones who'd been at my house the night of the gun battle. He recognized me and removed his right hand from inside his jacket.

"How's Ari doing?" I asked.

"He is still out," the man said in a heavy accent. "The doctor says he should make a good recovery, but it is too soon to tell until he awakens."

I reached into my plastic bag and handed him Ari's pistol. "When he wakes up tell him I killed the man who shot him." The man took the gun from my hand and nodded. "If there's anything I can do for him please call me." The man nodded again.

I pushed myself back away from the bed. Burnside took hold of the chair and rolled me out of the room. As hard as I tried to concentrate on Ari, as much as I sincerely wanted him to make a full recovery, I could not help but be glad I was not the one lying in that bed. It was not a thought that made me proud of myself.

Back in the hall I saw Sandra and the Widow with their heads together in conversation in front of the elevators. When I got close enough to hear what was being said the conversation stopped.

The four of us, followed by the teenaged volunteer, took the elevator to the main floor of the hospital. When we arrived at the front door there was an unmarked state police car sitting in the fire lane with a trooper behind the wheel. "There's my ride," Burnside said, patting me on the shoulder. "I'll be in touch." I felt abandoned, even though it was my choice, as I watched him drive away in the cop car.

I had almost been killed once already that Saturday. And I sincerely wanted to be at home with Sandra. But it was still hard to watch Burnside drive away and leave me. I was going home where it was safe while the real cops chased the bad guys. Life is full of choices.

The Widow soon pulled up in his vintage Jaguar. I expected to be bundled into the back seat wrapped snuggly in blankets as suited my new status as an invalid. But he pulled the car up to where the front passenger door was in front of my wheelchair.

"How do you feel?" he asked.

"I'm hungry and have a headache," I said. "But otherwise I feel pretty good considering."

"We'll stop by the restaurant for lunch on the way to your house," he said. Were it left up to me I would have opted for a big bag of fast food from a close by drive thru, but I needed to mend all the fences I could with both of them so I agreed.

It was a sunny day and the brightness made my headache worse. My sunglasses were in my destroyed cop car. I wasn't looking forward to telling the Maysville Town Council what had happened to

186

the car when I resigned on Monday. Or, more accurately, telling them whatever story White had come up with to cover up what had happened. I wasn't looking forward to resigning either, but I had promised Sandra so I planned to go through with it.

By the time we'd gotten off the Interstate and driven by the spot where this mess had all begun a few days ago I was as low and depressed as I can ever remember being. I have faced my mortality a number of times in my life. But it is much harder to face being one of those old guys you see puttering around with nothing worthwhile to do.

As the Widow pulled up in front of his restaurant I was much older and more infirm than I'd been when I'd gotten into the car a half hour before. I let him and my wife assist me getting inside. There were a dozen people eating lunch in the cozy space. Most stared openly at me in my beat up condition. When we were seated at his table in the back of the restaurant I had completely given up.

When the waiter approached with my usual beer I waved him away. For the first time in my life I thought about how the beer might react with the Advil I had been given for my headache. I thought I should probably just order oatmeal and warm milk and be done with it. But I mustered the gumption to have a fish sandwich and iced tea instead.

The Widow went off to take care of his business saying he'd drive us home when we were done. Sandra ordered a salad and sat watching me eat my lunch. I was confident that if I began to dribble my food onto my shirt she'd be ready with a napkin.

After I'd eaten I waited for Sandra to come around the table, help me up and guide me from the restaurant. The Widow held the door for us and we slowly made the short walk back to his car. As I was getting into the car I noticed a Maysville Police car was driving by. It suddenly occurred to me I was still the police chief and promised myself I would call the dispatcher as soon as I got home.

The Widow drove us the three short blocks to our house. When Sandra opened the door I was surprised to see new furniture in the living room. I had only been gone since yesterday morning but it seemed much longer. Before I could comment on the changes the phone rang. Sandra picked it up before the machine could get it.

"It's Miss Mamie," she said.

I took the phone, but before I could say anything Miss Mamie started, "Are you all right? Carl from the garage called hours ago saying he had picked up your car and it's a total wreck. Were you in an accident? What happened?" When she finally paused to take a breath I said, "I'm fine. I just got cut by some flying glass and have some stitches."

"Was it a car wreck or . . ."

"It had to do with the matter I was working on with Captain White," I said. I paused, but Miss Mamie didn't say anything. "I'll tell you what I can about it on Monday. I need to talk with you then about my plans . . ."

Sandra quickly placed her hand on my shoulder. I looked at her and she was shaking her head "No". So I changed the subject. "Can you send someone to get my stuff out of the car? I have my badge and gun, but my sunglasses, cell phone and other personal stuff should still be in the car."

"I'll send someone to get it right now," she said. "Do you want it brought to your house?"

"Please," I replied. "How's everything in town?"

"It's under control," she said. "Don't worry about it." I promised I wouldn't and hung up the phone.

I went over and sat down in the brand new leather recliner. I pushed the chair back and asked Sandra, "Would you get me a cover? I feel a chill."

She went into the bedroom and came back with a blanket. I was totally surprised when she threw it at me hard. "Damn it, Ricky," she said. "This crap has got to stop."

"What crap?" I asked meekly.

"This crap that you are too old to do anything anymore," she said angrily. I just looked at her. "This crap that you are going to quit your job as police chief. This crap that we are going to move to Florida. For God's sake, Ricky, you are not even 50 years old and you are acting like you're 80."

"But," I said.

"But nothing, Ricky," she replied. "A couple of days ago you burst into this room with a gun in your hand and killed a terrorist to save my life. Now you are an elderly invalid. If someone tries to kill me next week I doubt you will have the strength to throw your Metamusil bottle at them."

"But I thought. . ."

"No, Ricky, you did not think at all. You were a cop when I married you. I accepted that. I hope you are as careful as you can be but you can't hide in the house for the rest of your life." I just looked at her, stunned.

She looked back, exasperated. "Last week when that man chased us you saved my life. When you shot at the man with your little toy pistol and drew his fire toward yourself I was furious at you for risking your life. But you did not do it to be macho. You saved that woman trooper's life.

"Later you burst in here like John Wayne and saved my life. I am grateful for that even though it was even stupider than what you did to save the trooper," she said. "You are a great cop, my love, but you will make an awful elderly shut-in. If, and when, that happens I will deal with it. But I think we have a few more good years first."

Before I could regain my composure and say anything there was a knock at the door. Sandra opened it. Miss Mamie was standing there holding a plastic bag. "I'd sent one of the cops to take pictures of

188

the car. He came back with this stuff as I was getting off the phone with you." I thanked her and dug into the bag.

I dug out my sunglasses and cell phone which were covered in blood. The rest of the stuff, including my cigarettes and a disposable lighter, as well as the usual junk one finds in their car, wasn't worth sorting through so I wadded up the bag and carried it to the kitchen trash can.

When I returned to the living room I was not surprised to find Miss Mamie had installed herself on the couch and, I was confident, wasn't leaving until she found out what was going on. There was no reason not to tell her, assuming I had any choice in the matter anyway. I sat down in the recliner. Sandra made the customary Maysville offer of iced tea. We both accepted and she went to the kitchen to fix it.

"Are you okay, Ricky?" Miss Mamie asked. "I heard your car is a total wreck. What happened this morning?"

I didn't really want to talk about it, but Miss Mamie had been involved in our initial plan to find the bomb factory. I should have been keeping her better informed throughout the entire operation. And, if the truth were known, it was probably her relationship with Captain White which had gotten me accepted into the inner circle to start with. I decided to tell her everything.

"As you already know we have been scouring the area for the place where the terrorists are making their bombs," I began. "Chief Buford and I looked everywhere he could think of over the past week. We ran out of places to look day before yesterday so Burnside and I spent Friday chasing leads in Northern Virginia for White." Miss Mamie nodded her understanding.

"We grabbed up a couple of guys before they could carry out an attack so I guess it was productive. But we didn't make any progress on our local problem. While we were gone Chief Buford drove his wife over to stay with a lady from her church. On his way back he took a round about route and came across some Middle Eastern guys who were lost on a back road way over on the other side of Walton's Corner toward Charlottesville. He stopped to help. They showed him a map to the bomb factory." Miss Mamie laughed out loud.

Sandra came back into the room with our iced tea as I continued, "Anyway, it was after midnight by the time Buford got hold of us. As soon as we heard his news we started back here. In the meantime Chief Buford got in touch with Ari. You remember Ari?" Both women nodded that they did.

"So Ari and his associates got together with Buford and set up a command post in an old garage. They also put some guys to watch the bomb factory." I was careful not to categorize the guys as "snipers" in front of Sandra. I was being extremely careful in choosing my words period. "Anyway, the usual time to go in and make arrests is just at dawn when the bad guys are the least alert. But by the time we got

189

organized this morning it was too late to go. So they'll watch the building today while they get some more resources here and go in at dawn tomorrow. In the meantime White has set up to grab anyone who tries to go in or out of the area."

Miss Mamie nodded again, "But what happened to you this morning?"

"I was just coming home to take a shower and change my clothes. Ari needed a ride to the motel where they're staying so he could do whatever he needed to do. I gave him a ride."

Neither woman was satisfied with this explanation. Both stared at me intently until I continued. "When we got in the car I asked Ari about the location of the bomb factory so he told me to turn to the right instead of the left so we could go by the road into the place on the way back to Maysville. He pointed out the driveway as we went past. Then as we were coming across a small bridge, Ari was telling me the highway department was coming to block it off, we came upon two guys standing in front of a van with New York tags. They were apparently lost and looking at a map on the van's hood. I tried to turn the other way so I didn't have to drive past them. They must have figured out we were cops or something so one of them pulled a gun."

Not wanting to talk about shots being fired, I chose my words even more carefully as I continued, "When I saw the gun in my mirror I rammed the car into reverse and hit the one with the gun. The car's rear window exploded and I got sprayed by the flying glass. That's how I got the cuts in the back of my head. Ari got shot in the shoulder. I don't remember everything that happened between then and when I woke up in the hospital." I could tell Miss Mamie wasn't buying my evasion but she was enough of a cop herself not to cross-examine me in front of my wife so she let it go.

Although I could tell Miss Mamie was not completely satisfied by her visit she collected her purse and stood up from the chair. "When are you coming to the office?" she asked.

"Monday, first thing," I replied. "If you need me for anything I'll be here," I tried to say it as if I actually believed something might come up she couldn't handle. "Call the dispatcher and someone will pick you up," she said. I had forgotten I no longer had my own cop car.

After she'd gone I said to Sandra, "Do you want to move to Florida?"

"No," she replied.

"Do you want me to quit being a cop?"

"No," she replied again.

"Do you want to take a nap?"

"Yes," she replied, this time with a smile. She took my hand and helped me from the recliner. When I stood up, she kissed me hard then led me into the bedroom. We lay down on the bed, and she snuggled close in my arms. "I love you, Ricky," she said, "and it is going to piss me off big time if you get your dumb ass killed. But

190

somebody has to stand between the innocent victims and the terrorists. And as bad as I hate to admit it you need to be one of the ones who stands up."

I snuggled up closer to my wife. "I love you, Sandra," I said. "Who wouldn't?" she replied.

It was after six when I woke up. My headache was a dull thudding feeling. It was still fully light outside on a warm September evening. The rain had stopped. Sandra was already at work on dinner. When I went into the kitchen she was washing salad in the sink. She gave me my grilling instructions and I went to work. Lighting the gas grill on the small deck off the living room I could still see the blood stain from the man Ari's guy had killed here a couple of days ago. I would be glad to move out of this house and was sure Sandra would as well, but she'd never mentioned it. I would worry less about her if she would talk to me more about her feelings and problems. But since I wasn't willing to do the same with her I couldn't figure out how to make this happen.

I sat looking at my now tranquil back yard while the thick pork chops cooked on the gas grill. Five minutes after I thought they were done I took the chops into Sandra in the kitchen. She cut into them and pronounced them ready to eat.

Sandra had candles on the table, and as the Fall darkness fell we were snug at our dinner table together. She told me about the plans for the new house, and I agreed with everything she suggested. I was happy to be there with her and tried to put the morning's bloodshed out of my mind. Three more bad guys were dead and one of the good guys seriously hurt. I was so happy I wasn't one of them.

After dinner I helped with the dishes. Then we went back into the living room with our coffee. I pushed back in the leather recliner and began reading the latest pile of stories about the attack Sandra had found for me on the Internet. Most of the stories were from reputable news organizations about the aftermath of 9-11. Others were dire predictions of things to come. Some seemed to be based on verified fact while many others were "black helicopter conspiracies." It was truly a frightening time. About eight, I wondered how Ari was doing. I couldn't think of any way to call so I asked Sandra if she'd like to ride over to the hospital with me to check on him. She quickly agreed to go.

I changed into jeans while she did whatever women always do in the bathroom before going out. When she finally said she was ready I was waiting by the front door with my jacket on. "Do you have your pistol?" she asked. I nodded that I did. "Good," was all she said. She got her jacket from the closet and we were off.

I had pulled my keys from my pocket before I realized I no longer had my Chrysler. Sandra handed me the keys to her Mustang convertible as we walked to the curb. I opened the passenger door for her, then walked around and got in on the driver's side. By the time I was in my seat she had reached up and unfastened the latches for the top. As soon as I had the big Ford engine started she reached over and pushed the switch lowering the convertible top.

It was probably a little cool for having the top down, but Sandra puts it down just about anytime it isn't raining. If we were cold I could always turn on the heater.

As we drove through downtown Maysville I realized I was back being a cop. I carefully examined everything I saw for anything out of the ordinary which might be a potential problem. There were a number of people strolling on Main Street enjoying the warm night. The soft serve ice cream shop was the center of activity. Sandra was happily telling me about plans she and the Widow had made for decorating our new house, and I was pretending to be paying attention.

We came out of town onto the two lane highway toward the Interstate. As we approached the site of the first gun fight Sandra stopped talking. The little old muscle car hummed along. We drove by the new mall, its signs proclaiming it would be open in October, before getting onto the highway for the short trip to the hospital.

Once there I started to park in the fire lane as I usually did but realized no one would take the antique convertible for a cop car. To avoid the ticket and possible towing I drove into the nearby parking lot and found a legal parking space. When I do quit being a cop one of the things I'll miss the most is being able to leave my car any place I want. I'll have to obey the law like everyone else.

It was after visiting hours so the hospital was pretty much deserted. An officious looking woman security guard was about to tell us we couldn't go in when I badged her. She went back to reading her paperback while Sandra and I waited for the elevator.

We got off on three. The first thing I noticed was one of Ari's guys sitting in the waiting area just past his room. I still had my badge in my hand, but he recognized me and nodded before I could show it to him. I took Sandra by the elbow, and we waited while he said something into his cuff. He nodded again. I opened the door and we entered the room.

An older man I hadn't seen before was sitting by the bed. Ari was asleep, looking small and delicate, in the hospital bed. I introduced myself and Sandra to the man. He didn't tell us his name. I asked how Ari was.

"He has been awake briefly throughout the day," he said. "We are going to move him to a hospital in Washington as soon as the helicopter gets here."

I nodded and stood there looking at him for an awkward moment. I said the cliché, "If there is anything I can do" and we left the room.

During the time it took us to walk back to Sandra's car neither of us said a word. We were both thinking the same thing.

When I was back in the driver's seat Sandra asked, "How is your head?"

192

"The stitches itch but otherwise it's okay. The headache is gone," I replied. I sat there a moment listening to the throaty V8, thinking of many things, before pulling out of the parking lot and heading home.

Chapter 19

Neither Sandra nor I had anything to say to the other as we drove back to Maysville. She probably felt as guilty as I did about being glad it was Ari lying unconscious in that hospital bed instead of me.

As we turned back into Main Street Sandra asked, "Are you going to stop by the Police Department to get another car? I would like to have mine in the morning." I was taken aback by her question. Why did she think I needed a car?

"Sure," I said, "I can do that." I pulled up in front of the police station and got out of the car. Sandra got out on her side and walked around.

When she was beside me she put her arms around my neck and kissed me hard. "Be careful out there, Ricky," she said. "And call me once in a while."

I promised I would do both and stood watching as she drove away. She had just assumed I wanted to go back to the garage and be part of whatever was going to happen next. I wasn't so sure I did. My wife obviously thought I was braver and more dedicated than I think I am. Hopefully she was right.

The dispatcher, Bobby Williams, was surprised to see me. "How's your head, Chief?" he asked when I walked in.

"The stitches itch like the devil," I replied. "But otherwise I'm okay. I tore up my car though. Is there another one I can drive tonight?"

He nodded, "That old black Ford is sitting out back. It should run okay if it'll start."

"I'll try it later," I said walking into my office. My desk was piled with the mountain of junk mail I hadn't had time to go through over the last few days. I quickly looked through another, happily smaller pile of telephone messages. That reporter had called again. Apparently she'd heard about my car wreck, hopefully without any of the details. Chief Buford had called several times the previous night trying to find me but I'd seen him since then. I tossed the whole stack in the trash can. I didn't bother to check my email.

I leaned back in my high backed chair and closed my eyes. I knew I was stalling, but I wasn't sure I wanted to get back involved in whatever was going to happen next. I had screwed up badly this morning. My screwing up had gotten Ari seriously injured. It was pure luck we weren't both dead. I looked at the picture of Sandra on the desk and wanted to go home to her. Despite what she'd said I knew I was entirely too old for this stuff.

While sitting there it occurred to me I still had an out. I didn't know how to get back to the garage where I'd been that morning. It had been dark. Burnside had been driving, and I hadn't been paying any attention to where we were going. If I couldn't reach someone, and cell phones didn't work at the garage, I wouldn't be able to go back there. I'd be forced to go home.

First I dialed trooper Burnside's cell phone. To my chagrin he answered on the first ring. I told him who it was.

"Chief," he said, "how are you? I'm sorry I didn't get back to check on you this afternoon. I got hung up and . . . "

"Don't worry about it," I said. "I was thinking about coming back to the garage, but I don't know how to get there. Can you meet me and . . . "

"I'm on my way to meet some feds between Richmond and Charlottesville to hand over a prisoner right now," he said. "I don't know when I'll be back to the garage."

"You've got a new prisoner?" I asked.

"Yeah," he replied. "Some Iranian woman in a car with New York tags was wandering around lost in Walton's Corner. A trooper stopped her for some traffic thing and found another bunch of money and a couple of machine pistols in her trunk."

"How'd he get a look in the trunk?" I asked.

Burnside laughed, "The woman offered him a $1,000 bribe not to run a computer check on her driver's license, which turned up good as far as we know so far. The trooper arrested her for the bribe attempt. He found the money and guns during the inventory search. We didn't have a car with a cage so regulations require two troopers transport women prisoners. We would have taken her to the regional jail, but the feds want to talk with her. So here we are running down the road."

"Well, since I can't get anyone at the garage by cell phone maybe I'll just head on home," I said trying not to sound relieved. "Call me tomorrow when you get a chance."

"Wait, Chief," Burnside said. "You can call on that satellite phone of Ari's they have at the garage. Let me give you the number. Got a pen?"

I said I did and he gave me a string of eighteen numbers preceded by a 1 to dial. "Speaking of Ari, Chief, have you heard how he's doing?"

"Sandra and I went by to see him in the hospital about an hour ago. He was asleep. The guy with him said they were waiting for a helicopter to move him somewhere better and safer."

Burnside was quiet for a minute. "I guess it's like those mob guys say on 'The Sopranos', 'It's the life we've chosen.' Hopefully I'll see you back at the garage, Chief," he said before he disconnected.

Maybe Burnside was having second thoughts about the life he'd chosen as well. But I was still disappointed in myself. Sandra was right. I'm a cop, and protecting good people from bad people is what cops do. I was ready to go back and do my duty. I dialed the phone number Burnside had given me.

After a number of rings a voice with a heavy accent answered, "Yes?"

"This is Rick Harris," I said. "I need to speak with either Chief Buford or Captain White."

"Neither is here."

"Will you have one of them call me back when he returns?" I asked.

"What's the number?"

I gave him my cell phone number and he disconnected. Having finally made my decision to go back to the garage I found myself all dressed up with no place to go until someone called me back. Since I had time I decided I would do what the Town of Maysville pays me to do. I pulled up my email and got started plowing through them.

In the two days since I'd last been in my office to check I had received over 150 emails. Most were offers to sell miscellaneous cop stuff. I hit the delete button without reading them. Then there were emails from various organizations about what had happened since the attacks and what was expected to happen in the near future. About as many claimed to have information about horrific attacks in the future, many of these in my opinion "Black Helicopter" stuff, as claimed the attacks were finished, and life could go back to normal. Interestingly none of them talked about bombs in discount stores.

By midnight I had finished sorting through the emails as well as the junk mail on my desk. I settled into reading a lengthy proposed plan for providing security at the new mall. The plan was complicated by the fact it utilized resources from both the town's police department and the county sheriff's office. It was a split the baby solution that wasn't likely to work smoothly, if at all, but since it provided money for more officers in each department neither was likely to opt out. So far I'd left my department's efforts to Miss Mamie. Even with her conflict of interest as the sheriff's honey, however she worked it out was okay with me. I sincerely wished I cared more about the project.

My headache was gone, but the stitches were itching like crazy. I wondered what was happening at the garage. But I still hadn't heard back and had no way of contacting anyone there. I decided to give it until one and then go home to my wife and my bed. The shift had changed, but apparently everything was quiet in town since I hadn't heard from the new dispatcher to the contrary. I had spread the tools out on a newspaper on my desk and was giving my 9mm a thorough cleaning when my cell phone finally rang. It was Chief Buford.

"Ricky," he said. "How are you? I have been meaning to call

all day but you know. . .   "

I quickly assured him I was fine and told him about the plan to move Ari to another hospital.

"We heard about that," he said. "They moved him to a more secure facility in Washington about an hour ago. He was awake and talking. The doctors think he should make a full recovery."

"I don't know what happened this morning," I said. "We drove up to these guys on the side of the road. I tried to turn left to avoid driving right by them. They opened fire. I don't . . ."

"Ari told his people he recognized one of them," Buford interrupted. "Apparently the guy also recognized Ari."

That made me feel a little better. At least it wasn't completely a screw up on my part that had gotten Ari hurt so seriously. Thank God for small favors.

Chief Buford continued, "Are you coming back to the garage? A lot has happened since this morning. The SWAT team is planning to go in just after first light."

"I'd like to come watch," I said. "But I don't know how to find the garage. It was dark when we came before and Burnside was driving so . . ."

Buford laughed, "Meet me at the convenience store in Walton's Corner. I need to make a junk food run anyway. You can't have cops without doughnuts."

I told him I was on my way. I quickly reassembled my pistol, loaded and returned it to my shoulder holster. I grabbed my jacket, stuck my cell phone in the pocket, and left my office. I spoke to the dispatcher on my way to the small bathroom off the lobby.

The bandages were coming loose from the three cuts on the back of my head so I pulled them the rest of the way off. I couldn't see the wounds without another mirror, but I could feel the stitches in their individual shaved spots. I slathered Neosporin on the wounds from a tube in the medicine cabinet. I went back into my office and found a Yankees' baseball cap to cover the stitches.

Back at the dispatcher's desk I asked for the keys to the old black unmarked Ford. As he was giving them to me he said, "It's running, Chief, but the doors are locked. Bobby had the guys jump start it when the shift changed. The battery was just low. It should be okay." I thanked him and went out the back door to the small parking lot.

This old basic black cop car with its plastic seats was a far cry from the deep leather luxury of my wrecked Chrysler. It brought back memories of the NYPD. Hopefully it would run until I got it back to the police station. I was pleasantly surprised by the pickup of the old police interceptor engine as I drove past the ball fields, clearing the town limits. I cranked the window down and enjoyed the crisp night air.

I wanted to call Sandra. I knew she'd be worried about me. I longed to hear her voice. But I also hated to wake her if she'd managed to get to sleep. I was at the store before I could make myself act.

There were no cars in the convenience store lot when I pulled in. A dark skinned young clerk, whom I'd never seen before, was watching a tiny TV behind the counter. He nodded as I came in.

I collected my two Krispy Kreme doughnuts and Diet Dr. Pepper. When I paid for them I also bought a pack of Marlboro Lights and a new throwaway lighter.

I'd finished both doughnuts and was sitting on the hood of the Ford smoking a cigarette when Chief Buford pulled in to the lot driving his old pickup truck. He waved and went into the small store. I'd finished the cigarette and was anxious to get on our way by the time he came out carrying a good sized box. I opened the door on the passenger side of the old truck. He slid the box onto the seat.

Then he turned toward me. I was surprised when he grabbed me in a bear hug. "Ricky," he said squeezing me hard, "you scared the hell out of me this morning. Are you sure you're okay?" I nodded. "Why don't you follow me in your car?" I nodded again and we set out for the garage.

As I followed him through the tiny dark town of Walton's Corner, and out into the near total darkness of the rural Virginia countryside, I was alone with my thoughts. They were not pleasant company.

I couldn't avoid thinking again about the men I'd killed since that horrible Tuesday, less than two weeks before. It had been them or me in each case. Actually, in the shooting in my living room it had been him or my wife Sandra, whose life was much more important to me than my own. I knew if there was a line of men who were a danger to my wife I would gladly shoot them one by one until they were all dead.

One thing which oddly bothered me was the way the shootings had been handled by local authorities. Both the shootings in which I was involved in New York had been fully investigated in much more detail than I felt was necessary at the time. Here the first shooting, at my house, had been covered up by the state police. They had literally destroyed evidence instead of collecting it. Since no one had been to see me about the previous morning's shooting, in which I had after all killed three more men, I assumed it would be handled the same way.

I know I should be personally grateful for small favors, but I was not comfortable with the direction the country seemed to be headed in since 9-11. I had spent too much time with law enforcement to be happy giving them the power of life and death over people without any fear on their part of being held accountable. If America is abandoning all civil liberties the terrorists had accomplished their goal of destroying the country.

At the same time I knew if we didn't stop these local bomb builders before they could deliver their bombs a lot of innocent lives would be lost. Being a grown up can be very complicated.

Among the somber news reports and black helicopter conspiracies Sandra had downloaded for me from the Internet was the story of a redneck from Mesa, Arizona named Frank Rogue. After bragging to a beer joint full of his friends how he wanted to kill the "ragheads" responsible for the terrorist attacks he shot and killed a man named Balbir Singh Sodhi while he planted flowers outside the Chevron station he owned. Mr. Sodhi was not a terrorist, or a Muslim, or even from the Middle East. He was an immigrant from India who worked long hours in his gas station to provide for his wife and children. He came to this country for the American dream, and his family got a nightmare instead. I was afraid America was entering an orgy of hate crimes against "foreigners."

I knew Chief Buford would protect the foreign looking residents of Walton's Corner, but I was embarrassed by how little I knew about the people who live in Maysville. I promised myself if I survived until Monday I would make all the people of Maysville's safety my number one priority. That, after all, is why the town council pays me.

After what seemed like a long way in the near total darkness we finally came to a narrow road off to the right of the main highway. I followed Buford down the narrow two lane road to the garage. The overhead door rolled up as we arrived and we both drove inside. The building, which had looked so big and vacant the previous morning, was now nearly full of men and vehicles. There were small groups doing different things scattered throughout the space. Over in a back corner was the SWAT team, dressed in black, checking their weapons and getting ready to assault the bomb factory just before dawn. I didn't envy them their job in the least. They were at least as aware as I was that some of them were likely to die this morning.

Buford placed his box of junk food on an empty table and motioned for me to join him as he walked over to where White was talking with a small group of men. I only recognized one of Ari's guys. The others were strangers. White finished his conversation before turning to me, "What the hell happened this morning, Ricky?" he asked.

"I don't know exactly," I said telling the story once again. "I was driving Ari back to his motel. We decided to take the back way so he could show me the road into the bomb factory. When we got just past the little bridge there was a New York van on the side of the road with two guys standing in front looking at a map, trying to get a cell phone to work. Ari must have recognized one of them. He told me to turn left instead of driving by them. I tried to make the tight turn but the road was too narrow. I had to stop and back up."

My heart was racing remembering. "One of them opened up on us with a machine pistol. The car's back window exploded. Ari apparently got hit with a bullet. I just got cut." I paused. No one asked how I'd managed to kill all three of the bad guys, and I didn't volunteer any details. I did ask White, "Are there going to be repercussions from the shooting I need to worry about?" He shook his head, and I considered the matter settled. I guess I'm willing to make an exception to the need for full investigations under some circumstances.

Buford was also shaking his head. "Guys with guns seem to take an instant dislike to you, Ricky," he said with a smile. I couldn't help but laugh. I was tempted to say, "So far they've all regretted it," but thought better of it.

White went back to his conversation and, having nothing specific to do I went over and leaned against the hood of my car to observe what was going on.

There were at least a dozen SWAT guys gathered around a table looking at what I assumed was a diagram of the bomb factory. I also assumed there were more of them waiting somewhere else. One of the first things I learned in law enforcement is you never want to find yourself in a "fair fight." As a rookie patrolman I was taught the value of superior force in any situation. On the street, if a perp has no weapon the officer should use his nightstick. If the perp has a knife the officer should use his gun. If the perp has a gun there need to be enough cops on the scene to show him he will die if he doesn't immediately drop it and surrender.

The situation at the bomb factory was complicated by several issues. First, since we were cops, we were expected to identify ourselves as such and give the bad guys an opportunity to surrender peacefully. If they choose not to surrender we have lost the element of surprise. And to make matters worse, we knew they had explosives in the building, even if we didn't know how much.

It was more likely they would blow themselves up, taking as many cops with them as possible, than they would choose to meekly surrender. Nineteen of their fellow terrorists had committed suicide flying airplanes into buildings less than two weeks earlier. I felt guilty about how happy I was not to be a member of the SWAT team for this operation.

I moved over to where I could see the television monitors. Since I'd been gone they had added two more cameras to the video surveillance on the building. Now I could see all sides of the structure. The cameras had night vision capabilities. I could see detail in the shadows around the building. The lit windows on all sides of the building appeared as glowing blocks of light in the cinderblock walls. Several vehicles were parked close to the building.

The monitors were being watched by a sleepy looking technician who flipped switches from time to time for reasons I couldn't figure out.

A little after three the SWAT guys began getting themselves together to leave the garage. They lugged their gear out the back door apparently to vehicles parked in the rear. I heard several vehicles start up and pull around the side of the building. Only one of the black dressed guys was left in the garage. He sat in the corner by a large radio with a headset in place.

White was standing by himself looking at the back door. He had just sent fellow cops into harm's way and didn't appear too happy about it. I walked over to him and stood there without saying anything. After awhile he said, "They're going to go in just after daylight."

I was surprised. "They aren't going to try to get them to come out first?" I asked. He shook his head.

"The SWAT commander decided it was too dangerous," White said. "He thinks the element of surprise is the most important thing."

"Does he know the building contains explosives?" I asked.

White nodded again. "They can't use concussion grenades because of that," he said. "And I told him these folks are known to be 'suicide bombers'. But he makes the tactical decisions. It's out of my hands." We stood there together for a long time just looking at the door, lost in our individual thoughts.

There were about 15 men left in the building but the noise level had dropped to almost dead silence. Apparently the others were also thinking about what the men who had just left us were about to face. I wondered how many of them were sorry they weren't going to be part of the entry team; maybe some of the young ones. And how many, like me, were relieved not to be asked to do this extremely dangerous thing.

I asked White, "What have you learned from the ones locked up in Petersburg? Do we know anymore about who's in the building and what their plan is?"

White put his arm around my shoulder and led me to a battered desk in a corner away from the video monitors. There were three copy paper boxes stacked next to the desk. He took the lid off the top box. Inside were two stacks of paper. The top sheet of one pile showed an FBI report and the other was from the Boston Police Department.

"These boxes are just the stuff from yesterday," White said. "We are literally buried in intelligence, and no one has time to sort out the useful information." I ruffled my hand through one of the stacks. There were reports from federal agencies as well as police departments up and down the east coast.

"And this is just the cream that somebody thought was important enough to distribute in printed form, just the stuff that may be relative to our case. There is ten times, fifty times, a hundred times more of this in the computer data base. Usually in investigations we are looking for information. In this one we are buried in it.

"Remember that pay phone in the pizza parlor across from the Brooklyn mosque we got off the pay phone in the Petersburg lockup?"

I nodded. "Okay, the feds put a pen register on that phone, secret caller ID if you will, and collected a hundred numbers from calls that came in. Then they checked those numbers and put pen registers on half of them. Then they collected the numbers that called those numbers and so on. Suddenly they got tons of names and phone numbers. And . . ."

I finished his sentence for him, "And we've got these terrorists in a building with explosives in Nowhere, Virginia and we don't know squat about them."

"Exactly," White replied. "We aren't even trying to flip any more of the ones we arrest. We're just locking up anyone suspicious we can, figuring they can't hurt anyone from jail."

He looked at his watch and said, "It'll be another hour before the entry team goes in. Why don't you read some of this stuff and see if there is anything we should know in it?"

I started at the top of the top box and began reading reports. I spent most of the next hour at the task and didn't learn anything remotely useful. I could not keep the names straight and honestly do not even know where Yemen is on the map. All I had after my reading was a better appreciation for the problems of law enforcement since 9-11 and a massive headache. I thought about Caroline Barns. Hopefully any legal problems she might have would get lost in the deluge. Her friend would probably get fired from the DOJ for the marijuana, but I didn't owe her anything. Her father hadn't saved my life.

Burnside and another young man, who I assumed was also a trooper even though they were both dressed in jeans and dark jackets, came in. Each was carrying another box of reports. I motioned for them to put them down next to the desk. Burnside spent several obligatory minutes inquiring as to how I was feeling, but I could tell he wanted to go find out what was happening. I assured him I was doing great and sent him on his way. I went back to the reports with an eye on my watch and the window for the approaching dawn.

When I sensed the increase in activity, and tension in the garage I put down the report I was pretending to read and began paying more attention to what was going on around me. It was getting close to time for the SWAT team to hit the building. I moved closer to the video monitors so I could watch the action. The guy handling communications with the entry team had also moved to where he could see the building on screen as well. He was murmuring into the microphone of his headset.

Two technicians were fiddling with the video hookup to insure they could see every inch of the outside of the building. I had just heard the SWAT communications guy tell his troops they were going to make entry in two minutes when there was a bright flash on the screen which showed the back of the building. At first I thought it was an explosion. But I quickly realized a door had opened and I was seeing the light from inside the building greatly intensified by the infrared capabilities of the video camera. The door closed and the light was gone.

One of the video techs was zooming in on the figure of a man standing by the rear door. There was another flash of light as he apparently lit a cigarette. For a brief instant the man was seen brightly illuminated on one of the video monitors. I instantly knew something was not right about him but before I could figure out exactly what it was I heard one of the techs yell, "Son of a bitch!"

The communications guy was yelling into his microphone, "Hold your positions. Hold your positions!"

Then the tech yelled, "Captain White, I need you. Now!"

Chapter 20

All eyes in the garage were locked on the video tech as White rushed toward his corner of the garage. Everyone, including me, quickly followed. I found a spot out of the way where I could still see and hear what was going on.

The main video screen showed the man, in some detail, standing next to the back door of the building. The fire end of his cigarette glowed white like a star against the gray background in the thermal image. The tech was turning knobs, adjusting the picture to make it clearer. The bulk of his body seemed out of proportion to his head. Then I realized what had caused the tech to react so excitedly.

"Look at the guy, Captain," he said. White stared intently at the screen with a quizzical expression on his face. "He's wearing a hazardous materials handling suit."

White repeated the tech's earlier reaction. "Son of a bitch!" he said. Then he turned to the SWAT team's communication guy. "Tell them to quickly pull back as far as they can but still have a shot." The communications guy stepped back, talking rapidly into his headset.

"They're pulling back now, Captain," he said to White.

Chief Buford had moved up beside me, standing silently with his hand on my shoulder. It seemed like a very long time before anyone said anything. Finally White spoke. "Well, this is a whole new ball game," he finally said. The guy on the screen flicked his cigarette off into the darkness. It looked like a comet in the night sky on the monitor. Then he put the hood to his suit over his head and went back inside the building.

The guys White had previously been conferring with joined him in front of the video monitor. I could see their aggressive gesturing but couldn't hear what was being said. Buford and I moved back against the wall, leaning against an old work bench. I knew I didn't have anything to add to their discussion, and it appeared Buford didn't either. He seemed to be as grateful as I was not to be in charge of this operation.

After a while Buford asked, "What do you think, Ricky?"

I could only shake my head. "I'm glad that guy smokes," I said after some thought. "If those SWAT guys had gone into the building there is no way of knowing what kind of a disaster we would've had." I felt myself shiver even though it was warm in the garage.

Although we were both "chiefs" Buford seemed as happy as I was to be just an "indian" in this operation. We stood around watching the guys who were in charge deciding what to do. After a few minutes of sometimes animated discussion White turned to face the garage and said, "Can I have your attention for a minute?" There was no sound from anyone in the room as everyone turned their complete attention to what Captain White had to say.

"You all saw the Hazmat suit that guy is wearing?" There were murmurs from the group. "Needless to say this new development means we will have to reevaluate our strategy and change our tactics. No one is going into that building until we have better information about what is inside."

"The prisoners we have that may have knowledge are being re-interrogated. I'm pulling the SWAT guys back as far as they can go and still be able to shoot at the building if it becomes necessary. Hopefully a couple of the bad guys will try to leave so we can grab them up and find out what's going on inside," White said. "For now, we will just have to wait and see what happens next."

It was getting light outside. With nothing constructive to do, I hunkered down for a long day. Maybe White would think of some way for me to be helpful. In the meantime I watched the building on the four video monitors.

Many of the others seemed to feel the same way. All sense of urgency was gone. We were all just hanging around waiting for the next shoe to drop.

Around eight Chief Buford came over and invited me to make another junk food run with him. I wasn't doing anything anyway so I agreed. I enjoy his company, and it would give me a chance to call Sandra while we were closer to a cell phone tower.

As we drove back toward town in his old truck he asked, "How are you feeling?"

"My stitches itch and my eyes feel like they've been sandpapered, but otherwise I'm okay," I said. "How are you doing?"

"To tell you the truth, Rick, I'm exhausted. Hopefully this will be over soon," he replied. Neither of us was crucial to the success of the operation, and either of us could have gone home if he'd wanted to do so. But neither of us wanted to miss the excitement. Since he's at least 30 years older than me I didn't bring up my usual complaint about my age.

I looked at my phone when we turned onto the main highway and saw there was now service. I excused myself to Buford and hit the keys necessary to dial my home phone. Sandra answered on the first ring.

"Hope I didn't wake you, darling," I said.

"No," she assured me. "I've been up for an hour. How are you? Where are you?"

"I'm fine," I reassured her. "I'm with Chief Buford going to pick up more junk food for the troops."

"You aren't doing anything dangerous are you?" she asked.

"I'm eating doughnuts and other greasy stuff," I said. "I haven't been closer than at least a mile from anything dangerous."

She'd given up on getting me to eat right years ago so she just laughed. "I'm going to do errands. Call me on the cell phone if you get the chance. I love you, Ricky," she said.

She waited until I told her I loved her as well before she disconnected. We were nearly back at the store when I stuck the phone back into my pocket.

At the store I gave Buford all the cash I had and leaned against the truck smoking a cigarette while he was inside. He came out carrying a large box which he stuck in the bed of his truck.

When we arrived back at the garage nearly everyone was crowded around the video monitors. On the screens I could see young, casually dressed men carrying things out of the building and loading them into a car and a minivan parked a little way away from the building.

The trunk was open on the car. I watched a man carrying what looked like several backpacks out, placing them in the trunk. One of the men closed the trunk and they all went back into the building. These were probably the bombs we believed were destined for discount stores in the northeast. Both the side and rear doors of the minivan were still standing open.

I could hear White talking to the SWAT team communications guy as well as on the satellite phone in his hand. Plans were being made to stop the car on the gravel road before they got to the main highway. I couldn't help but think about the guy in the hazmat suit and wonder what evil stuff was in those bombs. And I couldn't help but be glad once again I wouldn't be one of the guys who had to stop the car, get the bad guys out and secure everything with those bombs so close at hand. These terrorists had proven over and over they are more willing to die for what they believed in than I am.

I could hear White still working out the details for the ambush when I saw men coming out of the building again. This time each man was carrying one of those large plastic storage containers which have become so popular. There were wires trailing from each container. We had some just like them in the garage at home. Each holds ten gallons of whatever you put in them.

Over the next few minutes we saw at least 10 different men come out of the building. Two got inside the van and the others stacked containers in from the rear. I couldn't see what the ones inside the vehicle were doing, but I had a strong suspicion they were connecting the wires from the separate containers together. Before I could say anything I heard White say, "It's a truck bomb! Son of a bitch, we can't let them get out of there with that." He took the headset from the SWAT communications tech. I could see him talking, then

206

pausing to listen, but I couldn't hear what was being said.

Once again I was happy I wasn't in command, and it wasn't my responsibility to decide what to do now. Although I could come up with several options, none of them were good. Even assuming all the men surrendered peacefully, if the bombs were radio controlled, they could be detonated at any time by whoever had the detonator in their pocket.

The others White had previously been conferring with crowded around him. While the discussion of what to do was taking place in the garage I saw a group of ten men milling around in between the building and the vehicles on the video monitor. There was handshaking among them. Then two men walked to each vehicle and got inside. The remaining six men turned and started back into the building. I didn't know what White had decided to do. But I knew whatever it was, he needed to do it now.

As the men were starting the vehicles the video tech zoomed the camera, on the side of the building we were watching, back to a broader view of the scene. Both the car and minivan started rolling down the driveway, away from the building, toward the road. The video camera panned to follow them. Were it up to me I would stop and contain them there. I couldn't see any advantage to letting them get onto the road.

White apparently agreed. I heard White say into his headset, "Stop them! Shoot the tires. Stop them!"

There was no sound from the video. It was like watching an old silent movie. First the tires on the lead car exploded and the car itself lurched into the shallow ditch next to the driveway, effectively blocking the minivan's escape. Then the tires on the minivan van exploded. All four men leaped from the vehicles and ran back toward the building. Two of them were firing machine pistols toward where I assumed the shots from the SWAT guys had originated.

White didn't give the order for the snipers to shoot them. This was probably the correct decision under the rules which law enforcement usually operates. But I couldn't help second guessing him. If I were in charge I would have had the SWAT guys drop them in their tracks. At some point before the day was over they would have to be dealt with. I thought of 'The Sopranos' quote from Burnside earlier. This was the life, and the death, these terrorists had chosen.

I watched the video camera zoom back in on the building. It stopped where we could still see the vehicles as well. After a few minutes of consultation with the other men around him I heard White ask into his headset, "Are all your guys far enough back to be safe if the building blows up?" He apparently received an affirmative answer because he then said, "Okay, on my signal in 30 seconds, take the windows out on all four sides of the building. Let's let them know they're surrounded."

All eyes in the garage were locked on the video monitors as

White counted off the time on his watch. Finally he said, "Go" and we could see windows exploding on all sides of the building, then nothing.

No one came out of the building to surrender and I didn't see any flashes of fire being returned. We all stood watching the monitors silently until one of the men next to White asked, "What now, Captain?"

"Beats me," White replied so we all continued to watch for another a long minute. After a consultation with the half dozen guys around him I saw him nod his head. "Listen up," he said. "Since they now know we're outside I'm going to go over to the scene. The ones of you I want to go with me will be informed by your various commanders. The rest of you stay here and continue to do what you've been doing."

I went back to leaning against the car since that's what I'd been doing. But as White walked to his car he motioned and said, "Ricky, come ride with me." I was surprised to be included but did what he said.

Inside the car, as we were waiting for the vehicles blocking us in to move, I looked to White to enlighten me on my role in the operation. We were outside the garage before he spoke. "Give me a cigarette, Ricky," he said.

I couldn't help but laugh. My important role had been defined. I had cigarettes in my pocket. I gave him one and my lighter. He lit it and took a deep puff. "How can anything that bad for you be so satisfying?" he asked.

I laughed again. "The cigarette wasn't the only reason I wanted you to come, Ricky," White quickly assured me. "I really need to know what you think I should do."

I shook my head. "I don't know," I said. "There aren't any good choices. But hopefully some of the bad ones are not as bad as some of the other bad ones."

When we'd arrived at the entrance to the bomb factory White pulled into the far end of the driveway, around a curve from the building. Two other cars pulled in behind us. We got out and looked around. Apparently this was White's first trip to the scene. While we were trying to get our bearings I noticed a SWAT guy coming from the far side of the road. "Over here, Captain," he said. We followed him back across the road and up a steep hillside. The black dressed guy trotted effortlessly up the hill. I vividly remembered why I'd quit smoking last time before we got to the top.

There were three of them behind a makeshift barricade at the crest of the hill. I could see the bomb factory but it looked tiny, a long way away. The SWAT guy who appeared to be in charge handed White a large pair of binoculars. He looked through them for a minute then handed them to me.

I was surprised at how close they brought everything in the clearing across the road to me. I could read the tag on the minivan in the driveway. When I put the glasses down I could barely see the vehicles at all. It must have been close to a thousand yards.

There were two shooters in position just behind the barricade. Each had a rifle mounted with a large scope resting on a sturdy tripod. They had apparently shot the tires off the vehicles and the windows out of the building from this vantage point. I was impressed.

None of the men wore any rank or insignia on their black coveralls. White apparently knew who was whom in the group. He asked the one who wasn't crouched behind a rifle, "What have we got?"

The man looked quizzically in my direction. White nodded it was okay to talk in front me so he began, "It could be a lot better, but it could also be a lot worse," he said.

"On the plus side, there are no occupied houses for nearly a mile in any direction. We have the high ground so we are shooting down into the target. All the land behind the building is National Forest. The highway department blocked off the little bridge in one direction and we closed the road with a roadblock on the other end.

"This is a good spot for us to shoot our rifles from, and the other team is a little closer to the building on the other side. We are on the diagonal and can hit windows and doors on two sides of the building from here. They can't get to their vehicles, which aren't going anywhere anyway, without coming into our field of fire."

"And the bad news?" White asked.

"There is plenty of that," the man continued. "There's no cover to operate any closer in. There are all these little skinny trees which block our shots but don't give us anything to get behind if we try to move in closer. I would like to use the shoulder launch rockets to take out the vehicles as a demonstration to whoever is in the building. But we'd have to be too close to use them.

"Those vehicles are packed with explosives and lord knows what else. Our guys need to be back several hundred yards when they fire the rockets. If we had a clear field of fire it wouldn't be a problem. The rockets don't have the range to use them from here. They have the range from the road but they'll blow up when they hit a tree well before they get to the vehicles."

White nodded his understanding. "What's Plan B?" he asked.

"I talked with 'our friends' and they say the only way to go in safely is with a tank."

"How soon could they get a tank here?" White asked.

"That's a major problem," the man said. "They have these over the road trucks they transport tanks on but they aren't sure some of the bridges between here and the Interstates could take the weight. Then, even if they managed to get to the turnoff from the main road, they would have to cut trees for a couple of miles to get the tank here. It would take several days."

"And," White continued for him, "by the time they got it here

CNN would be carrying this mess live to the world." The guy nodded his agreement.

"I guess we'll just have to figure out a way to get them out then," White said. He told the SWAT commander to hold his position and motioned for me to follow him back down the hill.

Neither of us had the wind to talk and navigate the steep hillside at the same time so White didn't say anything until we were back on level ground. "So what do you think?" he said.

"I think we have to try and talk them out," I said. We were cops after all. These bombers were really just extremely dangerous 'perps'. I have never been comfortable with the idea of killing them without first giving them a chance to surrender. "But can we get close enough without getting shot or blown up by the explosives in the vehicles?"

White motioned to one of the guys I didn't know who was standing on the side of the road. When he came over White asked, "Is there any way we can get a bullhorn speaker up close enough to the building for them to hear us without having to go in too close?"

"Sure," the guy said. "We have a radio bullhorn deal. Someone can place the speaker as close to the building as they can safely get while you're back on the other side of the road with the SWAT guys. Piece of cake."

White smiled. Something was working out. Then the guy said, "I'll get someone at headquarters in Richmond to bring it to us."

White turned on his heel and walked away from the guy without another word. When I caught up with him I couldn't resist saying, "The bullhorn thing will probably get here before the tank does."

He grinned in spite of himself. "So what's your plan, smart ass?" he asked.

I didn't return the grin. Once again I had put myself in a position I did not want to be in. I had just come back here to watch how the big kids did it. Now White expected me to be one of the big kids.

"Okay," I said. "Let's strip this mess down to its essence. What we have here is a barricaded suspect situation. We have both been through those before.

"On the minus side there are two vehicles full of bombs between the road and the building. The terrain is bad. The building is made out of cinder blocks. We have no cover up close, and we can't get a clear shot at the vehicles or the building with any kind of rocket launcher.

"But on the plus side," I continued, "They are contained. There are no hostages or other innocent bystanders. We are far enough away from anything else not to have to worry about using weapons. We just have to get close enough to use the bullhorn to convince them to surrender." I had wanted to say "You just need to get close enough"

210

but couldn't make myself do it.

"And if they won't come out?" White asked.

"Then we have to go to Plan B," I said. He looked at me intently. "And I have no idea what Plan B is," I admitted.

White stood there chewing on his knuckle for a minute. Then he said, "Let me go talk to some folks about Plan B then we'll go do this." I reluctantly nodded my agreement. It seemed I was going to have a bigger role in this than I wanted.

While White was talking to a couple more guys I didn't know on the side of the road I walked further down the road to where I could see the building through the trees. When I figured I was out of range of the machine pistols we'd seen previously I left the road and went a short distance into the trees. I could see a large fallen tree maybe a hundred yards from the door to the building and a little ways beyond it. If we went further down the road and came back through the woods it would provide some cover, assuming they didn't have any more powerful guns.

I made my way back to the assembled group standing in the road. White finished his conversation and motioned to me to follow him to the rear of a police car parked on the side of the road. He took a pair of bulky Kelvar vests from the trunk and handed one of them to me. I took my jacket off and put it on, being careful to make sure I could still get my pistol out of my shoulder holster. I tried to put my jacket back on but it was too tight over the vest so, after transferring my cell phone and cigarettes to my pant's pocket, I tossed the jacket into the trunk.

White was putting on the other vest. I didn't have the heart to tell him I'd been wearing a vest almost exactly like this one the last time I was shot and nearly killed. "Do you want a rifle?" he asked.

I shook my head. "I probably couldn't even hit the building with a rifle," I said.

White nodded, and then spoke into his radio apparently to the SWAT commander, "I need a sharpshooter to move in a little closer with us." Almost immediately one of the black dressed guys came trotting down the hillside across the road carrying a rifle with a scope on it.

Someone handed White a bullhorn and the three of us started down the road together. We walked two hundred yards past the building before we turned into the woods. We made our way past the building in that direction then turned back toward it. I pointed to the fallen tree and we made our way to it through the sparse saplings which provided no real cover. If the bad guys had longer range weapons than the machine pistols now was the time they would use them.

We made it to the fallen tree without drawing any fire. There was room for all three of us behind it. If it wasn't rotten it appeared to be thick enough to stop a bullet. The sniper quickly braced his rifle on the trunk and took aim at the door to the building. It took White a minute to figure out how to work the bullhorn.

When he was ready he pointed it toward the building, pushing a button. The device made an ear shattering sound. This was to get their attention I guess. Then he pulled the trigger on the device and said, "You in the building. This is the police. You are surrounded. If you will come out with your hands up you will not be harmed. I repeat, come out with your hands up, and you will not be harmed."

There was a pause and then someone started firing an automatic weapon toward us from a shattered window next to the door. White quickly told the sniper to hold his fire. I had ducked as far as I could when I heard the first shot, but it didn't sound like any of the bullets came anywhere close to us.

When I got back up to a kneeling position behind the tree trunk I asked, "What do we do now?"

"I guess we wait a few minutes and try again," he said. "If they don't come out then I guess it going to be Plan B."

I hadn't noticed how young the sniper was until he said to White, "Should I tell my commander to get ready to storm the building, Sir?"

White shook his head, "I don't know exactly what we are going to do," he said. "But I do know we are not going to storm that building." I couldn't tell if the young man's expression was of relief or disappointment. White looked at his watch. "Let's give them a couple of minutes and try again. This time," he said to the sniper, "if you see anyone take them out. It might get their attention." The young man nodded.

I turned to try and get more comfortable leaning against the tree. The stitches in my head were itching and, since I'd put on the vest, so were the places the bullets had hit the last time I had been shot. I knew this was psychosomatic, but they itched just the same.

White moved around into a more comfortable position as well. "Give me a cigarette," he said. I gave him one and offered the pack to the sniper. He looked embarrassed but took one for himself. I lit the others and then one of my own. We sat quietly smoking and waiting out the few minutes White had given the terrorists.

Finally White said, "Okay, let's do it." I saw the sniper speak into his headset. White hit the button for the screaming horn again, then spoke through the bullhorn. "You are surrounded. If you give up no one will be harmed. This is your final warning. Come out with your hands up."

I could see the door to the building start to open slowly. When it was opened most of the way suddenly there were shots coming at us again from the window. I ducked involuntarily. When I got back up to where I could see I saw two men come running from the door. They went in different directions around the sides of the building. More shots came from the building. This time there was a shooter crouched in the doorway firing at us.

212

I heard several separate shots coming from different directions before the young sniper next to me fired his rifle. Then it was quiet and the door to the building closed again.

The sniper spoke into his headset again, listening to the response before he said anything to White. "They got the two that went around the sides of the building. I got the one in the doorway square in the chest. If he wasn't wearing a vest he's dead too." White nodded his understanding of what the young man had said.

"Sir," the sniper asked, "My commander wants to know what you want him to do now."

"Tell him to hold his positions until I get back to him," White said. "Now let's withdraw and figure out Plan B." We slowly made our way back the route we'd come. The SWAT guy walked more or less backward to keep his gun on the building. When we were back on the road headed toward the others waiting by the entrance to the driveway I could see the body of one of the terrorists lying between the building and the back of the minivan. I assumed there was another dead one on the far side of the building as well.

Judging from the ten we'd seen earlier, when they were loading the vehicles, there were still at least seven of them inside along with an unknown quantity of whatever it was they were using the hazmat suit to handle.

When we got back to the group on the road White motioned to the pair of guys he'd been conferring with earlier. He left me standing there and joined them. They had a long conversation complete with head shaking and hand gesturing. After awhile White came back to where I was standing with the young sniper and Chief Buford.

"Listen up, people," he said. "I want everyone but the SWAT team to go back to the garage." There were a few murmurs but the men started toward their vehicles. I was asking Buford for a ride when White said, "I need you two to stay here with me." We stood where we were. White said to the SWAT guy, "Tell your boss I said for him to move his guys back as far as he possibly can and still be able to hit anyone who comes out." The young man nodded and spoke into his headset. The men had gotten into their vehicles and most of the vehicles were moving out.

The two men White had been conferring with earlier were standing together on the side of the road. One of them was talking into some kind of radio. When he was done he came over and said to White, "ETA fifteen minutes."

White nodded his agreement and the five of us started up the hill to the SWAT position. I was worried about Chief Buford as we climbed the steep hillside again. But when we got to the top he was not as out of breath as either White or I.

I wondered what they had decided for Plan B. There was no way anyone could get a tank here in the next fifteen minutes, and White had said there would be no SWAT assault.

Chief Buford was probably as curious as I was, but neither of us asked any questions. One of the guys I didn't know was still talking to someone on his radio.

We just crouched there behind the barricade, looking at the building until one of the men said," In one minute, Captain."

White said, "Everybody get down and stay down." Then I heard a sound. It wasn't loud, and I was surprised when I looked up to see how close the unmarked black helicopter was above us. The engine was well muffled but apparently they couldn't do much with the noise the spinning blades make.

I stayed flat on the ground but couldn't resist looking up. I watched the helicopter circle the building once at an altitude of a few hundred feet. Then it climbed higher and hovered in the air some distance away.

Suddenly there was burst of flame from the undercarriage of the helicopter and the building erupted into a massive fireball. Flames leaped hundreds of feet into the air. I could feel the heat from the explosion at our position a thousand yards away. The noise was deafening even at this distance.

My hearing came back quickly and I could hear the helicopter moving slowly toward our position. The man with the radio was talking to someone. It appeared the helicopter was lining up another shot when the flames from the building fire ignited the two bomb loaded vehicles. They blew up with nearly as much force as the building had.

The guy with the radio said something, and the helicopter flew off. He nodded to White, and he and his associate started walking down the hill.

White turned to Buford and me saying, "Okay, here's what I need you to do."

(Newspaper clipping)

Secret Drug Lab Explodes

Walton's Corner, Virginia - September 26, 2001

By Mary Johnson
May County Chronicle Staff Writer

Around 3:00 p.m. Saturday afternoon residents of the Piles Creek section of the county heard a loud explosion. According to Walton's Corner Police Chief Curtis Buford it was a secret, illegal drug lab blowing up.

On Friday Chief Buford said he received a tip from a usually reliable local informant that a methamphetamine, often called "speed", lab was operating in an abandoned shop building on Route 498 in Pines Creek. He went out Saturday afternoon with several Virginia State troopers to investigate.

"Apparently someone saw us poking around in the area," Buford said. "I don't know if they were trying to move the operation or destroy the evidence or what. Making these drugs requires mixing a number of highly unstable chemicals in a high heat process. These guys often blow themselves up."

It is not known if any of the drug manufacturers where killed or injured in the explosion. "When we got there after the explosion the back door to the building was standing open. We assume whoever was in the building got away."

According to Chief Buford there was a beatdown path through the woods to a fire road in the National Forest which adjoins the rear of the property. He also said there was evidence a vehicle had recently been parked there. Helicopters were used to search for the fleeing men but they were not located.

Although local residents said they heard gunfire Chief Buford said there was apparently ammunition in the building which went off during the fire. He said neither he nor the troopers fired their weapons during the operation.

Methamphetamine, and its derivative drug "Ecstasy", are becoming a major problem for law enforcement in the Valley. State police have made numerous arrests for the sale of the drugs in recent months.

(See **Explosion** on page 8)